Shenandoah Home

SARA MITCHELL

THE SINCLAIR LEGACY ~ BOOK 1

Shenandoah Home

WATERBROOK
PRESS

SHENANDOAH HOME
PUBLISHED BY WATERBROOK PRESS
2375 Telstar Drive, Suite 160
Colorado Springs, Colorado 80920
A division of Random House, Inc.

Scripture quotations are taken from the *King James Version.*

The characters and events in this book are fictional, and any resemblance to actual persons or events is coincidental.

ISBN 1-57856-409-3

Library of Congress Cataloging-in-Publication Data

Mitchell, Sara, 1949–
    Shenandoah home / Sara Mitchell.— 1st ed.
      p. cm.— (The Sinclair legacy ; bk. 1)
    ISBN 1-57856-409-3
      1. Shenandoah River Valley (Va. and W. Va.)—Fiction. 2. Sisters—Fiction. I. Title.

PS3563.I823 S54 2001
813'.54—dc21

                    2001023769

Printed in the United States of America
2001—First Edition

10 9 8 7 6 5 4 3 2 1

For Amanda and Gwen, our two daughters.

Thanks for being who and what you are.

Acknowledgments

I would like to thank Colleen Ritter, gift shop manager and tour guide for Old Town Winchester Welcome Center; and Jim Lonas, with the City of Winchester Fire and Rescue, for their time and courteous efforts to ensure historical accuracy for parts of this book.

Any mistakes made are the sole responsibility of the author, who has a tendency to allow fiction to outweigh fact when it comes to storytelling.

Northern End of
Shenandoah Valley
of
Virginia 1889

to Winchester

Cedar Creek

Strasburg

North Fork of
Shenandoah
River

Allegheny Mountains

Tom's Brook

*Sloan's
House

*Sinclair Run

*Sinclairs'
House

Massanutten Mountain

Blue Ridge Mountains

Woodstock

Valley Pike

N

* indicates a fictional place

Part I

GARNET

Prologue

SINCLAIR RUN
SHENANDOAH VALLEY, VIRGINIA, OCTOBER 1888

*M*ight never know whether all the choices I've made these past fourteen years have been the right ones, Jacob Sinclair mused one windswept autumn afternoon. But then a widowed Scottish furniture maker struggling to rear three motherless daughters faced obstacles that would doubtless try the soul of a saint. And the blessed Lord was fully aware that Jacob Sinclair was no saint.

Jacob stepped outside his workshop and heaved a gusty sigh, feeling the need for a draft of clean autumn air. He shaded his eyes while he scanned the meadow behind the run, his heart restive because Garnet still wasn't home from her day's wanderings. Why couldn't the girl be satisfied with drawing the wildflowers littering their property?

Och, but didn't he know better by now than to grumble over the nature God had given his middle daughter? He ran his hand through his thinning hair, tugging the strand that always fell across his forehead. It had been a day just like this, he remembered suddenly, when he'd settled on the special object for Garnet's heartwood chest. A paint box October day, trees dripping color, Indian summer air fragrant with cedar, wood shavings, and linseed oil. The kind of day that made a man thank his Maker for life. Jacob had needed such days back then, when the grief over Mary's passing was still fresh, the bright spots few and far between. What year *had* that been? '72? '73? No...Garnet had just turned seven, so it would have been the autumn of 1875.

But he'd been smiling that day, Jacob recalled...

He hummed an off-key Scottish jig while he worked, each stroke of the wood chisel in his hands keeping time with the beat.

At the end of the tune he straightened to study the grain of the board, a handsome piece of cherry. Stained, work-roughened fingers caressed the surface, while in his mind Jacob pictured a graceful woman with slim white hands, carefully tucking something inside a hidden drawer—the secret heart of the small chest he was in the process of creating. Perhaps a sprig of dried flowers? Lily of the valley, or that large pinkish flower Garnet brought home yesterday afternoon. Mary, God rest her blessed soul, would have known its name…

He banished the painful graveside memories. Over a year had passed; his girls had recovered, and that was what mattered. Giving himself a mental shake, he pulled out his watch, then removed his apron. Right now it was time to wake five-year-old Leah from her nap so they could fetch Meredith and Garnet from school.

An hour later he pulled old Dipple to a halt underneath a sugar maple burning the sky with brilliant scarlet leaves. Laughter and loud talk filled the crisp afternoon air as children scattered toward home on foot, mule, or wagon. Smiling, Jacob watched the exodus before turning his attention to the front of the school. He was a bit late today, but his two older daughters, instead of fidgeting on the porch steps, were nowhere in sight. Where were they? Jacob frowned as he scanned the almost empty school yard. Normally they raced for the buggy, pigtails and petticoats awhirl, Garnet with her longer legs usually winning despite being younger than Meredith by thirteen months.

Beside him, Leah began to wriggle, twisting on the seat to search the yard. "Papa? Where's Mer'dith an' Garnet?"

"I'll go find them." He cupped the bouncing little shoulders in his hands. "You must stay here in the buggy, muffin. Promise me."

Solemn now, she nodded. "I promise, Papa."

Jacob kissed the tip of her nose, then followed the sound of childish shouts to a grove of cedars some twenty yards behind the schoolhouse. Anger flared as he took in the scene. Several boys were pounding on the door to the privy, hard enough to rattle its flimsy hinges. Ugly words dirtied the air.

It took Jacob less than a second to realize the foulmouthed attack was directed at Garnet. Sunny, funny, sensitive Garnet. Rage to shame a thunderstorm poured into him. He wanted to lash out with fist and boot against the verbal sewage spewing forth. From the sons of neighbors—tousle-haired, gap-toothed boys his daughter had called her friends, who now mocked her form and face and striking red hair.

Gathered nearby the privy a cluster of girls watched, not one of them trying to stop the cruel baiting. Meredith stood trapped in their midst, tight-lipped and rigid, her eight-year-old face beet red, chin quivering.

Jacob descended with the swiftness of a vengeful guardian angel, reaching for the two nearest boys. Each of his hands closed over the backs of their shirts. They yelped as he lifted them completely off their feet; a single threatening look cowed the other two spineless mongrels. "I ought to whip the lot of you!" he thundered. "You, Slocum—'twas only last week Garnet spent all evening drawing you a picture, because your dog had died. And you, Otis Teasel—who gave you her own pair of shiny new brogans this past winter 'cause the soles of your own were full of holes?"

He shook the pair of them, then flung them against the other scoundrels. "Get on home, the lot of you. I'll be expecting apologies to my daughter come morning."

They scattered, the girls tumbling after them in a flurry of high-pitched squeals.

Meredith flew into her father's arms. "I couldn't stop them, Papa! I tried and yelled, but they just laughed and pushed me down, and Garnet ran but they chased her i-into the privy..."

Jacob hugged her, hard, then gave her a gentle prod. "Go on along now. Wait with Leah in the buggy."

Shoulders slumped, Meredith disappeared around the corner of the schoolhouse. He took four deep, calming breaths before he spoke to his middle daughter. "Garnet, it's all right. You can come out now, little one. The loutish halflins have fled. 'Tis just me, needing to fill my arms with my flower-loving daughter."

The door creaked open, letting loose its breath-stopping stench. Garnet's tragic freckled face peeked out from between long strands of tangled hair, and Jacob felt as though a hot splinter had lodged in his chest. This morning her face had been scrubbed clean, her bright hair meticulously braided with new green ribbons. Now the ribbons were gone, along with the braids, replaced by a squirrel's nest of dirt, leaves, and sticks. As though someone had poured—

Jacob closed his mind to the image. "Och, darling, come here."

"I'm all right," she whispered, but her arms wrapped tight around his neck, and her elfin frame shook. "Last week Miss Wimbish had the blacksmith put a new hook inside the privy door." A shuddering sigh tickled Jacob's ear.

He gathered her into a close embrace and wished he could absorb her wounds into himself.

The following Saturday afternoon Jacob had just finished unloading a pile of lumber from the buckboard when Meredith barreled into the workshop, her eyes wide. "Papa! You need to come—Garnet's…Garnet's…you need to see!"

Several sheets of prime yellow poplar thudded to the sawdust floor. "Is she hurt? What's happened? Where is—"

"Papa, Papa, come see!" Leah appeared in the doorway, puffing and equally wide-eyed. "Garnet looks funny."

Pulse racing, Jacob followed their flying figures out across the yard to the wash house, just off the back porch. A half-dozen paces away, Garnet stood, poker straight with her arms crossed, head lifted. But her lips trembled when she looked over at Jacob.

"I told you you'd get in trouble," Meredith began.

"Meredith, Leah—inside the house." Leah tugged on his trouser leg. "Go with Meredith, baby," Jacob said.

Instead Leah scampered across to Garnet, wrapping her arms about her sister in a fierce embrace. "Garnet hurts. You have to hug," his tiny mother hen ordered. Only then did she march up the back steps with Meredith.

Jacob didn't acknowledge his youngest daughter's plea, for he couldn't tear his gaze from the sorry sight of his middle daughter.

This morning Garnet's hair had been a glorious cloud of burning red, deep chestnut, and burnished gold—a color to make the angels weep. Now it was a repugnant shade of…black. Lusterless and lifeless.

Like the expression in Garnet's eyes.

Jacob gently lifted one stiff, damp braid between two fingers. When he dropped it his fingers came away stained. The front of Garnet's corduroy jacket sported twin black smears as well. "Why?" he asked. "Why do this to yourself?"

Her lips quivered again, and he saw her throat muscles working. *Ah, little one,* he thought. *If only you'd been given a personality to match the hair…* With a deep sigh he unwound her arms and picked up her hands. "Here, too?" He smoothed the stained, sticky fingers open on his large palm, trying not to wince.

Miserably she nodded.

"Did I ever tell you about your Granny Mae—my mother? Her hair was the envy of every lass in Glasgow, for no other was blessed with so fine a shade of red. Put a sunset to shame, your granddad always said. 'Twas just like yours, Garnet."

"It's not a blessing. I hate it."

Jacob knelt and cupped her chin. "This is because of what happened on Tuesday, isn't it?"

Narrow shoulders lifted. "Yesterday, too. Rowley Futch said I was ugly, that I looked like…like a monster threw up b-blood all over my head." A single tear pooled in the corner of her eye. "I…called him names too. But it didn't help."

"Your Granny Mae wouldn't have bothered with mere names— she'd have called down a curse on his head—turned him into a salamander on the spot."

"Curses only work if you have a brogue."

If he hadn't been staring directly at her from inches away, Jacob would have missed the flash of returning humor in her eyes. Relief filled him, lightening his heart, his voice. "Well now, lassie," he said in the rumbling brogue of his ancestors, "then I'll be workin' on helping ye tae cultivate one tonight, won't I?" They smiled at each other, and he wiped away the tear.

"I'm sorry, Papa. It—it'll wash out, won't it?"

" 'Twill grow out, if not." The smile in her eyes died, and Jacob relented. "We'll study on the matter after supper and chores." He tapped the end of her straight nose. "Learn a lesson from this, flower-face?"

Solemnly she nodded.

"And that would be—?"

"That Rowley's already a slimy salamander. And…when I finish school I'll join my friend Mary Mahoney's church and become a nun. Nobody will see my hair but me."

"Ah, Garnet, Garnet…" He surveyed the sticky black clumps of hair, then the rueful expression of a daughter whose personality remained as elusive and enticing as the wildflowers she loved to draw. "Do you think a cardinal complains because it isn't a sparrow or the mockingbird because it isn't a blue jay? God gave you red hair, and whether you believe it or not, it is a crowning glory. I pray that doubting heart of yours will someday believe that you are beautiful, not only inside where it counts, but on the outside as well."

❧

Ah yes, Jacob thought now, a bittersweet smile touching the corners of his mouth. That was when he knew what would go into the secret drawer of Garnet's heirloom chest, and he prayed that someday she would understand.

One

That's it! Garnet decided, eyeing the white flowers on the other side of the creek. The faint odor of licorice—typical of Sweet Cicely—teased her nose; beads of moisture clung to the flowers' shiny green leaves, a gift of random sprays of water from the gurgling creek. As she watched, a single droplet slid to the serrated edge of a leaf, then fell soundlessly to the earth.

To capture on her sketchpad enough of that precise moment—the instant a single droplet stretched thin as angel hair from the tip of the leaf… "That's it!"

The sound of her voice, loud enough in this deserted glade to summon a herd of cattle, made Garnet laugh. Eyes fastened to the wildflower, she tightened her grasp on the large cloth bag holding her supplies, took a flying leap across the creek, and landed with scant grace in a patch of loose earth that promptly gave way. Mud and humus spilled into her tramp-about shoes.

Undaunted, Garnet spent several moments studying the flowers from different perspectives, selecting the best angle from which to draw before she finally settled onto a patch of ground. Mind churning with possibilities, she absently removed her old brogans and poured out the dirt. Anticipation caused her fingers to twitch when at last she reached for sketchpad and pencil.

Someone sniffed, the tiny sound tugging at her attention.

Garnet paused, charcoal pencil tip hovering over the paper, but she didn't raise her head. Then, with the precision of a skilled craftsman, she finished a detailed rendering of the leaf she'd been working on. It was…credible, at least for a first draft, and captured the essence of the flowers. Enough for her to finish the work back in the attic room her father had converted into a studio for her, where—

From somewhere behind and to her right she heard a soft rustling, followed by another sniff. Garnet turned her head to see, since the brim of her sunbonnet limited her range of vision to what was directly in front of her. JosieMae Whalen was sitting in a clump of bluebells and red clover, her lantern-jaw face streaked with grime.

"JosieMae…child, what are you doing here?" Garnet thrust the sketchpad aside and scrambled to her feet, wincing when all her muscles screeched in protest. Spots danced across her eyes, and with a start she realized the air was late-afternoon golden. "How long have you been sitting there?" she asked, dropping down beside the heavyset girl, her arm automatically wrapping around JosieMae's shoulders.

"Dunno. You was workin'," she whispered, sniffing more loudly this time. "I like to watch." Dull red crept into her cheeks, and she ducked her head after meeting Garnet's gaze for less than a blink.

Garnet knew why. JosieMae's left eye had a tendency to drift upward, inflicting upon the hapless twelve-year-old the look of a half-wit. As a consequence the girl seldom looked directly at anybody. Garnet hugged her hard, resting her cheek against chopped-off, unwashed hair. "Want a drawing lesson?"

"Huh-uh. Ma'll skin me for a washrag if I don't be home for evenin' chores." She wiped the back of her hand across her nose.

Garnet dug around for a handkerchief, handing it matter-of-factly over. "Save a corner of that for me," she said with a conspiratorial smile. "If my face looks like the rest of me, I'll need to wash up a bit before I go home, or Leah will come after me with a mop and bucket."

JosieMae laughed. "She asked me to fetch you—said you'd forget to come home iffen you was drawing." She swiped her nose with Garnet's hankie, then candidly pronounced, "Your dress is covered with mud. So's your stockings and brogans, but your face isn't bad…I wish I looked like you, Garnet. Even when you're dirty, you're purty." Fresh tears welled.

A funny-queer sort of catch tightened Garnet's throat. "Well, I'm partial to my friend JosieMae, and I happen to think she's fine just the way she is."

Flushing, the girl clambered to her feet. "Gotta go." She ran a few steps, paused, then turned back. Her mouth opened and shut as if she were trying to work up the courage to speak.

"Don't forget our drawing lesson. We'll do it next week," Garnet called, understanding.

Relief flooded JosieMae's face. She bobbed her head, waved, then galloped clumsily up the long sloping meadow and disappeared over the crest.

The lump in Garnet's throat swelled. Why, she wondered as she slowly gathered up all her supplies, did God allow helpless children to suffer from the cruelties of a callous world? There was no answer, of course. The world was both cruel and callous, and all the prayers of righteous souls would not change that bitter truth. God sometimes responded to the pleas of His children—but sometimes, Garnet had learned, He chose not to.

She reached for the sketchpad she'd tossed aside in her haste to comfort JosieMae, and realized that it had landed on top of the Sweet Cicely she'd been drawing. Two of the delicate flowers were crushed, and the stalk of a third had broken. Garnet dropped to her knees, cradling the destroyed blooms as though her unspoken apology would restore them.

Overhead, a bird twittered in the budding branches of a willow tree, and somewhere on the other side of the hill one of Fergus Whalen's cows bawled a plaintive message into the wind. With a long sigh Garnet rose. Enough maudlin melodrama, as Leah would uncharitably point out. She looped her bag over her shoulder and set off toward home, turning her mind toward tomorrow, when she hoped to head out in the buggy, toward Strasburg. The north branch of the Shenandoah River, along with its Cedar Creek tributary, had carved out deep, rocky gorges, over the years leaving the banks alongside choked with all manner of flora.

Armed with knowledge, persistence, and pluck, Garnet hoped to unearth some twinleaf, a seven-petaled white wildflower similar to the common rue anemone. Unlike the anemone, however, the twinleaf was very rare. For months Mr. Smoot, her publisher in New York, had been urging her to include some lesser known species in her next batch of illustrations for his monthly magazine.

If she were particularly fortunate, she might at least find some of the more infrequent species—puccoon…fumewort, or Dutchman's-breeches.

"Puccoon and Dutchman's-breeches," she told the bird. "If names like that don't bring a smile to your face, nothing will." Mostly content, Garnet lifted her face to the slanting sunbeams and rising wind. At least she'd be home before sunset, so Leah could only scold her about the dirt.

❦

VALLEY TURNPIKE, SOUTH OF WINCHESTER, VIRGINIA

"God…why did You create humans in the first place? You'd have done better to endow a different species with a piece of Your divinity, if You were that lonely." Sloan MacAllister, M.D., late of Adlerville, Pennsylvania, kicked one of the many sharp-edged stones littering the Valley Pike, a broad swath of crushed gravel roadway traversing a godforsaken state in a godforsaken valley.

The blasphemous thought hovered in the air, tweaking a conscience Sloan was trying hard to forget he'd ever possessed.

All right, he conceded, watching the rock sail over the low stone wall next to the Pike. *All right*. He would concede, if grudgingly, that no place on earth was altogether forsaken by God. Just men.

Men like himself.

Grimacing, he stepped to the side of the road beneath a scraggly oak tree, dropped his medical bag, then shrugged off his knapsack to stretch out a few kinks. Unfortunately nothing seemed to relax the mental kinks that had been slowly choking him from the brain down these past months. Or was it years…?

Since breakfast, when he'd set out, he'd passed by rolling hills, patches of forest, and a couple of streams—runs, some locals called them, all guarded by blueish haze-covered mountains running north to south on both sides of the valley. At some point, the old Indian trail had metamorphosed into a wagon route, then to this macadamized Pike, complete with tollbooths every five miles between Winchester and Staunton, ninety-three miles to the south. Since Sloan was on foot, he'd been spared the frustration of waiting at the first two tollbooths for the keepers—both of them women—to raise the pole that blocked the road until they received a two-penny toll charged for a horse and rider.

Buggies and wagons, he supposed, would extract more. Not that he cared one way or the other. Regardless, his surroundings offered a tranquil setting, despite all the bloody battles that had swept this section of the country twenty-five years earlier. Sloan wondered whether any corner left in God's creation was still untainted by man's corrupted nature.

He picked up another stone, and without looking winged it into a meadow full of placid-faced bovines. Fortunately the missile landed harmlessly in a patch of bright yellow flowers instead of striking a cud-chewing cow. A few heads turned his way, but their massive indifference to the smoldering presence of an ill-tempered man almost prompted his first smile in weeks. Perhaps he should have been a veterinarian.

For the past six years Sloan had fought sickness of all kinds, arming himself with ongoing discoveries in cellular pathology, physiology, and bacteriology, claiming as his battle cry a verse from Psalms, where the Lord had promised to heal all of mankind's diseases. Too bad he'd forgotten that the greatest "disease" was man's heart. *You could have done more, Lord,* Sloan thought as he gathered up bag and knapsack. The pomposity and arrogance of fellow doctors…the ignorance and obtuseness of patients who refused to be honest with him about their conditions because revealing everything "offended their sensibilities." Tom… Amos Jorvik… *Jenna.*

His life had become a powder keg, culminating in an explosion the previous month that spewed pieces of his soul like shrapnel. Never again would he be able to face death with the naive confidence of years past. Right now it was life bleeding him dry, each breath he inhaled a reminder of two people—one of them his brother—who would never breathe again.

So he had chucked it all—home, profession, dreams…perhaps even a goodly portion of his faith—to disappear here in the backwoods of an unfamiliar culture. One as alien to his roots as the squalid railroad company town that had butchered his soul. He didn't know why he'd brought along his bag. Habit, probably. He'd sell it, in the very next town, and donate the proceeds to the first helpless beggar he passed. Sloan no longer considered himself a doctor. A man couldn't call himself a physician when he hated people, hated himself.

Why didn't You do more?

The only answer Sloan received to this silent accusation was a rumble of thunder from a line of black clouds oozing over the western ridges and a damp wind slapping his face like the kiss of a slobbering dog. With a sour grin Sloan flipped up the collar of his jacket and hunched his shoulders. April in the South wasn't turning out to be the sunny haven old Berta Schumacher had promised.

"If you got to run, Doc, you try the mountains of Virginia. They'll heal what's ailing your soul." The trembling hands, so twisted with rheumatoid arthritis they more resembled claws, fumbled for her bottle of Kakapo Indian Oil.

"That stuff won't help and you know it, Mrs. Schumacher."

"Dr. MacAllister, what'll help will be this tired old body lying in a cozy coffin, and me tickling the ivories with Jesus Himself singing along." She'd given Sloan a slow measuring look that to this day had the power to make him squirm. "Go to the hills and heal, son. But don't go because you're running away. Go because you're running toward the answer."

The answer to what? Sloan hadn't bothered to ask at the time, because he hadn't cared. He still didn't. Right now, running *away* took all his energy.

But this morning when his horse pulled up lame, he'd made arrangements to leave the faithful mare under the care of the man who owned the livery stable, then set out walking instead of waiting for the next southbound train. Nothing like a solitary hike to free a man's mind, give him time to think. As a boy, he'd tramped the Berkshires with his father and brothers—Sloan closed that particular memory door with a resounding thud and trudged stoically down the road, his face to the wind.

Two

$\mathcal{S}$ome while later Sloan rounded a bend, and his eye caught on a splash of color halfway up another of the interminable rolling meadows landscaping the Shenandoah Valley. His step slowed, then stopped altogether, and he lifted a hand to shade his eyes.

So. His eyes weren't playing tricks on him after all. It really was a woman, sitting up there in the middle of some purple flowers. Gauzy sunbeams dusted the meadow with ethereal light, blurring the lines of the woman's shawl and the splash of blue gown floating over the grass. The setting eerily mimicked a Whistler painting hanging in the drawing room of his family home in Baltimore, except the woman's back was to Sloan, and an old-fashioned sunbonnet completely covered her head and neck.

Had she materialized from a sod hut on the Nebraska plains or something? Sloan hadn't seen a woman wearing one of those contraptions since he was a small boy. Reluctantly charmed by the quaintness of it, he dropped his gear by the side of the road, then casually vaulted over the stone wall.

As he climbed through the long grasses and clumps of wildflowers, he debated whether to hail her or wait to speak until she heard his approach and turned around. His curiosity mounted with each step—what was she doing out here all alone? Her head was bent, her elbows tucked close against her sides, the line of her spine bowed, as though she were studying, or…God help him if she was weeping. Sloan had always been a sucker for tears, and his weakness infuriated him. Tears were one of a female's most effective weapons, because they reduced a man to the intellectual level of an earthworm.

A dozen paces away, and she still hadn't moved or given any indication that she was aware of his presence.

Sloan cleared his throat. There was no response.

Slightly miffed, curiosity replaced by determination, he kept walking until he was less than a yard away. "Hello, there," he began, assuming his best bedside voice to avoid frightening her. "I was walking along the road, and saw…" His voice trailed away.

Instead of a start or a scream of surprise, her only response was the irritable wave of an ungloved hand. She neither turned nor looked up. *Leave me alone, I'm busy,* the gesture stated as plainly as words.

It was an acknowledgment of sorts, but certainly not what Sloan had expected. Intrigued and irritated, he stood pondering her back and that ridiculous bonnet, wondering what to do. Good manners dictated he withdraw and leave her to her chosen isolation. Somewhat to his surprise, he realized he didn't want to do that.

What he wanted was…acknowledgment. "What are you doing?" he tried next. Hopefully a direct question would force a verbal response.

Nothing.

Sloan deliberately stepped in front of her, where he discovered that she was drawing on a large sketchpad. *Oh.* At least she hadn't been weeping. Smiling to himself over his effrontery, he knelt and waved a hand in front of her face.

Quick as a slap her head lifted, and she pressed the sketchpad against her chest. She was young, he saw, perhaps late teens to early twenties. Neatly framed by the bonnet brim and a lopsided bow, inquiring grayish-green eyes studied him out of an oval face sunkissed with freckles. Apparently she didn't always wear the sunbonnet.

"Hello," he repeated, a little stunned by the unblemished purity of her expression. It had been a long time since he'd seen one free of pain and bone-deep weariness. Disillusionment and dissipation. Coyness and calculation…the catalog was endless.

And yet…what shadowy emotion *was* lurking there? Fascinated, he stared at this fey creature with her otherworldly eyes until she spoke, her words a gentle, almost musical drawl.

"Hello. Did you want something?" She blinked owlishly, frowning. "If not, I'm rather busy. If you don't mind." She gestured to the sketchpad, then glanced over his shoulder toward the line of thunderclouds.

Sloan finally shook off his bemusement. This—this self-possessed Southern country maid had succeeded in doing what no woman save one had ever accomplished: rendering him as tongue-tied as a boy still in short pants. "Sorry for interrupting. Ah…I wasn't expecting to meet a young woman, all alone out here in the middle of nowhere."

He tipped his head sideways, trying to peer beneath the concealing shadow of the bonnet. It made an effective shield—he couldn't even ascertain the color of her hair. For all he knew, the girl was bald as an egg. "*Are* you alone? It doesn't seem very wise." The genteel young debutantes he used to escort around Baltimore and Philadelphia would sooner boil themselves in oil than appear in public unchaperoned. Jenna…he suppressed an inward shudder. Jenna had always demanded a male escort, even to walk down the block to a neighbor's house. If Sloan couldn't accompany her himself, Tom was quick to offer his arm. Tom…

"You sound like my family." She laid the sketchpad aside and stretched, rotating her head. "You're not from around here, are you?" she said. "Most everybody hereabouts is long used to my wandering ways."

To his chagrin, Sloan found his gaze dwelling on the graceful line of her apricot-tinted cheek. "No," he agreed dryly. "I'm not from around here."

Drawing room manners aside, he started to introduce himself, but saw that her attention was focused on her sketchpad. She even held it a little way out, obviously to better see whatever it was she'd been working on. Sloan might as well have been a tree stump.

Disgruntled, even more annoyed with his own increasing fascination, he forced himself to relax. Then he sat down as though they were friends enjoying a picnic in the park. The situation was bizarre. Three years of Adlerville, not to mention a lifetime of Jenna's Machiavellian ploys, should have rendered him immune to any vagaries of human nature. He should be unfazed by an unworldly looking young woman sketching without maid or companion in the middle of a deserted countryside.

But he wasn't.

Sloan leaned forward with a determined smile. One more attempt, he decided. If she snubbed him, he'd swallow his pride like a man and take himself off. "My name's Sloan MacAllister, originally from Baltimore, late of Pennsylvania."

"Well, I'm pleased to meet you, Mr. MacAllister, but I have to go. I'm trying to beat that storm"—she pointed toward the darkening clouds—"and make it to Cedar Creek while the weather's still pleasant." She smiled distractedly and reached for a large cloth bag beside her. "Do you happen to have the time?"

Sloan lifted a brow, but tugged out his father's gold pocket watch. "Twelve minutes past two, Miss—what did you say your name was?"

"Buttercups and bitterweed!" She jumped to her feet in a flurry of motion. "I lost track of time." With a graceful sweep of her arm, she stuffed sketchbook and writing tools inside the cloth sack, then looped it over her shoulder.

Sloan had risen when she did, his gaze lingering on the guileless features and the unpretentious charm of those freckles. His muscles twitched with the urge to grab her arm, to force her attention to him. "What's your name?" he insisted.

"Hmm? My name?" She blinked again. "Oh, if you're not from around here, I suppose you wouldn't know, would you?" Suddenly her eyes were wary, evasive. "Garnet Sinclair. My name is Garnet Sinclair."

"Garnet Sinclair," Sloan lifted his hand. "It's a pleasure."

Instead of giving him her hand, she stepped back, her gaze moving once more to the line of clouds over his shoulder. "I need to go."

"Can't you spare even a few moments?"

"I'm afraid not. I should have been up there an hour ago…"

Did the chit even notice that he was a man? Sloan stuffed his hands inside the waistband of his trousers. "You're the strangest young woman I've ever met, Garnet Sinclair."

"Probably. I gave up trying to be like everybody else years ago." She shrugged. "It was lovely to chat, Mr. MacAllister. But I do want to beat that storm. Good-bye."

She darted up the hill with the airy grace of a bird and disappeared inside a grove of cedar. Sloan continued to stare after her, hearing the unexpected refinement of that drawling voice…seeing the shifting shadows of a hundred moods in those eyes. Both lingered in the soft April afternoon like the faint fragrance of flowers and sunshine.

Eventually he realized he was gazing up the hill like a moonstruck suitor. Sloan turned away with a snort of self-disgust and marched back down the slope. *You never learn, do you?* He needed to remember Jenna Davenport, with her dazzling blue eyes and striking red hair. Needed to remind himself how he'd been beguiled from the beginning, especially that first year, when she'd tormented him with her feigned shows of indifference.

Fine. He remembered. So why was it, when this quaint Southern girl blazoned her lack of interest across the sky, all he could think about was contriving a way to meet her again? He'd also better remember that April showers produced violent storms as often as flowers and sunshine.

❧

The sky had darkened to the color of tar by the time Garnet pulled up in front of the Tweedies' and jumped down from the road cart. A gust of wet-smelling wind tugged at her sunbonnet. As she tied Goatsbeard's lead to the rusting iron gate, huge drops of rain splattered the dirt.

"I'll come back for you in a minute," she promised the horse. Then she grabbed her cloth bag and ran for Effie Tweedie's sagging porch. "Mrs. Tweedie!" she called, pounding on the door. Over the last year the elderly woman had grown hard of hearing.

The door flung wide. "Sakes alive, but you gave me a fright, girl! What are you doing up here, and a storm coming on?"

"I lost track of time. Mrs. Tweedie, if you'll let me put Goatsbeard in your barn until this blows over, I'll clean the stalls and do the milking, all right?"

"Bless you, child, but that's not necessary. Go on with you. Put yon beastie away and come back afore that rain hits." She shook her head. "Here. Give me your poke. You don't want your drawing doodads to get wet, I reckon." Chapped, stumpy fingers plucked the cloth bag from Garnet's shoulder. "Don't suppose you'd let me sneak a peek at your sketchbook in exchange for a couple of my nobby buns, fresh from the oven?"

Garnet brushed a kiss across the plump cheek. "You know better than that. But I'd still enjoy one of your buns. I ate the lunch Leah packed hours ago." She hesitated. "You…you won't…"

"No, child. No. I was pulling your leg a mite. But I did want to tell you that Nahum never meant nothing by his prying. He's a good boy, my grandson, and you know he's always been sweet on you."

"I know. I'm sorry." Ever since she'd caught him leafing through her sketchpad a month earlier, Garnet had tried to time her weekly visits to Mrs. Tweedie when Nahum would be out in the fields. She'd hoped Mrs. Tweedie wouldn't notice, but obviously she had. And had taken upon herself the responsibility of…meddling.

Garnet avoided the elderly woman's eye. Even though it had been a month, she could still remember the excruciating sense of vulnerability that washed through her when she'd seen her open sketchbook in Nahum's hands. It had made her feel as though her soul had been stripped bare. No one, not even her father or her sisters, had ever seen her works in progress. Nahum's inquisitiveness had been almost as wounding as—

"Now don't be going all bashful on me, child. You know I—"

"It's not too early to milk Sadie, is it?" Garnet asked in a rush. "Perhaps by the time I finish, the rain will have quit. Is…where's Nahum working today?"

"Boy's carried himself off to New Market for an auction. Won't be home 'til late this evening."

Concerned, Garnet glanced outside. "I can stay with you for a few hours, but you know Papa and Leah will have a conniption if I don't show up by sunset."

"And so they should." She folded her massive arms across an equally massive bosom. "Can't say as I blame 'em none, but I do enjoy your visits."

Garnet smiled. She knew that Mrs. Tweedie also appreciated the help, even if she was too proud to admit it. "I'll take care of Sadie for you," she promised, and dashed back outside, accompanied by an earth-shaking clap of thunder.

An hour later, with the bucket of foaming milk balanced on the seat of a high stool so the cats couldn't tip it over, Garnet finished raking the last of some fresh straw around Sadie's stall, then carried the soiled straw and droppings away in a rickety wheelbarrow. She made a mental note to ask her father if he could contrive a scheme to repair the thing without smacking into the wall of the Tweedies' pride.

One of the barn cats padded down the aisle, her white-tipped black tail gently waving. With a plaintive meow the animal nuzzled Garnet's feet and ankles, a hopeful look in her unblinking feline eyes.

"Babies hungry again? All right, I'll sneak y'all a cupful of Sadie's milk. Just don't tell the Tweedies. And"—she fixed a stern eye on the indifferent cat—"I get to play with your children as long as it's raining."

She was sprawled on top of a bale of hay with her chin propped on one hand, holding her sunbonnet with the other, ribbons dangling for four sets of furiously batting little paws, when Nahum strolled into the barn.

"Garnet? Hoo-ee, Garnet. Where are you, gal?"

Garnet scrambled to her feet, kittens scattering as she brushed straw from her clothing and straightened her rumpled skirts. Several pins had fallen out of her topknot so that stringy coils of hair hung limp about her face and neck. But there wasn't time to do anything about that now.

"Coming," she called, and lifted her chin. Had to face him sometime, after all. Might as well be now, even if she did resemble a bedraggled scarecrow. "I thought you were in New Market."

Nahum snatched off his hat, gawking at her as though she'd sprouted an extra head. Tensing, Garnet mentally rolled her eyes. "Did you buy anything?" she prompted, glancing behind him. "At the auction?"

"Aw, they sold everything I was interested in afore noon. Caught a ride home with a feller from Fisher's Hill. He let me off at the Tom's Brook tollgate. You know I don't like leaving Gran by herself at night." He cleared his throat. "Sure is nice to see you, Garnet."

"It's nice to see you, too." She hesitated. "I have to be going. It's getting late."

"Wait a spell, Garnet." Nahum's ears turned bright pink. His hands crumpled the soft felt brim of his hat. "I...um...dang it, Gran peeled my skin for trifling with your drawing stuff. That's why I haven't seen you these last weeks, hain't it?"

Garnet felt his embarrassment almost as keenly as her own, and that realization loosened her taut neck muscles enough for her to finally relax. "I suppose," she confessed, smiling at him. "I don't even let my family see my unfinished drawings, Nahum. It's not just you. All right?"

He nodded, a wave of greasy straw-colored hair falling over one eye. "I'm powerful sorry, Garnet. I won't do it again, ever." He blinked, his eyes anxious. "Will you stay for a spell? Gran's made her nobby buns, you know. She even hauled down her fancy crockery for us."

"It's late, Nahum. Perhaps another time." She smiled again to soften the rejection, wishing not for the first time that she'd been born with Meredith's flirtatious nature or even Leah's diplomacy.

Undeterred, Nahum trailed after her while she fetched Goatsbeard and insisted so vehemently on hitching the animal for her that she gave in. "Still raining," he pointed out, threading the traces through the loops. "Sure you can make it home all right?"

"A little dampness never hurt anybody. I'll be fine." Garnet stuffed the limp sunbonnet back in place. One of the ribbons, she saw in amusement, had been clawed to shreds. "I'm going to tell your grandmother good-bye."

"I wish you wouldn't wear that thing. It covers all your pretty hai—" he gulped, dropping the reins over the dash. "Beg pardon, Garnet."

"It's all right, Nahum." Garnet suppressed a sigh. "I wear a bonnet because it keeps the wind from blowing my hair into my face and ears when I'm drawing." After five years, the lie fell easily from her lips.

A short while later she climbed into the road cart, then turned to wave to the Tweedies. A basket full of sugar-dusted nobby buns wrapped in old newspapers was stashed beneath the seat. Garnet herself was wrapped neck-to-toes in a gigantic mackintosh that smelled of camphor and rosemary. "Pappy's got no use for it, now has he?" Mrs. Tweedie told her, fastening the garment about Garnet. "Reckon it don't rain overmuch in heaven. And if he went t'other way, I know it don't rain there. Now don't be a stranger, child. Nahum'll behave in the future, keep his nose out of your business. Won't you, boy?" she added with a good-natured buffet to her hapless grandson's head. "Watch that stretch of track at the bottom of the hill. Tends to wash out when it rains…"

"I will." She waved a final farewell, then turned Goatsbeard's head toward home.

But for the next mile or two she wished she'd given in and asked Mrs. Tweedie why she didn't know where her husband was spending eternity. For the past several years—a little over five of them, now—Garnet had struggled with uncertainty over her own eternal destination.

Three

By the time Garnet reached the Valley Pike, the rain had intensified to a steady downpour. Rumbles of thunder and intermittent flashes of lightning over the mountain warned of another deluge, so Garnet urged Goatsbeard to a brisk trot. Several years earlier her father had modified the one-horse road cart for better protection from the elements, using parts from an old coupe rockaway. But an open front remained, still leaving the driver somewhat vulnerable.

Which was why Garnet had promised to always keep an eye on the weather and return home in plenty of time to avoid a drenching. Guilt lashed her like the rain lashing the wooden panels, soaking into her spirit like the moisture dampening Mr. Tweedie's old mackintosh. She should have known after becoming distracted by those bird-foot violets that she wouldn't make Cedar Creek today.

The memory of the meadow brought to mind her brief encounter with the dark-haired stranger. What an odd gentleman he'd been, tramping all the way up the hill just to speak to her! At first terror had all but paralyzed her, until she realized that he *was* a stranger to the Valley, his presence in the meadow benign. Of course, the bonnet had covered her distinctive hair, so even if they had finally hired someone to track her down after five years—*Hush up, Garnet.* The notion was beyond absurdity.

The man had seemed a trifle put out when she refused to linger. What was it he'd said? Something about her staying a few more moments? She hadn't paid much attention, because after realizing he hadn't been sent after her, all she'd been thinking about was Cedar Creek.

Had she been rude? She supposed Meredith would have lingered, drawn him out until she knew all about the tall, forbidding Yankee. Leah would probably have invited him to dinner. Her sisters didn't understand Garnet's attitude toward men, even though over the last few years they had finally ceased harping on her indifference. Indifference, she thought with an inward flinch. If only they knew… Indifference was much more acceptable than the terror.

She knew her family loved her, that her father and sisters might even sacrifice their lives for her. Yet she had never been able to explain what had happened, that summer when she'd turned sixteen.

Goatsbeard came to an abrupt, tail-swishing halt, hooves digging into the soggy roadbed. A brook had overflowed, spilling muddy water across the Pike. "It's all right, you old goat." Garnet leaned forward to pat the soaked flank, then firmly urged him forward until both animal and cart navigated the fetlock-deep flooded roadway. "Now, that wasn't so fearful, was it?" she asked, jiggling the reins.

Fearful…

Papa had tried once to talk with her, she remembered. Right after she began wearing the sunbonnets. It had been raining about like this, and she'd holed herself up with her heartwood chest, in the attic her father had converted to a studio for her. Jacob had come looking for her, and she'd asked him again about the cardinal feather in the hidden drawer.

"Why not a flower, or one of Mama's handkerchiefs, since you say I'm the most like her? I don't even like birds that much."

Jacob hadn't gotten upset or even impatient. Just stood there, fondling the bright red feather, his gaze wistful, a little sad. "Why don't you tell me why you've taken to wearing your mother's old sunbonnets when you wander about the countryside? Or why you no longer go with Meredith to the Sunday school socials or picnics. You didn't even go the annual Fourth of July celebration. "

"Meredith's interested in young men. I'm not. I'd rather be drawing. And I wear Mama's old bonnets because I got tired of my hair blowing in my face when I'm outside."

She'd managed the words without batting an eye, even though after five years the memories still chilled her. But it was the truth, Garnet reminded herself fiercely, even if it was only a portion of it. The rest would remain buried. She must never reveal what had happened that day when she'd returned home by herself from the high school in Woodstock, because Meredith had stayed behind to help Tate Zickle clean blackboards.

For a long time, she'd wondered if God was punishing her because she couldn't be like other young ladies, couldn't seem to discipline the wild streak in her nature. Couldn't stifle the doubts: Why hadn't God given her a fiery temperament along with red hair or plain brown hair to match her unexceptional disposition?

Instead the Lord had chosen to create a...a patchwork personality. An even-tempered redhead. A restless gypsy with an equal need for home and hearth. Likely as not she would never fit anywhere beyond Sinclair Run, especially after what had happened to her. Which meant Garnet must accept her solitary lot in life. Besides, defying her world by revealing her secret would result in shame, probable banishment, and threat to her family. So she lived a lie and strove to accept God's will with grace and humor. But ever since that summer afternoon five years ago, she hadn't been able to trust Him.

If only loneliness didn't strike like a poisonous snake at odd moments, biting deep with its venom, filling her with an unnamed longing for something more. For someone.

With an impatient sniff Garnet tossed her head, resolutely flinging off her melancholy along with the raindrops. She was healthy, with a family who loved her regardless of her eccentric ways, and lately a rewarding profession unheard of for most ladies, especially here in the Valley. She should be grateful that the Lord allowed her to make use of her artistic gift, not whine because no man would ever feel about her the way Papa did about the mother Garnet barely remembered.

And as long as she covered the beacon of her hair when she was out, she—and her family—should be safe.

One of the wheels rolled into a rut, throwing Garnet sideways and causing her to yank the reins. "Sorry, Goatsbeard," she called, swiping muddy water from her eyelashes. "Did I pull your mouth?" Better keep her mind on the task at hand, she decided. Returning home in a downpour would be forgiven. Riding home astride because of a snapped axle or a broken wheel…well, that was a fate to be avoided at all costs.

A prolonged growl of thunder reverberated over the mountains, initiating a chilly deluge. In seconds her head was drenched, the sunbonnet clinging to her scalp in limp defeat. The fresh blast of rain soaked into the mackintosh's heavy wool. The pungent odor of mildew and herbs took her breath away. Oh, she was in for a rare scolding for sure. And yet…

Exhilaration pulsed through her veins. Since she was going to be soaked, she might as well enjoy it. In reckless abandon Garnet lifted her face to the sheeting rain and laughed aloud.

❧❦❧

By the time Sloan reached another of the tollgates situated every five miles along the Valley Pike he was shivering and soaked through. For the last half hour he'd had to slog through relentless rain and gusting wind, leaving scant energy to fume over Garnet Sinclair, or anything else.

Of course he could have waited out the storm in a local drygoods store in the small community of Tom's Brook. But due to the rain, the store had been crawling with locals and other travelers, and when he'd passed by, Sloan had shuddered more over the cluster of horses, buggies, and buckboards crowded along the hitching post than he had over the weather.

When the middle-aged woman who collected the toll at the next gate invited him to dry out by the fire and share a meal with her and her husband, Sloan accepted at once. He was far too miserable to nurse his foul temper any longer. Even her sideways study of his medical bag didn't deter him from the promise of food and warmth.

An hour later, clothes dry and belly full, Sloan politely refused Ebenezer Wickham's invitation to join him for a smoke, earning instead Katie Wickham's flustered gratitude when he helped clear the table. "Least I can do, after enjoying the best meal I've eaten in months."

He stacked plates and bowls, then carried them to a large wooden tub Mrs. Wickham was filling with hot water in the kitchen. When she firmly shooed him off, he joined Ebenezer in front of their parlor stove,

27

sitting down opposite the older man in an identical cane-bottomed rocking chair.

"Where you be headed, Doctor?" Ebenezer tamped his corncob pipe against the stove's grate, a benign expression on the long-jawed face. "Mighty poor weather for travelers this evening, 'specially ones on foot."

"My horse drew up lame, back in Winchester. It was a pretty morning. I decided to walk."

A low chuckle rumbled up from Ebenezer's chest. "Weather here in the Valley takes a notion more often than not to surprise us with a tantrum."

"So I discovered." They shared a companionable smile.

Sloan leaned his head against the chair's high back. The peace of the cozy stone cottage was seductive; laziness lapped around his feet, winding its way up his legs, softening his bones and the bitterness that festered inside like a canker. "Since I'm no longer a practicing physician, how about calling me Sloan."

Ebenezer harrumphed, pursing his lips around the pipe. "I go by Eb. Might as well tell you, Sloan"—he cocked a bushy white eyebrow— "I was sorry to hear you say that. But the way I see it, when a man makes a decision, he's obliged to stand behind it, no matter what folks comment behind his back."

"Appreciate it." Sloan set the rocker in motion. It was the first time in weeks he hadn't felt compelled to justify or defend himself.

For a while they sat in silence, content to listen to the snapping fire behind the isinglass windows on the front of the stove. Rain drummed a steady rhythm on the roof, the creaking of Sloan's rocker beating a counterpoint. The homey sound of rattling dishes and cutlery floated through from the kitchen. Eyelids half closed, Sloan absorbed the essence of his humble surroundings. The rectangular room functioned both as dining room and parlor, where the Wickhams apparently spent most of their waking hours. It was sparse, even plainly furnished, almost absent of frills and ornamentation other than a set of inexpensively framed pen-and-inks tacked to one wall.

He would have given half his inheritance for a place of his own that exuded the same aura of quiet contentment.

"The pen-and-inks are nice," he remarked after a time. "I've always been partial to watercolors myself, but those are some excellent renderings."

"Ah-yup. Garnet did those for the missus some years ago, when she was scarce knee-high to a grasshopper. Local girl, bit odd, some folks claim. But it's nice to see an educated feller like yourself appreciate her work."

Sloan quit rocking. "Those were done by someone you know? A young girl? Named Garnet?"

"Mm. Lives a couple of miles south of here, over on Sinclair Run. Reckon she's nearer a woman grown now though."

Years of practice at hiding his expression from patients was all that allowed Sloan to utter nothing beyond a noncommittal grunt. Slowly he forced his hands to relax on the rocker arms, while memory roared through him like a brush fire. "Well, she does nice work," he commented without inflection.

"Oh, are you talking about Garnet?" Mrs. Wickham came into the room, dabbing her perspiring face with the hem of her apron. "Such a sweet girl. Shy as a fawn, but a more tender-hearted soul I've never known." She blessed Sloan with a twinkling smile when he rose and insisted she take his place in the vacated rocking chair. "You're a charmer, aren't you, Dr. MacAllister? But I do appreciate it, thank you kindly."

"Call him Sloan," Eb corrected her around his pipestem. "Since he don't do doctoring anymore, he prefers it."

"And here I was all ready to ask him about my bronchial catarrh. Been plaguing me all spring."

"Tell me about the young lady—Garnet?—instead," Sloan said with a coaxing smile, ignoring the leading comment. "You say she's shy?" That certainly didn't sound like the young woman he'd encountered in the meadow.

"Never struck me as shy," Eb observed. "Just because she's not a flap-tongued chatterbox like some of the young girls hereabouts don't mean she's shy." He took the pipe out of his mouth and pointed it across the room. "Grab that chair over there at the table and drag it over here, Sloan."

"Thanks. I'll do that." As he walked by the two prints he paused, studying them, flabbergasted by the delicacy and precision of style. He could almost smell the flowers. The scene back in the meadow made more sense now; she'd been working, not dabbling, not being coy. "Does she draw anything but flowers?"

"Don't rightly know," Mrs. Wickham said. "She won't talk about her work much. I know a biggity New York publisher pays her to do some work for his magazine, so she doesn't have as much free time as she used to. Meredith—that's Garnet's oldest sister, told us last year before she hared off to Winchester that the gentleman had seen some of Garnet's work in the hotel lobby, up in Strasburg. Seems he appeared on the Sinclairs' front porch the next day, wanting to carry her off to New York, have her get 'professional training,' or some such flummery."

"Uppity Yankee outlander," Eb grumped. "Begging your pardon, Sloan."

Sloan turned back around. "I've been called worse myself. Don't worry, Eb. Far as I'm concerned, the War's over. Besides, human nature's not much different regardless of one's accent." He snagged one of the pressed-back chairs at the table and stationed it in between the Wickhams, gesturing toward the pen-and-inks as he sat down. "If that's a sampling of her early work, looks to me as though she could teach an art instructor a thing or two."

"God blessed her with a gift." Mrs. Wickham reached behind her into a large wicker basket, pulling out knitting needles stuck in brown yarn, and a half-finished sweater. "All those girls of Jacob's are lovely, but I confess Garnet's always been my favorite. All the young uns flock around her after church like a gaggle of geese. She's so…unassuming about herself and her art. Why, she doesn't even realize half the young men in Shenandoah County would give her the moon for one of her smiles."

Ebenezer nodded. "Local feller's been courtin' her for several years now, but far as we know there's still no smell of orange blossoms in the air."

Sloan bit back a stinging comment. He'd wager his left arm Garnet Sinclair knew exactly what effect those big eyes and the air of teasing indifference kindled in those hapless young men. Abruptly he rose to his feet. "Rain's slackening," he said. "I need to be—"

A desperate-sounding voice shouted outside. Frantic pounding erupted against the front door. "Eb! Ebenezer!"

In seconds Sloan was across the room. The door burst open, and a dripping, wild-eyed man staggered over the threshold. "A-accident, quarter-mile south," he gasped, swiping a bloody hand over his rain-soaked face. "Whole family, flung all over the Pike—buggy wheel snapped off…Man's hurt real bad. So's one of the young uns. Me'n Ike were hauling molasses up from Woodstock."

He sucked in lungfuls of air. "Said I'd fetch you, then head out for Doc Porter's." Then, glancing at Sloan, "Mister, could you help? Buggy's a big un. It's flipped, and the man's pinned beneath the axle."

Rage vibrated through his muscles, and Sloan almost shook a fist toward heaven. *Why can't You just leave me alone?* he wanted to shout.

"Sloan?" Eb's voice was tentative.

"I'll get my bag." Sloan shot the bewildered newcomer a look, his smile more like a baring of teeth. "I'm a doctor."

"Here," Mrs. Wickham thrust the familiar brown leather bag into his hands. "I'll put on water to boil, rip some cloths for bandages. Ebenezer, go on with Billy and Sloan." She looked into Sloan's eyes, compassion softening her face as she laid a bracing hand on his forearm. "Thank you," she said, "Dr. MacAllister."

Four

*G*arnet would have missed the child crouched against the stone wall flanking the Pike, but as the cart jogged by a dark shape leaped up, waving sticklike arms. Goatsbeard shied violently sideways. Garnet calmed the snorting animal, pulled him to a halt, then leaned around the panel.

A pale little face with desperate eyes emerged in front of her. "Please help. I want to go home."

"Oh, you poor scrap...quick, now. Pop up here beside me." She held her arms out, and the boy scooted into the cart like a terrified puppy. "You're shivering." Garnet hurriedly opened the heavy mackintosh. "Come here."

"I'm all wet."

"Well, I'm a trifle damp myself. So is this mackintosh, but if we snuggle close together, perhaps we'll be a bit warmer."

He obeyed, but his nose wrinkled. "It stinks."

"Mm. It does, doesn't it? But it's better than being wet and cold and all alone in the rain, don't you agree?"

He nodded his head vigorously, soaking Garnet's shawl. "I'm Timmy Bottoms. Who are you?"

"Garnet Sinclair. Do you belong to the Jefferson Bottoms clan, the ones living in Skunk Hollow?" Their farm was tucked at the base of some hills about four miles distant. What on earth was this little tyke doing so far from home?

"Huh-uh. That's Uncle Jefferson 'n' Aunt Rose. Me an' my brothers come down from Mount Olive, to help with spring planting."

Garnet jiggled the reins, and they set off down the road. "So how did you come to be out here all by yourself, Timmy?"

"Fell outta the wagon. We'd been to that store with all the barrels and smells—Cooper's?"

"That's right." Maude Cooper wouldn't care for the unflattering description, even though it was uncannily accurate.

"Aunt Rose boughten us candy sticks. Mine was wintergreen. I dropped it in the road, tried to fetch it. But I fell out instead."

"Why didn't they stop?"

For a moment Timmy didn't reply, the thin face a study in misery. He sucked on his bottom lip, and Garnet felt the bony shoulders lift in a shrug. "Uncle Jefferson didn't see. The others—they thought it was funny. They was laughin', like. I thought it was funny too. But then I—" He stopped, and Garnet glanced down in time to catch his convulsive swallowing. "I couldn't run fast enough to catch up. And it was rainin' real hard, so Uncle Jefferson whipped the mules, and they…I couldn't catch up."

Why hadn't his cousins and brothers told Mr. Bottoms to stop? Garnet wondered, her heart aching for Timmy. "Well, I've got you now. We'll pass by Cooper's in a few moments. I can leave you there—don't worry, the Coopers love little boys. Did you know they have four sons and two daughters? Or"—she eyed the averted head, adding more slowly—"you can come home with me until the rain stops."

"I don't care," he muttered. "I wanna go home."

"I know you do, laddie. But if I don't make it to my own home soon—" She stopped, realizing that Timmy did not need to hear how upset her own family would be if she didn't turn up by sundown. "Buttercups and bitterweed."

"Huh? Why'd you say that?"

"Say what?" Diverted, Garnet glanced down, then laughed. "Oh, you mean 'buttercups and bitterweed'? I say that when I'm frustrated or…or thinking hard," she amended, lest Timmy assume the burden of her frustration.

"That's a stupid saying. Why don't you say—" He'd managed several ear-burning obscenities before Garnet clapped her hand over his mouth.

"I don't talk like that," she sputtered, "and neither should you,

Timmy Bottoms. Nobody should say words like that, no matter how provoked or—or whatever." She moved her hand to his chin and gave it a light pinch. "My father would wash my mouth with alum or persimmon juice or something." Or worse, he'd let her see his disappointment. That tactic had devastated both her and Meredith when they'd gone through a spell of tossing out cuss words for effect. Unfortunately for Papa, it only annoyed Leah.

"Uncle Jefferson says those words all the time, 'specially when he's angry." Timmy blinked hard, and pulled away from Garnet's hand. "He probably didn't come back 'cuz he was angry."

Garnet hugged the stiff body, then let him go. She fiddled with the reins a moment, thinking hard. "Tell you what," she said. "We'll stop at Cooper's long enough for me to buy you a new stick of wintergreen candy. Then I'll drive you home. We should be there by suppertime. All right?"

"What if they don't want me anymore? What if that's why they didn't come back for me?"

"I don't know why, Timmy. But there's only one way to find out, isn't there?" Garnet was interested to hear it herself. And if she didn't like what she heard, she just might pay a visit to Sheriff Pettiscomb. Or drive Timmy back to his home in Mount Olive.

After a moment the bony shoulders shrugged again. "I reckon you can take me home."

For a little while they traveled in silence. Garnet wondered if he'd fallen asleep. Then, "Do you think they didn't tell Uncle Jefferson 'cuz of the bottle of castor oil Aunt Rose bought? I dipped their candy sticks in it when they weren't looking."

Garnet barely managed to swallow a gasp of laughter. "Timmy, if you'd done that to my candy, I would have left you in the middle of the road too!" She slanted him a downward glance. "Are you sorry now?"

He grinned an urchin's grin that turned wobbly at the end. "They looked funny, spittin' and hollering. But I didn't like being alone. And the thunder…" His voice trembled, and all of a sudden he burrowed into Garnet's side. "If I say I'm sorry they have to let me stay, don't they?"

"I have a feeling," Garnet volunteered as she guided Goatsbeard off the Pike and pulled up at the entrance to Cooper's Hardware and Dry-goods Store, "that they'll be as glad to see you as you will be to see them. Especially if we take your cousins and brothers a fresh batch of candy." The pungent odors of glazed calico, buggy harness, and ripe cheese met them at the door, overlaid by the musty smell of smoke on rain-dampened wood. Next to the potbelly stove in the middle of the room, two gaunt farmers huddled over a game of checkers. The men scarcely glanced up when Garnet and her tiny charge came dripping through the wide double doors. Keeping Timmy's hand in a firm clasp, she led him down the crowded aisle, past open drawers full of jumbled brogan shoes and the glass showcase with its meticulous display of toiletries.

Mr. Cooper appeared in the doorway to the side room, a burlap sack of feed on his shoulder. When he saw Garnet, his bearded face lit in a welcoming smile. He dumped the feed against a large wooden barrel. "Sure, I'll clean the whippersnapper up," he promised after Garnet explained the predicament, holding his hand out to the docile boy. Garnet hunted down Mrs. Cooper, who was arranging a display of ladies' millinery in the upstairs room. After waving away the woman's dismay over her drenched appearance, Garnet asked if a message could be sent to Jacob and Leah, explaining why she'd be home after dark.

It was almost three hours later by the time she finally pulled a droopy-headed Goatsbeard to a halt in front of the house. Garnet herself barely had enough energy to stumble out of the cart and up the porch steps.

As she reached for the knob, the door was flung wide and her father's wiry figure filled the entry. "Don't worry, I'll see to the horse and cart. Come in now and let's take care of you." He stepped aside, and Garnet dragged into the hall. "Did you get the lad home then?"

She nodded. "They didn't hug him or tell him they were wor-ried…didn't even save supper for him." She lifted a hand to her throat, as though massaging the tightness could ease the burning constriction. "His aunt, Mrs. Bottoms, cuffed the side of his head for not being there to do his chores, and his cousins were threatening to—" She had to stop, but Jacob seemed to understand.

He enfolded her in a comforting hug, pressed a kiss against her forehead, then rubbed noses. "You can't save the whole world, lass. That's the Lord's business. You did what you could."

"Seems like the Lord's not doing a very good job," Garnet mumbled. She summoned a weak smile. "More likely it's me. Timmy was clinging to my hand so tight my fingers went numb. I don't think he wanted me to leave. But I…I pressed a bag of candy sticks I'd bought for him to give everyone into his hands and told him everything would be fine…" She leaned against the doorframe and closed her eyes. That only made her misery worse: She could still see Timmy's defeated slump, the hopeless eyes in a face years too old for a child of eight.

With an effort she straightened, fumbling for the buttons on the mackintosh. The fragrance of Leah's ginger-and-garlic pork roast teased her nostrils, overlaying the smell of wet wool and camphor, soothing Garnet's raw senses. Her father's sturdy presence wrapped her in security. *Lord, it's good to be home.* "Did you have roast pork and"—she took a deep, appreciative breath—"baked apples for supper? I'm sorry I missed it."

"You didn't," Leah announced coming in from the hall. "I left a plate on the stove."

Her younger sister looked as fresh and neat at nine o'clock at night as she had that morning when Garnet left. She surveyed Garnet, her disapproving look at odds with the concern that darkened her observant brown eyes. Leah didn't miss much. "But you can't have anything until you get out of those wet clothes." The brown eyes twinkled all of a sudden. "While you eat, Papa and I will have another go at clipping the wings of our ruby-haired hummingbird."

Five

*J*acob fretted over his middle daughter. Lately, when she wasn't aware that he was looking, a soul-wrenching dejection would settle over her freckled face. It never lasted long—Garnet's sunny nature usually dominated the dour Scottish streak she struggled with at times. But Jacob fretted all the same. He was careful, however, not to let Garnet see. She hated to be fussed over, hated undue attention of any kind, even from her family.

He studied the corner china cabinet he'd stained two days earlier, walking from side to side to make sure the golden oak tones darkening the grain were equally blended. At least the Brauns had given in and allowed the cabinet to be stained instead of painted, as was the current fashion in the Valley these days. Why in the name of Bonny Prince Charles did folks insist on covering up God's natural beauty? To Jacob's way of thinking, there were few things on earth to rival a fine piece of wood. Three of those being, of course, his daughters.

Och, but Garnet was a puzzle. Lovely and long-limbed, with that mass of glorious hair, at twenty-one in the prime of womanhood—and the girl as oblivious to young men as a knothole in a tree. Meredith claimed Garnet was actually *afraid* of men. Pure nonsense, it was, as both Garnet herself as well as Jacob had insisted.

Meredith had tossed her head and told them that if they wanted to be blind moles, that was fine, but not to expect her to play along. Shaking his head, Jacob picked up a clean rubbing cloth.

Garnet wasn't like other young ladies, he told himself, not for the first time. That was all. Why, didn't she always natter with the neighbor boys when they crowded around her after church? And hadn't Nahum Tweedie sidled up to Jacob at Cooper's store this past March to tell him how much he and his grandmother enjoyed her visits? Then there was Joshua Jones, steadfastly courting the past few years in spite of Garnet's equally steadfast indifference.

No, Jacob decided as he rubbed in boiled linseed oil to seal the wood, there was simply no basis for Meredith's claim. Garnet was just different. A…a wild violet nestled in the middle of a rose garden.

Pleased with his analogy, Jacob began to whistle. At least she'd finally completed her latest batch of drawings and was no longer spending all her days and evenings hunched over her easel. First thing this morning, she and Leah headed out for the post office in Woodstock. With a bit of luck—and gentle bullying—Leah would manage to keep them out all afternoon. Both girls needed more outings, more frequent companionship of friends and neighbors, especially with his gadfly, Meredith, gone. When his eldest still lived at home, the old place always seemed to be filled with young folk.

In truth, it was less than an hour later when Jacob heard the buggy pull to a halt in front of the barn. Tossing aside the rag, he sluiced his hands in a bucket of water and stepped outside, just in time to watch Garnet scampering toward the house like a fox fleeing the hounds. The midday sunlight washed over her willowy figure, turning her hair to a blend of burnished copper and flaming mahogany. Jacob couldn't help but admire the sight, any more than he could help noticing her stiff posture.

"There's my two lasses." He leaned down a bit so Leah could give his cheek a kiss. "What's with your sister?"

"She's upset. With me." Arms folded, her expression rueful, Leah waited until Garnet disappeared inside. "I suppose I shouldn't have lectured her all the way home."

"And what were you lecturing her about this time, little wren?"

She favored him with one of those particularly feminine looks that blended impatience with resigned tolerance. "This time, Papa, you'll be surprised."

Jacob tugged the drooping plume of her go-to-town hat. "Very well," he countered with a wink, "Surprise me."

"After we mailed the drawings, we ate lunch at Mrs. Booth's Café.

Everybody there was talking about this mysterious outlander from Pennsylvania or Maryland or somewhere. There's even a wild tale about him being a miracle-wielding doctor who saved the lives of some travelers or some such flumadiddle. But apparently he's bought the old Pritchett place. Paid cash, according to Mrs. Booth, who heard it from the banker's wife. But the most startling—"

"Och, that farm's been vacant for going on five years. No telling what manner of repairs he'll need to make it habitable. Why would a rich Yankee doctor purchase a place like that?" Bemused, Jacob shook his head. "Does he have a family?"

"Don't know. I don't think so." She waved her hand. "That's not important. *Listen* to this, Papa. Garnet's met him! She admitted it, calm as you please, then asked would I please pass the rolls."

"Garnet met him? Where? When?" Leah had the way of it—Jacob was surprised. He was even more upset, however, because Garnet had not mentioned the incident.

"You remember the day she found the Bottomses' nephew out along the Pike? Came home late, looking like a drowned kitten? Well, it was the very same day she met this mysterious stranger." Leah brushed specks of road dust off the points on her lace collar. "He…ah…he climbed up the hill to where she was working and introduced himself."

"He did *what?*"

"To hear Garnet tell it, he didn't do anything beyond disturb her concentration and act mildly annoyed when she wouldn't stay to chat. She doesn't recall his name, much less remember what he looked like, beyond having dark hair and a straight caterpillar mustache." They exchanged looks of mutual exasperation.

"I think," Jacob said after a moment, "it might be time to sit the lass down for a talk."

"Papa?"

"Hmm?" Preoccupied, he set about unhitching the horses. When Leah hadn't responded by the time he'd removed the shafts, he glanced over, frowning, then slowly tied the horses to the paddock gate.

Leah was by nature straightforward. Even as a scrap of a lass she had little use for prevarication in any form. Right now, however, her gaze avoided his, and the dainty frame fairly hummed with agitation. Jacob folded his arms and waited.

"Papa, is Meredith right?" she finally ventured, her voice reluctant. "Is Garnet...well, afraid of men?"

Something hot and bitter tightened his throat. "Just because your sister's no' like Meredith nor you doesn't mean—" He stopped himself. "I don't know," he admitted at last, equally reluctantly. "She's never said anything, never indicated an aversion—" Again, he stopped.

That summer, he realized. It all started in Garnet's sixteenth summer. She'd been driving old Dipple home from school all alone, and the horse ran away with her when a rabbit ran across the road. Chowder, the family dog, had chased the rabbit and apparently run off himself. He hadn't come when Garnet called, and they'd never seen him again.

"Aversion or no, she acts as though every male she meets is between six and eight years old...or ninety-six years, perhaps," Leah said. "Even poor Joshua. Meredith and I used to talk about it a lot, whenever Garnet wasn't around."

Jacob ran a weary hand around the back of his neck, his resolve crumbling. "I know what Meredith thinks. It isn't so."

"But Garnet never used to be like that, not when we were young. I always wondered...people don't change without a reason." Her fingers combed through Goatsbeard's mane. She still wouldn't look at Jacob. "What if someone—I mean, what if a—a man..."

The pain in Jacob's belly cramped suddenly, viciously, and he reached into his pocket for one of the bismuth tablets. Closing his eyes, he chewed the medicine and waited for the searing pain to ease. For years he'd fought—but kept to himself—the niggling suspicions. Now 'twas plain as the barn door he'd not done right by his daughters. He'd buried his concern, pretended that Meredith and Leah hadn't noticed anything amiss. Pretended that their innocence shielded them from all knowledge of the world's capacity for wickedness.

He looked Leah straight in the eye. "Your sister was not...violated," he stated, bluntly because the time for shielding was over. "Not like poor Olive Lindemann, four years ago." For months the entire community had been shaken by the vile incident involving a local young woman.

Leah's gaze jerked up to his at last, her expression confirming Jacob's hunch both about her reluctance, and her determination. He hooked his thumbs through his suspenders, "But I do think Garnet is holding on to a dark secret. Don't know why she won't share it, and I tell you plainly that hurts my soul something fierce. I reckon whatever it is, it's painful enough to her that she's spent these past years convincing herself, her family, and the rest of the world, that this secret—whatever it is—doesn't exist."

"You truly don't know what it is? Only what it isn't?"

"Lass, I'd almost be willing to sell my immortal soul to know. But she's never told me." And as he'd confessed to Leah, the bitter pain of it was a monstrous thorn in his flesh.

"Papa...if someone had done that to Garnet, we'd know. We'd *know*."

Jacob lifted her clenched fist, tucking it close against his chest. They stood in silence for a long time before he lifted her face to rub noses, then gently set her aside. "About this...miracle-wielding doctor. Tell me everything you heard about the Yankee outlander and everything Garnet said."

Six

*M*ay. Ever since she was four years old and waved her very first picked flower under Papa's nose—a dandelion that made him sneeze—Garnet had loved the month of May. March and April vacillated too much; balmy sweetness one day, snow and sleet the next. Flowers tended to be timid and short-lived. Lovely, of course, because they were flowers and part of God's gifts to the earth, but Garnet still preferred the exuberance of May.

It was as though the Lord finally allowed Mother Nature to indulge to compensate for the monochrome winter, incorporating all the rainbow colors in His palette. Above her, a deep blue sky hurt her eyes with its jewellike brilliance. Around her, infinite shades of green from fragrant gray green cedars to emerald meadows. And the flowers! Bright yellow buttercups, hot pink lady's slippers. Purple violets and periwinkle. Scarlet poppies and trumpet honeysuckle. Just this morning she'd stumbled across a breathtaking *Rhododendron calendulaceum,* blooming in flamelike brilliance beneath a stand of beeches. The clustered flowers decorated the towering bush like gigantic brooches. Garnet remained bowed over her sketchpad for hours, determined to capture enough detail to achieve that effect with her pens later on, back in the studio.

Perhaps one day she would take up oils or watercolors, instead of pen and ink. More likely not. It was a contradiction that baffled her sisters. "How can someone who loves flowers so much prefer to draw them in shades of gray and black?" Meredith always asked. "It doesn't make sense."

"We're talking about Garnet," Leah usually responded. The two sisters would nod at each other, then run shrieking when Garnet pretended to toss an open bottle of ink between them.

Fifteen years earlier, a stubby pencil clutched in matchstick fingers, she'd painstakingly drawn her first flower on the back of some crumpled butcher paper. Jacob hung the finished product on the parlor wall, and the next week wheedled an old set of draftsman's pens from a civil engineer in Strasburg—all they could afford at the time. Garnet, transported by a joy that had yet to fade, still occasionally fitted one of those old pen points to the worn wooden barrel, just to savor the memory.

And to remind her why she stayed with the medium.

Part of it was the challenge, she thought now as she trudged up a tree-choked hill near Cedar Creek. The perfection of detail, of reproducing one of the Lord's creations as faithfully as one of Mr. Eastman's cameras. Smelly oils and temperamental paintbrushes just weren't the same. Likely she'd still be lining and crosshatching when she was a bent old lady.

Near the top of the wooded rise she paused to catch her breath, listening to the muted song of rushing water, the endless whisper of wind weaving through the trees. And pressing down and around and through her—the magnificent silence of an ancient mountain chain washed in sunlight. A rush of gratitude flooded her being, stinging her eyes with tears. *Thank You for this day.* Then, feeling almost shy, she darted through the trees, nimbly hopping over half-buried stones and around massive boulders, until she came to the crest.

At the bottom of a steep rock-strewn slope Cedar Creek babbled its way toward the north fork of the Shenandoah. Some hundred yards or so west was the old Valley Turnpike Bridge, momentarily free of travelers. *At last,* Garnet thought, rubbing her hands in a fever of anticipation. She was here at last, after weeks of more pressing obligations.

Now…all she needed was a nice healthy selection of twinleaf, or perhaps some vivid yellow puccoon? The blood in her veins all but hummed with eagerness. She examined the bank on both sides of the creek and abruptly saw a flash of color at the bottom of the hill. Red. Not a vivid scarlet, but definitely red, which ruled out puccoon and twinleaf. She squinted, peering more closely.

Why, it looked like…yes, it *was* an animal.

Surprised but unalarmed, Garnet watched without moving for a while, puzzlement growing when the animal didn't stir at all. Sleeping, perhaps? More likely it sensed her presence and was playing possum, except she'd never heard of another animal that employed that tactic. And this was definitely no possum, not with that coloring. A noisily jawing bird landed on a branch overhanging the creek, directly opposite the animal, which didn't so much as twitch. Garnet belatedly realized something was wrong, that the splash of red might in fact be blood. Without further thought she searched for and found a way to negotiate the steep, rocky slope.

Halfway down she was close enough to tell that the animal was a fox, obviously injured because it was so still, lying on its side, paws and tail limp. Uncertain, Garnet fiddled with the strap of her cloth bag. She knew next to nothing about foxes except that, around here, the animals were considered thieving varmints. Farther east, Meredith once told her, rich folks enjoyed fox hunting solely for the sport of galloping their fancy horses over meadows and woodland. But Doc Porter said foxes carried rabies, like raccoons and bats, and that if Garnet ever happened upon one while she was wandering, she'd best keep her distance.

Yet she couldn't blithely go about her work, knowing the poor creature was hurting and she'd made no effort to help. "I can at least determine if it's still alive." The actual sound of her voice seemed decisive.

Her heavy bag would make it awkward to maintain her balance, so she laid it in front of a large sumac bush, anchoring the straps with a heavy rock. "Don't run off," she said, then looked back down toward the inert animal.

A loose stone turned beneath her left foot. With a choked-off gasp she wavered, pitched forward, then tumbled down the hill in a painful kaleidoscope of rocks, dirt, and flailing limbs. Dimly she felt blows to her head, an icy-hot knife scoring her shoulder…blood spurting warm and wet into her face, soaking her shirtwaist.

Her out-of-control descent slammed her to a stop against flat-sided boulders by the creek. Pain and shock swirled around her in a thick black cloud, sucking her toward unconsciousness. Grimly she clenched her teeth and lay without moving, trying not to panic, focusing instead on the little fox, only a yard or so away.

After a time she realized that its head was turned toward her. And its eyes were open. "I won't hurt you," Garnet croaked. She tried to reach out her hand. The effort was so agonizing tears flooded her eyes. Bile, thick and hot, crowded her throat.

The fox whimpered, a thready sound like that of a tiny baby. It stirred, then collapsed and lay still once more.

Resolve flooded Garnet's noodly limbs; after a few sickening moments she managed to drag herself to a sitting position with her back against the boulder. When the sky ceased spinning, she gingerly lifted her right arm to her aching forehead—her left arm was useless, the pain accompanying any movement so awful she knew further effort would send her hurtling into unconsciousness for sure.

Her right hand came away covered with blood. "B-blast," she mumbled. It was the strongest epithet she'd ever heard her father utter, but she was too woozy to feel guilty. An errant thought surfaced: What would happen to her cloth bag? Panic flared briefly, but the starburst of pain in her temple forced her to remain still. She should be grateful to be alive. After all, drawings could be recaptured on paper. Life could not.

Lightheaded and dizzy, she tried to decide how to proceed. *Hard to tell who needs assistance more—me or the fox.* It hurt to move, though she didn't think any bones were broken. *So don't whine, Garnet. Go and see what you can do for that poor little critter, before it's too late.* Setting her teeth, breathing in shallow pants, and ignoring the pain, she set about dragging her uncooperative body across the intervening space.

She might not know a lot about wild animals, but she did know herself. Never again would she helplessly stand by. Didn't matter whether it was an injured child or an animal reviled as a pest. She would do what she could, or she could never look in the mirror again.

Sloan grumbled all the way down the weed-choked lane that meandered past his recently purchased house, grumbled all the way down the two-track road leading into Tom's Brook, and vowed with every step after he headed north on the Valley Pike that he was turning around and returning home. Now. By four o'clock though, when he was twenty minutes past Strasburg, he had changed tactics. He badgered God instead, demanding answers.

He still couldn't believe he'd given in to this inexplicable but infuriatingly persistent urge to *walk* to Winchester to retrieve his horse, for crying out loud. All right, yes. He'd known since he'd taken possession of the gone-to-seed farmhouse that eventually he'd have to either fetch Dulcie or sell her to the livery owner who'd been caring for her.

Mr. Grigsby had written Sloan twice in the past two weeks, wanting to know what Sloan planned to do. Dulcie had recovered completely from her lameness, and Mr. Grigsby had declared a liking for her malleable disposition. She'd be a fine addition to his stable...

Feeling a strange reluctance to doom the faithful mare to the ofttimes brutal life of a livery hack, Sloan had balked at selling. Until this morning he'd also balked at interrupting his work to fetch his horse. Over the past week he'd been installing new mantels over the fireplaces—marble in the front parlor, carved mahogany in the sitting room and his bedroom. The trip to Winchester would waste an entire day, even if he caught a northbound train at Tom's Brook.

Adding insult to injury, at dawn he'd been pulled from a dreamless sleep, awakened by the vague notion that there was something important he was supposed to do that day. As though something had grabbed the back of his neck and shaken him, demanding his attention. But he knew it had been Someone, not something, and he'd been angered at the intrusion.

Two years earlier Sloan would have listened without questioning for what he had come to recognize as God's spirit-manifestation in his life. He would have waited, confident and alert, for the Lord to reveal how Sloan could serve Him this time. Usually it required a middle-of-the-night trip to deliver a child, set a broken bone or two...with depressing frequency to offer comfort to the dying. Once, heeding that inner urging, he'd woken a brakeman and his wife, both healthy as market-bound hogs, from a sound sleep. The wife shrilled invective, while the bleary-eyed brakeman threatened to break his interfering nose before slamming the door in Sloan's face.

Sloan had barely climbed back into the buggy when the brakeman yelled his name. Seemed as though the surly fellow had stopped on his way back to bed to check on his mother, who lived with them. Turned out the woman had awakened and was suffering a cardiac asthma attack, complicated by hysteric angina. If a qualified physician hadn't been on the spot, she could have died within an hour.

On this particular morning, however, instead of heeding the call, Sloan grumbled defiantly, rolled over, and went back to sleep.

When he jerked awake a second time to that prickling sense of urgency, rebellion rather than obedience dictated his actions. "I won't listen to You!" he'd shouted, stomping down the stairs to the kitchen to grind some coffee. No longer was he a healer, a shepherd to God's wounded sheep. *Sheep, ha!* More like jackals, snapping and snarling, biting into his soul until it bled dry. He'd devoted his life to a profession that had crushed him, pledged his fidelity to a woman who had betrayed him, and trusted his soul to a God who demanded the impossible.

So why was he here, sweating and coated with road dust? Sloan asked himself for the dozenth time in the last hour. He glared at the medical bag he'd picked up out of habit on his way out the door, then lifted it above his head. "I'm selling this in Winchester!" he shouted to the sky. "I'm through with doctoring, do You hear?"

The echo of his voice mocked him. But a cool breeze blew across the road, caressing his perspiring face. The bitterness he wore like a suit of armor could not deflect a sensation of...of an understanding hand, patting him on the back.

And gently nudging him down the steep incline toward the rickety old bridge that crossed Cedar Creek.

Half ashamed, Sloan stopped in the middle of the structure to listen to the running water, reluctantly enjoying the way late afternoon sunlight poured into the creek. Light and shadow, changing with every ripple. Like life, he supposed, except he wasn't in the mood to wax poetic, so he turned his attention to an indeterminable shape on the bank, about fifty yards east of the bridge. Looked like a pile of clothes, he decided, wondering with brief amusement who had lost their shirt.

Then the pile of clothes moved. Sloan leaned over the bridge, hands gripping the stone abutment. Seconds later he was running, slipping, rapidly maneuvering his way down to the water.

Seven

A woman. It was a woman lying there, a scant yard from the creek. She wasn't moving anymore. He didn't know if she was alive. Sloan clambered over a jutting boulder, dropped onto a narrow strip of damp sand, saw the blood—and the old-fashioned bonnet covering the woman's head.

Garnet Sinclair.

She was curled on her side beneath a clump of shrubbery growing between several large boulders. And, thanks be to God, she was alive: Blood still oozed from beneath her concealing bonnet, smearing her forehead. More stained the whole left side of her dress from shoulder to neck. Her eyes were closed, the lids translucent from blood loss, shock—Sloan automatically noted symptoms, none of them comforting. Nestled against her right side, her right arm curled protectively around it, was some sort of bundle wrapped in a blood-spattered shawl.

Sloan's mind recoiled from what appeared to be a fox's narrow snout and pointed ears peeping out of that shawl. *A fox?*

He dropped down beside Garnet, who did not stir. But the creature's eyes blinked open, and a faint yip emerged from its sharp-toothed mouth. It was a fox, all right—not a domestic animal or a pet. Even a baby would have been less shocking than a wild red fox.

Over the years Sloan had faced numerous frightening encounters, from angry mobs to a grieving father who thrust the muzzle of a gun against Sloan's chest. This present terror, intensified by anger, eclipsed all other occasions. His mind was mush, his hands trembling. To think the girl had actually tangled with a rabid fox and—from the look of it— with some idiotic notion of *helping* the animal.

He eyed the swaddled form with loathing, calculating how best to destroy it while evading a disease-infected bite. He'd have to move fast, for Garnet's sake as well as his own. His fingers closed over a sharp-edged rock. How many times had the animal broken her skin before she subdued it in the shawl? In order for her to have captured it, the rabies would have progressed to the latter stages.

Sloan's medical bag contained no vials of Pasteur's life-saving serum.

A whine sounded deep in the fox's throat.

Garnet Sinclair's translucent eyelids flickered. "Shh…'s all right… don't be afraid." Her hand fumbled, barely missing the fox's black nose. "Need more…water?" She stirred. "I'll…find help. Don't die. Please."

The poignant plea, soft but audible, caused something inside Sloan to twist painfully, some remnant of feeling he wanted to deny but couldn't. Even when semiconscious, the girl's instinct was to help. To protect. In spite of his training, logic, and common sense, Sloan was unable to ignore that plea.

He would have to try to help the fox as well as Garnet.

Reluctantly his gaze focused on the animal, which needed to be moved out of the way so he could determine the exact nature of Garnet Sinclair's injuries. After a long moment of concentrated study his hand opened, and the rock dropped back to the dirt. Something was wrong with the fox, all right, but it wasn't rabies. He hoped.

Garnet's right arm twitched, half lifting. "Find help. I…" Her hold on the animal loosened. The shawl unwound, and the fox collapsed in a limp, bloodied heap at Sloan's feet. Late afternoon sun revealed the ugly wound that had ripped open the animal's belly. Torn strips of cloth dangled uselessly above and below, attesting to Garnet's efforts to bind it closed.

Once again logic urged Sloan to make short work of the creature, toss it aside so he could find out how badly Garnet herself was injured. But he couldn't do it. He simply could not do it. Not when the girl had all but killed herself over a dumb animal—and not when that dumb animal looked directly up into Sloan's face with an eerily human expression of resignation…and trust. Sloan wondered if *he* was the one who had gone mad.

"If I find out you do have rabies along with that gash in your abdomen, I'll turn you into a rug."

He shucked off his jacket, then reached for the unprotesting fox. Now that he had settled on a course he worked with speed and deftness, his hands sure. In seconds the blood-soaked cloths were back in place, holding ragged edges of furry skin together. Sloan figured his ministrations must be painful, yet the fox never attempted to struggle, much less bite. Just kept watching him through unblinking eyes with elongated pupils and an unnerving anthropomorphic trust. Pity pinched his heart. Sloan ignored it. He securely wrapped the small animal, a young juvenile from its size, back in the cleanest portion of the shawl, then laid it underneath the nearby bush. Its fate rested where it belonged, in the divine hands that persisted in meddling in Sloan's life.

He washed his own hands in the cold creek water, thought about his bag, but because she seemed to be unconscious decided to check Garnet before he retrieved it. A faint moan whispered past her lips as he knelt beside her. "It's all right. I'm here, and I'm going to help you."

A swift once-over reassured him that she'd suffered no broken bones—all that would have deterred him from moving her—though movement might be the least of his concerns. From the appearance of the churned earth and trail of blood on the other side of the boulders, the injuries had been sustained elsewhere. The girl must have literally dragged herself over to the fox. Foolish, soft-hearted, impetuous female…

Her skin was softer than a doeskin glove and alarmingly cold. In spite of the gathering dusk and old-fashioned sunbonnet, Sloan could still discern the freckles dusting her face. For a month now his memory of that first meeting had kept him awake many a night. He'd worked every day since like a man bent on punishing himself because of it. Their present circumstances only stoked that ruinous fire. She was injured and vulnerable and had made it clear she had no interest in him. She needed a doctor, and he was the only one around. God made it plain he was here to help her.

But what he wanted was to touch each one of those freckles.

He was actually lifting his hand when her eyes fluttered open. Sloan yanked his hand away. She moaned again, lines of pain bracketing her mouth, furrowing her brow. "Shh. Don't be afraid," he murmured. He brushed his fingers against her cheek, his only intention now to reassure. "Don't try to move. It's all right. Tell me where it hurts." Relief filled him when awareness seeped into her eyes. "Miss Sinclair—Garnet. Can you tell me where you hurt?"

"What—?"

"Looks like you've suffered a fall," Sloan began, keeping his voice calm and soothing. "I need you to tell me where you hurt, so I don't cause you unnecessary pain, or more damage. Don't worry—I'm a doctor. I know what I'm doing." Blood from the gash in her forehead had dripped over his fingers. He tugged out his handkerchief, wet it in the creek, then carefully pressed it against the wound.

She tried to lift her arm, but the movement was uncoordinated, jerky. "Fox—?"

"I took care of it—no! You mustn't move." He pressed her struggling body back down. "The fox is alive, all right? I promise."

"Help…"

"I will. Don't worry. I'm going to help you."

She shook her head weakly. "No. Help…fox. First. I'm all right." Glassy eyes fixed on his face. "Take care of the fox."

"You're in no position to give orders," Sloan began, shutting his mouth when he realized how overbearing he sounded. Abruptly his gaze sharpened.

There was something about her expression, a current of tension that had manifested itself in a deep inner trembling he could feel beneath his fingertips where he held her down. "Relax," he said, watching her closely. "I'll see to the fox, I promise. I reclosed the abdominal wound with the strips of cloth you fashioned—very resourceful. As soon as I take care of you, make sure you're resting comfortably, I'll do the same for the animal, hmm? How about it?"

"Don't hurt…"

"I'll be as gentle as I can."

"Not me—fox."

Obstinate girl! "The fox is safe." Hopefully it was also still alive. "Do you remember meeting me?" he asked, hoping to divert her not only from that wretched animal, but also from his examination of her person.

For some reason she was manifesting the symptoms of extreme fear. Beneath his fingertips her pulse was racing, her lips were white, her pupils dilated. *Fear, not shock. For the fox? Herself?* Certainly the situation warranted some anxiety, yet Sloan had done his best to relieve her mind, even when she wasn't entirely sentient. Instinct warned him to tread with extreme caution. Considering their radically opposing reactions to his presence, it might be easier to win the fox's trust than Garnet Sinclair's.

Casually Sloan began a chatty monologue while he examined her. Besides the gash on her forehead, she'd suffered a jagged tear from high on her left shoulder to the middle of her collarbone, along with numerous contusions and scratches. The shoulder wound would require stitches.

Just like the fox. Sloan flung a sour glare toward the sky. The Supreme Creator of the universe possessed a bizarre sense of humor.

Well, of course. He'd created human beings, after all.

Sloan lifted Garnet Sinclair's slender wrist, positioning his fingers over her pulse. Still too fast. Frowning, he continued his rambling monologue, and suppressed all hint of impatience. "So I'm walking to Winchester because my horse, Dulcie, went lame a month ago. Turned out to be minor, a stone bruise, and I'm glad of it. She's a great little mare. Owned her for years, right after I started private practice." He almost choked on the words. "At any rate, I bought her from a family friend who raises saddlebreds. I was on my way to bring her home—did you know I've bought a place about a mile east of Tom's Brook? Left there right before lunch. I like to walk, you see. Good for the legs, heart, lungs. I stopped on the bridge, decided to get a drink of water because it looked so cool and fresh. Caught a glimpse of your dress."

She was relaxing, her pulse no longer racing. Incredibly, something that might have been humor flickered across the bloodied face, and a corner of her mouth tilted. "You're…not from around here, are you?"

"No." The words and gently amused tone matched with uncanny precision those she'd spoken to him a month earlier. The first flicker of true alarm prickled beneath Sloan's skin. Had his diagnosis been erroneous? Head wounds were unpredictable, after all. "I'm from—"

"Yankee...too bad..." Those otherworldly eyes, the color of fog-draped cedar, dimmed, as though she were withdrawing to some distant sanctuary. "Thanks for taking care of the f—" With the suddenness of a dropped curtain, she passed out.

Lips pressed together, Sloan wrapped her in his jacket and lifted her into his arms. She was surprisingly light. He held her limp weight close against his chest in an effort to provide as much of his own body heat as possible. She needed warmth and medical attention, and she needed them immediately. With shelter and care, other than a scar or two she should heal without permanent damage. Sloan was less certain about the fox. Once again he thought about a merciful end for it while Garnet was unconscious.

He'd given his word to help—both of them.

The quiet inward nudge set his teeth on edge. "Then You'll have to do it. I'm no veterinarian." And this was positively the last time he planned to practice his former profession.

His glance dropped to the quiescent fox. "I'll come back for you," he growled, feeling like a jinglebrain for talking to an animal. Picking his way with care, he followed the narrow creek bank downstream, aware with every passing second of the deepening twilight.

Moments later he came upon a small finger of well-grazed meadow that had reached the water through a fissure in the rocky cliff. Sloan's breath expelled in soundless relief. At some point in the past, a crude lean-to had been erected to protect an equally crude hayrick. He laid his burden on the driest part of the ground, hurriedly arranged a bed within the lean-to from scattered remains of hay, then settled his patient in her nest. She never stirred. After checking her vital signs again, he left.

Dusk was closing in fast. Darkness would follow even more swiftly.

Some twenty minutes or so later, with a blessed heat-and-light-giving fire to keep the encroaching night at bay, Sloan was finally able to focus all his energy on a still unconscious Garnet Sinclair. He'd stopped the bleeding before laying the fire, and every five minutes had been checking her vital signs, each time reassured by the strong heart-beat and steady pulse. If only fever didn't set in. Or worse.

That shoulder needed to be stitched, but he'd decided to examine her head more thoroughly first, based on her questionable lucidity and continued unconsciousness. The bonnet would have to come off.

He began working the knotted ribbons, ignoring the tingle of anticipation at the thought of finally seeing Garnet Sinclair without the infernal head covering. With a grunt of satisfaction, he carefully peeled the bloodied, dirt-smeared scrap of fabric away from her head.

Behind him the fire crackled, sending up a shower of sparks, and a burst of revelatory light shone directly onto Garnet's bared head. Even matted with blood and perspiration, arranged in an unflattering topknot on the crown of her head, the color of her hair was unmistakable.

Red. Even more striking than the fox's. *Red hair.* Sloan dropped the bonnet, his hands curling into fists.

Why did she have to have red hair?

Eight

Hen Garnet opened her eyes, she focused first on a campfire. She lay in dreamy languor, wondering when and why she'd built a fire, vaguely aware of a multitude of aches and pains. Eventually she turned her head and discovered that the world beyond the campfire was black as her father's boot polish. It was long past sundown.

"Oh no."

"Ah. You're awake." A man appeared by her side, and memory descended with the force of a deluge. "No—don't try to move just yet," he said, his hand pressing against her right shoulder. "You might start the bleeding again." He laid two fingers against her neck, monitoring her pulse, then checked her for fever.

"The fox?" Her voice emerged in a strained whisper. Garnet searched the face hovering over her, but the shadows revealed little other than light-colored eyes, dark unruly hair with a hint of wave, and a thick, straight mustache. "Where's the fox?"

"In the hayrick. Don't worry, it's still alive." A short pause ensued. "I don't know for how long. It was a bad wound. Aren't you interested at all in your own status, Miss Sinclair?"

She wanted to wince away from the biting tone. She supposed her dogged insistence concerning the fox seemed irrational, especially when there didn't seem to be any part of her that didn't now throb with pain. But she couldn't explain. "Am I—can I be moved? My family was expecting me home by sunset. They'll be...concerned."

More likely panicked. By now Papa would have called out all the neighbors, Sheriff Pettiscomb, and Banjo Scoggins's hounds. Oh, she was in a barrel of molasses for sure. And all for a fox...

"Are they nearby?"

"Not exactly." She tried to piece together where she'd left Goats-beard, but all that came to mind was a winding path through some woods, a huge bush drooping with clusters of flame-colored blooms. A steep slope—and the heart-stopping seconds when she fell. "I— This is Cedar Creek?"

He nodded, the restive shadows giving his face a sinister cast. Why was he looking at her like that, almost as though he were angry? Or was it another, darker emotion altogether? Garnet's heart began to pound. Her throat was arid, her lips rubbery. "I live about eight miles south of Strasburg, perhaps less…" Her voice cracked. Hating her fear, her help-lessness, she turned her head away.

"Wonderful," he said after a moment. "You might weigh less than my pack, but there's no way I can carry you for eight miles." The curt words might have been dragged over a bed of gravel.

Shocked embarrassment flooded her veins. "Of course not. I have a buggy." Instinctively she started to lift her hand. A knifelike pain pierced her shoulder, cutting off her breath.

The man's hand whipped out to stop the movement. "Careful! You gashed your shoulder when you fell. I've stitched and bandaged it, but you need to keep still." Unlike the curt admonishment, his touch was gentle as he rearranged the sling Garnet belatedly realized he'd fashioned. It bound her left arm and shoulder, keeping them largely immobile.

When he finished, he sat back on his heels and frowned down at her. "Tell me about the pain. Where does it hurt the worst?"

"Well"—*sort of everywhere*—"mostly my shoulder. A bit of a head-ache. Not too bad, really."

Stitched? Bandaged? The fingers of her right hand twitched with the instinctive need to check for herself. Surely a man who had gone to so much trouble intended no harm. And that day, the day in the meadow when she had been alone and vulnerable—he hadn't followed her then. Hadn't taunted or teased or grabbed. Hadn't…threatened.

He'd even taken care of the fox. Though as she lay there, her gaze fastened to his face, she realized sickeningly that she hadn't seen or heard the animal since she regained consciousness.

"What's wrong?"

"N-nothing. It's…ah…I feel much better. Perhaps you could help me up." She pinned a confident smile on her face.

Without warning, he leaned over her again. His fingers wrapped around her wrist as though he was about to hold her down. Reacting without thought, Garnet attacked, even as her panicked mind struggled to remember her father's instructions on how to defend herself against unwanted attentions. Burning talons of pain gouged her body, ripping her to shreds. Not much of a fight… Her vision blurred, dimmed, but she refused to give up.

"Shh! It's all right! I'm not going to hurt you! Listen to me, Miss Sinclair—Garnet. You must keep still or you'll tear the stitches. Garnet! Be still." The whiplike authority of his voice penetrated the miasma of pain and panic. She obeyed, primarily because she knew he was right. At this point, resistance would be counterproductive. Confidence and cunning, that was the way she would regain her freedom.

"That's better." His fingers were still wrapped around her wrist, but after a moment he carefully laid her hand across her middle and sat back. "Your pulse is racing." He stared at her, and Garnet watched in rising confusion as the harsh aggression on his face faded away, leaving behind a smooth impenetrable mask. "Do you promise not to move if I leave you for a moment?"

Warily she nodded.

He studied her for another long moment, and a flicker of something softened the harsh features. Then he turned and moved to the other side of the fire, disappearing into the shadows. When he returned, he was carrying the fox. "He's still alive. I thought you'd rest easier if you saw for yourself."

Without warning, tears brimmed. Garnet tipped her head up to keep them from spilling, ignoring the lash of pain at the movement. "Thank you…for taking care of him."

"I was afraid not to. Have you always been this intransigent, Garnet Sinclair?"

Was that a thread of humor she heard? It seemed so uncharacteristic of this dark, brooding man who acted the good Samaritan with a conflicting blend of irritation and compassion. "My sister Meredith's

the stubborn one. I'm"—she hesitated, then mentally shrugged—
"thought of hereabouts as the wild one, I'm afraid." *Oh, my.* That
sounded provocative as well as inaccurate.

"No wonder you were so stubborn over the fox then." He carefully
deposited the small bundle against her right side. "The little fellow's
asleep, or unconscious, which is the best thing for him. Hopefully his
presence will prevent you from any more outbursts—wouldn't want to
scare him, would we?"

"I—no."

Another of those indecipherable expressions flickered across his face.
Then he made an abortive gesture of his hand and abruptly turned
toward the fire. "I've made some sassafras tea. Found some roots growing near the creek. I want you to drink some. You lost a bit of blood."
When he turned back around, he held a collapsible metal cup in his hand.

Discomfited, Garnet watched the steam spiraling from the cup. It
was plain he resented the role of good Samaritan—but it was equally
plain that without assistance she was helpless. She doggedly held on to
her composure as she met the frowning gaze again, trying to apologize
with her eyes for all the trouble.

After a moment the man muttered something under his breath,
then deftly slipped his free arm beneath the back of her neck. "I'm going
to support you. Try not to expend any effort." His strength as well as his
nearness were overwhelming. Garnet automatically tensed. But the
impersonal skill of his hands was somehow reassuring, so she tried to
remember that he was a doctor, and doctors were allowed the privilege
of such intimacy. His hold was comforting, not threatening, and in spite
of her uncertainty, she relaxed beneath his hands.

"That's it…slowly now, don't add a scalded mouth to your list of
injuries."

The pungent tang of sassafras and some other unfamiliar aroma
filled her nostrils. The tea was weak, bitter, but its warmth comforted
her chilled insides. "Thank you."

"Any nausea?"

She thought for a moment, shook her head in relief.

"Good." He helped her drink the entire cupful, his aid experienced and capable. "If this stays down, in a few moments we'll try some solid food. The remains of my lunch, I'm afraid—half a ham biscuit, some cheese and soda crackers from the general store in Tom's Brook." His expression was wry. "They're fairly squashed, but your body needs the nourishment. About your buggy... Do you remember where you left it?"

Though still muzzy-headed with pain, she groped in her memory for a clear image. "Edge of a meadow. There's a lane that leads back to the road." It wasn't far, less than half a mile...but she couldn't make it. The pain battered in relentless waves, making her lightheaded.

"Not yet, my girl. Don't give in to it yet. Come on, talk to me. Help me to help you. You say you have a buggy, so your horse is waiting for you, isn't he? Tell you what, in a little bit I'll go find them. Garnet— may I call you Garnet? What's the name of your horse, Garnet? I've told you about Dulcie, tell me your horse's name."

"Hmm? Oh..." Garnet tried to smile despite the inferno of agony threatening to engulf her. "Goatsbeard."

He blinked.

"It's...a wildflower."

The man, MacAllister—was that his name?—smiled back, the first time Garnet had seen him do so. "Unusual name for a horse. But a young lady who draws beautiful flowers, and rescues wounded foxes at the expense of her own life and limb, is also unusual."

He reached beyond her head, and a moment later Garnet felt the balm of a cool, damp cloth against her face and neck. After a while the world stopped dipping and swaying. "You're...my sister and I ate lunch in town. We heard...they said you're a doctor."

"Not any longer." The emphatic denial registered with the force of a blow, yet the gentle strokes of the cloth against her skin never varied. "But you don't need to worry," he added, sounding as though the words had been squeezed through their wringer washer. "I didn't happen to be passing this way by accident."

"Going to Winchester, you said. To pick up your horse." Garnet fumbled, searching with her hand until she felt the soft fur and pointy shape of a fox's ear.

Sloan MacAllister gave a short bitter laugh. "Yes, but that's not—

never mind. You wouldn't understand. Even though I do, I don't like it." He muttered something else beneath his breath. "But I will take care of you, so don't worry. I *was* a very good doctor. And I've given you something, something that will help the pain while we're on the road. Relax. Stop struggling in your mind and relax. Trust me to take care of you."

"I'm taking the fox with me."

"Miss Sinclair. He's a wild creature, badly injured. Taking him with you will only frighten him, in all likelihood finish him off."

Garnet ducked her head, squeezed her eyes shut, and swallowed repeatedly until she could control her voice. "I have to try." *No good,* she thought, wincing at the thick wobbly sound. "What if…what if God brought me to this spot, because He didn't want one of His creatures to die so cruelly?" Not again. *Don't make me endure this again.* "I know, that doesn't make sense to you. It's just an animal, after all." She bit her lip, kept her head down, unwilling to face Dr. MacAllister's condemnation.

It was absurd to expect him to understand. Even worse, the height of presumption for her to interpret God's purpose. The almighty Creator of the universe neither required nor requested the cries of a doubting Thomas such as herself. She was behaving like a hysterical female, instead of graciously thanking this man for saving her life. "I'm sorry. I'm imposing on your kindness."

Odd, but Dr. MacAllister's face was indistinct, as though she'd smeared her charcoal pencil over it. "You're right, about the fox." She caressed the soft ear with trembling fingers, then slid her hand away in a gesture of renunciation. "Will he suffer, do you think? Or just…drift off?" Her throat closed up again.

"Oh, for—" All of a sudden fingers softer and warmer than a slice of Leah's fresh-baked bread traced a delicate path from her forehead to the vein fluttering in her neck.

"Ill-tempered lout," she heard him mutter. Then, "I'll take care of the fox, with as much diligence as I plan to take care of you. And we'll bring him along, I promise. I'll see both of you safely home, Garnet Sinclair." Incredibly, she thought she heard resigned humor drifting through the words. "Rest easy. I'll see you home."

Nine

*J*acob Sinclair stared between the horse's ears, his hands clutching the buggy reins like a lifeline. It was past ten o'clock. *Jesus, blessed Savior…it's past ten…* The vise around his ribs that made every breath a struggle now tightened with each passing second. Garnet. Garnet. *Where was the lass?*

Over the past four hours he had run a gauntlet of harrowing emotions, from annoyance to anguish. At this moment he was fighting to keep Leah from guessing how close he was to breaking down.

The entire neighborhood had roused to search for Garnet, gathering momentum as hours passed without word of her appearance. Bobbing lantern light speared into the countryside on both sides of the Pike, and a cacophony of sounds filled the moonlit night—plodding hooves, wheels crunching on the macadam. Occasionally Banjo's hounds bayed, halting the murmur of voices until Banjo scolded the dogs for sniffing out a raccoon or possum. As yet, the dogs hadn't found Garnet's trail. Nobody had found the trail, nor any sign of Garnet.

"Papa?"

"Aye?"

"I…nothing."

Jacob glanced sideways, to Leah's hunched figure. The buggy lantern shone onto her hands, those small but capable hands, not so steady now, smoothing endlessly over the pile of blankets she'd insisted on bringing along. A basket of food sat between her feet, along with a dry bonnet she'd dug out of the bureau in Garnet's bedroom.

Lord, forgive me. He'd been a selfish lout, locked inside his own fear. For all her self-possession, Leah was still only nineteen years old. "We'll find her," he promised now, shifting the reins to one hand to give her a hug. It was about like embracing a porch column.

"I know." Unspoken words hung thick in the cool night air, possibilities too horrific to voice aloud.

Finally Leah cleared her throat. "Since the Magruders have a telephone, I asked FrannieBeth to send Duncan back home, to call Meredith. No matter what, she'll want—" She stopped. "You know Meredith. She'll rent a hack, or be on the first southbound train, never mind her job."

"There's a good lass," Jacob murmured, patting her restless hand. "I never would hae thought of all that." But his Leah had.

"Um…what about Joshua? I mean, he's been courting her for years, even if Garnet doesn't see—" This time, her voice broke on the last word.

"Ho, Jacob!" Amos Pettiscomb cantered up, waving his hand. "Found her! We found her, man!" He pointed toward the north. "Half-mile along, headed this way in that runabout of hers."

Scattered cheers burst all around as the news spread among the searchers. Beside him, Leah choked back a sob.

"Thank God." Jacob closed his eyes, squeezing her in an exultant hug. "Thank God." Right now, he couldn't frame another coherent thought.

"Ah, um…" Pettiscomb hesitated. His horse tossed its head, spraying lather, hooves restlessly stamping.

Jacob peered upward. "Amos? She's all right, isn't she? I mean, she's driving, and all."

"Well, now, Jacob, I can't rightly say, 'cept she's—"

"What's happened? Is she hurt—what?"

"Papa, let Sheriff Pettiscomb finish."

Automatically Jacob covered Leah's fingers, which were digging into his arm.

"Ah well, as to that—Miss Garnet, she ain't exactly driving." He muttered something under his breath, and spat a stream of tobacco onto the road. "Listen, Jacob, best tell it to you straight. Your daughter's been injured, don't know how bad 'cept the feller driving the buggy reassured me she'd be fine. Sounded like he knew what he was about. Funny thing that, now I think on it—hey!"

His startled shout was drowned in a clatter of hooves. Jacob slapped the reins to the horse's flanks again, catapulting the buggy down the Pike at a reckless gallop.

❧❧❧

He shouldn't have stayed here, Sloan thought for the third time in as many minutes. The Sinclairs' parlor was stifling, the silence after this past hour thick enough to choke a buffalo.

Shouldn't have stayed, shouldn't have acquiesced to Jacob Sinclair's pleas. Should have resisted the hollowed-out desperation in his eyes, the frantic grip of his hand while Sloan explained what had happened to his daughter. *You're a feeble-minded softhead, MacAllister.* Right now he could have been halfway back to his place, instead of languishing in this room like a tame tabby cat. After all, there'd been plenty of offers from the neighbors, all of them eager to rub shoulders with the—Sloan clenched his hands so hard the knuckles ached—with the Yankee *doctor.*

Oh, he could have been on the way home, all right, forced to share a buggy with some yokel picking at his soul, demanding answers and asking questions, trampling on his privacy and Garnet Sinclair's. Sloan winced at the memory of the avid faces crowding around when he and Jacob Sinclair lifted her from the buggy.

Words formed somewhere deep inside him, gradually snagging his attention with their conviction. Scraps of Scripture, the notion that he was being chided like the apostle Paul for kicking against the pricks, resonated in the silent room as clearly as if they'd been spoken aloud. Shoulders sagging, Sloan forced his hands to relax, flexing the fingers until the circulation was restored. A corner of his mouth twitched. All right, he deserved to be smacked, and hard. The local folk had been concerned, their manner caring more than curious. Several faces bore the trace of tears.

More to the point, Sinclair and his youngest daughter deserved something beyond the curt words of reassurance he'd flung their way.

It was just…"It's a fox, for crying out loud," Sloan said. An injured, dying animal whose presence, because of his promise to Garnet Sinclair, was the primary cause of Sloan's foul mood.

It had been the unanimous opinion of thirty or so neighbors that the fox be tossed to the hounds. Even Jacob Sinclair, mindful of his daughter's tender nature, had been reluctant to shelter the injured varmint. That left nobody but Sloan to protect the animal, and by inference Garnet's "tender nature," an unpalatable choice because Sloan didn't want anything to do with either of them.

He ran a hand around the back of his neck, his mind tormenting him with the picture of an unconscious Garnet cuddled against his side like a helpless child.

At some point during the ride the wind had blown her hair across her face and onto his forearm, even though the darkness muted the brassy shade. She'd roused momentarily when he tried to stuff her hair inside the collar of his jacket to keep it out of his way. Sloan remembered with a grinding sort of disquiet that Garnet had even been concerned about ruining the blasted jacket. "I'll replace it," she'd whispered, her voice slurred from the injection he'd administered. "Did I…thank you? For the fox? My father…care for…"

Sinclair would have promised to house a family of skunks if she'd asked. The fox had been deposited inside a hastily scrounged orange crate and transported to a corner of the Sinclairs' wash house. Sloan figured its chances for survival were negligible.

Well, it was no longer his problem. He'd done what he could, for both his "patients," and as soon as the Sinclair family doctor gave his report, Sloan could leave Sinclair Run in the dust.

Resigned to the inevitable for now, he prowled the parlor, for a long time scarcely noticing his surroundings because he was arguing with God, albeit silently. Eventually, however, the peaceful atmosphere of the room worked on him, calming the resentment, the sensation of being trapped.

A smile finally teased the corner of his mouth when he approached the table where the youngest daughter had left him a tray loaded with food, along with the choice of hot tea or spiced cider. Leah was her name, he remembered. Sloan wondered whether she was ever still. The moment she'd sprung down from the family buggy, she'd taken over with the forcefulness of a field marshal, thanking the crowd at the same time she was directing Sloan where to carry her sister, making sure her father would take care of the horses.

He wondered what the oldest sister was like. Leah and Garnet appeared on first acquaintance to share little beyond the family name. Leah's slight frame and unremarkable coloring disguised a dictatorial personality. Garnet, on the other hand... Sloan tipped his head back, squeezing his eyes shut against the memories.

The self-possessed young woman with haunted eyes. The semiconscious, blood-soaked girl with a head of blood-colored hair, whose stubbornness defeated him even as her inexplicable fear unnerved him. Trying to understand Garnet Sinclair was like grabbing a handful of mist.

A ship's clock quietly ticking above an old horsehair chair in the corner showed it was approaching midnight. Upstairs, a floorboard creaked. Sloan poured tea into a sturdy earthenware mug and selected a square of some sort of bread. His stomach growled, reminding him that he hadn't eaten for over ten hours, having fed Garnet the remains of his box lunch from Tom's Brook. He swallowed some tea, which tasted good, actually, then took a cautious bite of the bread or biscuit or whatever it was.

Flavor burst over his tongue in a flood of incredible sensation. Sloan eyed the laden tray thoughtfully, then shrugged and sank down in a comfortably worn overstuffed chair. After wolfing down two squares, he settled back to savor a third more slowly.

While he ate, his gaze explored the room. Nothing like the luxurious mansion where he'd grown up, but a palace compared to the cramped and leaking company house where he'd spent the last three years. Furniture was simple, for the most part, though beautifully finished. All the wood gleamed satin in the soft glowing light. Examples of needlework here and there spoke of taste and skill. Garnet, Leah, or the oldest daughter—Meredith, was it?

Dusting his hands free of crumbs, Sloan rose for a closer look at a walnut and burl bookcase with as fine a finish as he'd ever seen; his mother had purchased an antique sideboard from Sotheby's in New York whose finish was no better. Perhaps not even as good.

Intrigued, he circled the room, examining objects more closely. A small rectangular chest sitting on the floor next to the door of Jacob Sinclair's bedroom caught his eye, and Sloan knelt to better study it. It was plain, but like the sideboard some of the best craftsmanship he'd ever seen. Curious, he picked it up. It wasn't large, about the size of a jewelry chest, and surprisingly heavy. *What kind of wood?* he wondered, his fingers tracing the pattern of the grain. There was an interesting irregularity on the right panel. Curiosity aroused, he carried it to where the parlor lamp cast a brighter light. Moments later, he found what he was looking for.

"It belongs to Garnet," Jacob Sinclair's voice announced quietly behind him. "I see you found the secret drawer."

Ten

*J*acob Sinclair stepped into the parlor. "I call it her heartwood chest," he continued. "Meredith and Leah each have one as well."

"Sort of small for a hope chest," Sloan said. "More like a jewelry box. Superb workmanship."

"Thank you."

Sloan carefully set the chest down and straightened to his full height, keeping his face expressionless.

Garnet's father stalked across the room and with scant ceremony dropped into the chair Sloan had vacated earlier. "Why don't you join me, Dr.—I'm sorry. 'Tis *Mister* MacAllister, you claim, is it not? Been a long evening, Mr. MacAllister, hasn't it?"

Weary to the bone, Sloan sank into a chair. "Yes, it certainly has."

He'd half expected the older man's attitude—Sloan after all was a stranger, and a Yankee. And he'd returned Sinclair's daughter injured and unconscious. But the sting of it caught Sloan off guard. He didn't want to care what Garnet Sinclair's father thought, any more than he wanted to care about the daughter. "Is your family doctor planning to stay the night?" Shouldn't be necessary, but he decided not to point it out.

The *orbicularis oculi* muscle next to Sinclair's left eye twitched. Interesting. Possibly not a good sign. "Doc Porter tells me you drugged her with some medicine he'd never heard of, something you had in your bag, an injection, he said. I must tell you, sir, that I'm no' comfortable with such. Ye claim tae no longer be a physician, so seems to me you've no right to act like one. Even if you were, I dinna hold with trifling in matters best left in the Lord's hands."

Why hadn't he escaped when he'd had the opportunity? "You're right. I should have let your daughter writhe in agony. Pain and suffering are God's will, after all—is that what you think?"

He could have relieved the man by assuring him that the half-grain of codeine was neither harmful nor addictive, but goaded by Sinclair's hostility, his temper flared. "Should have left her wounds untended as well. Just prayed over her, then hurried on my way. God knows I didn't want to be there in the first place. But I was, so I did what needed to be done."

He made an abrupt slashing motion with his hand and surged to his feet. "Forget it. Believe what you want to believe." He started across the hall.

"I'm sorry."

Sloan checked his stride but didn't turn around. He heard Jacob Sinclair noisily clear his throat.

"If I promise to explain, would you give a protective father another chance?"

Begrudging every movement, Sloan faced the older man. "No explanations are needed. You were right. If I'm not going to acknowledge my profession, I shouldn't practice it. Don't worry—I won't make that mistake, ever again. My medical bag's by the front door. Tell Porter I left it for him." Not that the old croaker would know what to do with the contents. "Or you can throw it away. I don't care."

"Mr. MacAllister, I believe something happened to my daughter, when she was sixteen years old. What I mean to say is"—he coughed, tugging at a strand of graying hair that had fallen over his forehead—"I believe she may have been…harmed, in some manner, by a man or some men. Don't you ken, when you brought her home I thought—I couldn't but wonder if…" His voice trailed away. He looked exhausted —and ashamed.

Sloan felt as though he'd been broadsided with a singletree. Slowly he retraced his steps, sat back down. "Are you trying to tell me your daughter was raped?"

Sinclair winced, but to give the man his due, instead of upbraiding Sloan for his bluntness he answered with equal bluntness. As he spoke, his brogue gradually disappeared. "Nae—she couldn't have hidden so detestable an act."

He splashed cider into a mug, took a quick gulp, then clutched the mug with white-knuckled fingers. "We're a close family, and a trusting family. My daughters, they *tell* me things, don't you see. Her sisters... Garnet wouldn't be able to keep a monstrous offense to herself." He swallowed more cider. "But I do know something happened. Because, after that summer, she changed."

In an abrupt movement he rose, crossed the room, and snatched up the small chest, hugging it as though it were Garnet herself. "She changed."

Sloan sat in silence, unable to respond. Memories of the past hours seared his conscience, because at the time he'd been seeing not an injured red-headed girl with frightened eyes but—Jenna. He didn't want to face the ugly truth about himself, but Jacob Sinclair's revelation left no room for self-deception.

Garnet had been afraid, all right. Afraid of *him*. He had never intentionally hurt a woman in his life—but Garnet had felt compelled to defend herself.

Bitterly ashamed, Sloan repeated the thought aloud, as an indictment against his self-absorption. "She was trying to defend herself."

He looked across at Jacob Sinclair, and the tiny hairs on the back of his neck lifted. "Take it easy," he said, raising his hands in a pacifying gesture. "She was in pain, barely conscious. I was too close. She didn't realize I was trying to help her." He kept his gaze steady. "I didn't hurt your daughter, Jacob Sinclair. From what you've told me, her reaction was to be expected." Not, of course, that Sloan deserved absolution...

"I'll carve your heart out with an awl if you've treated her with anything less than the respect she deserves."

His brogue was so thick Sloan could easily picture him in full Highland dress, brandishing a claymore. "I thought vengeance belonged to the Lord," he observed mildly. He eased back, crossing one leg over the other and letting his arms rest openhanded in his lap. "You can be proud of your daughter," he said. "Even out of her head and incapacitated, she almost knocked me backward into the creek. You taught her, didn't you?"

Jacob nodded. "Aye. I taught all my lasses how to fend off unwanted attentions." Some of the rage began to fade; the veins in his forehead no longer bulged, and his skin color was returning to normal hues. After returning to his seat, he balanced the chest on his knees and exhaled a deep sigh. "Felt it was my duty as a father—I can't always be there to protect them. Not all men honor their God-given responsibility to be mindful of those physically weaker than themselves."

"Not all men honor God."

"Aye, that is all too true. What about yourself, Sloan MacAllister?"

Silence stretched between them.

"Hmph." Sinclair scratched his beard-roughened chin, then shook his head. "Never mind. I'll decide for myself then. So, I can't say I like what you did, sticking needles in her, I mean. But you did bring her home. And Doc Porter told me he'd never seen better stitches." He leaned forward, planting his hands on top of the chest in his lap. Eyes narrowed, he stared long and hard into Sloan's face. "Och, man, 'tis for sure I've seen more expression on my chisel. Yet when you carried the lass upstairs—"

"Don't read anything into it," Sloan interrupted. "I did as much for that wretched fox."

"Mm. So you did." Jacob didn't smile, but the lines furrowing his brow eased, and after a moment he sat back. "Will the fox live, do you think?"

"Probably not."

"But you brought it along because you promised Garnet?"

"Its presence calmed her, that's all." For the first time Sloan noticed the numerous scars crisscrossing the skin on Sinclair's hands. The nail bed of his left thumb was mangled, as though it had gotten in the way of a saw or some other destructive tool. Sloan looked up.

"You made the chest," he stated, stunned anew. "And…all this furniture? You're a-a—"

"Cabinetmaker. Aye. Third generation. My grandda apprenticed with Robert Adam himself, my da with Duncan Phyfe in New York. I suppose you could say it's in the blood. Will you stay awhile? I could use the company, since Leah's not budging from her sister's bedside."

Sloan was too tired to soften the edge in his voice. "Let's make it easier on both of us. I'll leave."

He half rose, then sank back into the chair as though pushed by an invisible hand. Every muscle tensed in denial of the knowledge permeating his consciousness and gradually settling into his mind: He was supposed to *stay* here. Resigned, Sloan forced himself to relax. He might not like the decision thrust upon him, yet he couldn't quite bring himself to ignore it.

But if Sinclair himself stood up—an indication that he agreed with Sloan's desire to leave, then—

"Please stay, Mr. MacAllister."

"What?" Sloan shook his head and passed a hand around the back of his neck. He was exhausted, that was all, his mind playing tricks. And Sinclair wasn't in much better shape, to be asking a man he didn't know or trust to keep vigil in his family parlor. "There were any of a score or more of friends angling for an invitation. Why me?"

Garnet's father studied his ruined thumbnail for a moment. "Because I'm convinced you're a better man than I might have thought at first. Possibly a better man than you yourself realize," he finally said.

A half-smile appeared, and he jerked his chin toward the stairs. "Because I'd like to tell you about Garnet, if I may. I—I *need* to talk about it. You were willing to bind up her external injuries. I'm asking you now, as her father—and as a man—for you to help me try to heal the injury to her spirit." He hesitated. "Sometimes wounds to the inside hurt worse when they're suffered in silence. She's carried this pain for all these years, not even sharing it with the ones who love her the most. I don't know why, don't know what it is she fears so that she won't talk to her family, her friends. But perhaps you—"

Sloan surged to his feet, the sweat of panic misting his skin. "I'm a stranger to you, to your daughter." He wheeled, stabbing his index finger toward Jacob Sinclair. "I'm the last man you need to talk to about her. Blast it all, I just want to be left alone." *God, why won't You leave me alone?*

He jammed his hands into his pockets to keep from snatching up the chest and dashing it against the fireplace. "You're not a fool, Sinclair. Why on earth would you trust someone like me? You don't know me, you know nothing—*nothing* about me." It didn't make sense. Nothing made sense, except the violent urge to flee.

"I don't care about your past, Mr. MacAllister. As to why I trust you…" He rose to stand directly in front of Sloan. "Any man who takes the time and trouble to try and save a badly injured critter of no use…well, somewhere inside that man must be a piece of the Lord. You hide it well, son. But that fox out in my wash house is why I trust you. Most anyone who'd found her would have brought my lass home, or gone for help. None I can name would have done the same for the animal."

Defeated, Sloan finally admitted the truth to himself, and for the first time in hours…days…months, the tight knot lodged beneath his breastbone began to loosen. Garnet Sinclair had intrigued him from the moment he'd seen her on that sun-dappled hillside. Even learning the color of her hair—a red flag if ever there was one—hadn't stifled the need.

Might be he possessed a fatal weakness for redheads. Might be a congenital easy mark for sufferers. But, for whatever mysterious divine purpose, apparently he was also being obedient. He raised his hands in capitulation. "Very well. I'll stay, for a while anyway."

"Thank you."

"But no promises. I make no promises."

"No promises. Of course, I wasn't asking for any, Sloan MacAllister."

Both men sat back down. For several moments they didn't speak, studying each other with the wry camaraderie of two males who had survived a couple of rounds in the ring. Sinclair wasn't a tall man— Sloan easily topped him by a good six inches. But there was strength in those sinewy arms, and a matching strength in his face. Dressed in faded corduroys held up only by the suspenders, with a cheap collarless shirt that looked as though he'd slept in it, the man looked stereotypically Southern dirt-poor.

But the furniture, particularly the heartwood chest, took Sloan's breath away. And the plea was one he couldn't ignore, even when his soul was blackened almost beyond redemption.

"Tell me about Garnet," he said.

Eleven

ix days after the accident, Garnet stepped gingerly onto the front porch and discovered her cloth bag sitting by the front door. No note, no explanation. She glanced out into the yard, but saw nothing, heard nothing beyond the steady rasp of sandpaper against wood—her father, out in his workshop—and the hollow hum of a lazy breeze.

Mr. MacAllister wanted as little to do with her as she with him.

Garnet wondered why that should depress her. She ought to be relieved that he had returned her supplies at all. Annoyed with the fluttery bout of nerves, Garnet knelt to pick up the cloth bag, her movements slow, careful. Straightening, she hugged it to her chest and waited until the lightheadedness passed before making her way to the wicker settee. What a bother. These past days she'd been nursed and bullied by her family, poked and bled by Doc Porter, and fussed and fretted over by friends.

The convalescence had been more of a trial than the injury itself. She had suffered the consequences for her rash decision to rescue a fox, but mercysake—everyone acted as though she'd almost died.

By noon the day after the accident, Meredith was sitting beside her on the bed and spooning hot soup down her throat, all the while talking nonstop about her job in Benjamin Walker's fancy hotel. Garnet dearly loved her older sister, but by the time she departed after two days to catch the train back to Winchester, even Garnet's ears drooped with exhaustion.

Of course, Meredith was only her first visitor.

FrannieBeth came twice, juggling nine-month-old Jessup on her lap while three-year-old Alice played at the foot of Garnet's bed.

Her best childhood friend, Chloe, who had moved to Luray the previous year, even surprised her with a visit. "I've been spending a couple of weeks with Great-aunt Louise. Her gout's acting up. Coming to see you is a relief. Don't be silly," she hushed Garnet's protest, her endearingly homely face and mild brown eyes full of affection. "Just because I moved away doesn't mean I don't care about you anymore." She stroked damp strands of Garnet's hair away from her forehead. "After all, you're the only person in the Valley who never called me 'Horseface Henderson.' "

"You're the only person in the Valley who never made fun of my hair."

A pleasant but exhausting stream of neighbors rode or drove up every afternoon to see how the patient was faring and to indulge in as much gossip as Jacob would allow. Except for FrannieBeth and Chloe, the visits were usually brief. Her father brooked no criticism of Garnet's actions, nor speculation about the black-haired Yankee outlander who had rescued her, brought her home—and left her.

Garnet shifted on the seat cushion, relieved when the motion resulted only in a middling tug. For the past week she had concentrated on healing as rapidly as possible, not only because she hated being a burden, but because loss of drawing time meant loss of tuition for Leah. Fall classes at Mary Baldwin College commenced in September, and the funds for her share of Leah's studies wouldn't be available unless Garnet was well enough to complete her illustrations on schedule.

She gave another experimental shrug. Good. The throbbing ache in her shoulder had definitely subsided; the stitches only pulled when she forgot and tried to do something she shouldn't, like move her arm. Dressing remained…a challenge. As for arranging her hair, for the past couple of days all she could manage was to gather it with a clip at the base of her neck.

It would be a tremendous relief when the stitches were removed, even if she didn't look forward to Doc Porter's less than gentle ministrations. But the brusque fumbling of his moist hands was still preferable to the skilled touch of the stranger whose gray eyes had chilled every time he looked at her.

Like splinters embedded under her skin, thoughts of Sloan MacAllister were not easily dislodged. The man was a troubling enigma. He plainly disliked her, yet according to her father Mr. MacAllister had taken the fox home, promising to do the best he could for the animal. Garnet did not delude herself by imagining any sanguine motivation on his part: Doubtless once he reached the Pike, he'd dumped the creature along the side of the road. Still, he'd known how much the fox's welfare meant to her and had made at least a pretense of acceding to her wishes. But why?

Thinking about the fox depressed her as much as thinking about Mr. MacAllister. The animal was a nuisance, cursed by farmers and hunted for sport. There was no divine purpose in what had happened. The little creature had simply suffered a stroke of ill fortune—clawed by a bobcat, shot by a farmer, or some other mishap. God had not arranged circumstances to ease the burden of guilt Garnet carried. Far better to accept bittersweet reality than cling to flimsy hopes.

Papa, of course, would argue with her about her lack of trust. Joshua, as well.

Ah, Joshua… Talking, lecturing—preaching almost—Joshua Jones spent most of the time they were together battling Garnet's doubt-riddled conscience. An upstanding bookkeeper, son of a minister over in Saumsville, he had been alternately arguing with her and wooing her since they'd met at a county fair three years earlier, when Garnet was helping out at a taffy-pulling booth.

Twice since the accident he'd come calling, his cowlicked hair slicked down and his pale blue eyes anxious. Each time, he knelt by the davenport where Garnet reclined, and with heartfelt sincerity and bouquets of blandishments he prayed for her heart as well as her health.

Garnet yearned for such an uncluttered faith, but she always struggled against laughter at Joshua's grandiose expression of it. The man should have been a preacher instead of a bookkeeper. Garnet pondered her fingers, then absently lifted her hand to chew off a hangnail on her right thumb while her mind chewed over the dilemma of Joshua Jones.

Her father entertained hopes of an eventual match. After all, Joshua hadn't given up even after three years, in spite of Garnet's equal intransigence. She blew a ticklish strand of hair off her forehead. There had been times, these past few years, when she almost blurted the truth.

Prudence, and fear, prevailed.

The threat was five years old, but the men might still live in the Valley. Until Garnet was an old woman, her signature red locks grayed to anonymity, her sisters long gone and Papa safe in the grave…her life must be dictated by that threat. Joshua deserved a faithful companion with an untroubled soul.

A bird warbled from the branches of the tulip tree that shaded the porch. Startled, Garnet jumped, and her shoulder squawked in protest. With a long sigh, she rested her head against the curved wicker back, closing her eyes until the discomfort passed.

What would it feel like to have somebody other than her family with whom to share her fears and her secret dreams? Not just a good friend like Chloe, but—a man. A man who understood her flawed personality but still accepted her. Who wouldn't demand or even expect her to sacrifice the very essence of her being in order to fulfill his own dreams.

A man who would love her, whom she could love in return.

A man her past could destroy.

Garnet gazed blindly across the yard through the sunlit branches of the cedars her parents had planted as a hedge thirty years earlier. *God? Please help me to be strong enough to bear it. Especially if Joshua is supposed to be that man.* Joshua certainly thought so. No matter what Garnet said, he remained secure in his delusion that time and God's sovereign will would change her heart.

Life had yet to teach the preacher's son that some circumstances could never be changed, because God's sovereign will seldom manifested itself in the lives of His less-than-saintly children.

Oh, Joshua, Garnet thought as she sat on the porch and held her precious cloth bag with fingers that wanted to tremble…*if you knew what I know and what I've done, you'd be thanking God that I'm not interested in you.*

"Garnet, where did you put that pile of mending you were working with?" Leah opened the screen door and stopped. "I wanted to—your bag! Did Dr. MacAllister return it? What did he say, why didn't he come inside?"

"I found it on the porch." She forced a smile. "And we can only assume *Mr.* MacAllister left it because he's the only one who would have known where to look for it. Since there's no note—and no person—attached, it will have to remain speculation."

Leah blew out an exasperated breath. "Well, of course it was Dr. Mac—oh, don't look at me like that. He's a doctor, and we all know it even though he claims to have renounced both profession and title." Her head tipped sideways as she studied Garnet, fingers tapping her cheek. "He's also rude. I don't care what Papa says. The least he could have done was to deliver your supplies in person."

"What does Papa say about him?" Garnet asked. She met Leah's bland look with one of determination. "I'm not helpless or hurting anymore, miss priss. This time, I want some answers." Especially since certain memories made her uncomfortable. Unfortunately, like stubborn weeds inching their way between the floorboards in the wash house, they refused to be vanquished.

"It might upset you."

Garnet's throat went dry and tight. "Oh?"

"Well…you seem to think Mr. MacAllister doesn't like you. You mumbled a lot of absurdities those first few days, you know, all of it a lot of stale stuffing." She tugged Garnet's sloppily bound hair over Garnet's shoulder and began to plait it with nimble fingers. "I wish you'd let me help you dress," she muttered beneath her breath. "Um…Papa won't tell me much. But I do know Mr. MacAllister asked a lot of questions about your heartwood chest—remember Papa was rubbing all of them down with fresh linseed oil and beeswax, and yours was sitting off by itself on the floor? Strange, isn't it, that it happened to be yours, since—"

"Leah, get to the point."

"Fine." She finished the braid, refastened the clip, and tossed the tidier rope of hair back over Garnet's shoulder. "Mr. MacAllister found the secret compartment, and your cardinal feather."

Leah was right. The words did hurt, like the stones that had gouged her head and shoulder when she tumbled down the slope at Cedar Creek. Garnet quailed from the likelihood that Sloan MacAllister had leafed through her sketchbook before he returned it. But that disquieting probability paled beside her sister's revelation. Mr. MacAllister had examined her heartwood chest. Had in fact discovered the secret compartment that nobody else, including Joshua, had ever found.

Garnet felt as though her insides had been scraped raw with a cheese grater, but what could she do? Self-consciousness, no matter how intense, was not a fatal condition.

"Do you know if Mr. MacAllister said anything? Or what Papa said to him?" she asked when she was certain she could speak without emotion. Excessive outbursts made Leah cross.

"That's what Papa refuses to tell me." She made a face. "Claims it has nothing to do with me." Her hand crept over Garnet's, gently squeezing, and only then did Garnet realize that her own fingers were colder than Sinclair Run in early spring. "What he did tell me was that he believes Mr. MacAllister is 'carrying around a tortured spirit,' is the way he put it. Most vexing. I know Papa's dander was up when Doc Porter told him that you'd been given some kind of pain medicine with a syringe. Papa was ready to call Sheriff Pettiscomb back to haul Mr. MacAllister off to the county jail. Instead the pair of them end up talking in the parlor half the night like they're old friends."

"Mr. MacAllister found the feather…"

"Perhaps after church Sunday we should drive up to Tom's Brook and pay him a visit." Her eyes glinted with speculation. "You could always express your profound gratitude, invite him to dinner…"

"I'd as soon parade through Woodstock in my unmentionables." Garnet took her bag and stood, concealing a wince of pain. "Leah… don't. I can see you planning something, but—don't."

"Don't you want to *know?*" Scowling, Leah stood as well. "If it had been my heartwood chest, and Mr. MacAllister offered any explanation, however ludicrous, as to why Papa stuffed a dried-up flower bulb in mine, while he put a bird feather in yours and that ugly cookie cutter in Meredith's…well, I'd be on his front porch by sunrise. Mercysake, Garnet, sometimes you—"

Abruptly she broke off, pressed her cheek against Garnet's, and stepped back. "Never mind. I need to go check the Irish potatoes I put on to boil for this week's batch of yeast. Thanks for doing the mending. Don't tire yourself out; you still look too pale."

After she disappeared inside, Garnet remained on the porch while she pondered what Leah had read in her face that practically set her to babbling.

Abruptly her hands closed into panicked fists.

That day, the day of the accident, when pain and medicine and malaise kept her locked within a dark maze, there were gigantic chunks of time she couldn't remember at all. What if, during those unremembered hours, she had revealed the secret—no. No. If her tongue had babbled even a portion of the truth, she wouldn't be brooding out here on the porch while Papa happily sanded in his workshop and Leah bustled about inside the house.

She was behaving irrationally, that was all. Too much time alone with her thoughts, unable to draw, shorn of mobility, nothing to do but grapple with shadows. In a few more days she'd be fine. Fine.

A horse snorted from the bottom of the lane just beyond the cedars, followed by the muffled thud of hoofbeats. First visitors of the day, no doubt, except they usually waited until afternoon. Garnet's gaze darted over the porch in search of a hiding place for her bag. She managed to stuff her supplies behind the ficus plant Leah moved outdoors during the summer months just as the buggy, a fringe-topped surrey laden with four passengers, came into view.

Left arm hugged against her side, Garnet waited while the visitors, townswomen from Woodstock, alighted from the surrey like a flock of colorful birds taking noisy flight.

"Why, Garnet, what a lovely surprise, finding you out here on the front porch today." Lurleen Mosely and her husband owned a butcher shop. Lurleen's ample bosom was offset by a surprisingly sharp-featured face that reminded Garnet of a badger. "I know it's early, but we were just over to Mrs. Booth's Café, and we heard some news of interest to you."

"We wanted to be the first to tell you," Elmira Whitaker added with a girlish giggle that belied her matronly status. "So even if you've already heard, don't let on."

"You're no longer the only artist in Shenandoah County," Mavis Kibler announced, elbowing past her companions. "An artist from

California—a *lady,* moved into the best rooms at the Chalybeate Springs Hotel in Strasburg, for the rest of the summer."

"—doing a series of paintings—scenes from all over the country."

"—famous, according to my husband. Felicity Ward's her name."

Mrs. Whitaker reached Garnet first, studying her with the frankness of a woman who'd reared seven children and a passel of grandchildren. Her youngest daughter, FrannieBeth, was Meredith's best friend. "I'm sure she'll be calling on you, dear. Everyone's talking about her—you know what gossips we townsfolk are."

"And you're the worst, Elmira. Good gracious, but you're still looking mighty puny, Garnet. I could count your freckles from a dozen paces. I gave you my remedy for those, didn't I? The almond paste, followed by a poultice of English mustard powder and lemon juice? You ought to try it…"

Garnet scarcely took in the excited flow of words. Her smile was fixed, a frozen slash of her lips. She could have kissed her father's sawdust-coated face when he hailed everyone from the doorway of his workshop.

Felicity Ward, she thought. Felicity Ward had come to the Valley.

Twelve

*A*nd I reckon this load'll keep you busy for a spell." Breathing hard, the young boy from the hardware store wiped his palms on the bib of his overalls. He glanced from the pile of stacked lumber, to Sloan's house, to Sloan. "Um…Mr. Gutermann says you're doing all the work yourself."

"I am."

"Well…if you change your mind, want some help, be obliged iffen you'd think of me. I'm a strong worker and dependable—ask Mr. Gutermann."

Sloan wiped the sweat from his face and neck, studying the bean-pole of a youth with round, pale blue eyes. He folded his damp hand-kerchief into a compact square and tucked it away with deliberate slowness. "What's your name, son? You helped deliver the mantels for my fireplaces last month, didn't you?"

"Yes sir. Name's Raymond, Raymond Critchley." He shuffled his feet in the trampled grass, then crammed his hands into the side pockets of his overalls with such force Sloan was afraid the suspenders would tear. But the candid blue gaze never wavered. "I helped my pa build our new place, in town. He's a foreman, out at Kreuger Mines."

Sloan lowered himself on top of the neatly stacked lumber and stretched out his legs. He'd been up since dawn, taking advantage of the cool early morning hours for hard labor—which over these past few days had been to replace rotten, cracked, or warped clapboard siding. Not an easy task for a lone man. But he had enjoyed the solitude, savored the silence. There was a deep satisfaction, watching his painstaking endeavors achieve tangible results. Sort of like helping a mortally ill patient recover from—Sloan squashed the intrusive comparison.

"I'll give it some thought," he said to the hopeful Raymond. Regardless of ulterior motives, the boy was right. Sloan could use some help.

The admission annoyed him, but his thwarted hermitic yearnings weren't Raymond's fault. Sloan scraped up a smile. "Thanks for the offer."

"Well…you're welcome." Raymond hesitated for another awkward moment before he finally scrambled onto the seat of the delivery wagon.

Sloan watched him steer the two mules down the bumpy, overgrown track that led to Sloan's house. What was that all about anyway? He supposed he should be grateful that he'd been asked about a job instead of medical advice. Over the last month, the stream of hopeful patients approaching him whenever he went to town had taxed his remaining humanity to the breaking point. Several even knocked on his front door. Fortunately, inspiration supplied a tactic that thus far seemed to have staunched the flow.

"Infernal nuisance," he grumbled, but without heat. It was a beautiful day, and the old place was starting to look pretty good, if he did say so. Soon as he finished replacing all the clapboards, he could paint. Yellow, he'd decided some days ago. A nice, creamy yellow, and he might even put some shutters on either side of the windows. Front porch roof still sagged, and the tin roof was rusting…

No matter. He had all the time in the world. All right, so sometimes the nights were lonely, and restlessness tweaked him every so often. At least twice a week he saddled Dulcie for long rides about the countryside. The day after he'd found Garnet Sinclair at Cedar Creek, he found himself back at the bridge, and it seemed absurd, even craven, not to spend an hour poking about for her bag of art supplies. For a week it sat, unopened and accusing, on a shelf near Sloan's back door.

Because of what Jacob had shared about his daughter, and because Sloan himself valued privacy, he hadn't so much as glanced inside the bag. He doubted Garnet would appreciate his forbearance…especially since it was due more to indifference than nobility of character. Didn't matter any longer, as the previous evening he had taken the coward's way out, dumping the bag on the Sinclairs' front porch in the middle of the night.

He wondered in spite of himself how the girl was doing, wondered if that old sawbones Porter had managed to speed the healing process, or if he'd induced infection instead. Man probably never set foot inside a medical school, or any other institution of higher learning.

Wasn't Sloan's problem. Garnet Sinclair was not his patient, and whatever real or imagined trauma had occurred when she was sixteen was none of his concern. He'd let Jacob talk, much the same way he used to listen to the stream-of-consciousness ramblings of patients' loved ones. All they needed was a listening ear, a pat on the shoulder, a word of encouragement. So he'd provided that courtesy for Jacob Sinclair, but as far as Sloan was concerned that ended the obligation.

No promises. He'd made no promises, therefore he wasn't breaking any. He'd renounced the past—his background, his family. His profession. Jenna. Most especially Jenna. The last thing he needed was to become embroiled in another woman's life, no matter how vulnerable or intriguing.

And yes, he could *feel* God's waiting Presence. Always there, crowding Sloan with almost good-natured persistence. Never rushing, never demanding. Never yielding. Just—waiting.

"Well, You'll just have to keep waiting." Sloan snatched up the flat work cap he'd removed earlier, crammed it back on his head, and headed for the porch.

Before he returned to work, it was time to check on the one patient he had committed to. At least this one didn't talk back. In a matter of speaking, that is. To Sloan's surprise—he would never admit to relief, much less thankfulness—the fox had lived. Now, six days later, the wound was healing nicely, and for two days the animal had been lapping milk from a bowl instead of the baby bottle Sloan had purchased. It had also eaten the meat scraps he'd left the previous night. Most of the time, however, the animal slept, curled in a catlike ball with the long bushy tail draped over its face and body.

"How ya doing today, little one?" He stepped over the makeshift wire mesh pen he'd fashioned at one end of the porch.

The fox unwound, yawning as it lifted its head.

"Good boy." Sloan scratched behind the large pointed ears, then beneath the perennially smiling mouth. "You're doing all right, aren't you?" The eyes had lost their cloudiness, and even the burnt orange fur had taken on more of a luster.

He paid no attention to the color, gently pressing the animal onto its side so he could examine his sutures. "Any tenderness here, hmm? No? Well, that's amazing. Did you know you're lucky to be alive, pal?"

The fox watched him through those uncanny rust-colored eyes in a gaze devoid of fear. It was unnerving. Sloan had the feeling that even if he'd wrapped his fingers around the white furry throat and squeezed, the fox would have allowed it with that same trusting expression.

"What happened to your survival instincts?" Sloan mused, settling into a relaxed sprawl, his back against a weathered corner post. "You don't act wild at all. Remind me more of a child's lost puppy—no. Not a puppy. They make a whole lot more noise than you, and they're far less graceful."

Almost shyly, the fox inched over and laid its narrow head in his lap. Shaken, Sloan felt a tightness in his chest, a prickling sensation in the back of his throat.

"What do you think you're doing?" The question emerged hoarse, almost gruff. He cleared his throat, feeling more of an idiot than ever, sitting here on the porch and talking to an animal as though they were the best of friends. "Look, I have work to do. Go back to sleep. Best of my knowledge—limited, I admit—you're supposed to be nocturnal."

He moved to lift the relaxed creature aside. Instead he ended up rubbing its head and shoulders, marveling in spite of himself at the delicate bone structure, the rough-yet-silky feel of the fur. A light breeze puffed through the porch, bearing with it the heady aromas of fresh lumber and the honeysuckle that grew in glorious abandon all over his property. Giving in with a rueful smile, Sloan leaned his head against the column and closed his eyes, his hands gently stroking the fox.

❦

Garnet smiled and nodded as the group of visiting ladies trooped down the porch steps.

"...be sure to send word when Mrs. Ward comes knocking on your door. Shouldn't be waiting much longer, I'd reckon, now you're up and about again."

"…and do take this chastisement from the Lord to heart, Garnet. Get yourself hitched to Joshua, instead of traipsing—"

"Hush your mouth, Lurleen." Elmira Whitaker patted Garnet's cheek. "You'll be all right, child. You just eat that beef soup I left in the kitchen, you hear? Put some color back in those cheeks."

"What she needs is three glasses a day of my clover tea," Mavis chimed in. "Leah, you make sure your sister drinks the entire jarful. It provides equal benefit imbibed warm or at room temperature."

By the time the last farewell faded in the languid summer air, Garnet felt as limp as an overcooked snap bean.

"Let's stay outside, settle on your favorite porch perch," Leah said. "Mrs. Kibler's toilet water is so overpowering I feel like I've bathed in it along with her."

"I agree, but she loves it," Garnet said. " 'Sweet Bye-and-Bye', it's called, for some reason. She purchases it from a mail order catalog."

Leah wrapped a firm arm about Garnet's waist and bullied her into the settee. "There. Might be hotter, but right now the humidity's easier to breathe than the air inside the parlor."

They both laughed. Garnet's muscles slackened, and her eyelids drifted down.

"Papa's going to Cooper's," Leah said after a while. "Reckon I better go make a list." She rose, stretching her arms.

"Perhaps I'll go with him," Garnet mused drowsily. "A drive would be nice."

"Don't be ridiculous. Can't risk tearing Dr. MacAllister's neatly sewn stitches." With a saucy grin and flick of her hand, Leah scooted back inside the house.

Years ago her younger sister had mastered the art of a well-timed exit to get her way. *Little saucebox,* Garnet thought, smiling. She closed her eyes again, savoring her solitude.

The moment was fleeting. Only a short while later, Joshua's buggy rounded the curve and climbed the gentle rise toward the house. Garnet remained seated, more spent than she cared to admit, dispirited as well by the news of Felicity Ward. Buttercups and bitterweed, but Joshua was persistent. She cared for him. Enjoyed his company—Joshua was one of the few gentlemen Garnet felt comfortable around, for in all the time they'd known each other, he had never…well, crowded her.

But she wished he'd chosen to visit another day. She wished more fervently she could scrape together an ounce of resolve and convince him not to call at all. It would be a kindness to them both.

Today, however, she was too drained. Too…twitchy, Meredith would say, though Garnet avoided examining whys and wherefores. A vivid memory surfaced without warning, of narrowed smoke-colored eyes in a lean face stamped with contempt and compassion. Strong hands that—

"It's a blessing to see you looking so fit," Joshua called, pulling his horse Ruth to a halt in front of the porch.

Garnet blinked. The disturbing memory vanished. "Tactful as always." She smiled, watching him set the brake, double-check it, secure the reins, double-check that they were looped just so, and finally feed his horse a carrot. "How is Ruth these days?" The swaybacked piebald was ugly as a mudhole, but Joshua doted on the animal.

"Been a tad stiff lately—I asked the smith to have a look at her last month when I took her in to be reshod." He gave Ruth a last pat and stepped up onto the porch. "Won't make that mistake again. That bounder told me she was twenty-five if she's a day and ought to be sold to a glue factory." The pale eyes filled with indignation.

"At least you appreciate her, Joshua."

"I do. But not as much as I appreciate you, Garnet." He removed the fawn-colored fedora he favored and sat down opposite her, drawing his long legs up. "I've been in earnest prayer, as you know, entreating the Lord to heal you." The corner of his mouth lifted in a shy smile. "Looking at you now, how beautifully He has answered my prayers."

"Joshua, you should pray for better eyesight." In reality Garnet knew she looked more like a washerwoman after a hard day's scrubbing.

"You never take your faith seriously." He cleared his throat. "I know, you think I take mine too seriously."

"I think you live your faith, and I envy you for it. No—don't say anything else. I'm not up to a debate today. Half the neighbor ladies just left. They wore me out."

"I passed them on the way up. Garnet?" He hesitated, his long-boned fingers tracing the crease in the crown of his hat. "Are you…I heard about Mrs. Ward. That's one of the reasons I stopped by. I know you've always felt that the Valley is your domain, that the Lord called you in a sense to be His emissary through your drawings."

Sometimes Joshua could be endearingly stuffy. "Perhaps I do, but that doesn't mean I've a deed for the land between Winchester and Roanoke. Anyone—including Felicity Ward—is free to make use of the scenery."

He smiled at her, his crooked teeth boyishly charming. "I suppose we're all free to enjoy God's beauty, though until now I thought you were the only one who insisted on capturing it on paper." He paused, adding after a moment, "I may not approve of your habits, Garnet—wandering about unaccompanied, I mean. But I admire your drawings very much. Don't trouble yourself over Mrs. Ward's stature. Remember how, in the book of Galatians, Saint Paul instructs us to not compare ourselves to others?"

"Comparing myself to Felicity Ward would be about like comparing Signal Knob to Pike's Peak in Colorado. I read an article in *Harper's Magazine* that said Pike's Peak was over fourteen thousand feet high. Can you imagine?" She shook her head. "I'd love to see a mountain that high, but I wouldn't want to live in its shadow."

"I wish you wouldn't do that."

Garnet stiffened at the reproving tone. "Joshua, I am not hiding my light under a bushel. I'm merely agreeing with you. Besides…" With relief she heard Leah and her father approaching. "Paul also admonishes us not to think more highly of ourselves than we ought."

"Humility is supposed to be a spiritual conditioning of our hearts, not a catalog of our inadequacies." Joshua, too, heard the voices. He leaned forward, determination blazing from the pale eyes and jutting chin. "But perhaps the doubts I see in you reflect a restlessness in your heart. Perhaps what you need more than anything is the security of place—something that your art can never provide. Garnet, I—"

"Papa's making a run over to Cooper's Store. There's an item or two

I need to remind him to purchase." Ignoring the fiery jab of pain, Garnet rose, forcing Joshua to do the same. His manners, if not his perceptions, were impeccable.

"A fine afternoon, is it not, Joshua my boy?" her father said as he stepped through the front door. "Don't tell me you're leaving then?"

"Garnet's tired." He sent her an apologetic smile that belied the determination. "And I have an appointment in Woodstock." In a clumsy, unexpected move, he grabbed Garnet's right hand and squeezed it tight. "I've given her something to pray about." He released her and settled the fedora on his head.

"What was that all about?" her father asked moments later, his gaze on the dust curling out from Joshua's departing buggy.

Garnet examined her fingers, still numb from Joshua's almost frantic grip. It was the first time in three years he'd been less than the perfect gentleman. "I'm not sure. He's never so much as held my hand at a picnic before."

"What do you expect?" Jacob said, giving her braid a light tug. "You never let on you'd welcome it."

The lash of loneliness struck hard, raising welts. "I still don't," she managed.

Another image of Sloan MacAllister flashed through her, as startling and forceful as Joshua's impromptu gesture. Mr. MacAllister had held her in his arms. Had bound her wounds, soothed her fears, treated her with a familiarity Garnet had experienced only within her family.

He had also intimidated and frightened her.

Yet when his hand engulfed hers, the grip hadn't left red marks.

An unwelcome sliver of knowledge more painful than the wound to her shoulder forced its way to acknowledgement. If Sloan MacAllister had been sitting opposite her on the porch instead of Joshua Jones, she would have welcomed a handshake—and more.

For the rest of the afternoon, Garnet closed her mind to all thoughts of Mr. MacAllister.

At a little before five Jacob returned from the store. He poked his head inside the parlor where Garnet was plowing her way through one of

Leah's scholarly books on botany. "I'm going to clean up," he said, "then I want to have a talk with you, Garnet."

"This sounds serious. What about?"

Her father searched her face for a long moment, then heaved a sigh. "Doc Porter happened to be at Cooper's while I was waiting for our order. Tells me he's got to go to Roanoke, won't be back 'til the first of the month."

Leah had followed Jacob into the parlor. She scowled at the news. "Typical of the man. Never around when you need him."

"That'll be enough of that, miss."

"I'm doing well, Papa," Garnet hurriedly inserted. "I don't need— oh. The stitches." She bit her lip. "You and Leah can—"

"Don't be ridiculous," Leah interrupted. "We'll ask Mr. MacAllister. After all, he put them in." She nodded in satisfaction. "Should have been checking up on her all along, of course. This serves him right, I'd say."

Jacob lifted an eyebrow at her, and Leah subsided. "I'm going to wash up," he repeated mildly, "and then we'll talk. Did Lurleen bring any of her Republican Cake? I'll have me a piece of that, lasses, and we'll discuss what's best for Garnet."

Thirteen

here's going to be a storm. What if I catch a chill, in my weakened condition?"

Jacob chuckled. "Aye, you've a fine head on your shoulders, lass. These past few days I've been taking note of all your canny excuses. Let's see…'a chill' would be, yes, number seven. But we're still not turning around, Garnet. It's been two weeks. You need those stitches out."

He glanced up at the sky, then jiggled the reins. "Let's pick up the pace a bit, lads," he said to the two horses, a tacit agreement that earned a small smile from Garnet. Without turning his head, Jacob shifted the reins to his left hand so he could tug the brim of her bonnet with his right. "How did you persuade your sister to tie the ribbons for you?"

"Didn't even try. I tied them myself."

A deer fly was pestering Goatsbeard. The horse swiveled his ear and gave a vexed headshake that set the harness to jingling. Jacob watched the battle for a little bit before he dispatched the deer fly with a single well-aimed flick of the whip. Finally he spoke. "And was the pain worth it?"

"It was better than listening to a lecture."

When Garnet spoke in that flat monotone, further badgering would only result in a quiet but unbridgeable withdrawal. Jacob hunched his shoulders and began to whistle between his teeth.

A mile or so from Tom's Brook, Garnet's spine relaxed, and Jacob heard the slow exhalation of her breath. Her reluctance to visit Sloan MacAllister might be nothing more than shyness; of his three daughters, Garnet had always been the most sensitive, and Jacob was willing to concede the awkwardness of today's visit. Still and all, her protest over the past days rang more of inexplicable anxiety than shyness.

Jacob turned the horses down the narrow road that he'd been told led to Sloan MacAllister's place. He longed for Garnet to share her fears instead of facing the world with that heartbreaking smile and wrenching humor. But she hadn't been that open with him for five years now.

Lord Jesus…but why? If he just understood, he'd move heaven and earth to give her back the joy of her salvation.

Jacob swallowed the aching knot of regret. "According to Mr. Cooper, the Pritchetts' old place is 'bout a quarter-mile down this road. We should be there soon. Good Lord willing, Sloan can see to your stitches, and we'll be on our way back home long before the rain hits." Mentally Jacob crossed his fingers and prayed for a gullywasher.

"You're assuming he'll make an exception and be willing to perform the service, Papa. Haven't you paid any attention to all the stories?"

"This is different. He'll not mind seeing you. Trust me, Garnet. He'll not mind."

"It's no different," was her toneless response, "and he's more likely to mind very much."

Neither of them spoke again. Moments later, Jacob turned the horses onto a rough track that dipped down, crossed a shallow creek, then undulated out of sight up a gentle hill. In the distance he could hear the rhythmic pounding of a hammer.

So could Garnet. "I told you. He's busy, Papa."

"How long can it take to snip a few pieces of thread?" Jacob injected jocularity in the words, but the girl's reluctance was beginning to spook him as well. The pale freckled face was almost ethereal, still as a corpse. It made no sense. No sense at all.

But didn't it remind him of that afternoon five years ago? She'd returned home then with this same look of—of awful serenity, splattered with mud and her eyes full of desperate lies, while she promised him over and over that she was fine, just shaken because the horse had taken a notion to run off and their dog, Chowder, hadn't come when she called.

Jacob prayed fervently that he hadn't misunderstood Sloan MacAllister's nature.

The man stood at the top of a ladder while he fastened unpainted boards onto the side of the house with the skill of a seasoned carpenter.

Jacob suppressed a pinch of guilt, and a bit of uneasiness. The back of Sloan's shirt was damp with sweat, and he'd rolled up the sleeves to reveal strongly muscled forearms. Sunbeams poured over Massanutten Mountain, glinting off a shaggy black head of hair that hadn't seen barber's shears in a long time.

He resembled a sober physician not a bit. *Aye, Lord, and what would You be having me do then?* A warning flicker gnawed in his innards, but Jacob resolutely pulled the buggy to a halt beneath a giant chestnut tree. He set the brake and turned to Garnet. "I'll help you down."

"I'll just wait here, while you go speak to him." Her chin lifted. "It will save time."

The lass could outstubborn a tree stump. "Very well." He settled his flat cap on his head, climbed down, and strolled across the yard. "Mr. MacAllister! Good day to you. Could we have a moment of your time?"

"Medical advice costs fifty dollars up front. No exceptions." He didn't even turn around, adding insult to injury by not even pausing in his work.

Fifty dollars? Glory be, but Jacob hadn't anticipated that response. Sloan had refused any payment whatsoever the night he'd brought Garnet home. And he'd fixed a clear-eyed glare on Jacob that could have hewn an oak timber when Jacob tried to insist. He stared up at the broad back in consternation.

Behind him, Garnet's soft voice called his name, the undertone of pleading igniting a spark of anger. He took a deep breath, planted his fists on his hips, and bellowed, "I ought to knock the ladder out from beneath your feet, ye stiff-necked, prideful young fool. Come down here and face me like a man, and tell me to my face that you'll be charging so—"

"Jacob?" Sloan interrupted, his head twisting to peer downward. A rueful smile lifted the corners of his mustache, and a second later he'd shimmied down the ladder, landing with light-footed grace in front of Jacob. "Sorry. Didn't know it was you."

"Fifty dollars?" Still rattled, Jacob felt like gathering a handful of Sloan's damp shirt and shaking him. "And where would you be getting the gall to commit such extortion?"

"Same place as the folks who see fit to knock on my door at all hours, even though I've made it plain I'm no longer doctoring." Unabashed, Sloan wiped his sweating face on his forearm. "What brings you up this way, hmm? Come to tell me all the mistakes I'm making? Don't keep me in suspense. How am I doing?"

"I…um…ah…"

Sloan dropped the bantering, frowning a little. His gaze lifted toward the buggy, narrowed. "Garnet's with you? Is she all right? She found her bag, didn't she?" He cleared his throat. "It was late; that's why I didn't knock."

"Aye, she's fine, fine. Very relieved to have her things." Jacob ran a finger back and forth over his knuckles. "That is…Sloan, well, Doc Porter's left town for the summer, don't you know, and she needs the stitches removed. I thought…well, I hoped you'd not mind so much doing the job yourself. In light of your initial reception, I can see I might have presumed a wee bit, and for that I'm sorry."

"Been a while since I saw a grown man blush," Sloan said after a prolonged pause. Then he thumped Jacob's back. "Since I put 'em in, it's only fitting that I remove them. Just don't go around telling everyone, is all I ask."

"The fifty dollars ought to keep folks from the door regardless."

"If not, I can always raise it to seventy-five."

He started for the buggy, leaving Jacob staring at his back, the niggling doubts swollen enough to choke a mule.

"I would invite you to wait in my parlor while I clean up a bit, but there's no furniture," Sloan said when Jacob drew abreast. " 'Fraid it will have to be the kitchen, if you don't mind."

"Front porch'll do. No need to intrude in your home. No furniture, you say?" An idea sprang to life, and it was all Jacob could do to keep from rubbing his hands.

"Haven't needed it. I've arranged for some things to be shipped from my home up in Baltimore. They should be arriving in a couple of weeks."

They reached the buggy, and Jacob watched in relief as gentleness transformed Sloan's hard-edged inscrutability. The burning inside his stomach subsided to a negligible twinge. *Och, Lord, for a while there, I doubted, but 'tis plain to see the man's heart is to heal.*

"Hello," Sloan was saying to Garnet. "You look a lot better than the last time I saw you, Miss Sinclair."

"Call her Garnet," Jacob suggested. "With three daughters, it makes things simpler."

"I can see that it might. All right, then…Garnet?" Sloan asked her. He didn't even look Jacob's way, which pleased Jacob, though 'twould also please him if the man smiled a bit more.

"Mr. MacAllister, this trip was my father's idea. I told him Leah could remove the stitches." For the first time the solemn gray green eyes lit with humor. "She's an excellent seamstress, you know."

"I'm sure she is."

Jacob helped her climb down from the buggy, but when Garnet winced and bit her lip, he found himself elbowed out of the way by Sloan. "What kind of pain did you feel just then? And where?" he asked, his gaze sharp.

"Don't make a fuss, please. It's just the stitches. They pinch a bit, that's all. The past few days Leah and my father practically carry me off to bed if I so much as grimace. They're about to set me to howling at the moon."

She stepped back, pulling free of Sloan's restraining hand, distancing herself, Jacob knew, from the man. To his eternal relief, Sloan was having none of it, though he was astute enough not to crowd her again.

"We can't have that, can we?" he said. "Tell you what. While I wash up, why don't you have a chat with my patient up there on the porch. If I'm fortunate, perhaps he'll convince you to trust me enough to let me examine your shoulder."

Garnet shook her head, her eyes anxious. "I think we'll just wait here, in the buggy."

A patient? Jacob moved to Garnet's side, laid a comforting hand on her uninjured shoulder. "Didn't realize anyone in the Valley could afford that fifty dollar fee. Besides, you told me you weren't hanging out your shingle, Sloan."

"I haven't. I won't. This particular patient, like Garnet"—he finally smiled, looking almost boyish—"is an exception. Go ahead, you've met him before. I'm sure he remembers. Just be careful. No sudden moves."

Beside him Garnet had turned to a pillar of salt, her face a study in confusion and budding hope. "Mr. MacAllister?" she whispered. She took a step toward the porch.

"He's very tame, believe it or not. Perhaps it's because a compassionate young woman taught him that some human beings can be trusted."

In a gesture that tore at Jacob's heart, Sloan lifted his hand toward Garnet, his fingers just skimming the bonnet's brim. "It's all right, Garnet," he promised in a deep, soft voice. "Your father wouldn't have brought you if it weren't. Think about that, while I go clean up and fetch my bag."

His hand dropped, he nodded once at Jacob, then turned without a word and loped toward the house. Jacob glanced at Garnet. She looked stunned, but her gaze was not on the tall commanding figure of the man. She was staring at the porch, and the splash of reddish color visible behind the weathered railing.

Fourteen

*H*ope squeezed her heart. Garnet all but tiptoed to the porch one tentative step at a time, not so much because she couldn't believe her eyes, but because she did.

"I'll stay back," she heard her father say behind her.

Garnet lifted her uninjured arm in response but did not speak.

The fox was confined in a crude pen fashioned from mesh poultry netting, and upon first glance Garnet wondered if it could possibly be the same animal she had rescued. This fox's luxurious rust-colored coat gleamed in the sunlight; the tail, which she remembered as thin and droopy, now dominated the small body with bushy magnificence. Alert eyes the color of ripe pumpkin watched Garnet from a collection of rumpled blankets, obviously its bed.

Garnet crept forward until her knees brushed the wire. "Hello." The word emerged in a husky murmur because she was fighting tears. "Remember me?"

The narrow head tilted. Black-tipped ears pricked forward. After a moment of breathless suspense, the bushy tail wagged once, and the fox rose slowly to his feet. Garnet didn't move, didn't so much as inhale as she watched the catlike creature gliding toward her on dainty black paws.

He stopped a foot away, lifting his pointy snout as though to sniff the air. Then his mouth opened in an absurdly human grin. A single tear spilled over Garnet's eyelid, dribbling down her jaw line as the fox walked right up to the wire and thrust a damp black nose through the holes, into the folds of her skirt.

"You're alive." Carefully, ignoring the dull ache in her shoulder, Garnet lowered herself until she was kneeling on the uneven porch. "You're *alive*." She started to lift her hand.

"Perhaps you should wait for Sloan."

The fox blinked and backed a step.

"Don't, Papa. You'll frighten him. He knows me, it's all right." Her voice dropped to the croon a mother uses with her baby. "He won't hurt you, I promise. You're so pretty…won't you let me pet you? Mr. MacAllister's taken good care of you, hasn't he? I'm sure he wouldn't have wanted me to see you if it wasn't safe."

Her father cleared his throat several times. "I ken you well, lass. Just…be careful, for my sake, hmm? I'm no' used to my daughter flirting with a wild beastie." After a short pause she heard him blowing his nose, loudly.

Garnet understood. She swallowed the lump in her throat, then held out her hand. "See? He's not wild at all, not really."

Seconds later the fox returned, sniffing her fingers. Long whiskers spiked from the muzzle, tickling her wrist. After a moment, she turned her hand. The fox didn't flinch away. Tentatively Garnet brushed the white fur just behind his jaw, astonished when the animal butted his head against her hand.

"He wants you to scratch behind his ears, and on top of his head," Sloan said. The toes of his work boots nudged the folds of her gown. "I've accused him several times of being a cat in fox's clothing. If he starts to purr, however, I just might have to sell him to Mr. Barnum. Sure to draw a larger crowd than General Tom Thumb."

He knelt beside Garnet, so close she could feel the heat of him, smell the clean aroma of soap. A strange sensation fluttered through her, but she resisted the urge to rise.

"He does smile like a gentleman who hopes to take all your money, doesn't he?" She scratched the tufted ears and hoped Mr. MacAllister would attribute the breathlessness in her voice to her gladness over the fox's presence.

"Mm. Now that you mention it, I believe you're right. Would you like to name him, Garnet? I planned to give him to you, of course, so it's only fair that you name him. He's never going to be strong enough to make it on his own in the wild, I'm afraid."

"A fox for a pet?" Jacob's voice rose, and Garnet could almost see the tips of his ears turning pink as they did when he was taken off guard. *"A fox?"*

She risked a quick peek at the man beside her, disconcerted to find him watching her. "I think he'd make an excellent traveling companion," she offered, looking everywhere but Mr. MacAllister. "And I think…in honor of Mr. Barnum, that Phineas is a good name. Um…what do you think?"

"Phineas the fox? It does have a nice alliterative ring, doesn't it?" His hand slid under Garnet's elbow, holding her steady in a light but firm grip. "So, Phineas. How would you like to keep your mistress diverted while I remove her stitches, hmm? You can prove your worth to Mr. Sinclair, and secure yourself a position in their home."

Utterly flummoxed by his manner—so congenial, so downright good-humored—Garnet did not resist when the hand beneath her elbow tightened. Before she could blink twice he had helped her to her feet.

"Come along," he said. "Do you mind that your father will have to chaperon?"

"Chaperon?" She glanced toward her father, who looked equally confused.

"You have to remove your arm from the sleeve of your gown—also whatever shift or chemise you're wearing—for me to get to the stitches."

"No!"

Garnet stepped back too quickly. Mr. MacAllister dropped her arm and lifted his hands as though she were something repulsive.

The absurdity of her involuntary retort brought a shamed flush to her cheeks. "I…I beg your pardon, I'm being silly," she stammered. "You've taken care of me before, and you didn't hurt me then. I mean…I hadn't given you cause. I mean—" *Dear Father in heaven, what have I done?*

She closed her mouth and her eyes. Her stupid panic might have just secured a death warrant for herself as well as her family. They would want explanations, they might demand them, and she was so tired of the lies…

"Take it easy, Garnet. Look…you're frightening Phineas. Reassure him for me, won't you? He's very gentle-natured, but shy. Jacob, why don't you fetch my case? I left it in the kitchen, on a table. You can't miss it. We'll stay on the porch. She might feel safer if I just remove the stitches out here."

"Out here? But anyone could see—"

"We'd see them first. She'll be sitting down in that old kitchen chair, over there by the window. Go on, please. I want Garnet to know she's safe even if you're not in sight."

Muttering, he obeyed.

Garnet listened to the slow scrape of his footsteps fade, disappear. "You don't have to talk as though I'm not here." Her mouth was powder dry, but she managed to meet head-on Sloan MacAllister's watchful gaze.

"I'd like to know who caused you to fear a man's touch, to have you look at me like that," he said, very quietly.

"I don't…it wouldn't make any difference. There's nothing you can do—nothing anyone can do." She half lifted her hand. "I know I was irrational. But I can't explain. Mr. MacAllister, I—"

"Sloan. Call me Sloan."

"What?"

"If I call you Garnet, you're entitled to call me by my Christian name. Here, come over here, to the chair. It's inside the enclosure, so you and Phineas can get reacquainted without barriers. Will you let me help you step over the wire?"

"I—step over?"

"Mm. I'm going to put my hands on your waist, to steady you. Shh, it's all right," he murmured close to her ear. "Up and over."

Before she had time to gasp, she was inside the pen, with Mr. MacAllister close behind her, his firm grip guiding her to an old pressed-back chair. The warmth of his hands burned through her clothing all the way to her skin. No man—not her father, not Joshua, had touched her with such intimacy in five years.

"Will it collapse?" she asked, just to diffuse the tension in the air with words.

"Will you?"

Her spine stiffened, her head going back. "No." She planted her feet on the floor and breathed through her nose. "I won't collapse. But I'm not certain about this chair. It's…well…a fresh coat of paint would help. My father would strip and stain it. He hates painting over wood."

"That's easy to understand," Sloan said, as though this were a conversation taking place in the family parlor. "Your father loves wood. For him, covering it up would be tantamount to desecration, or at least hiding its light under a bushel."

Garnet gawked—there was no other word for it—at him. He was so close she could see the individual hairs that formed his mustache, the shadow of a beard darkening his neck and face. And his eyes…for the first time since she was a young girl, she risked looking directly at a man she did not know, accepting his proximity, absorbing the intelligence and the strength. Fear and shyness wrapped around her like vines, along with revelation: There was no threat to her here.

Until this moment Garnet had never comprehended that fear for her family's safety was not her predominant motive for spurning male companionship. "You're very perceptive," she said, watching fascinated when understanding turned those gray eyes the color of smoke.

"Only when I'm not being pigheaded," he murmured. His teeth flashed in a quick smile. "Not afraid of me anymore?"

Her gaze dropped to Phineas, who was sniffing the dusty toes of her sturdy buttontops. "You don't understand."

"Then help me to, Garnet." He dropped to one knee, then grasped the chair with one hand to balance himself. "Your father thinks you're afraid of men. He talked with me, you know, the night I brought you home. Did he tell you?"

A blush tinted her cheeks. "Leah told me. My father refuses to discuss it. I don't understand why he felt compelled to burden you"—*and betray me*—"but I know he would have a good reason. You…Leah said you asked about our heartwood chests."

"I only saw yours. I think your father's one of the most highly skilled craftsmen I've ever known."

"Leah said…Leah said you found the drawer, with the cardinal feather," she finished in a rush. Lightly she brushed her fingers over the fox's narrow snout, rubbed the patch of white that splashed his throat and jaw. *What did you think?* she wanted to ask. *Do you know why my father put it in there?*

"Mm. I found it…intriguing."

"You wondered why there wasn't a piece of heirloom jewelry?"

"No." He hesitated. "At the time I didn't want to know anything about you or your family history," he said. "But sometimes we don't get what we want, Garnet Sinclair."

The door opened behind them and Jacob appeared. Mr. MacAllister finally turned away then, leaving Garnet to flounder over that uncomfortable truth while he thanked her father for fetching his medical bag.

"Best let you do the job then," Jacob said. "Those clouds are moving in fast." He shuffled his feet. "Um…what do you want me to do, Sloan?"

"How about," Mr. MacAllister said after a thoughtful pause, "if you stand opposite Garnet and me, by the railing over there, where you can keep a watch out for visitors?"

"Ye wouldn't be needing me tae hold something then? Your scissors or…or wipe away blood or—"

"There won't be any blood, Jacob," Mr. MacAllister promised soothingly. "And no, I don't need you to hold anything unless Garnet needs you to hold her hand."

"I'll be fine, Papa," Garnet added as confidently as she could. "It will help me more, if you watch for someone who might be coming up the track."

"Aye, well." He sidled toward the front of the porch and stepped over the pen. "This ought to do it, about here, I reckon."

"That's fine, Jacob." Mr. MacAllister smiled down at Garnet. Amazingly, he winked. "Keep your eyes peeled on that track now."

Flustered anew, Garnet scarcely noticed what else he was doing until his hands deftly untied the bonnet strings and removed it from her head. "There," he said, and she felt the brush of his fingers against the back of her neck. "Now I can see the buttons on your gown."

She went rigid.

"Remind me to write out a list of the foods I've been feeding Phineas," he commented. "I've been meaning to do a spot of research on foxes, you know. Just haven't taken the time, with all that's been going on lately."

The resonant baritone voice flowed around Garnet. Instead of what he was doing, she tried to concentrate on the sound of his voice, with its not unpleasant clip so different from the slow mountain drawl she was used to hearing. He was talking about Phineas, how the previous day the fox had been watching him munch on an apple with such longing that Sloan had sliced off a piece. How he'd watched in astonishment when Phineas ate the piece and begged for more…

"Breathe, Garnet. You're doing fine. I'm not going to hurt you."

Breathe? Oh. A breath shuddered through her, but when he gently maneuvered the long sleeve down her left arm and exposed her flesh from fingertips to neck, her right hand flew up and she flattened herself against the chair.

"Easy. Remember, I've done this before. I'm a…" There was another pause, so fleeting Garnet might have missed it except her gaze had fixed blindly on his throat and she watched in a sort of stupor as dark color spilled over the collarless neck of his shirt. "A doctor," he finished. "For you, right now, I'm a physician, Garnet. Sworn to heal, to do no harm. As God is my witness, I'm not going to harm you."

"I know that." She closed her eyes, but the swarm of memories that had been buzzing around her intensified when her eyes closed. So she kept them open, fastened on Sloan MacAllister's intent face.

He could be harsh, bitter, intimidating, she knew. And in spite of his present manner, she was convinced he didn't like her very much. But her father trusted him, and there was a helpless animal sitting quietly pressed against her ankles that owed its life to this man.

She had been a naive sixteen-year-old girl when she wandered off onto a sun-dappled path and her life had changed to a constant battle with fear and darkness. Perhaps the time had come for her to take a step toward a path that might lead her back into the sunlight.

Surely God would not punish her—or her family—for trying.

Fifteen

*L*eah was absorbed in her dog-eared copy of *The Brothers Karama-zov* when a knock sounded on the front door. Grumbling, she marked the page and rose, padding into the hall on stockinged feet. If JosieMae begged to talk to Garnet one more time—

Leah flung open the door. Instead of the pesky JosieMae, a strange woman dressed in a bottle-green silk gown waited, poised as a duchess. A matching green parasol was hooked over her arm, and beneath her smart straw Empire hat, thick black hair had been swept up in elegant coils.

"Good afternoon," she said. "Mrs. Elmira Whitaker was supposed to accompany me for introductions but was unable to come at the last moment. I couldn't wait any longer, so I took a chance and stopped in anyway." She smiled, a toothy smile, Leah decided critically. "I'm Mrs. Felicity Ward. Would you by any chance be Miss Garnet Sinclair?"

"I'm her younger sister, Leah." She glanced behind Mrs. Ward, toward the slouched figure of the young man still sitting on the driver's side of a fancy surrey. "Garnet's not at home."

"Oh." She waved long gloved fingers. "I assume I'm to take that literally to mean that she is not inside at all? I do understand she'd been injured, which is why I waited until now."

"She's out with my father," Leah acknowledged reluctantly. "I don't know what time to expect them home." Curiosity was an itch begging to be scratched, so she opened the door and stepped back. "But you're welcome to come in for some refreshments, if you like."

"Thank you, dear, but I wouldn't dream of intruding. If you could just give your sister my card. I do want to meet her, very much." She extended a heavy vellum calling card, her gaze wandering over Leah's plain shirtwaist and skirt down to her shoeless feet.

Leah resisted the urge to apologize over her appearance. She decided Mrs. Ward was a snobbish woman, plainly convinced of her superiority over backwoods rustics. Without blinking an eye she stuffed the card in her pocket. "She's looking forward to meeting you too. Unfortunately, she stays very busy. I'm sure, since you're also an artist, you understand. Were you needing to ask her advice on your work? Garnet knows every inch of the valley hereabouts, from Woodstock to Winchester." In a precise mimicry she allowed her own gaze to roam over the statuesque woman, feeling a certain satisfaction when Mrs. Ward's nostrils flared, and the patronizing smile froze in place. "I'll be sure to give her your card."

"Thank you." The artist turned her back in a rustle of starched petticoats and watered silk. But at the top porch step, she whirled around, marching back across to an astonished Leah. "I offended you, didn't I?" she demanded.

Leah's mind went blank. "Why do you ask?" she finally managed, feeling young and gauche.

Mrs. Ward gave a peal of laughter, her gloved hand lifting to pat Leah's burning cheek. "So I can apologize," she said. "Everyone tells me I'm an unforgivable snob—doubtless due to my heritage. My grandfather owned one of the richest plantations in the Carolinas, and my mother never let me forget it."

"Your father fought for the Union," Leah said. "That's why you grew up in California. So claiming snobbery due to your heritage doesn't make a lot of sense." She wished her family were home. "But you can still apologize if you want to."

"You're an outspoken young lady. I like that, especially since I'm one myself, though no longer so young." She tapped a long elegant index finger against her chin, studying Leah. "It would seem you've been doing a little digging about me. It wasn't necessary. I'm not a threat to your sister. I've seen her work. She's very good."

"She's better than very good."

"Fine. She's excellent. But her medium is pen and ink, mine oils, and for the most part she prefers floral illustration while I work on canvases to produce scenic works of art. We both want to…to share the Shenandoah Valley with the rest of the world. Her, with her magazine illustrations, me with a collection of paintings." A look of frustration clouded the pleasing roundness of her face. "I was counting on her assistance. Someone with an artistic eye to help me settle on locales."

Knowing Garnet, Leah thought her sister would share every one of her cherished places with this brash outlander, while inside her vulnerable heart would be shrinking from the intrusion. "Why did you select this end of the Valley?" she asked, half to herself.

Mrs. Ward smiled. It was a peculiarly ironic smile, one that rendered the older woman more approachable. "I haven't told anyone else," she confided. "But since you're so protective of your sister, I'll tell you." She leaned forward, and Leah caught a whiff of a heavy fragrance. "I saw one of her works in the *American Monthly*. 'Flowering Dogwood, A Shenandoah Spring,' was the caption. It took my breath away."

"I remember it." Leah swallowed the prick of chagrin for her disrespectful thoughts.

"Of course you'll know that, for the last several years, I've been painting various scenes from different parts of the country."

"You have a traveling exhibit, part of the Chautauqua Literary and Scientific Circle, don't you?"

"Why, yes I do. You certainly are knowledgeable for—never mind." Another deep-bodied laugh escaped. "I can tell by your expression it would be better to leave that remark unsaid. By the way, you have a very paintable face. Did you know? It would be fascinating…" She pursed her lips and studied Leah through narrowed eyes.

"Thank you, but I prefer my face—unpainted," Leah said.

"What a shame." Mrs. Ward waved her hand. "At any rate, when I saw that dogwood illustration by Garnet Sinclair, I knew that the Shenandoah Valley would have to be my next project. I contacted Mr. Smoot, persuaded him to tell me where she lived."

"I see." Oh, she saw all right. Prying, pretentious busybody, treating them like a family of paper dolls she could dress and undress as she chose. "Mrs. Ward, I'm sorry but I have—"

"I really will leave now," the other woman interrupted. "I do hope you'll think about everything and realize the mutual benefits your sister and I could enjoy. It was lovely to meet you, Leah." She stood for a second longer. "I hope your sister appreciates what an effective watch-dog she has."

A rolling thunderclap accompanied her as she swept down the steps, one hand waving away the driver's assistance. They disappeared into the cedars that lined the drive just as the approaching storm clouds snuffed out the sun. Leah sat down on the steps, her mind on the departed guest while her eyes watched the approaching storm. It looked to be a nasty one. She hoped Garnet and their father wouldn't be caught in it.

Felicity Ward, on the other hand, could probably benefit from a soaking.

❦

Sloan tried hard to ignore Garnet's fear while he methodically bared her arm and shoulder. It was more difficult—all right, it was impossible—not to notice the fine-grained alabaster skin, and the light smattering of cinnamon-toned freckles.

The healed wound was an obscenity, the ugly black stitches protruding from that tender skin offensive.

Garnet's eyes, an unblinking rainwashed green, filled her face. Her earlier response to him had made him feel like Jack the Ripper. As far as Sloan was concerned, whoever was responsible for that look deserved to be—he stifled the stew of conflicting emotions and bent to examine the cut. When he pressed it lightly with his fingers Garnet's breath hitched, her arm reflexively jerking.

"Hurt?" Sloan asked, keeping his voice impersonal.

"N-no. It's not that."

The pause that followed brought his head up to search her face. Uncertainty, fear, doubt...nothing he hadn't expected. But what raised his eyebrow was the resolution, shining like gold amid a pile of rubble.

"What is it then?" he asked finally.

"My father trusts you." Both of them glanced over at Jacob's stalwart back. When she spoke again, her voice was low, the words a hurried jumble. "I don't understand it, but I-I trust you too. Even so, I don't know if I should say anything; it's been five years. But I'm afraid if I don't take a chance now...he wouldn't have, I mean I see now how he, well *arranged* to come here, because he trusts you. But if I tell you, it could put you in danger—"

Put him in danger?

A long rumble of thunder boomed a warning, and he glanced out in surprise. The sky had darkened to the color of his black riding boots.

"Sloan, this looks like a nasty one," Jacob called without turning around. "Ah... You 'bout finished there?"

"Not quite," Sloan said, thinking rapidly. "Tell you what. No sense in either of you racing a storm. Why not put your horses in the barn, stay here 'til it passes? I should be finished with Garnet by the time you return. I don't have much to offer, but for the duration, my house is yours."

Jacob turned around, his gaze barely grazing his daughter before darting away. His face blanched, whether from the exposed wound or her exposed skin, Sloan wasn't sure. "Garnet?"

"You better hurry, from the looks of the weather," Garnet said. "Don't worry, Papa. I'm...I trust Mr. MacAllister."

"Aye. Well, then..." He nodded once, then jogged down the steps and across the yard, accompanied by another peal of thunder.

"Thank you," Garnet said. "I-I didn't want him to hear this. Not yet. How..." She lightly stroked Phineas's head, which seemed to have found its way onto her lap. "How did you know?"

Sloan shrugged. "You need to tell me something, but you were having trouble. If it wasn't because you're still afraid of me, I thought it might be because you were afraid of your father's reaction." Especially if she was about to confess to physical assault, or worse. In spite of Jacob's vehement assertions, Sloan's opinion of mankind was jaded enough not to preclude the obvious reason for Garnet's aversion to the male of the species.

Right now she looked resolute, but her manner remained uncertain. "Tell you what," he said. "How about if I remove the stitches, and you tell me whatever you wish. Talking will keep you distracted from what I'm doing, and when your father returns we both know he'll be relieved."

A ghost of a smile flickered. "Will it hurt?"

"Might pinch a bit. I'll be as gentle as I can. I'm going to swab it with this"—he showed her the bottle of benzoic acid—"then cut the knots and tug out the sutures. You needn't watch. Talk to me, Garnet. Tell me why you think I might be in danger."

While he waited for her answer, Sloan went to work on her shoulder. Her skin quivered when the soaked cotton wool first touched her skin, but her right hand continued to stroke the fox's head. "I was sixteen," she said after a while. "And I had a…crush on this boy at school. Only my older sister, Meredith, fancied him too. She's a born flirt, not in a bad way…all the boys liked her. Meredith's fun to be around, so full of life—sorry. This is difficult."

"You're doing fine, take your time." He snipped the first knot, then tugged the thread out. Garnet emitted a tiny gasp, then resolutely continued her tale.

"Meredith convinced Tate to stay after school with her, to help clean the chalkboards. I was hurt. Jealous…but I understood. Meredith's beautiful, and she doesn't have this hair." She gestured at her head.

Sloan stared at her in surprise, jarred from his concentration on her shoulder. "What does your hair have to do with it?"

"The color," she said impatiently. "I've been teased about it ever since I was a child. It's a curse. People with red hair stand out—especially if they don't have the temperament associated with the color."

Jenna's teasing face flashed through Sloan's mind. "And you don't?" He clipped off knots, deftly tugged threads loose.

"No." Her face was lowered, her right hand pausing from its ceaseless stroking. "I don't have much of a temper. Compared to my sisters, I'm dull. Eccentric but colorless, except for my flaming sunset hair." Her tone made it plain that the description was not a compliment.

Dull. Colorless? How could anyone be so blind about herself? "So you left Meredith at school and started home on your own," he prompted.

"Yes. Did Papa tell you that?"

"He said you changed, your sixteenth summer. And that the change occurred after the day you told him the horse ran away from you. That's not what happened, is it?"

Garnet didn't answer.

Sloan removed the last thread and laid his scissors and tweezers aside on the fresh towel he'd placed on the porch floor. He cleaned the scar, pleased with his handiwork—no sign of infection, redness diminished, complete healing—then secured a light gauze pad in place.

A strong breeze, smelling of rain and honeysuckle, swirled beneath the porch roof, stirring loose tendrils of the hair Garnet thought of as a curse. Sloan contemplated her for a moment. She still hadn't spoken.

In a dispassionate sweep, he stroked his fingers over her bare skin, starting at the downy hair on the nape of her slender neck, following the trapezius muscle to her biceps, on to the inside of her elbow. Not until he reached her wrist did she finally react.

"What are you doing?" She lifted her hand, as though unsure whether to push him away or slap his face.

"Forcing a reaction. Tell me what happened that day, Garnet. It won't take your father long to unhitch the horses. If you don't want him to hear this, you need to tell me now."

Sloan sensed the automatic mental recoil as though he were inside her head. *She won't do it,* he decided, disillusionment battling with the instinct to comfort. He couldn't blame her—in all his years as a practicing physician, none of the physically and emotionally brutalized women he'd treated had been willing to admit it. For some bizarre reason, they seemed to blame themselves.

Then he remembered Jenna—and his brother. Some women *were* born Jezebels, after all. "Never mind. We can talk later," he said. "Here, I want to see how much range of movement you—"

"I left the road to follow a path through the woods. I was disobeying. I wasn't allowed to leave the main road back then." She was breathing rapidly, and beads of perspiration dotted her forehead and upper lip. "I—there were some men. Four. They…they smiled at me. I didn't realize they weren't just being friendly. And I didn't realize what they were doing, what I was seeing, until it was…too late."

"Garnet." He couldn't help but lift her hands to hold them between his, his gaze on her anguished face. "It's all right. Not your fault. Tell me how they hurt you, Garnet. I won't condemn you, I won't blame you—" He broke off when a sobbing laugh bubbled out of her throat.

"You should." She swallowed hard. "I do. One of them…he told me what pretty hair I had. He was the first boy, except he was grown—

a man—but he was the first other than my father to tell me I had pretty hair. So I-I…" She yanked one hand free and covered her eyes. "I flirted with him. *Flirted.* Tried everything I'd watched Meredith do. I wanted them to like me. *God, forgive me!*" The wrenching cry tore from her chest. "I was stupid and shallow and vain—when I saw the body I didn't understand, at first. I remember tossing my head, hoping the sun would shine on my hair, that the young man would notice and pay me another compliment. Then I caught sight of the body. When they saw me staring…everything changed."

A body?

The first raindrops spattered on the tin roof. Sloan picked Phineas up and placed him on the floor. "Tell me what happened." Without making a fuss he knelt and took her hands again. Her fingers dug into his. Sloan gently ran his thumbs over her knuckles in a calming motion. "Garnet," he said very quietly, "what did you mean about seeing a body?"

She went deathly still. After waiting a moment, Sloan disengaged their hands so he could cup her chin, forcing her to look at him. "Take your time; just tell me." He stroked the soft skin with the tips of his fingers, then finally released her, though he didn't allow her any distance between them.

"They'd killed a man." Her dilated eyes fixed on his face. "Dug a hole, and were about to bury him in it. The back of their wagon was full of boxes of dynamite. I didn't know until much later, of course, when I saw similar boxes in Mr. Cooper's store that he'd ordered for Kreuger Mines. And I remember him remarking that this was a repeat order, because the first batch had been stolen.

"Th-the men… I think they stole that dynamite. And they told me if I said anything, told anyone, that they'd find me. They'd hurt me, my family—nobody would be safe. To prove the point, they shot our dog. His name was Chowder. He was barking…they shot him…"

A clap of thunder shook the earth, and with a whooshing roar sheets of rain cascaded from the heavens.

A sad smile curved Garnet's mouth. Sloan thought it the most poignant smile he'd ever seen. "I love rainstorms," she murmured. The gray green eyes blinked once, and her throat muscles tightened. "They hauled me out of the buggy. The one man…began to kiss me. When I struggled, another one held me. They were so strong, I couldn't—I didn't know how. I was helpless." She paused. "I always wondered about my father, because it was after that summer that he taught us how to defend ourselves. But…" Her voice trailed away again.

Sloan waited, fighting a desperate internal battle not to haul her into a protective embrace.

"They…they would have done more than—well, more," she confessed, "but another of the men stopped them. He was older. He made them stop. They dumped me back in the buggy, told me it didn't matter who I was or where I went, that my hair would be easy enough to spot. So I came home, and I told Papa the horse had bolted when a rabbit ran across the road, and that Chowder ran after the rabbit. I told Papa lies…so many lies. But I didn't know what else to do. I had to protect my family. And…I was sc-scared."

Her voice broke. She blinked again, looking around as though waking from a nightmare. "He'll get soaked if he doesn't stay in the barn."

"I'm sure he'll do the wise thing and stay there." With calm authority that belied his inner fury, Sloan began to work Garnet's arm back into the sleeve of her shirtwaist. "You don't need to catch a chill either. Come along, let's go inside. I'll make you some coffee. Nothing like Leah's tea, of course, but it should be drinkable. I'll even let you help. I want you to start exercising your left arm, so the muscles don't atrophy."

He helped her to her feet, and for just a moment allowed his hands to remain on her forearms. When she didn't flinch or pull away, he gave in to the need to hold her. Slowly, carefully he drew her close, and pressed her cheek against his chest.

"You're safe," he said, knowing even as he spoke the words that they might well be as much a lie as the flimsy story Garnet had concocted to provide her family with the same illusion.

Sloan didn't care. Right now, more than his skill as a physician, Garnet Sinclair needed comfort. The fact that she allowed this level of intimacy after what she'd been through humbled him. It also alarmed him.

He had no business feeling what he was feeling toward her right now.

He was in almost as much trouble as Garnet Sinclair.

Sixteen

Garnet listened to the roar of the rain while she watched Sloan MacAllister efficiently move around his large, bare kitchen, lighting the stove, filling a battered tin kettle with water from a rickety pump. Moments later the sound of percolating and the scent of coffee filled the room.

"Will Phineas be all right?" she asked once, when a frenzied gust of wind rattled the door.

"He'll curl up inside the den I fashioned for him out of empty fruit crates. It's snug against the back corner of the porch, and won't blow away. Didn't you see it?" He turned from the stove, a slight smile lifting the corner of his mustache.

"I'm afraid I only noticed Phineas." Among other things...like the man standing at the stove, and what he'd been doing to her. She lifted her left shoulder experimentally, wincing even as she marveled at the freedom of movement.

"How does it feel?"

"Much better than before. Thank you. You were right, it is stiff."

Sloan handed her a mug of the steaming liquid. "I'll give you a series of exercises. Within a week or two, your shoulder should be good as new."

"You're a very good—" She swallowed the word.

"Go on and say it." His voice was resigned. He handed her a mug of steaming coffee and dropped down across from her into a dilapidated chair that matched the one on the front porch. "I'm a good doctor, right?"

A lopsided smile stretched her lips, faded. "Well...yes. You are. Even if you don't want to acknowledge it."

His fingers drummed on the tabletop, then massaged the back of his neck. After a moment an exasperated breath exploded through his tightly pressed lips. "God's not going to let me run away from it, I suppose."

Despite sharing her secret and his insistence that she call him Sloan, Garnet hadn't expected such a personal comment, and it made her feel awkward. She wrapped her fingers around the thick stoneware mug and took a sip of coffee, which was strong enough to strip paint.

Through the window over a cavernous sink she could watch the storm with a cozy intimacy that reminded her of home. How amazing, to sit here listening to the howling wind and the relentless tattoo of raindrops. Her father was stranded inside Sloan's barn. She was stranded—alone—inside Sloan's house. He had bared her shoulder, and she had bared her troubled heart. Yet she wasn't afraid. *I'm not afraid of this man.*

Unfortunately, she was afraid *for* him, and more than ever afraid for herself. Was her decision to tell right and responsible, or had she selfishly made the second greatest mistake of her life?

Regrets were futile. She would simply entreat Sloan to say nothing, even to her father, and everything would continue as before—No. If regrets were futile, denial was as childish as trying to turn her head from a spoonful of medicine. For better or worse, another person—who happened to be a man—shared her secret now. And in a corner of her heart, Garnet welcomed the knowledge, because for the first time she didn't have to bear the burden alone.

She felt as though she were wearing new skin, fashioned from cheese gauze. Light, airy. Tentative. Oh, but it was extraordinary. A strange man had touched her, *handled* her—never mind that it was in the role of a concerned physician—and she had been safe.

Safe. Shielded. Protected, cared for, and sheltered. She hadn't understood Sloan MacAllister then, and in spite of a growing familiarity she didn't understand him now.

But she wanted to.

Garnet dropped four lumps of sugar into her mug, stirring distractedly while her mind grappled with how to proceed. Meredith and Leah would ask questions, she thought: Engage him in conversation, not sit here in silence, inwardly debating over procedure.

She took another sip of coffee without shuddering, set the mug aside, and propped her chin in her hands. "Would you tell me what you meant about God not letting you run away?"

"Ah." Head tipped back, Sloan contemplated a smoke-blackened beam in the ceiling for a long time. Garnet tensed. For some reason, he looked almost angry. "Your father's a very godly man, isn't be?"

"A saint," Garnet agreed with a wistful sigh. "I always wished I could have a faith like his."

"In my experience, that kind of faith generally springs from a simple mind or a simple heart. No offense to your father, of course."

He shrugged, his expression chilled with bitterness. Garnet's nascent confidence faltered even further. "For me, faith is no longer a matter of simplicity," he continued. "Perhaps it never has been. I don't know. I'm not sure I can answer your question. In the past I enjoyed a spiritual life, if you want to refer to it that way. I talked to God, He… talked to me, in a sense—is that what you want to hear? Right now there're some problems, all on my part, of course. I'm not deluded enough to believe it's God who went astray."

A thunderclap shook the house, and Sloan saluted with a mocking gesture. "He's agreeing with me, no doubt. You looked disbelieving, or rather as though you're wondering if perhaps I deserve a lightning bolt for my irreverence."

Garnet managed to shake her head. Well, she'd asked, hadn't she? His anger and bitterness coiled about him like hissing snakes, threatening to strike anyone within reach. Including her. A tortured spirit, her father had told Leah. But, like her father—like Joshua, for that matter —Sloan MacAllister still felt confident enough to talk to God as though the Lord really heard the words. Despite his obvious hostility toward this discussion, Garnet pressed forward, desperate to understand, herself as much as him. "Sloan?"

"What?"

"Why did you…go astray?"

He stiffened, a muscle twitching in his jaw as he raked her in a furious glance. "That, my dear, is none of your business." He rose abruptly, sending the chair screeching across the linoleum floor with such force it toppled. "Baring your soul doesn't give you license to trample mine. I'll go fetch your father. Wait here. Spend your energy figuring out how to tell him about *your* secret past instead."

Garnet stared after the inflexible wall of his back as he stalked across the room. He turned at the doorway. "You didn't learn much about caution five years ago after all, did you?" He disappeared through the doorway.

She was alone. All the lightness had fled, leaving her more isolated and confused than ever. Sloan had touched her so gently with his hands—then wounded her so cruelly with his words.

Perhaps she needed to be afraid of Sloan MacAllister after all.

⋘⋙

Sloan found Sinclair's two horses contentedly munching hay in a couple of stalls that Jacob had cleaned. Man certainly didn't mind making himself at home. He'd even broken open a bale of straw and scattered it on the floor of the stalls; Sloan looked closer and discovered that Sinclair had cleaned Dulcie's as well, even groomed the mare. For the first time in a week her tail flowed free of tangles, burrs, and bits of straw. He'd kept himself busy, the past hour or so.

Now, however, Sinclair himself was fast asleep on the seat of his buggy, hands laced over his chest, his cap pulled over his eyes. The deluge outside hadn't disturbed his slumber any more than it troubled the three placid horses.

Sloan grabbed a rag off a nail and mopped his face. Water from his mackintosh pooled at his feet. Glowering and foul-tempered and fighting guilt, he stomped over to the buggy and gave the seat a hard shake.

"Wake up, Jacob. Nap time's over."

The older man sputtered, staring wildly around before blinking himself awake. "Sloan. Didn't realize I'd dropped off. Och, but this buggy's a terrible bed. And it sounds a terrible storm." He stretched, then cleared his throat. "What'd you come out here for, with it raining fit to float another ark?" All of a sudden he sat up straight. "Garnet? Did you finish taking out the stitches? Is something wrong with the lass?"

Sloan hunched his shoulders. "Not physically, no. But I probably hurt her feelings." *No, you oaf, you did hurt her.* Might as well have back-handed her, the way he'd responded to her tentative query.

Jacob climbed down, slapped his cap against his thigh, and settled it back on his head. "And you decided a soaking retreat was better than an apology."

"No doubt I deserve to be showered with a bucket of hot oil." He felt cornered, but matters had gone too far to bolt now. "Here. I brought you a slicker." He pulled it out and tossed it to Jacob. "Garnet has something to say—things you need to hear. You won't like them, but we may as well get it over with."

"She told you what happened, didn't she?" His hand gripped Sloan's forearm with crushing force. "That summer? She's told you! Lord be praised, I knew you were the man, I sensed it from the first. All these years…"

"Be careful how you thank God for His machinations. They tend to sneak up when you least expect them and deliver a swift kick." He pulled free. "Hurry up. I don't like the sound of the wind."

Jacob snorted. "Just a summer thunderstorm. 'Twill pass within the hour." He yanked the garment over his head and followed Sloan into the deluge.

All around them the wind shrieked, blowing rain in their faces, setting the trees to wild swaying. Halfway across the yard, a loud *crack* rent the air. A thrill of warning iced down Sloan's spine. He jerked his head up, just in time to glimpse a dark shape through the curtain of rain. It was a tree limb thick as his torso, hurtling down toward them with the speed of a thrown spear.

There was no time to shout a warning, no time to even think. Sloan threw himself against Jacob, wrapping his arms around the wiry body as they fell to the ground in a welter of tangled legs and tree branches. Rain and wet leaves blinded him, twigs gouged his head and mackintosh-swathed torso, and something hard whacked his back and shoulders with enough force to take his breath.

Wheezing, still hanging on to Jacob, he rolled once, twice until they were out from under the severed branch. Rain pelted the side of Sloan's face, blinding him. He sucked air into his lungs and hoped their mackintoshes had protected them from puncture wounds. He'd hate to have to stitch himself up as well as Jacob.

The other man squirmed beneath him. Sloan managed to roll off into the sodden grass, where he lay, still winded, indifferent to the pummeling rain. *Ought to move,* he supposed. *Be a shame to escape being crushed to death only to drown.*

"Sloan?" A trembling hand bumped his nose. "You all right, son?"

"Nothing's broken." Sloan sat up with a groan to squint sideways at the blurred lump that was Jacob Sinclair. "How 'bout you?"

"Feel like a cliff fell on top o' me, but nae doubt ye saved us both from a worse fate. Twigs scratched my cheek, and my hip's complainin' a bit. But God is gracious. If the entire tree had fallen, might have been a different story, don't you know."

Sloan opened his mouth, thought better of it, and settled for a churlish assent. He put out a hand to Jacob. For a moment they stood in the pouring rain, staring through a dripping gray veil at the mass of leaves. "Might not have been the whole tree," he said. "But it certainly felt like it."

"Limb's big enough for one." Jacob took a couple of steps, nudging the jagged end of the severed branch with his muddied boot. "Almost a foot in diameter here where it tore—'tis a shame. It was a fine old shagbark hickory. A difficult wood for cabinetry, but ideal for tool handles, wheel spokes, and the like. Good firewood, too," he added reluctantly.

"Help yourself."

They continued to stand there, staring at each other like a couple of shipwrecked survivors, until a grin winked in Jacob's blood-smeared face. "You look like someone poured a bucket of muddy water over your head, lad."

"So do you." Sloan wiped mud and grass from his fingers so he could examine Jacob's cheek, where pink rivulets ran into the collar of his shirt. "A twig did get you, here—left cheekbone. But it's shallow."

"Reckon we should go inside, Sloan? Garnet's bound to be fretting."

"Mm." He finished examining Jacob's head for lumps. "It would be drier."

At that moment the sky brightened, infusing the air with golden sunbeams that poured over the earth in streams of light. The storm slackened in the blink of an eye from deluge to melodious drips. Somewhere a lone songbird warbled an all-clear, and the scent of freshly washed earth filled Sloan's nostrils. He lifted his gaze toward the sky, filled with a grudging admiration for nature's extravagant display.

"All we need is a rainbow," he muttered, unaware that he'd spoken aloud until Jacob took his arm and turned him around.

Arching over the blue-washed eastern sky, a rainbow coalesced in shimmering iridescence, stretching toward the earth from the wake of tattered charcoal clouds. As real as the ancient mountains beneath it— as impossible to grasp as God's grace.

Seventeen

he screen door banged shut. "Papa!" Even from this distance Sloan saw quick alarm flood Garnet's face. "What happened?"

" 'Tis not so bad as it appears!" Jacob called back.

"Don't—" *worry,* Sloan intended to say, except Garnet whirled about and disappeared back inside. "We better get on up there, reassure her," he finished instead. "She's enough on her mind, without adding this to it."

He ached from his teeth to his toes. He was soaked, he was covered with mud, his knees still knocked from how close they'd come to a serious mishap. He was in no condition to soothe the overwrought nerves of a semihysterical female. On the other hand, this was Garnet Sinclair, who deserved not only his consideration but an apology. A very handsome apology.

When they trooped up the back stairs and through the door into his kitchen, however, Sloan encountered a determined red-haired fairy instead of a tearful female. Her movements competent, every gesture graceful despite her proclaimed stiffness, she flitted about heating water and rummaging in his cupboards. His medical bag had been placed on the table, the instruments he'd used to remove Garnet's stitches by the sink, as though waiting to be cleaned. She'd even discovered the pile of threadbare towels Sloan kept stacked on a shelf.

When they shuffled into the room, she peered from behind the cupboard door. "Papa...your face is bleeding." She shut the cupboard and took several steps toward them. "Mr. MacAllister? What happened to you? You look like you're in pain."

He hung the soaked mackintoshes on a row of wooden pegs, then managed to walk toward the sink without limping. "I'm fine. Your

119

father's fine. Tree branch fell, caught us as we were crossing the yard. Don't make a fuss."

"Lad saved us both, more like." Jacob took the towel Garnet thrust at him. He swabbed his face, then dodged out of the way as Garnet tried to examine it. "Sloan's already pronounced it naught but a wee scratch. Leave be, lass."

"You both need dry clothes." She handed Sloan a towel, avoiding both his fingers and his gaze.

"I'll see what I can scrounge up." Casually he positioned himself so that she had no choice but to acknowledge him, before adding in a soft voice, "Thanks for your help, Garnet. Feel free to rummage while we change, but try to limit extreme movement in that shoulder, hmm? And don't lift anything over five pounds."

"That won't be hard. Your cupboard's almost as bare as a dandelion in the hands of a four-year-old."

Bemused, Sloan gestured Jacob toward the back stairs. All the way up to his bedroom he wondered at Garnet's expression. Had it been a trick of the light, a twinkle of humor he'd spied whisking through Garnet's eyes like a will-o'-the-wisp? Or a flash of fear?

Thirty minutes later they were gathered outside on the veranda, sitting in not quite companionable silence while Sloan and Jacob sipped Garnet's much better tasting coffee. ("I washed the pot and only ground half as many beans," she'd admitted.) Droplets of water plopped from the eaves. Birds twittered among the dripping trees. The ululating wail of a passing train floated through the steam-scented afternoon air.

Feet together flat on the floor, Garnet perched next to her father. A half-smile curved her lips as she and Jacob exchanged idle chitchat. Thus far the topic uppermost in their minds had been ignored.

Sloan, by design, slumped in a chair on the other side of Garnet. He maintained a restless scrutiny and wondered how many years would pass before he forgave himself for his earlier insensitivity toward her. She might be smiling and chatting, but he could see tension in the taut wrist bones protruding from her neat shirtwaist. She'd trusted him, and he'd ground that fragile gift to dust with his cursed temper.

So Sloan sipped coffee and waited, wrestling with his own internal adversaries. Garnet's tentative question about his faith only heightened his dilemma: He no longer viewed her as his patient. Even more dangerous, he could no longer use her surface resemblance to Jenna as a barrier, no longer cared that Garnet's hair was red. *Red!* he thought, almost choking on the coffee. Unlike Jenna's, Garnet's hair gleamed in the sunshine with every shade from cinnamon to russet, infused with gossamer gold-tipped threads. Jenna's had never reflected so many shades, nor captured the sunlight in such a flaming nimbus. How could Garnet regard her hair as a curse? Jenna's vanity had been enormous; with the advantage of hindsight Sloan saw how deliberately she had drawn attention to hers by tossing her head, fiddling with a dangling strand while her eyes peeped out from the screen of her lashes. She was forever patting it, especially when she—

"We need to go," Garnet announced. Sloan watched her produce a determined and completely artificial smile. "I'll see that your clothing is returned to you, Sloan."

She wasn't going to say anything at all. In a reflexive motion his arm shot out, his hand closing over her slender wrist. "There's time yet." An expression of desperation flashed across her face, but Sloan pushed ahead. "Sun won't go down for three hours at least. Wait a bit. Let the water run off the road."

Jacob's chair creaked as he stirred and made uncomfortable noises in the back of his throat. "Ahem...Sloan indicated there was something you needed to be telling me," he finally got out.

Garnet went stiff as a plank, but she'd had five years of practice at living a lie. "Oh? Well, it's nothing important. I'm sure the Pike is fine. I—you'll not protest about Phineas, will you, Papa? We don't keep chickens, he won't be any trouble...I'll take care of him." She tried to free her wrist.

"Boils," Sloan murmured into her ear, "need to be lanced in order to heal."

His fingers tightened. Scarcely aware of his actions, he began stroking the racing pulse in soothing circles. He knew he was confusing her, probably alarming her, but he couldn't help it. Someday, hopefully soon, he would try to explain. Until then, all he could do was to try and earn back Garnet's fragile trust through whatever options presented themselves, gentlemanly or not.

The angle of Jacob's chair prevented him from noticing Sloan's unprofessional behavior. "Lass, a fox is a wild thing," he argued, albeit kindly. "You can't turn him into a pet. He needs to be free."

Garnet stilled. "You heard Sloan. He's been injured, Papa. He'll never be the same, never be free in the wild again." Her voice faltered. "If we don't take care of him, he'll die."

"Och, you were ever the soft-hearted one, weren't you, flowerface." Jacob stiffly rose and leaned over her, cupping her cheeks in his scarred workman's hands. "Garnet, don't you ken I know you too well? This isn't about that fox, and I'm no' fooled by these great big eyes. For over five years I've waited, hoping you would come to me, tell me what monstrous thing was eating up your soul."

"Papa," she began, her voice thick. "I didn't mean—I don't want to hurt you."

Sloan released her wrist, sat back, and folded his arms, feeling like a hulking intruder. Feeling more than ever the sterile isolation of his exile from his own family.

Jacob gave his daughter a hard hug. "Ye canna hurt the man who loves you more than his own life. I was there when you came into the world, lass. A wee precious gift from God. I held you, and your tiny fingers took hold of mine, gripping with strength enough for ten. You trusted me then, completely. Blindly. Trust me now, lass. Whatever it is, we'll face it together."

Three beats of silence passed.

Then a shudder rippled through Garnet. "Trust. So easy to say—so hard to feel, put into practice. I meant to ask Sloan not to say anything to you. I"—her hand lifted to smooth a damp strand of gray off Jacob's broad forehead—"the silence is…safer. Easier."

"Not for me. Not for your sisters. That silence builds walls, not bridges."

Garnet winced but didn't speak again.

Sloan abruptly rose. Two giant strides brought him to the back door, and he propped his shoulders against the doorjamb. Three months earlier he'd dynamited some bridges of his own, and there would be no loving family member handing him bricks and mortar to rebuild. Black longing spilled through him, and the bitter taste clogged his throat.

He focused on the troubled woman before him, and the longing intensified, narrowing until Garnet alone was at the heart of it. Sloan marveled at the paradox of her personality. She was as different from Jenna as a ruby to a river stone. Certainly no other woman in his "privileged" life could have carried the burden Garnet had borne alone for five years, borne with grit and grace and a dash of unexpected humor. If he were honest with himself, he'd acknowledge that her courage far surpassed his own. She hadn't run away, hadn't renounced her life, disguising cowardice by claiming self-preservation.

I don't want this, Lord.

Trouble was, it was too late. Better he should concede and ask for God's help instead.

"Garnet, I've waited all these years." Jacob jostled her chair leg with his foot to gain her attention. "Just get on with the telling, girl. Whatever it is can't be worse than the waiting."

"Even if I'm an accessory after the fact to a murder?" she finally said, her voice not quite steady. "Even though by telling Sloan, and now you, I might be responsible for your deaths? My sisters'?"

"Don't forget your own." Sloan jerked away from the doorjamb to loom over her. "While you're busy hefting the cross of responsibility for all our lives, you might remember that you'll be the first one those men will be coming for."

Eighteen

an't be helped." Sheriff Amos Pettiscomb shoved his derby off his perspiring forehead. " 'Twas a long shot, at the best."

"Garnet, lass, are you sure this is the spot?" Her father's eyes were clouded with anxiety.

Swallowing, Garnet searched the peaceful glade once again. Nausea rolled greasily up into her throat. Oh yes, she was very sure. A squirrel churred its indignation amid the stand of beech trees off to her left, where years ago she had brought her buggy to a halt. Over there, the men had stood beside those ancient boulders, a mud-coated shovel propped against the granite surface. Instead of a scolding squirrel her ears filled with the memory of Chowder's deep-throated growls.

The trees had grown a bit, and since it was late June instead of early May, a canopy of leaves cast shadows over the churned up earth where a cluster of sweating deputies now waited in stolid silence. Two hours of digging the half-dozen holes had yielded nothing but stones, crumbling dirt, and tree roots.

But five years and two months ago, unforgiving sunbeams had spotlighted the chilling lifelessness of a sprawled body.

"This is the place." Garnet fought to keep her voice shorn of emotion. "The body was lying at the foot of those boulders, next to…the hole they'd dug for a grave." She'd always known that one day she would have to return. Lay the ghosts of the past to rest and conquer the jolt of terror that spiked through her every time she passed the turnoff to this sheltered glade.

What she had not anticipated was the disbelief. It wrapped her in numbness, stifling the queasiness. All the terror had flattened out, as though the stick of dynamite she had been juggling for so long had

124

detonated with a wet pop instead of a deafening bang. She wandered back over to the empty hole at the foot of a mangled sumac. "I'm quite sure of everything I've shared."

She faced the group of men, seeing her own disbelief reflected in their faces. Disbelief—and boredom. To them, Garnet's story was no more than a hysterical girl's implausible concoction. "I know every inch of this end of the Valley. This is where I came that day. And I saw what I saw."

"We're not disputing that, Miss Garnet," the sheriff said. "Don't fret yourself none. Likely they buried the corpse somewhere else after you stumbled upon this spot, for just this eventuality."

"So why didn't they just kill her off as well?" one of the deputies muttered.

"Shut your mouth, Will. Ain't no call to bring it up again. Miss Sinclair's told us the ringleader stopped 'em from doing just that. We'll never know his reasoning either." His eyes crinkled at Garnet, though his bulldog face remained somber. "Let's just say the good Lord was watching after one of His lambs real good that day."

Jacob wrapped a protective arm around her shoulders. "Let's go back to the courthouse. You can go through the wanted posters one more time. That all right with you, Amos? Perhaps after being here, something will jog her memory."

"Papa—" Garnet bit her lip to keep from voicing the protest. The lines on his face had deepened over the past several days, and she knew his stomach was giving him problems again.

So she leaned into the sturdy embrace, slipping her own arm around his waist. "All right, Papa. You may be right. I'll look through everything again, if Sheriff Pettiscomb doesn't mind."

The sheriff nodded, dismissed his deputies, then walked with Garnet and Jacob back to their buggy. "If you still don't recognize anyone in those fliers, reckon you both realize there's not much else I can do," he said gruffly. "I searched the records back a full six years, all the way back to '83. Only missing persons unaccounted for were a young gal, and an old man whose grandson warned me was still fighting the '62 battle at New Market. Couldn't find a soul we can match with your man's body. And with no confirmed grave site and no suspects, there's nothing to investigate."

"Can't we question folks?" Jacob's fist pounded the buggy wheel. "What am I to do for my daughter's safety? Her peace of mind? She can't live looking over her shoulder for the rest of her life."

The sheriff stroked the side of his nose, his gaze sliding away from them. "Well now," he said after a while, "You know where I stand on this matter, Jacob. I've been straight with you all since you came to me with the tale four days ago."

"My daughter told you the truth, and I'll no' have any man think otherwise!"

"Now, Jacob…I ain't saying that. I'm just saying she was sixteen and frightened."

Garnet laid her hand on the bunched muscles of her father's arm. "It's all right, Papa," she said. "Truly. I understand how difficult this is— for all of us." She took a deep breath. "Sheriff Pettiscomb, it would have been wiser if I had come straight home five years ago and told my father what had happened. I didn't…because you're right. I was only sixteen, and I was frightened. But I was as frightened for my family's safety as for my own. My judgment may have been faulty, but it was based not on misunderstanding of the circumstances, but what I considered a very real threat to my family."

"And yourself." Her father's warm hand came down to quickly cover hers. "Amos, you've known us for twenty years."

"Let it rest," the sheriff interrupted wearily. "Let it be, Jacob. I'm just telling you that there's naught else that can be done."

"What do you recommend that I do then, Sheriff?" Garnet asked, her voice low.

Pettiscomb spat in the dirt, then settled his hat back firmly on his head. "I recommend you forget the whole blamed mess. They're long gone, that's what I think." His gaze touched on her bonnet. " 'Cause— beggin' your pardon, Jacob—you'd be easy to find, Miss Garnet. For all you're the sweetest-natured young lady I've ever known, not a prideful bone in your body…everybody from Strasburg down through New Market knows about the red-headed gal who draws pictures for the

American Monthly magazine. If these men wanted you, they'd have tracked you down by now."

Garnet barely controlled the flinch. After talking to Sloan MacAllister, she had reached the same conclusion herself. How could she have been so naive, all these years? Ever since that day on his porch, she'd wondered how she would scrape together the courage to once again ramble about her beloved Valley with the same freedom, believing the bonnet would shield her from discovery.

Sheriff Pettiscomb mounted his horse. "Get on with the rest of your life," he said. "Just…get on with your life."

"But you will keep an ear to the ground?" Jacob said.

Pettiscomb gave a curt nod, then left.

Garnet and Jacob drove home in a silence heavy with thoughts neither of them was inclined to air.

June melted into July. The air thickened like syrup, hot and sticky; afternoon thunderstorms blustering over the mountains provided the only relief. Farmers cut hay, half-grown calves gamboled in wildflowered meadows—and Jacob spent almost as much time interrogating the neighbors as he did fashioning a maple highboy in his workshop. In spite of Sheriff Pettiscomb's counsel, her father wouldn't lay the matter to rest. These days he wandered up and down the Valley Pike more than Garnet.

A garden slug had more freedom than Garnet. For the first week or so, she didn't care, clinging to the security of home, of friends and family. Then the restlessness crept in, followed by the longing. Now she grudgingly abided by her father's wishes, yearning to test her recovered fortitude while she waited until he satisfied himself that stirring old ashes wouldn't ignite a fire. Fortunately she had a number of drawings to complete, left undone while her shoulder recovered its freedom of movement. Even so, if it hadn't been for Phineas, she might have bolted.

To the mystification of the entire family, the fox adapted to life in the Sinclair household as though born to it. He clearly doted on Garnet, trotting by her side whenever she was out in the yard, sleeping at her feet, or even in her lap when she was drawing or reading. At night, when every other fox on God's green earth was out chasing mice and moles, Phineas sat on the window seat in Garnet's bedroom, almost as though maintaining watch.

"The two of you make a good match," Leah liked to remark. "Both of you red-haired, both of you paradoxes."

"I finished the picture," JosieMae announced, halting Garnet's restless musings. "Can I pat Phineas now?"

Once a week JosieMae faithfully appeared for a cherished art lesson. Occasionally one of her brothers or sisters tagged along, but most of the time JosieMae came alone.

Garnet smiled at her childish depiction of the sleeping fox. "That's much better. I can tell from the smoothness of your lines that you're holding the pen at the proper angle. But look"—Garnet covered the sweating fingers with her own—"press the point *lightly* to the paper. Let it sort of glide like a drop of water sliding down a block of ice."

"I'd like to be sitting on a block of ice." JosieMae flashed her a walleyed grin. "It's so hot my feet stick in the dirt."

"It's so hot Leah can bake her biscuits on the porch steps," Garnet returned, and they both laughed. She stood from her seat at the sturdy square table set up in the dining room by the bay window, where she taught JosieMae and the few other children whose parents allowed them the luxury of art lessons.

"I'll go fetch us some limeade while you finish drawing. Then you'll have to scoot, so you'll be home in time to do your chores."

"Why aren't you ever in the meadow anymore, Garnet? Is it because of those bad men?"

"No, sweet pea. Mostly it's because I've drawn all those flowers." Garnet escaped from the dining room before the girl could pepper her with more questions she didn't want to answer.

Even the children knew. Thanks to Jacob's mule head and bugler's mouth, the Secret of Sinclair Run was now the Talk of the Valley, from toddlers to the hard-of-hearing Effie Tweedie. On alternate days Garnet longed to either pluck the remaining hairs from her father's balding head or curl into the sanctuary of his loving embrace.

On her way to the kitchen she detoured through the parlor, where Leah was absorbed in a book on calculus. She was absently chewing a lock of her fine brown hair, a childish habit that unexpectedly made Garnet's eyes sting. When September arrived and Leah left for Mary Baldwin, at least both of her sisters would be safe from even the remote possibility of threat. "Want some limeade? I'm fetching some for JosieMae."

"Thanks." Leah marked the page and shut the book. "I could use a break. Why don't I get it?"

"Leah, you're not a paid servant." The words hung suspended in the sultry air. "Sorry." Garnet straightened the edge of a fraying antimacassar and avoided her sister's eye. "I didn't mean to snap at you."

"That's not snapping. Turtles snap…beans snap. Meredith and I— well, we won't compare our respective tempers with what passes for yours." Leah rose, came over, and wrapped a comforting arm around her waist. "You're just in a pother because you haven't been confined to the house and yard since you were six years old. Honestly, sissy, you remind me of a cat in a cage."

"The sheriff told us to forget about it," Garnet burst out. "If those men were still around, we'd have known by now. Thanks to Papa, everyone from Winchester to Woodstock knows the story." Which was why she *hadn't* mentioned that after she mailed Mr. Smoot her finished drawings, Garnet planned to head for the hills. Alone. "I never should have told him what happened."

"It was a mistake for you to keep quiet about it all these years." Leah moved away. "Garnet…Oh, never mind. Let's go fetch the limeade."

"It was a bigger mistake to tell."

Leah whirled on her with an exasperated groan, fists on hips. "It was not a mistake to tell! Far as I'm concerned, the only mistake was telling Sloan MacAllister instead of your family."

Garnet winced, instinctively cupping her palm over the scar while she confronted her sister. "Sloan found the secret drawer in my heartwood chest," she finally said. "Do you know he's the only one in all the years to have discovered it? Papa keeps all of our chests in the parlor— I never thought about it because…well…that's where they've always been. People make remarks about them the same way they do the furniture. It's Papa's craftsmanship they notice—not the unique nature of each of our heartwood chests."

Leah sniffed. "They're advertisements. People see them and then order one. It's sound business, not sentimentality."

"The other chests he makes are seldom from the heartwood. And he doesn't add secret compartments in them."

Phineas ghosted across the floor. Garnet scooped the fox into her arms, nuzzling the soft fur. "Our chests are different, Leah. For Papa, they're…somehow they represent his hopes for us. His dreams. I still don't understand…I just wish—" She lifted her head, her hands burrowing into the fox's thick ruff. "Sloan discovered the differences," she finally continued. "Differences that nobody else took the time to search for or talk with Papa about."

She gently set the animal down. "Did you know that Doc Porter never went to Roanoke at all? Leah, Papa contrived circumstances. *Arranged* them so I would agree for Sloan MacAllister to remove the stitches."

"Papa…lied? Our Papa? Why, he's so honest he could tell Preacher Hunsacker it was Abraham who led the people out of Egypt, and the preacher would believe him. Our father despises lies."

"He despairs of your flippancy."

"He's well used to it by now. He and I have clashed over faith for years. Garnet," she said, her acorn brown eyes round with disbelief, "Papa lied."

"So he did." Garnet poured limeade into three glasses, then filled a saucer of some for Phineas and set it on the floor. "But since I've been living a lie myself, I can't exactly throw stones, can I?" She paused. "Neither can the one who hides all the sweets and tells Papa they're gone or who reads under her covers past midnight after promising that she'll turn out the light."

"All right. You've made your point." Leah snatched a tray and loaded the glasses on top. "Hiding sweets from Papa is for his own good. They make his stomach hurt."

"Mm. And to Papa's way of thinking, arranging for Mr. MacAllister to remove the stitches was for *my* own good." Though whether he'd trusted Sloan more as a physician or a skilled interrogator was a question for which Garnet had no answer. "I wonder," she half whispered, avoiding Leah's abruptly narrowed gaze, "every day, I wonder why Papa trusted a stranger. Why I trusted him."

"So do I. So does Meredith. Did you know she even wrote to me, asking the same thing? Sloan MacAllister…well, he's not family; I'm not sure he's even a friend."

"Leah, he saved my life."

"All right, he saved your life. He even saved this—this creature." Leah glared at Phineas, contentedly lapping the limeade. A smile was building before she pursed her lips in a vain attempt to hide it. "And he found the secret compartment in your heartwood chest. But he's a Yankee! Why not Joshua, for heaven's sake? He's impossibly conventional and naive, but he's besotted with you, and, well, at least he's a Southerner."

A curious sensation swelled, part feathery tickle, part coal-sized lump, squeezing Garnet's heart. "Joshua's besotted with his own image of what he wants me to be. He thinks the chest is nothing but a trinket box, something to gather dust on a bureau. The only time in three years he made a comment was to ask why we didn't keep them in our bedrooms."

At the time Garnet had been unable to explain. Like her sisters, every so often she would carry her chest upstairs to her bedroom. She enjoyed holding it, enjoyed studying the cherry wood grain. She would close her eyes, finding the secret compartment through touch alone, and the cardinal feather tucked inside. Somehow her heartwood chest offered comfort along with the enticing pinch of mystery.

But it didn't belong in her bedroom, any more than Leah's or Meredith's belonged in theirs. Didn't fit. The chests belonged in the parlor. Always had, like the ship's clock behind Papa's horsehair chair and their mother's needlepoint pillows.

Sloan thought the chest some of the most remarkable workmanship he'd ever seen. He'd held it on his lap, Jacob had told her, his fingers stroking the grain of wood, just as Garnet loved to do. *He'd found the cardinal feather.* What had her father told him—what? Jacob refused to talk about it, no matter how Garnet contrived to worm an explanation out of him.

More than the revelation of her secret, more than lingering fears over possible repercussions, that question tormented her thoughts and haunted her dreams.

"Garnet?" Leah's voice was puzzled. "You have the most peculiar expression on your face." Her head tilted sideways, the little wrinkle in her forehead deepening as it did when she was thinking hard. Her eyes opened wide. "You look like Meredith did when she went chasing after that salesman! Garnet, are you falling in love with Sloan MacAllister?"

JosieMae appeared in the doorway. "There's a buggy coming up the lane," she said. "With a man driving. I think it's that doctor man."

Nineteen

And I ain't never rode in a fancy buggy like this one!" JosieMae's pudgy torso twisted from side to side on her perch between Garnet and Sloan. "Wait'll Matthew an' Barney an' Pansy sees me! Wait 'til Ma sees!"

Garnet smiled. Within moments of his arrival, Sloan had expertly maneuvered her father into admitting that a buggy ride would be beneficial for Garnet's emotions as well as her physical health, coaxed JosieMae into admitting that a lift home would be a "wondrous fair" treat—and lulled Garnet into charmed acquiescence when he removed his cravat to engage in a game of tug of war with Phineas. When they left, the shredded cravat was indifferently stuffed away in his jacket pocket.

Oblivious to peril as well as dust, JosieMae leaned forward over the dash.

"Be careful, JosieMae," Garnet began indulgently.

At the same moment, a stagecoach thundered around the bend in the turnpike—in the middle of the road.

Sloan's hands were full controlling Dulcie and the buggy, pulling hard to the right without landing them all in the ditch. Garnet lunged forward, wrapped her arms tight around the girl, and hauled her back against the seat as the juggernaut of a stage racketed past in a whirlwind of thundering hooves, spinning wheels, and swirling dust. JosieMae screeched in terror.

Sloan brought Dulcie to a halt and set the brake. "Everyone all right?"

Garnet managed to extricate herself from JosieMae's ferocious choke hold, but her sunbonnet had been knocked askew, effectively blinding her. Abruptly the girl's weight disappeared; large masculine hands brushed her throat and her chin, gently tugging the bonnet away.

"How's the shoulder?" he asked. "That was pretty quick thinking, by the way."

"I'm fine." Garnet coughed, clearing her throat of dust. Sloan was so close she could see the shadow of a beard darkening his cheeks as clearly as she could see the concern that had darkened the gray eyes to slate. "Um…shoulder's fine too."

Flustered, she reached for the sunbonnet, which Sloan had tossed over the arm rail. "Somebody ought to do something about those stage-coach drivers."

Sloan started to reach toward her before he turned abruptly away. "And are you all right as well, little lady?" he asked JosieMae.

"Didn't mean to hurt Garnet." She wouldn't look up.

"You haven't hurt anybody. But I need to make sure you haven't hurt yourself. Here, now. Let's see, did you knock your forehead against the socket? It's made of steel, unlike your forehead…easy, now. I won't hurt you, child."

Garnet watched in amazement as he gentled the frightened, embarrassed girl into looking up, watched his fingers skim over JosieMae's dirt-streaked forehead, then teasingly tweak her nose. "Fit as a fiddler's fiddle," he announced, and smiled. "So, Miss Whalen, you've survived your first near mishap on the Valley Pike. As a reward, when we turn onto the lane leading to your farm, how about if I let you hold the reins?"

"M-me?" Incredulity flushed across the plump sunburned face. She didn't even duck her head. "Hold the reins?"

"Long as you promise to do exactly as I tell you."

"I promise." The rounded shoulders straightened. "Did you hear, Garnet? The doctor man said I can hold the reins!"

Thirty minutes later, having deposited JosieMae safely at her back door, Sloan guided Dulcie north toward Tom's Brook instead of south toward Sinclair Run. "Now that she's out of hearing range, how severe is the pain?" he asked.

Garnet smiled sheepishly. "It's fine, truly. Just a momentary flareup, like you warned me. No worse than when I help Leah hang the wash. Thank you for not making an issue of it in front of JosieMae."

"She's enough of a confidence problem, with the divergent strabismus…"

"You mean…her eyes?"

"What?" Beneath the mustache a corner of his mouth twitched. "Yes. The walleyes. And before you ask, no, I couldn't help her even if I wanted to. There're a few physicians I've heard of, most of them in Europe, who might be able to. But under the circumstances the only suggestion you might make to her parents is to cover the normal eye, try to force the muscles of the walleye to bring it into better alignment."

A large wagon loaded with bales of hay lumbered by; after exchanging nods with the farmer, Sloan urged Dulcie to a trot, and Garnet settled against the tufted seat with a murmur of delight. She guzzled the summer day, her spirit reveling in the joy of her release from captivity as she inhaled the baking hot breezes. Most of the wildflowers were gone, but she spied clusters of fat clover, their pinkish blossoms bobbing when they passed almost as though they were tipping their heads. Occasionally a bright patch of goldenrod flashed by, heralding autumn's approach, and once she leaned over in JosieMae-like abandon to savor a bright ribbon of delicate lavender-colored chicory.

"We might not be able to persuade your father that you'll be safe with me if you tumble out of the buggy at this speed."

Garnet laughed. "I was admiring the chicory."

"The what? Oh, flowers. Those pale blue ones?"

"Yes. Aren't they beautiful? Their perfect petals, each flower designed with the same precision. And the color…" She lifted her hand to her cheek, feeling a flush heat her skin. "Sorry. It's—I've missed this."

"You really do need to be free, don't you?" He wasn't looking at her, and the ungloved hands remained supple and confident on the reins, but Garnet still felt as though he had touched her. "I've never known a woman like you."

A herd of brown-and-white cows plodded in a ragged line toward the barn, its roof barely visible over a rise. From the Whalens, Garnet had learned that each of those seemingly placid creatures was assigned its place in a rigid bovine hierarchy. Any new cows introduced to the herd would be forced to butt heads with all the other cows to find their position in that ragged line. "I know I'm different. Years ago, I gave up trying to be like everyone else."

"Different," Sloan returned, "doesn't imply deficient." After a soft pause he said, "Your father told me that once, when you were a child, you dyed your hair black."

She groaned. "He told you about that? I was seven, and hated the color. Unfortunately, I ended up not only with this sticky black hair, but black hands, a black-streaked face, and I ruined my favorite corduroy jacket."

"Must have made a pretty sight. Garnet...I'd like you to do something for me." Now his right hand did leave the reins, reaching across the seat. His fingers toyed with the brim of her sunbonnet. "Take this off."

"I...you don't understand." Her voice sounded breathless, and fresh perspiration dampened her palms. "The bonnet keeps me...anonymous. Safe. I know it's naive of me to believe that. But there's still a chance, don't you see, that if those men...it's because they were strangers to me at the time, so if I still hide my hair—"

"You're right about the naiveté." Sloan's frank pronouncement halted her fumbling words. "If those men learned your name five years ago, it's doubtful you'd be sitting in this buggy with me. Your—let's call it your nature—doesn't lend itself to anonymity, after all. Garnet Sinclair, the eccentric artist who wears an old-fashioned sunbonnet? It marks you even more than your hair, especially since your father's done his best to shout what happened from every treetop and ridge line."

His voice deepened. "If those men are still in the area they'll know who you are, where you are." Long fingers reached up and stroked her cheek, a fleeting brush whose unexpectedness caught Garnet completely off guard. "But it's not just those men you're hiding from. Is it?"

Her cheek burned to the bone. Her tongue was frozen. Garnet needed to see his expression—but the bonnet brim deprived her of all peripheral vision. For five years she had tolerated the handicap. For five years she had told herself it was necessary for her family's safety as well as her own.

Now…now a thousand doubts swirled about her head. Her heart pounded, her jaw ached with uncertainty. As though the image were painted into the buggy's forest green dash, she could see Sloan MacAllister as he had appeared that long-ago day in the meadow, a formidable, dark stranger who first disrupted her concentration, then her entire life. "Did my father ask you to do this?"

"No." A beat of silence passed. "Do you really want me to tell you the reason, Garnet?"

"I—yes. I think you'd better tell me."

A short laugh burst from Sloan. "Well. You surprise me, Miss Sinclair. And I thought I was long past the age where a woman could surprise me."

Garnet finally pried her gaze from between Dulcie's ears and turned toward him. He did look surprised. Fair enough. "You don't like women very much, do you?"

"You may have noticed that I don't like *people* very much."

Perhaps he didn't, unless he was forced into the role of physician. Then, Garnet knew well, his compassion welled up in a spring of infinite, almost Christlike gentleness. In a flash of insight she realized her own self-perceptions might be as skewed as Sloan's.

Without warning he turned Dulcie off the road. They bounced along a grassy two-track path until they reached a stand of hardwoods— locust, sycamore, maple. A dead tree reached forlorn, skeletal branches skyward, while tendrils of Virginia creeper encircled the trunk, binding it to the merciless earth. Garnet ran her tongue around suddenly dry lips and upbraided herself for demanding answers that were better left unexamined and unstated.

Sloan pulled the horse to a halt on the far edge of the woods, out of sight of the turnpike. In front of them the Massanutten ridgeline marched straight across the horizon. Then his hands closed over her shoulders, turning her to face him. "Garnet, we—" He stopped, a peculiar expression dimming the silvery gray eyes. "I'm not going to hurt you. Garnet? Don't be afraid of me. Please."

His hands fell away, and his head dropped, but not before Garnet glimpsed a raw vulnerability that made her want to weep.

"I'm not—it's not you I'm afraid of. That is…I know you won't hurt me, physically." Somehow she had known almost from the beginning that despite his fierce temper, this man would never harm her physically.

And yet, forced to confront emotions that had quietly been intensifying over the past weeks, despair choked her as surely as the vines choking that dead tree. Words at the moment were unprofitable. Garnet faced a choice, a choice that might lead to unimaginable joy. More likely she would suffer pain far more devastating than five years of isolation and secret fear. Especially if Leah was right.

Possible joy—probable heartache. The choice remained Garnet's alone, since she could not depend on the hope of divine intervention. She possessed neither Jacob's unswerving faith, Meredith's stubborn optimism, nor even Leah's skepticism. And yet…freedom of choice was a gift from God as surely as the Son He had sacrificed because of it.

Slowly her hands lifted. She began to untie the ribbons with fingers that felt like jumbled kindling. Even more slowly she pulled the bonnet from her head.

Sloan, of course, had seen her without the bonnet, and had even seen her partially unclothed. This was different, and she knew they were both aware of the difference. The cloying summer air seemed to collapse, pressing down, forcing air from her lungs. A bead of moisture slipped down her temple. A rebellious strand of hair, freed from restraint, drifted along her cheek, tickled her chin.

"Thank you." Sloan's hands covered hers, gently prying her fingers away from their death grip on the bonnet. His gaze, serious, absorbed, moved over her face, lingering on the strand of hair. "The first time I saw you," he murmured almost absently, "I wondered about the color of your hair. And I wanted to touch each one of these freckles."

"My freckles?"

Beneath the mustache one of those rare half-smiles appeared. "You sound so astonished. Don't tell me—you don't like your freckles either."

A curl of bewildering heat spiraled from her toes to her flushed freckled cheeks. Embarrassment…yearning…the chill of hopelessness. "I've never been able to do anything about them. Most of the time I forget they're there, until Mrs. Kibler urges me to try another remedy she's concocted."

His eyes had gone all smoky and warm, their expression tender. Yet he wasn't a physician right now. He was a man. Only in her most secret dreams had a man looked at Garnet like that—*seen* beyond the red hair, beyond the facade of cheerful indifference.

But she couldn't stem the rising panic, "Sloan—don't. I've changed my mind. I don't want this. You didn't like me at first, I knew it. I sensed it. Whatever you're doing now…it's even more difficult to bear. If you leave—"

In a move that startled them both, Garnet leaped from the buggy. She took several halting steps, then stopped. Beneath a shaggy-barked sycamore a dogwood tree grew, its slender trunk bowed outward, away from the sycamore as the branches sought the sun. For a moment she stood, her heart thrumming like a flock of panicked birds. Then Garnet pressed her clammy forehead against the smooth trunk and willed the nausea to subside.

She heard Sloan approach and steeled herself.

"I owe you an explanation," he said.

He made no further statement, nor did he touch her. Garnet's muscles loosened, one by one, until she was able to face him. She clasped her hands behind her back and leaned against the dogwood. "I want to hear whatever you need to say," she admitted. "But I'm afraid to ask."

His breath exhaled a long sigh. "I know. That day, in the kitchen, I was a bad-tempered oaf. My brother used to tell me—" His head jerked suddenly, and the broad shoulders turned as rigid as the Massanutten ridge. "I told you earlier that I didn't much like people."

She nodded, trying not to smile, and a thunderous scowl crossed his face. "An understatement, I know. But the truth is, until I stumbled across you that day at Cedar Creek, I was determined to consign humanity to the devil. I'll…tell you the story," he continued, his voice low and hard. "It isn't pretty, but you deserve to know."

He stood in front of Garnet, his feet planted solidly apart, his mouth a grim line. "You need to know, because you're the reason I can no longer renounce my faith in God, along with people."

Twenty

*H*e'd never felt less confident of his ability to control a situation. As clear as a pane of new-blown glass Sloan sensed Garnet's anxiety. She was drawn to him, he knew, because she lacked the artifice necessary to hide her interest. Yet she was equally determined to deny it. He wondered if she had any idea how transparent she was. He marveled as well at the transformation within himself: His need for her to trust him with her heart as well as her life deepened with every breath.

But until he overcame his past—until he stopped blaming both himself and God, Garnet Sinclair would remain beyond his reach. *Physician, heal thyself.*

In abiding relationships, trust was a two-sided coin. Like Garnet, he would have to relearn how to expend it. For both of them, he also needed patience. Self-control. Gentleness. *I hear You,* he thought. *I hear.* And for the first time in months, he was willing to hear with submission instead of resentment.

"I have a lap robe stored under the seat," he said. "Why don't I spread it on the ground, under that dogwood tree?"

"All right."

She waited, passive and still while he fetched the blanket. He was careful not to touch her, allowing her to settle, hiding his smile at the unselfconscious way she unlaced her ankle boots and tugged them off. She tossed them aside, tucking her stockinged feet beneath her plain gingham skirt and a single eyelet-trimmed petticoat whose hem peeped from beneath the skirt. A woman of contrasts, was this elusive Southern wildflower. Reserved yet artless. Candid yet closed. So vulnerable that she blushed like a wild rose at the merest brush of his fingertips. Intrepid…yet filled with fear.

Sloan sat down with her on the blanket and braced his arms across his upraised knees, clasping his hands because he wanted so badly to hold Garnet. *Lord, You're going to have to fill me with a buckboard full of that self-control.* "My family home is in Baltimore," he said. "My paternal grandfather was a shipbuilder, my father as well, though in later years he invested more heavily in railroads."

"Your family must be very wealthy."

"Blue bloods for generations." He plucked a blade of grass and twirled it between two fingers. "I probably would have been a profligate scoundrel like my older brother if it hadn't been for my grandfather. He died from a particularly vicious cancer when I was ten. I watched him deteriorate from a vigorous strapping man with fire in his eyes and a great booming voice, to a gaunt shadow so weak from pain he couldn't lift his finger off the bedclothes."

"That must have been dreadful. My mother died when I was six. Typhoid. Painful death scars children, doesn't it?" She reached out, as if to touch him, then dropped her hand back to her lap. "Or at least some children."

Filled with despair, Sloan gazed sightlessly at the blade of grass between his fingers. She was afraid to touch him, even with a simple gesture of empathy.

He'd done that to her, with his misconceptions and self-absorption. In his bitterness he had wounded her, slicing her spirit to shreds with a thousand scalpels. *God...what have I done?*

At that moment he wanted to give up, take her home to Sinclair Run and flee the Valley as well as Garnet. Because he didn't deserve a woman like her. Didn't deserve the chance to explain. To atone for his behavior.

Because shame burned the back of his throat like gall, he retreated behind verbosity and vocation. "Your father mentioned your mother's death to me once. The, ah...the germ theory of disease causation—advocated by a Frenchman, Louis Pasteur, and a German by the name of Koch—has been slow in catching on in the American medical community. When I was practicing in Adlerville, it was a constant battle—sorry." He crushed the blade of grass, wishing he could do the same to his tongue.

The fleeting pressure of her fingers against his forearm brought his head up with a jerk. His muscles tensed, and he could have lost himself in the mist of her compassionate gray green eyes.

"You love medicine like I do my art," she murmured. "I think you miss it as much as I've missed my freedom. It's like a calling…hard to turn your back on."

"Mm. I'm beginning to accept that. God knows how I tried to turn my back"—he smiled a little—"as do all the good people hereabouts. But you're right, sweetheart. I considered it a calling for too many years to disagree with what you say."

The endearment had slipped out. Sloan was relieved when both of them decided to ignore it. He leaned back, propped on his elbows, and watched a fat white cloud puff soundlessly across the blue-washed sky. "I've known I was supposed to practice medicine since I was a boy, watching my grandfather die. Watching an army of bearded physicians strut in and out, all of them pretending they knew what they were doing. They dispensed pompous, empty words to the family and worthless nostrums to my grandfather. Even as a child I knew their presence was a sham. A farce. The day we buried my grandfather, I made a vow to God that when I grew up I would be a doctor. A doctor who would heal, who could stop pain. I asked Him to help me, but I also knew that learning was vital. Education. For the next five years my appetite for medical knowledge was insatiable."

The white puffy cloud thinned, its contours softening like melting wax. A lone bird drifted above them in the humid stillness. *Say it,* Sloan ordered himself. *Tell her and be done with it.*

"When I was fifteen, Jenna Davenport moved down the street from us. She was a year younger, and I thought she was the most beautiful girl in the world. I fell in love with all the passion and intensity and mindlessness that inflicts half-grown boys." It was an effort to maintain the level tone, but he plowed ahead, determined not to spare himself. "An experience I wouldn't wish on a mongrel, but have you ever tried to reason with a young man in the throes of first love?"

"My father would tell you it's just as impossible to reason with young girls. Meredith—our older sister—has fallen in love a half-dozen times since she was fifteen. Last year, she moved to Winchester to follow a charming salesman who'd taken her fancy. Stubborn and impulsive, that's my older sister. Meredith's always had to learn things the hard way."

"I look forward to meeting Meredith. Sounds like we have a lot in common."

"You'd love her. People do—especially men. She's generous to a fault, full of fun, and so beautiful. She loves fine clothes—teases Leah and me all the time about our lack of fashion, then mocks herself for being a slave to it."

If he hadn't been watching her closely, Sloan might have missed the shadow drifting through her eyes like the drifting cloud above him. "Meredith," he stated very deliberately, "might be beautiful, but so are you."

"I'm not, but thank you." She fingered the dusty, windblown ends of her hair, which she'd hurriedly gathered at the base of her neck when Sloan had invited her to go for a drive. "Red hair and freckles…no, there's nothing beautiful about me."

The temptation was almost more than a man could resist, but all Sloan allowed himself was a single brush of his knuckles against the delicate line of her jawbone. "I told you that I thought Jenna was the most beautiful girl I'd ever seen?"

Garnet nodded, eyes wide and unblinking, the enchanting blush heating skin he'd scarcely touched.

"Jenna's hair was red, Garnet. A fiery red-gold flame. When she walked into a room, all heads turned, female as well as male. She was beautiful…on the outside."

"I can tell you thought so. It's all right, Sloan. I understand what you're trying to do, but it isn't necessary."

"I don't think you do understand. And it is necessary." He paused, remembering a cardinal's feather and a very wise father. "When I met you, it wasn't you I hated. Just…your hair. It reminded me of Jenna. But you're nothing like her, Garnet. Nothing. I should have recognized it from the first." Except he was a blind, embittered fool.

"Humans are irrational creatures. We're supposed to learn from past mistakes. But I've come to the conclusion that we tend to learn the *wrong* lessons most of the time." His gaze touched on the tangled rope of Garnet's hair. "I learned to detest redheads, instead of discerning Jenna's flawed personality and adjusting my attitude accordingly. Jenna's hair was her glory and her pride. She used it like a weapon, a snare for hapless males. Like me. It blazed in the sunlight, and under the glow of crystal chandeliers, it mesmerized. Jenna knew just how to go about achieving maximum effect—and would have if her hair had been the color of coal or dirt."

He sat up. With each word he leaned closer, closer to Garnet until his breath drifted across her temple. "Comparing you to Jenna is like comparing a newborn babe to a corpse. As for your hair…compared to yours, Jenna's has all the shine of tarnished silver."

"Sloan…"

He watched the pulse fluttering in the hollow of her throat, watched while she struggled to find words to refute his. He thought about telling her that her efforts were useless.

"Are you…" She closed her eyes, then opened them again. "We should leave."

"Haven't finished my story. You're too distracting."

He couldn't help it, could no more stem the overwhelming need anymore than he had been able to ignore God's relentless Spirit leading him to Cedar Creek that long-ago day. He wanted to smile at Garnet, reassure her, explain to her that he wasn't toying with her, wasn't "trifling with her emotions." He wanted, or rather needed, to show her how beautiful she was—outside as well as inside. Wanted to spend the rest of his life—*wait a minute, Lord.*

Garnet had scrambled to her feet in a flurry of skirts. "I'm not like Jenna," she stammered. "Sloan, I don't tease men, don't flirt. Not any longer. Never again. And I can't think of my hair as anything but a—a cross to bear. I'm going home. Take me home, please."

"All right," he said very gently, rising to stand beside her. "I'll take you home." *But not just yet.* His fingers closed around her balled hand, pried it open until he could run his thumb over the damp little palm. "You took your bonnet off," he whispered, and lifted that palm to his lips. Then he placed it on his shoulder and laid his own palm against her cheek. "For yourself as well as for me, Garnet. You took the bonnet off."

He could feel her trembling, hear her quickened breathing, and tenderness flooded his soul with a heat he'd never felt before in his entire dissolute life. "Don't back down now. You're safe with me, Garnet. I'm not going to hurt you in any way."

"Yes. You will." She covered the hand on her cheek with her own, and her eyelids fluttered down. When they lifted, tears were swimming in her eyes. "You're a good man, Sloan MacAllister. Like my father. A man after God's own heart. You…talk to Him like I wish I could. Even when you claim to be angry with Him, even though you've run away from something that's hurt you badly…you still talk with Him."

She tugged his hand away from her face. For the space of two heartbeats her fingers clung, then slipped free. "I—don't have that kind of relationship, not with God, not with any man. But I can't run, Sloan. And I can't ask you to stay when I know that, someday soon, God will call you to go back to your home."

"How about if you let me and God work out the rest of my life?" Sloan took her shoulders and drew her forward, ignoring her resistance. "Garnet, tell me this: Do you and that preacher's son have an understanding?"

"J-Joshua wants one. I don't." She had quit resisting with her body, but her mind was a more formidable obstacle.

"Because you don't care for him that way, or because you witnessed a murder when you were sixteen? Because you're afraid those men might harm Joshua?"

"Neither. Both…he's a friend, nothing more. A friend," she repeated faintly.

"Would you take off the bonnet if you went for a buggy ride with this Joshua?"

One quick shove and she had freed herself, retreating three steps out of arm's reach. Her back was straight, chin lifted. "Why don't you tell me what you want from me, Sloan?" Her gaze flickered toward the buggy.

She was inches away from bolting. Good. Sloan wanted her off balance, on the verge of panic. He wanted to push her until she faced her feelings toward him—and realized she had no reason to run. "I told you part of what I want," he said, and took a step forward. "I want to touch every one of your freckles. But I also want very much to bury my face and my hands in your hair, savor its color. The softness. And I want to kiss you. I want to hold you in my arms, not as a physician comforting a patient, but as a man holding a woman."

Instead of slapping his face like a proper young miss or batting those mink-brown eyelashes...or even hiding her scalding blush behind her hands like a shy innocent—Jenna had employed these and more—Garnet tilted her head to one side and asked a simple one-word question.

"Why?"

It was at that precise moment that Sloan admitted he was in love. "Because I want to, more than I want to take my next breath."

He took another step, and when she didn't retreat, he drew her back into his arms. "Because for reasons beyond my comprehension, God seems to have brought us together, and I'm tired of fighting it."

He began to touch each cinnamon freckle, featherlight touches that singed his fingers nonetheless. When he at last cupped her face in his hands, she closed her eyes. Her arms lifted to rest upon his chest, her right palm directly over his heart.

Sloan lowered his head and kissed her.

Twenty-One

*G*arnet at last finished the rhododendrons. This project had proven a challenge because she'd gone with the engraving effect, which lent a distinctive texture appropriate for this distinctive flower. Brow puckered, she stood back to study the finished work. Phineas, roused from his nap, padded over to sit at her feet, his head tilted as if to ask why she'd woken him up.

"What do you think? Better than the calendula I finished Tuesday? Be honest with me, please. And don't think you can just sit there and smile without committing yourself one way or the other."

The fox grabbed the hem of her skirt in his jaws and tugged.

"I'll come outside with you after I clean my pens." She knelt and took the narrow head between her hands. "You're such a scallawag... and I don't know what I'd do without you, especially with Leah leaving in less than a month." Abruptly she sank onto the wide plank flooring and gathered Phineas into her lap. Not a day passed that she hadn't thanked God for sparing this creature's life, not an hour passed when she hadn't thanked Him for the man who had been His instrument. Not a moment passed when she was free from the awful burden of an impossible love, seemingly placed in her heart by that same unknowable God.

Twice a week Sloan paid a call, his manner scrupulously proper even as his gaze kindled with sparks every time he bowed over her hand or helped her into the buggy for a drive. Only once had she gathered the courage to broach a tentative question about his circumspection.

"I don't want to hurt you again," he answered, searching her face. "Garnet, if I thought I could—" His lips had clamped together then, and a shadow of that old bitterness reappeared. "Bear with me..."

"All right." She had no choice. She'd fallen in love with this dark, difficult man. And she fought demons of her own.

For some reason, Sloan appeared at times to be almost as afraid of her as she used to be of him. The realization bewildered Garnet, for after her one tentative query, she'd made no more demands, even preventing herself at each visit from asking when she would see him again. Uncertainty was as familiar as an old friend, since for years she had lived with the constant worry of exposure; Sloan's refusal to commit himself might hurt, but she dreaded renunciation far more than uncertainty.

Garnet wished she could talk to Meredith, because she was the only person who would understand at least a small portion of Garnet's turmoil.

"Garnet?" Leah called up the stairs. "Mrs. Ward is here."

Sighing, Garnet set Phineas aside with a reassuring pat and headed downstairs for the parlor. Over the past weeks she and Felicity Ward had met on several occasions, mostly due to Felicity's persistence. A childless widow in her forties, obviously accustomed to having her own way, the woman was determined to gain Garnet's cooperation. But Garnet was equally determined not to be bullied, charmed, or maneuvered, regardless of Mrs. Ward's stature as an artist. She had agreed, however, to show Felicity some favorite scenic spots, and the two of them had made several forays about the countryside.

Most of the time Felicity felt compelled to point out alternative sites that Garnet, of course, had missed, by being "much too focused on the minutiae of your flowers, instead of framing the landscape. Look"—she was forever grabbing Garnet's arm as though Garnet were a misguided toddler—"see how those rocks offer a stunning contrast to the blowing meadow grass and the wisps of clouds?"

Zeke, the rawboned son of the Chalybeate Springs Hotel's concierge, functioned as driver and protector. Garnet concealed her qualms about their "chaperone," not telling her father that, while she and Felicity explored field and forest, Zeke pulled his hat over his face and went to sleep.

"Can't you at least keep that animal outside, in a pen, when visitors pay a call?" Felicity asked when Leah and Garnet returned to the parlor with Phineas shadowing Garnet's feet. "For heaven's sake, what if he bites someone?"

"If he bit anyone, it would be only because he was defending himself," Garnet responded with a slight smile. "Which means the person deserves to be bitten." Behind her, Leah smothered a giggle. "But if he makes you nervous—"

"Certainly not, it's just that—"

"I'm sure he wouldn't mind snoozing on the window seat in the dining room."

"I'll take him," Leah offered, coming forward to scoop the docile fox up into her arms. "It's a mystery, this strange bond he and Garnet share," she told Felicity. "I'm on your side as far as animals in the parlor. But who can resist this innocent furry face?"

"I can, quite easily." Felicity tugged off her white kid gloves, and even this pedestrian act seemed graceful, practiced. She was outfitted today in a pretty striped silk visiting dress embellished with lace. Chosen to impress, Garnet knew. She wanted to laugh, because the effect was wasted on her and Leah. Neither of them cared a fig about fine fashion.

"I once had a lovely fox stole," Felicity said. "Striking shade of red...always received compliments when I wore it. Your little pet's tail is mighty tempting, so full and lustrous—oh, do pull in your claws, girls. I was merely teasing." She watched Leah march stormy-faced through the doorway, setting the portiere's fringes to waving. "Your sister doesn't care much for my sense of humor, does she?"

"Leah tends to be a literal-minded person."

Felicity waved a hand in dismissal and fastened her bright blue eyes on Garnet. "Well? Have you thought about my offer?" The artist wasn't one for wasting time or mincing words. It was very un-Southern for someone who prided herself on her mother's heritage.

"Yes, I have." Garnet kept her expression bland and gestured toward a couple of parlor chairs. "But much as it might be beneficial to me, my answer is still no. Leah leaves next week for Mary Baldwin College. My father would be alone."

"I've talked to your father. He very much wants you to go, Garnet. He's a grown man and can feed himself fried ham and a dish of greens or something for a few weeks. He agrees with me, you see. Accompanying me on my lecture circuit would open doors for you, far beyond the limited exposure your charming sketches reap in the *American Monthly.*"

She leaned forward, her skirts whispering like hundreds of hushed voices. "Garnet, I've come to know you over the summer. For the most part, you and I are complete opposites. You're a composed young lady content to hide your light in the rural backwoods of the Valley. I, on the other hand, am an ambitious upstart." She grinned, unrepentant. "An interfering, obnoxious woman meddling in your affairs."

"I wouldn't go quite that far."

"Do you know, I believe you smile like that fox of yours."

They both laughed. Then Felicity clasped her hands, and her expression sobered. "Garnet, you have a lot of talent. But you're squandering it, no matter how much you protest. With the right kind of guidance—and yes, I do believe I can offer that—within a few years you could be putting on shows of your own. Certainly I'll ensure that you commission more work than monthly illustrations. How much does Jan Smoot pay you?"

She sneaked in the last inquiry, but Garnet wasn't fooled by the too casual tone. "How much do you sell your paintings for?"

After a trenchant pause Felicity sat back, one black eyebrow delicately arched. "Very good. Point taken, my dear." Garnet could almost see the thoughts churning behind the elaborate rows of ringlets arranged across her forehead.

Garnet silently admitted to a prick of envy over the other woman's indefatigable confidence, though fame no doubt fueled Felicity Ward's dominating personality. A master at controlling conversations, she enjoyed tossing out questions and opinions, all the time holding her listeners with the intense focus of those thickly lashed blue eyes. She reminded Garnet of the chipmunks that darted about the barn, searching for ways to raid the grain barrels.

Well, she'd have to dig in a new barrel in another barn. Garnet kept her smile in place and tried for a bright-eyed expression of her own.

"You consider your talent a gift from God. Am I correct?" Felicity tried next.

"Yes, I do. And I'll tell you before you bring it up, I also consider that how I make use of the gift is between God and me."

"Do you honestly expect the Almighty to provide you with that insight? How do you *know* what you're supposed to do?"

"I don't always know," Garnet admitted. "I just know that, when I sit in a meadow full of flowers or beside a rocky creek with a row of lady's slippers along the bank, a—a need arises in me to capture them on paper. And I know I can do it."

"That's how I feel too. Don't you see, Garnet? Call it God, call it whatever you care to—both of us are artists, and we need to fulfill that destiny. But I've learned to reach for a destiny far beyond the childish dabbling of a schoolgirl. And I like to feel that God has rewarded my efforts. Oh, do say you'll reconsider accompanying me."

She hesitated, her hands smoothing the V-shaped velvet trim on her basque. "Garnet, I…this is difficult for me. I like you," she finished, a diffidence in her voice Garnet had never heard. "And I think the two of us would get along famously together. I'd introduce you to my acquaintances in the art world, and you would be my traveling companion…"

"I'll think about it," Garnet said and stood. "But that's all I can promise."

"It's more than I've managed to wrest from you before." Felicity rose as well, the fragrance of roses enveloping Garnet when the other woman took her hand and gave it a brief squeeze. "I'm having a soiree in my hotel suite. A week from today. I'd like for you and your family to attend."

"I don't think—"

"You don't have to stay long, no more than an hour. Say yes."

"I'll talk it over with my family."

A mischievous smile spread across Felicity's face. "I already have. They're willing and agree the outing would be good for you. Bring your doctor friend, if you like." She squeezed Garnet's hand once more, then let it go. "I confess I've longed for an opportunity to meet the infamous Dr. MacAllister, but all my little schemes thus far have failed. I've even considered feigning some monstrous illness or exotic condition. Of course, from what I hear, if you requested his services as your escort—"

"He'd feel just as inclined to turn me down." Garnet walked into the hallway, forcing Felicity to follow. "If you're that interested in meeting Dr. MacAllister, you could always make an appointment. I understand his fee is fifty dollars." She opened the front door. "I believe I'll be busy next week and won't be able to attend your soiree. But thank you for the invitation."

"It's unusual for someone with your coloring to lose her temper with such quiet dignity." The artist patted Garnet's cheek before working the kid gloves back onto her hands. "When we're on the road together, you'll have to ignore my brashness. And perhaps I'll learn to emulate your dignity."

Garnet closed the door behind her, almost catching the trailing hem of Felicity's fancy visiting gown. When she turned around, Leah was clattering down the stairs.

"I heard—was on the landing. What a bucket of slop. *Soiree*," she mimicked Felicity's patrician, unaccented tone. "Perhaps we should attend. We can wear our favorite flour-sack dresses. I'll borrow one of your older sunbonnets, and Papa can purchase a pair of overalls from Cooper's."

"We can even stick some straw in our hair."

But after Leah returned upstairs, Garnet fetched Phineas and headed for Sinclair Creek. She spent a pensive hour there, sitting on the bank, splashing her bare feet in the shallow water, wondering what to do about Felicity Ward's incredible offer. About Sloan and the raw uncertainty of the love that had pushed its way into her heart.

About a God she had believed in all her life, but whose will remained indecipherable. She wanted to talk with Him as her father did. As Sloan did.

But what if Felicity was right and God didn't answer?

Sloan finished scrubbing the last corner of his bedroom floor, staggered to his feet, and dropped the filthy rag into the bucket. Sweat plastered his shirt to his skin and made his scalp itch like the very dickens. His muscles felt as though they'd been trampled by a herd of buffalo. Sometimes he wondered if he'd completely lost his mind, wasting himself in manual labor. Scrubbing floors! He'd never take such menial chores for granted again, that was for certain.

Yet the satisfaction in watching the old house gleam with new life outweighed the exhaustion and helped to ease a pervasive sense of... incompleteness.

Groaning, he headed outside to sprawl at the base of the hickory tree, the one that had hurled a limb down on Jacob and Sloan that momentous afternoon. Seemed like yesterday. Seemed like forever.

Garnet...

He should be too exhausted to need to see her, and in fact his intense labors over the past ten days had been calculated to pummel the need to numbness. Thus far his plan had proved unsuccessful. The feel of her in his arms, that miraculous moment when their lips had met and a spring of indefinable joy had welled up in him—the memory still rocked him beyond the exhaustion, beyond the pain of his self-imposed exile.

More often than not over the past weeks, Sloan still felt the same kick of stupefaction and helplessness as when he'd been tangled beneath the branches of that shorn limb. Nothing like falling for a woman to mess up a man's mind. Whenever Sloan was with Garnet, love clouded his brain, turning his resolution to cold oatmeal, his reason to emotional mush. All Garnet had to do was to look up at him through those great vulnerable eyes of hers, and he was ready to saw his arm off with a dull pocketknife to avoid causing her more heartache. Yet heartache was all he had to offer.

Garnet, he knew, admired his so-called relationship with God. And Sloan, egotistical hypocrite that he was, couldn't bear to disillusion her with a confession of the depth of his—

With a half-stifled imprecation he banged the back of his head against the peeling bark.

His shame.

Christians weren't supposed to feel shame. The ugly emotion, with its corrosive patina of unworthiness, its humiliation and stench of guilt, were alien to Jesus' gospel of grace.

Sloan knew—and could not heed. The spiritual silence of the past few weeks cloaked him in a desolation that overshadowed even the love he felt for Garnet.

He wanted her more than he had ever wanted anything in his life, including the childhood dream that had propelled him into medicine. But he was afraid he could not live up to Garnet's expectations of a faith Sloan could no longer claim.

And he was…ashamed.

If he possessed an ounce of integrity, he'd amputate his presence from Sinclair Run in order to save her life.

Even now, Lord, I think in medical analogies. If I go back… He stopped the thought, leaned back against the tree, and closed his eyes.

Jacob watched from his workshop as Mrs. Ward's carriage departed. Watched when, a short while later, Garnet slipped wraithlike onto the porch and drifted toward the run, the fox hugging her heels. *Lord,* he prayed, regret in his heart and acid churning in the pit of his stomach, *what are we to do about Garnet?*

The girl was a mixed-up mass of contradictions. Uncertain as an orphaned fawn with Sloan, wise as a fox eluding a hunter with the charming Mrs. Ward. What would she have been like, this red-haired lass of his, if she hadn't stumbled onto that band of murderous no-count varmints? Jacob chewed over it for a bit, wishing for words, for wisdom. "Even for wit, Lord." Garnet usually responded to the pull of humor when she couldn't be reached any other way.

Thus far, neither his cautious meddling nor Leah's logical arguments nor Mrs. Ward's forthright machinations had elicited a response from the girl. Garnet, Jacob knew, was hoping Sloan would pay a call, even though she wouldn't talk about him or even refer to his last visit ten days ago now. As for Sloan…*och, what's the problem with the lad? It's almost September, Lord. He's the one, isn't he? The one You've chosen for Garnet?* Sloan understood the significance of the cardinal feather, after all. And 'twas plain as oak grain that Garnet was smitten.

The very first time he'd taken her for a buggy ride, when Garnet returned with cheeks blooming like wild roses and Sloan gazing at her as though she were the most precious gift in the universe… Jacob had been beside himself, waiting for the fellow to speak to him as a prospective suitor for Garnet's hand.

Instead, Sloan's subsequent behavior toward the lass would put Joshua Jones to shame. And now, 'twas ten days since Sloan's last visit. He'd not even sent along a note.

Timing.

"Aye, to everything there is a season, I know." He tugged a rag from his back pocket and mopped the perspiration from his forehead. Seasons came, seasons went in accordance with a grand plan, and there was naught a man could do to alter or control the timing.

All Jacob could do was follow the example of the humble Jewish carpenter who had become the earthly father to God's Son. Doubtless Joseph hadn't understood either the timing or the significance of God's leading—but he had obeyed without question.

Obeyed and faded quietly into the background.

Shoulders sagging, Jacob accepted the gentle rebuke. Resolutely he returned to the only work for which he could assume control, the walnut kneehole desk for a banker down in Harrisonburg. But for a father, 'twas a hard task, waiting patiently in the background for God to accomplish His purpose in the lives of Jacob's daughters.

Especially when they all seemed to be making a fine muddle of things.

Twenty-Two

*I*t was refreshingly cool for late August, with a deep Ming blue sky momentarily free from humidity. For some reason Sloan had awakened that morning with a smile on his face. Head bared to the sun as he sat astride Dulcie, he found himself simply enjoying the beauties of God's creation, laid out for his pleasure on either side of the winding road into Tom's Brook. Yellow butterflies drifted in the clear sunshine. Energetic grasshoppers jigged about the tall grasses on either side of the road. Cicadas droned from the trees.

Only when he caught himself admiring a cluster of purplish flowers and wondering how Garnet would depict them on paper did the glory of the morning dim. It would be today, he realized. Today he would hitch Dulcie to the buggy and return to Sinclair Run. He still didn't know what to do, but for the first time in weeks he was willing to relinquish the outcome to God's will instead of his own.

By the time he reached the drygoods store in Tom's Brook, he was focused on the business at hand. After tying the mare next to a flop-eared mule, Sloan stepped inside and threaded his way down the narrow center aisle of the store, squeezing past showcases crammed with articles of clothing from shirtwaists and shirtfronts to paper collars, corsets, a tilted tower of derby hats, and several neighbors.

"G'morning, Doc!"

"Morning, Dr. MacAllister!"

"Saw you finished painting your house, Doc! Never seen a yeller house, but it turned out mighty fine."

"Thanks, Homer." He stepped around a rack of overalls and jumpers. "I'm starting on the shutters next—thought about black, or maybe dark green."

Sometime over the summer Sloan's curmudgeon act with local folk had waned with the moon. Most people no longer pestered him about their medical complaints, though they persisted in calling him Doc. Sloan conceded the honorary title. It was the truth, and since he'd slipped up twice, treating a couple of emergency cases, it was ludicrous to take umbrage any longer.

"Fact is," he said to Homer now, "I'm here to place an order for the paint. Say, how about giving me a hand? Which color would you choose?"

Homer, plainly flattered, launched into a detailed comparison of the two colors. Within moments, two graybearded farmers who had been hunched over the checkerboard in front of the stove joined in, followed by several other customers and Mrs. Rawls, the proprietor's wife. Sides were drawn between those favoring green versus the ones arguing for black. Sloan found himself trapped in the middle, against the counter, his back pressed to a display case of J&P Coats Company sewing thread.

"Here now, this ain't the town square!" Vernon Rawls emerged from a back room, his arms full of a stack of men's dungarees. "You all know I try to keep this center aisle clear. You want a debate, you take it outside or over yonder behind the stove."

Muttering, he elbowed his way behind the counter and caught sight of Sloan. The craggy face registered surprise. He handed the dungarees to his wife and thrust out a nail-chipped paw of a hand. "Doc MacAllister—didn't see you there."

Sloan understood the man's consternation. Lately he surprised himself with his sporadic flares of amiability.

"Got a letter for you," Vernon announced after they shook hands. "Came the other day. Baltimore postmark. Meant to have Homer carry it by your place, seeing as how you're neighbors. Now the both of you are here, so's it won't be necessary." He chuckled. "Hang on, let me just fetch it for you."

"Thanks, Vernon."

An interested silence bloomed. A half-dozen pairs of bright eyes watched Sloan. He waited with his arms folded across his chest, his heart thudding in a hard, arrhythmic beat far above his normal sixty-two per minute. The letter was probably from his lawyer, who had been managing Sloan's affairs since he left Adlerville. After the first two months, everyone else had given up trying to correspond.

Surely it was just a letter from his lawyer.

Most Southern country stores also functioned as the community post office, complete with an official oak partition, locked mailboxes, and a stamp and delivery window. Vernon grabbed a thick oblong envelope from Sloan's numbered box and thrust it through the window.

"Here you go, Doc. Ah…something wrong?"

"No." He felt as though an axe blade had been embedded at the base of his skull.

"Well, can I help you with—"

"No."

He no longer cared about ordering paint. About being amiable. Sloan crammed the letter in his pocket and left the store without a backward glance. One look at the return address had confirmed his worst fears: The precise sloped lettering identified the sender as his mother. Regardless of what tone she affected in the contents, nothing good would come of this. Why now? She'd made it plain that she considered her youngest son a murderer, a traitor to his family and his "class."

He mounted Dulcie and urged her into a hard canter the moment they were free of the cluster of mules, wagons, and buggies. By the time he turned onto the grassy lane that crossed the pasture in front of the house, Sloan had kneed the mare into a breakneck gallop.

He pulled the lathered horse to a halt in front of the barn, the first shock and much of his anger already fading. Sloan apologized to Dulcie, alternately praising her and berating himself while he removed the tack. He walked her until the lather dried, then spent a penitent hour giving the winded mare a thorough rubdown. He even cleaned her stall and fetched fresh water and a handful of grain, scratching beneath her forelock while she munched the oats.

The letter waited, its presence burning in his mind like a live coal.

Finally Sloan tromped heavily out of the barn and down the rock-stubbled meadow behind the house. Along the back edge of his property, a tangled hedge of Cherokee roses partially screened the remains of an old vegetable garden and an ancient apple tree whose gnarled branches sagged with ripening fruit. At some time in the past, one of the Pritchetts had placed a handmade wooden chair beneath the tree.

Sloan lowered himself onto the low, age-worn seat. Slowly he withdrew the crumpled envelope. For a long time he didn't move, just sat with his eyes closed and his arms resting on the rough chair arms. The letter lay untouched in his lap.

He could trash it without even opening it. He could even send it back. What was the point, exposing himself to all that misery again when he'd finally found a sliver of peace? The past was past. He couldn't undo the wrongs, couldn't restore lost or ruined lives. *Lord, why won't You let the dead bury themselves along with the past?* The whisper of a thought insinuated itself deep inside. He was still hiding. Still running.

No. He was trying to heal. Regain perspective. Protect himself until he could view things rationally again. Recover his relationship with God. Reconcile the sordid disintegration of his family. And finally—until he was sure in his own mind that he could separate his feelings about Jenna from his feelings toward Garnet—he needed…time. Room to think, to breathe. He was convinced that he understood Garnet, that his perceptions about her character were accurate, in spite of knowing her for only a few months. Yet those first years, he'd been equally certain that Jenna was sweet-natured, genteel—the mate God had designed for Sloan.

Lord…I was full of myself back then, wasn't I? Certainly he knew there was a world of difference between the snap judgments and emotion-based certainty of a stripling boy from those of an experienced man. But it was painfully obvious that experience and so-called maturity had not been sufficient to prevent equally monumental errors in judgment. What would happen if he committed himself to the wrong woman a *second* time?

All right. Fine. Yes. He *was* still running from the past. Hiding. *But so are You. Do you hear me, God? So are You.* Even as he hurled the accusation, Sloan knew what the response would be. He might yearn for restoration, but he continued to reject it because he was afraid of what God might demand of him.

But Sloan wasn't afraid—he was terrified. The blood of two men stained his hands, one a patient who had trusted Sloan with his life, the

other…Sloan's brother. One family left fatherless. His own family's reputation destroyed because of Sloan.

He'd given his life as well as his heart to God, and for a score of years
he had devoted himself to honoring the vow he'd made when he was ten
years old. But like King David, Sloan had stumbled over a woman. He
should have seen Jenna's true character, but instead he'd been so consumed with medical studies and high-flown ideals that he'd committed
the ugly sin of arrogance. Arrogance and pride.

He'd been a self-righteous prig back then. Now he was a bitter,
defeated…*coward*. The darkness roiled through him, snuffing out the
summer day. Anger, shame, grief suffocated his soul. He deserved to be
punished, deserved not mercy but retribution. Trying to build a new life
was a fool's dream. Instead he was doomed to repeat the mistakes he'd
tried to leave behind.

My blood has washed you clean…look at My hands. Not your own.

Sloan jerked upright in the chair. Blinking, he sat frozen, gripping
the chair arms with such force that pain streaked up his wrists. He stared
at them, uncomprehending, until he thought to relax his death grip.

Bright and airy, a butterfly drifted in front of his face. Then it
dipped and alighted on one of his white-boned knuckles. It was a small
butterfly, with burnt umber wings scarcely two inches across, yet it
rested fearlessly on a hand which could crush it with no effort. Sloan
quit breathing, his gaze fixed on the fragile insect. He could see the intricate pattern of veins, the threadlike legs and antennae—because the
butterfly perched motionless with outspread wings right there on his
hand. As though Sloan's knuckle offered a safe harbor instead of cruel
destruction. A place where it could absorb the sunlight, gathering
energy to seek out another flower.

Trancelike, Sloan watched the tiny messenger from God, until the
vise crushing his chest began to loosen, until he realized in a dim sort of
astonishment that his eyes were wet. Carefully, calling upon the patient
skill of a surgeon, he began to turn his hand. Unconcerned, the butterfly crept along to stay upright. When Sloan's hand stilled on the chair
arm, the butterfly remained, its gossamer legs fearlessly planted in the
cup of his palm.

Time hung suspended in a shimmering gold void. Soundless, weightless, as vast as the universe.

When the butterfly fluttered once, twice, then floated into the air, Sloan watched its ascent with something close to reverence.

Then a groan wrenched from the depths of his being, and he buried his face in his hands. When the redemptive storm finally passed, he mopped his face with his shirttail and opened his mother's letter with rock-steady hands.

❧⚜☙

WINCHESTER

Garnet stood in the doorway to the back wing offices of the Excelsior Hotel, watching Meredith attack a monstrous black typing machine. Over the *clickety-clack* of the keys she could hear her sister grumbling to herself. That, at least, was typical Meredith. At another desk a young man with a neat bow tie and wire-rimmed spectacles studied some papers. On the far side of the room a gray-haired woman leafed through the contents of a dark walnut filing cabinet. Nobody had noticed Garnet.

Their concentrated efficiency was intimidating. To be truthful, the setting itself intimidated her. It had taken enormous courage for Garnet to cross the hotel lobby with its gleaming parquet floors and Grecian-style columns and slip down a secretive hallway into the equally imposing suite of offices.

Her elder sister looked as though she belonged here.

The whole family—the entire community, for that matter—had been convinced that Meredith Sinclair would have a ring on her finger and a passel of little ones by the time she reached her twentieth year. Instead she'd found herself with a career. Garnet swallowed a bubble of nervous laughter. With the impulsiveness that dominated her character, Meredith had joined a new breed of independent single young women. Young women who eschewed home and family in the pursuit of, to Garnet, nebulous goals with illusory rewards.

Her younger sister's goals, on the other hand, were rooted as deep as the two-hundred-year-old elm that shaded the porch. Leah was determined to become the first Sinclair to earn a degree in higher education.

As always, she, the middle sister, was…in the middle. A career she still thought of as a calling. A decided lack of interest in the pursuit of knowledge. Little hope for a home and family of her own.

Desperation had propelled Garnet onto a northbound train this morning. Now, standing unnoticed in the midst of this prosaic, *professional* setting, her ill-defined turmoil of the past weeks seemed insignificant, her unannounced intrusion into her sister's place of employment a gross breach of manners. Meredith's fellow workers would not welcome an interruption, especially a personal one. Even worse, what if Benjamin Walker appeared and found his employee gabbing with her sister?

She'd been a self-absorbed picklebrain. Garnet stepped back, hoping she could slip away. Instead, the heel of her shoe caught on the fringe of an oriental carpet laid over the parquet floor. She lurched sideways, the heel of her shoe landing on the wood with an audible *thunk*.

"Garnet! What in the world are you doing here?"

Meredith leaped up and dashed across the room, her face a study of alarmed delight. "What's wrong? It's Papa, isn't it? No? You've finally run away, the caged bird finally broke her bars?" Talking nonstop, she held Garnet at arm's length, the hazel eyes conducting a thorough inventory.

"I should have waited at your boardinghouse. I needed to see you, talk to you. But I should have written a letter first." Flushing, Garnet eyed the door, aware of the cessation of activity as all attention focused on them.

"Nonsense." Meredith hauled her across the room, toward a closed solid walnut-paneled door with a brass nameplate fixed in its center. "Mrs. Biggs, if the chef rings up from the kitchen, Mr. Walker's suggestions for the Banker's Association banquet are on my desk. Lowell, I'm leaving. Could you finish these letters for me when you're through there?"

She focused on Garnet. "Now. Ignore these gawking busybodies. They're actually quite nice, even when they're being rude." She jostled Garnet's arm. "Something's wrong. I can see it in your face. Don't tell me—there's been word on those men who…hurt you?"

"No, not yet. But that's one of the—"

"Whew. That's a relief!" Her gaze narrowed. "Are you sure Papa's all right?"

"Not…exactly. What I mean is," Garnet hastily amended when Meredith's complexion lost color, "he's all right, though I have caught him taking more of those bismuth tablets than usual. But he is one of the reasons I—" Garnet tried to grab the medallion back of the velvet sofa they were passing. "Meredith, wait. What are you doing?"

"Telling Mr. Walker I'm leaving. You're going to stand beside me and look"—she paused, firmly wresting Garnet's clutching hand free of its grip on the mahogany trim—"convincingly distraught. Which you do."

"Meredith, this is your job."

"And you're my sister." She rapped on the door, swinging it open when a deep baritone voice gave permission for them to come in. "Mr. Walker, this is my sister Garnet. Something's come up—a family matter. I have to leave immediately."

Torn between exasperation and embarrassment, Garnet had only a vague impression of Mr. Walker. He'd been sitting behind an oak desk the size of a fishpond but rose courteously when the two women intruded into his domain. Taller than their father, taller even than Sloan, his impeccably styled cutaway frock coat and blinding white shirt spoke of vast wealth and a flair for style equal to Meredith's.

"This family matter is of the utmost importance? An—emergency, similar to your frantic visit home in June because of a serious accident one of your sisters had suffered?" Light eyes seemed to flicker over Garnet then refocus on Meredith.

"Yes. It's an emergency." Meredith's head angled forward, a clear signal that though she knew her position might be weak, she was prepared to fight to the death anyway.

"Then you may as well leave." The austere planes of his face relaxed in a brief smile. "But this time, I'll have to dock your salary."

"Fine. I'll be gone the rest of the day."

She linked arms with a bemused Garnet and swept both of them back through the door, but not before Garnet glimpsed the fleeting expression of admiration on Mr. Walker's face. As Meredith closed the door behind them, he had already bent to his work once more, looking as though there had been no interruption at all.

Twenty-Three

*H*ave you made it a habit, then—this testing the patience of your employer?" Garnet asked as they walked outside into the bright August sunshine. They waited until a stage loaded with passengers had gone by, then crossed the street and headed toward Meredith's boardinghouse.

"Yes." Meredith raised her parasol and held it over both of them. "One of these weeks, I'm hoping to jar him enough that he'll lose his temper. I'd like to satisfy myself that he possesses one. But you didn't come all the way up here to discuss Mr. Walker. And we have the rest of the afternoon now. Tell me what's troubling you."

At a loss all of a sudden, Garnet opened her mouth, then closed it. She could sense Meredith's impatience and was both relieved and surprised because for once her sister refrained from badgering. They strolled along the walk side by side, companions as well as sisters, exchanging nods with passersby. A sweating laborer hefting blocks of ice onto a dray chipped off a couple of finger-sized shards, which he bestowed upon them with a gap-toothed smile; two blocks later, when a bright blue ball rolled to a stop at their feet, Meredith cheerfully waved to a sailor-suited toddler while Garnet tossed the ball back.

Yet nonetheless a sensation of aloneness bound her in sticky cobwebs that she couldn't sweep away from her mind.

"I don't know what to do." The words finally burst forth when Meredith reached for the latch gate in front of her boardinghouse. "Meredith, I don't know what to do. I'm afraid Papa's health is deteriorating because of all this mess over...over..."

"The 'Secret of Sinclair Run?' "

Garnet nodded miserably. "We're all trying to convince each other that there *is* no threat, that Sheriff Pettiscomb is right. Those men left the county, probably even the state, that same day. There was never any danger, to any of us." She flicked a hand upward to the neat straw bonnet she wore instead of a sunbonnet. "All those years, I thought I'd been protecting my family by shielding my identity." One of her many self-delusions. "Do you know, it's still an effort, not to reach for a sunbonnet every time I go out?" She stopped. This was far more difficult than she had imagined.

"I'd think you'd be dancing a Highland fling. I'd like to." Meredith grinned. "Has Leah burned those bonnets or just cut them up for rags?" She opened the gate and tugged Garnet inside. "At any rate, I wouldn't fret over it. You wore the old things for five years. Give yourself time, redbird."

"That's not all." Garnet took a determined breath. "It's the solutions to my—my problem that I'm struggling over. I…well, I think I have two—solutions, I mean, and I don't know which to choose. So it might not be a matter of choice at all. Mine, I mean—oh, buttercups and bitterweed!" She felt like stomping her foot. "Felicity Ward has invited me to be her companion on her lecture circuit this fall. I'd be introduced as an artist as well. Mrs. Ward promises that this would be…ah…beneficial, to my 'artistic endeavors,' as she puts it."

"That woman! For someone I've yet to meet, she's beginning to annoy me. FrannieBeth wrote that she orders all her clothing from France, even her unmentionables, and until now I was willing to forgive a certain amount of condescension."

Garnet was unable to respond in kind to the teasing tone, and Meredith heaved an exaggerated sigh. "On the other hand, her idea merits consideration. That gown of yours must be three years old. I'm relieved you at least removed the bustle but mercysake, Garnet, hopefully Mrs. Ward would also bully you to improve your sense of fashion."

They reached the foot of the porch steps, and Meredith turned toward her. "Me and my jibber-jabber mouth. You know I wouldn't care if you wore Effie Tweedie's castaways. I was only trying to—" She wrinkled her nose and gave Garnet a quick hug. "Sorry. No more flippancy, I promise. But fashion aside, I wasn't teasing about the benefits of Mrs. Ward's offer. I do think you ought to consider it. Um…what's your second solution?"

Hopelessness plucked at Garnet with grasping fingers. Why was it so difficult to confess the words out loud? She closed her eyes, wishing she could pray, wishing with all her heart she could *know* that God would supply the answer. Fill her with even a portion of Meredith's courage. Certainly her older sister wouldn't be standing here like a dressmaker's dummy, incapable of expressing a simple phrase.

Behind them a delivery wagon trundled past. Somewhere a church bell tolled the hour.

"If it's that bad, why don't we sit on the porch?" Meredith said. "It's cooler than my room. Don't worry, the porch is deserted this hour of the day. Mrs. Allgood—that's my landlady—and Mr. O'Gill, are the only ones about, I daresay. Mr. O'Gill's eighty, and deaf. The only time he steps outside anymore is for his morning constitutional to the corner and back. Mrs. Allgood sweeps the porch and keeps an eye on him. A couple of clerks have rooms on the second floor. They won't return until after six." She paused, then continued sharing tidbits about the other boarders, her words splashing together until they turned into a soothing stream.

Her tacit forbearance at last unlocked Garnet's frozen jaw. "The first time Sloan took me for a drive—after the 'secret' was out?—he…he asked me to take the bonnet off. And"—his fingers, warm and tender, had brushed beneath her chin, against her cheek—"I did. But that's when I realized that I'd been wearing it for more than anonymity."

Her neck was stiff. Her wrists ached with tension. "You see, I finally realized that I was afraid of what might happen if a man thought I had given him any sort of encouragement."

"I knew it! I was right!"

"Yes." Garnet looked at her sister. "All these years I told Papa and Leah you were wrong. I told *myself* you were wrong because, until Sloan, I believed that you were."

Meredith hugged Garnet again. "I must meet Sloan MacAllister."

She was so lovely, with her thick chestnut hair and dancing eyes. No wonder everyone was drawn to Meredith. Garnet returned the fierce hug. When Sloan met Meredith—she stopped the thought instantly, ashamed of herself. Afraid. She pulled away and tried to smile. "When you meet him, you'll fall in love with him too," she said very quietly before she turned without another word to climb the steps.

Hundred-foot elms shaded the two-story clapboard house. Lush green ferns were hung from rusting iron hooks all about the wrap-around porch, and a profusion of greenery potted in every kind of crockery was scattered between an equal assortment of mismatched rockers, gliders, and a row of oak pressed-back chairs.

The chairs reminded Garnet of Sloan's porch. Of Sloan. She sank onto a white wicker settee and curled her fingers tightly around the cushion to still their tremor.

Meredith sat across from her in a glider and set it to rocking while she studied Garnet. Rueful understanding replaced the banter. "I'm sorry. I should have realized it, from the way Leah carries on so about the man. With Leah, of course, it's not personal. She admires him simply because he's a proficient physician. As for me, doubtless I'll develop a monstrous crush. Of course, that's all it would be. I don't think I'm capable of loving anyone like Papa and Mama loved each other."

For a moment the only sound was the glider's squeaking rhythm as it swayed back and forth. "But you're not like me. If you love Sloan MacAllister, Garnet, then it's a love blessed by God. Of the three of us— you, Leah, me—I've always known your capacity to give and receive love far outshone ours. Leah and I, well, we're too selfish. I," she paused, blinking rapidly, "I've always wished I could be more like you."

Stunned, Garnet peeled off her second best pair of go-to-town gloves. Stalling, she wiped her hot, itching hands with her handkerchief. "I came up here," she said at last, "because I was hoping to learn how to be more like *you*."

They both leaned forward, knees bumping as they exchanged unselfconscious hugs and tearful giggles. When they resumed their relaxed poses, Garnet felt more at peace than she had in weeks. The words flowed naturally.

"I'd reconciled myself to a lot of things," she said. "I would never have anyone who loved me like Papa loved Mama. And I would never leave the Valley."

Meredith made a rude sound. "That is, of course, absurd. Ridiculous. Muddle-brained. Which I hope you've realized by now, since you've fallen in love *and* you've been offered the opportunity to leave the Valley. So…what's your dilemma?"

Garnet spread her hands, then let them drop to her lap. "For one thing, Mrs. Ward's motivations are more transparent than she thinks I realize. She might introduce me around, so to speak. She might even hang one of my drawings in a back corner of a room. But my primary purpose would be to function as a glorified maid and companion, a more tolerant soul than my predecessors because, after all, I, too, am an artist." She tipped her nose at an appropriately supercilious angle. "I would understand the vicissitudes of her artistic personality."

Meredith stopped rocking and leaned forward, elbows planted on her knees. "Well. How…undiscerning of her. Do you know, sister mine, sometimes you even surprise me." She pondered Garnet, then grinned. "I think you should tag along with Madame Ward and teach her a lesson."

"I'm afraid I lack yours and Leah's more forceful personalities. As long as Felicity allowed me the free time to wander about whatever countryside we were visiting so I could sketch the local flora, I'd ignore her idiosyncrasies. I doubt I'd notice them after the first week or two." She removed the straw hat, elated but still uneasy with the newfound freedom. "I've enough of my own, remember."

"You needn't look so frightened. You're quite safe here. And in the shade your hair's not all that noticeable. Tell me about Sloan then. He's the second solution, I take it."

"Yes—no! Oh, this is hopeless."

"Mm. Indecisiveness is a good sign. All right, let's try this. He's not married, is he?"

"No, of course not."

"His affections aren't spoken for?"

Jenna, Garnet thought. *His first love.* "I…can't answer that."

"Pish-posh. Has he kissed you?"

Color scalded her cheeks. "Yes."

"A circumspect but otherwise unremarkable liberty? Or the kind of kiss that speaks of great passion?"

"Your reading material needs to drastically improve!" Garnet covered her face with her hands, but she knew Meredith could hear the smile in her voice. "I...I can't answer for Sloan," she managed levelly enough, "but...I'm afraid he wasn't left in any doubt about—about mine." And every time she relived the memory of her abandoned response—her rapt, willing participation, she marveled at herself. She despised herself.

If she had been secretly afraid she would be incapable of feeling any emotion besides repulsion when being held in a man's embrace, her response to Sloan had incinerated not only the past, but her fear. Helplessly she gazed across at her slack-jawed sister.

"Oh, dear," Meredith said. "That means he knows you're in love with him, doesn't it?"

Absently Garnet began fidgeting with her gloves. She grew more certain with each day that her transparency was the reason for Sloan's emotional—and physical—distance. "Except for Papa, Sloan's the most perceptive individual I've ever known."

"That's either very good or very bad." Meredith snatched the wadded gloves and set them aside. "From the quality of the silence, I'm thinking it's the latter."

"The last time I saw him, he didn't speak a word on the ride home. When he helped me out of the buggy, he"—she bit the inside of her cheek and swallowed hard—"he laid his palm against my face. His expression...Meredith, he looked as though he'd been handed a staff that had just turned into a poisonous snake. He...started to speak. I don't know what he wanted to say. But instead he closed his eyes. His hand—" She stopped again. His fingers had touched her freckles, one by one as though he were memorizing them. "He dropped his hand to his side and clenched it into a fist. Then he climbed into the buggy and left. I haven't seen or heard from him since."

"And how long has it been?"

"Two weeks."

"Ah, in that case, I recommend that you start packing for a lecture tour."

Twenty-Four

On a damp September dawn with mist draped over the Valley like wet cotton, Jacob set off for Strasburg with the lawyer's bookcase he'd finally finished. A week earlier, all of them pinning on brave smiles while they choked back tears, he and Garnet had accompanied Leah to Mary Baldwin College, sixty-odd miles south in Staunton. 'Twas a wrenching time in a father's life, this season of letting go.

Garnet will be the next. The last…

Oh, the girl had fought it, to be sure, though not with words. Stoic and silent, she had written down lists of all the fripperies she'd need for a thirty-day lecture tour with Mrs. Ward. She'd compiled a collection of her work to carry along in the fancy leather portfolio Mrs. Ward had presented her as a gift. She'd even hired a girl to cook and clean for Jacob and a laundress to spend two days a week with his washing.

"Lass, I can putter around the kitchen quite happily," he protested. "Even Mrs. Ward agrees."

"Felicity's opinion is her own. She's welcome to it. Now…shall I find someone for you, or do you want to ask around yourself?"

That was his middle daughter. Never raised her voice, never argued. But once she made up her mind, a body might as well try to whittle an oak tree with a feather.

Part of that resolve, however, was inherited from her father. Which was why Jacob set out for Strasburg this morning despite the dour day. He'd business, right enough—but an important portion of it was to be transacted at the Tom's Brook Mercantile.

The store was a combination drygoods, depot, and post office. If there was news to be had concerning Sloan MacAllister, surely this was the

170

place to unearth it. After warming his hands at the stove and exchanging pleasantries with the storekeeper's wife, Jacob spent another quarter-hour picking through an array of ladies' soaps and lotions. For the sake of Garnet's reputation, he couldn't very well launch into an interrogation at the outset.

"Daughter's off to see a bit of the world outside the Valley," he confided to Mrs. Rawls. "Thought I should give her a little present before she leaves."

"The Pear's Soap you're looking at's a fine choice." Her hands, quick and neat, rummaged among the bottles and jars arranged on top of the glass showcase. "There's also these—Latour's Violet Soap? We just received the shipment yesterday. I thought the fragrance was quite nice. We also have some toilet water in several fragrances."

"She's partial to violets." He set the soap to one side, then eyed a squat little jar that promised to remove all manner of facial blemishes. "Ah...my daughter's always mindful of her freckles."

No matter that after a score of years failing to rid herself of them, she'd declared it hopeless and refused any further suggestions. But he discussed sundry remedies with a diffident Mrs. Rawls, all the while waiting for an appropriate opportunity to quietly mention Sloan's name.

He was about to risk a frontal approach when the bell over the door jangled and a stoop-shouldered stick of a man stepped inside. "Foul day out," he announced with a congenial nod in their direction. "Say, Miz Rawls, Sloan asked if I'd check on that paint he ordered a couple weeks back, next time I stopped in. He said if it was in, and I went ahead and toted it to his place so it'd be waitin' when he got back, he promised he'd see what he could do for my...my mi-algae, I believe he calls it. No charge."

"*No charge?* My, yes. Lately he is a changed man. Why, when he stopped by before he—" Her cheeks went pink. "I'll be with you in a moment, Homer." Mrs. Rawls glanced at Jacob, embarrassment as well as a question in her eyes.

"You go right ahead and check on the paint," Jacob said, curiosity raging like the onset of a fever. "I'll study on which of these would please my daughter the most. Ah…this Sloan feller? Would he be Dr. Sloan MacAllister?"

Mrs. Rawls had started down the aisle, but at the question partially turned. "Why, yes. Do you know him then?"

"I've made his acquaintance," Jacob admitted. "But I haven't seen much of him lately."

"Headed off somewhere up north, week before last," Homer said. He shuffled past a barrel of autumn fruit and helped himself to an apple. "But I reckon he'll be back most any day now—told me no later than the second Sunday in September. I'm his nearest neighbor, don't you know." He took a huge bite out of the apple, chewing noisily while he studied Jacob.

"He's gone?" Jacob struggled to hide his disappointment. "Well…sorry I missed him." But he did thank the Lord that Sloan planned to return.

Mrs. Rawls joined them, her lips pursed as she watched Homer crunch into the pilfered fruit. "The paint's in the back. I'll have Vernon fetch it for you. And you owe me a penny for that apple, Homer Davies."

"Aw, don't go gettin' in a lather." Homer winked at Jacob. He rummaged in a side pocket of his faded overalls, then slapped the coin onto the counter. "There you go. Say, you want me to tell the doc you were in the neighborhood? What's your name, mister?"

"You might tell him that Jacob asked after him." He grabbed a jar at random and thrust it toward Mrs. Rawls. "I'll take this one. Best be headed out. Got to make Strasburg before noon." The curiosity rode him hard, and while Mrs. Rawls wrapped the jar of something called Hind's Honey Almond and Cream, Jacob gave in to temptation. "You mentioned Dr. MacAllister changed. What kind of change would that be, if you'll forgive my asking?"

Mrs. Rawls's somber expression deepened to worry, and she darted a quick glance around as though afraid to be caught gossiping. Homer, on the other hand, whapped Jacob's back and laughed.

"Some folks hereabouts are calling it a revelation from the Lord. Myself, I'm more inclined to think it was fairies casting a spell. Whatever it was, I'm grateful. Before, those eyes of his could freeze a blue flame.

Took my life in my hands every time we met on the road and I ventured a hello."

"Homer, you watch that wicked tongue of yours."

"Sorry, Miz Rawls." He winked at Jacob again. "These days, now, he's as likely to talk my blamed ear off. Wants my opinion of the land, soaks up local agriculture like a sand hill drinks rain after a two-month drought. Sure do hope this trip north and being surrounded by all them Yankees don't afflict his brain."

Jacob finally managed to escape. But for the rest of that long day to Strasburg and back, he pondered what he had heard at the Tom's Brook Mercantile.

⌘

Berta Schumacher's square frame house sat at the end of a row of ramshackle "company houses." Built by the owner of the Central Pennsylvania Railroad as a token feudal gesture toward his employees, Adlerville regrettably bore scant resemblance to George Pullman's Hyde Park community outside Chicago. The workers' dwellings here had been hastily erected, with shabby materials and sloppy workmanship. Worse, the Central line had gone into receivership the previous year. It was a surprise to Sloan that any of the Adlerville houses still stood. But the remaining workers knew better than to complain.

Slaves might have been freed in the South, but slavery without preference to the color of a man's skin still existed. And its borders extended miles north of the Mason-Dixon line.

Sloan walked along a muddy path, as familiar with its route as though he'd trod upon it the previous day. He wondered half whimsically what he'd find at the other end. It was a little past five, and chimneys chugged clouds of dingy smoke into an ocher-tinted sky. The acrid stench of coal blended with that of cooking cabbage and onions. Few souls were about. The men wouldn't return home until long after dark, and the women's labors inside their meager households lasted even longer. Sloan had spoken to exactly three people since he'd left the depot, none of whom knew him.

An emaciated mongrel tied to a frayed rope yapped when he passed by. Two houses farther down, where an amiable Swedish bachelor used to live, a wide-eyed waif disappeared through the door when Sloan waved at him. Before the door slammed he heard the wretched squalls of a colicky baby. Six months ago, Sloan would have knocked on the door, introduced himself, then tried to persuade the mother to let him examine her baby.

Another life, another time...

It was a curiously detached sensation, returning to a place he'd lived in for three toilsome years, the place where he'd spread himself out like an unguent until there'd been nothing left. Now he felt little beyond the vague curiosity of a casual stranger just passing through. An unwelcome one at that.

Not precisely the prodigal son's reception here, Lord.

He could almost hear a gently ironic reminder that Adlerville had never truly been his "home."

Still and all..."Don't believe I'm ready to face Baltimore."

Even as he murmured the words aloud he yielded to the inevitability of it however. But not this trip. When he did return to Baltimore to accept his mother's grudging olive branch, he planned to have Garnet by his side.

As always, longing coursed through him, along with an uncertainty that threatened his newfound peace. Perhaps he should have at least written her—no. Garnet deserved neither his personal demons nor his doubts; she certainly didn't deserve to be dragged through the sewer of his past, or rather—any more of it than the surface he'd already inflicted upon her. This way was best. He could come to her restored. Revitalized. Re...created.

When he explained she would understand. She *had* to understand.

But what of the gut-wrenching desolation that had filled her face the last time he saw her? God help him, he had turned away from her. He wasn't sure, but he didn't think he'd even told her good-bye. *Lord? How could I have been so cruel? So unbelievably insensitive? She'll forgive me, won't she?* When he explained...she'd understand.

Sloan dodged a sludge-filled pothole, his thoughts far away. He was relieved when he reached Mrs. Schumacher's cottage and spotted the delicate lace curtains still hanging in the two front windows. Determinedly bright yellow window shutters, though peeling and faded, still defied the dreariness. Thin smoke drifted from her chimney. Sloan loped up the steps and rapped on the door, feeling more trepidation than he would have liked.

"Mrs. Schumacher? It's Dr. MacAllister."

Relief filled him when through the thin wooden panel he heard the sound of a hearty "Alleluia! Praise Jesus!"

Moments later the door creaked inward. "I knew you'd come back someday." One swollen-knuckled hand clutched the duckbill-shaped handle of the cane he'd given her the previous year. She beckoned with the other, and Sloan suppressed an exclamation of dismay at the pathetically twisted old fingers. Tears swam in her almost colorless eyes. "Thanks be to Jesus."

He took the wrinkled hand in his, careful not to apply pressure, and kissed her papery cheek. "I figured out what I was running away from." He cupped her elbow and steered them back into her tiny sitting area, gently easing her into her rocking chair. "And then I allowed grace to bring me back."

After stoking the fire, he tucked a fringed woolen throw back over her waist and legs, then dragged over a stool and sat beside her.

"I've been praying for you, all these months," Berta said. A deep sigh brought a faint bloom to her waxen complexion. She smiled. "Tell me about it."

"That's why I came back." He studied her for a moment. "Hannah still looking after you? You look like you've lost a bit of weight. And the pain's worse, isn't it? Did you take the medicine I left for you?"

"Now, Dr. MacAllister, don't you start in with that business. You tell me your story, young man. That will ease pain better than those unpleasant nostrums you tried to foist off on me."

Sloan sat back with a sheepish smile and obeyed. "I met a young woman. Or rather…God more or less kept thrusting her in front of my face until I gave in and fell in love with her. After that, all the bitterness started to fade. I couldn't nurture the love with my past still festering inside like a putrid wound."

He fingered the corners of his mustache, scratched his stubbled jaw—stalling. Then, with a kind of wondrous relief, he committed himself aloud for the first time. "When I go back to Virginia, I'm going to ask her to be my wife."

"Ah, to find the mate the blessed Lord has designed for you, there's a gift indeed." Her gaze, old, infinitely wise, wandered over him like loving hands. "She must be very special, this girl. I trust her walk with the Lord is as sure and strong as your own."

"Mm. As to that…I'm thinking that's one of the plans He's incorporated as part of my…let's call it my restoration. Garnet's faith, you see, is a convoluted mixture of reverence, service, and doubt. She doesn't seem to grasp that God loves her, just as she is."

The need to hold her, to pour out his heart until all the gray in her misty eyes was swallowed up by the green, twisted his heart until every beat hurt. "I want to teach her. I want her to trust me. She's not said the words, but I think she's in love with me. She can't hide it—there's no guile in her, none of the barriers society trains in women from infancy. I took advantage of that, to my shame. And I took advantage of her father's trust. That's why I left her. Before I could return, explain my behavior—there was a letter. From my mother. And I knew I had to come back here first. Until I faced the cause for the—the blackness in my soul, I had no right to help Garnet with *her* struggles."

"Hmph."

She sat there, a dried-up wreck of a woman riddled with painful rheumatoid arthritis. Yet armed with a powerful dignity and that single piercing look, Berta Schumacher shredded the last of Sloan's well-intentioned arrogance. "Dr. MacAllister, as a physician you're a noble servant of our Lord, a model of the Great Physician if ever I saw one. As a gentlemen courting a young lady, I can tell you've made a mess of things."

"Yes ma'am." He barely resisted the urge to squirm like a scolded schoolboy. "As soon as I pay a visit to Mrs. Jorvik, I'll do my best to rectify those shortcomings."

"Don't you be sassing me. I may be crippled and half-blind, but this old schoolteacher can still rap your knuckles." Her eyes twinkled. "However, I will permit you to hold my hand again while I pray for you.

You're the only person whose touch doesn't pain me dreadfully. I miss that bond, you know…since Emil's passing and your departure, I've had only the Lord's hand to hold."

"Mrs. Schumacher—"

"My Jesus offers that comfort to be sure. But—long as He sees fit to confine me to this human form—there are moments when even His blessed spiritual Presence does little to quench the longing for the corporeal touch of a fellow believer."

"I'd be honored to hold your hand and pray with you," Sloan whispered. He had to clear his throat. Very carefully he folded his strong warm fingers around Mrs. Schumacher's fragile cold ones again.

"Almighty Father, strong to save. Shepherd to the weak and the wayward…I thank You for Your unwavering pursuit of this troubled young man. For restoring the joy of his salvation. For Your unrelenting Spirit, who banished his bitterness, his wrath, and his anger. Who is helping him to learn to forgive others for their flawed humanity. And now, blessed Savior, continue to help Sloan to forgive himself, not only that he may live to serve You, but that he may be the man You designed him to be. Bless this young lady, Garnet, of Virginia. May hers and your son Sloan's hearts and souls be united by You, through You—and for You, that the light of their union shall serve as a beacon for all. That all may see how great and wonderful and unfailing is Your love for Your children. Thine is the glory, both now and forevermore. Amen, and amen."

Silence filled the small dark room. God's Presence had never been more real. Sloan opened his eyes almost reluctantly, blinking in the yellowish glow of the smoky kerosene parlor lamp on the table by Mrs. Schumacher's chair. His throat tightened. He blinked again. Was it his imagination, or was the glow spreading throughout the room, except now it was infused with a white radiance bathing the two of them in unearthly peace?

"You're a good man, Sloan MacAllister," Mrs. Schumacher said. The gnarled fingers tightened in his, a light fleeting pressure. "Now. Go visit Kristen Jorvik. Purge your soul. Then return to the Shenandoah Valley." A beatific smile lit her face. "Told you those old hills would heal you, now didn't I?"

Twenty-Five

SINCLAIR RUN

$\mathcal{A}$t precisely three o'clock in the afternoon, Joshua's buggy pulled up in front of the house.

"I wonder," Garnet mused to her friend Chloe Spindle, "if he borrowed a manual on manners so he could memorize every one of the 'rules on the etiquette of paying calls.' "

"Will you put the poor man out of his misery today?"

Chloe rose from her chair to stand over the couch where Garnet relaxed lengthways, legs stretched across the seat, Phineas asleep in her lap. The couch faced the parlor window, and both women watched through the lace panels as Joshua climbed down, carefully secured Ruth to the hitching post, brushed road dust from his waistcoat, and finally straightened the brown derby hat he'd worn to match his brown-checked suit.

"You have to stay for a while longer now," she told Chloe, who had arranged to spend the day with Garnet while Jacob was in Strasburg. For the last quarter of an hour, however, her friend had been making going-home noises. "I need a chaperone."

"What's wrong with Phineas?" Chloe tugged a lock of Garnet's hair. Then, laughing, she languidly stretched her arms. "Don't fret, I'll function as a crotchety maiden auntie for you. Stay there. I'll answer the door."

Garnet watched her friend amble toward the hall. A frown gathered, and regretfully she woke Phineas. "Sorry, pet. You know how Joshua feels when you're curled up in my lap." Actually, it resembled, well…pouting. Of course, he was equally outraged by errant strands of fox hair clinging to Garnet's clothing.

She scratched the furry tufts behind one black-tipped ear. Phineas yawned, then licked the fingers Garnet had unknowingly balled into a fist in her lap. "It probably won't matter much longer," she murmured, setting the fox on the floor. Unblinking, Phineas watched her. "I know, you can tell something's not quite right with me, can't you?"

From the entrance hall she heard the sound of Joshua's slow drawl, his courtly inquiries after Chloe's family, whom he hadn't seen since they'd moved to Luray. Abruptly their voices dropped to heated whispers. Garnet sighed. Joshua had come expecting her father's presence to observe propriety. And Chloe, loyal friend that she was, was taking her promise to Garnet seriously. Perhaps she should have sent Chloe out the kitchen door after all.

Phineas growled, sounding so much like a protective watchdog Garnet had to smile. She swung her legs to the floor and brushed all the betraying orange-red strands away from her blue gown. "It's a shame our hairs don't match. Here." She plucked a large slice of pear from the tray of refreshments. "Run along to the kitchen. Don't worry. I can handle Mr. Jones."

Phineas accepted the offering daintily, the sharp white teeth barely closing over the juicy morsel. Garnet administered a discreet shove to his narrow flank. "Go along now. Scat. We'll go for a ride later, I promise."

"Garnet."

She straightened, surreptitiously wiping her hands behind her back. "How are you this bleak afternoon, Joshua?"

"Quite well. Thank you." His gaze skittered from the fox—disappearing through the doorway to the dining room—to Garnet's stockinged feet peeking from beneath her petticoats. He cleared his throat. "Garnet…will you walk with me? Miss Spindle has agreed that propriety will be well served so long as she remains on the porch, and we remain in sight of it." The high cheekbones turned a dusky red. "I hope you realize I would never do anything to compromise your Christian character."

"Of course you wouldn't, Joshua. I—"

"Nor do I want to shirk my responsibilities as a-a friend." His hands turned the derby round and round. "We need to talk. If your father were here, which I gather he is not"—the tone conveyed Joshua's disapproval—"I'm sure he would agree."

"I, on the other hand," Chloe piped in, "have been a trifle more… unbending."

She and Joshua exchanged keen looks that reminded Garnet of the flash of drawn swords. *Hmm.* Joshua and Chloe? "I'll walk with Mr. Jones." She smiled at her friend's consternation. "Don't worry, Chloe. As Joshua has said, he's a perfect gentleman."

"I'll be right out front, on the porch, should he decide to change his mind."

"Miss Spindle has adopted some unseemly traits since her move." Joshua paused. "She's always been a godly young woman. I would hate to see that virtue tarnished."

"She cares about me," Garnet refuted quietly. "And she's been a true friend."

"Yes, well, I hope you hold me in equally high regard." His stride was slow but decisive as they made their way across the yard. He wouldn't look at her. "Garnet, you know how deeply I care about you."

"I know you do."

Garnet kept her own gaze on the scarlet-tipped leaves of a maple sapling that had sprung up in the middle of the cedars a decade earlier. Though surrounded by the brushy evergreens, the slender maple had somehow endured until now it cast its shadow over the cedars. "If you've stopped by to try again to change my mind about accompanying Mrs. Ward—"

"Of course I'm going to try!" He stopped walking. "Garnet, did you read those verses I suggested? Wisdom dwells with prudence—'the fear of the LORD is to hate evil: pride, and arrogancy…the froward mouth …'? Mrs. Ward might be a fine figure of a woman, and I'm all too aware that she enjoys a national reputation of sorts, but she's a brazen…professional woman. An *artist.* And she's convinced you that because you draw pretty flowers for a ladies' magazine—"

"*American Monthly* is not a ladies' magazine, Joshua. It's—"

"Whatever. The point is, Mrs. Ward has flattered you into thinking that you're her equal. She's manipulating you. Don't you see? Lucifer cloaking himself as an angel of light to lead the unwary astray?"

Incredulous, Garnet searched his face. All right, yes, she was aware of Felicity's manipulative streak, and she had also come to realize that, token appearances for Sunday morning worship aside, Felicity wasn't even a believer. But she wasn't evil. And she needed compassion more than censure. As for Joshua... "It would appear that Felicity Ward is not the only one trying to influence my thoughts and actions."

"I see that she's already blinded you," he shot back. "See how quickly you act indignant on *her* behalf, instead of respecting the carefully thought out and, indeed, the more objective, observation by the man who's been courting you these past several years." He reached toward her, a fleeting brush of his gloved fingers just above her elbow.

Garnet jerked back.

"I beg your pardon." Joshua took a step backward and crammed his hands in his pockets. His flushed cheeks darkened, and the genuine hurt Garnet saw in the cloudy blue eyes caused a splinter of remorse to lodge just beneath her breastbone.

She pressed her hand to the spot. "I'm sorry, too. You—it's just that I'm not used to a man's touch—" *No, that wasn't honest.* She gnawed her lower lip for a moment, then gave a mental shrug. "I'm not used to your touch," she amended.

"At one time I had hopes of remedying that," Joshua said, his voice stiff. "That's one of the issues we need to address. This—this incident which occurred when you were sixteen...was something of a shock to me, Garnet."

"Not as much as it was to me, I imagine," Garnet retorted beneath her breath. She strolled over to one of the many ancient lichen-covered boulders dotted throughout their land and sat down.

"Here." Joshua removed his waistcoat. "You'll soil your garment."

"Better that than your new suit. It is new, isn't it?"

He nodded, but stood above her with an obdurate aura, holding the coat out. Dear, stuffy Joshua. "Thank you," she said after allowing him to spread it across the rough surface.

"You're welcome. Garnet, I have prayed for weeks about this. You must understand, I'm not trying to judge you. But I am convinced that God has been trying to reach you ever since that—that incident. Trying to teach you. 'For whom the Lord loveth he chasteneth,' remember?"

"You think He allowed those men to—to…You think that God *arranged* what happened, to teach me a lesson?"

"Of course not," he responded so quickly Garnet wondered if he was deceiving them both. "But I do think that, so long as your behavior lacks modesty and discretion, you compromise your faith. We're not to test the Almighty, remember. When you do, I think He more often than not chooses discipline to curb disobedience."

The boulder's dank chill seeped through Garnet's clothing. Shivering, she contemplated this dismal explanation for her ongoing spiritual struggle. "You sound as though you're telling me that God will only love me if I embrace proper behavior. That's not the God my father brought me up to worship."

"Yes, well…your father has always tended to err on the lenient side with all of you, to my way of thinking."

"My father is not the subject of this conversation. Joshua, why did you come today? We've known each other too long to tiptoe around unpleasant topics. You disapprove of my behavior. Lately, I've begun to think you disapprove of *me.*"

"There's no need to be defensive, Garnet."

"Oh? Perhaps I wouldn't be, if your remarks were less…offensive."

"You misunderstand." Abruptly he dropped down beside her, searching her face in a kind of desperation. "Don't go with Mrs. Ward, Garnet. Not until we—resolve matters between us. Please."

"Joshua—"

"I prayed all night," he continued rapidly, his voice low, almost hoarse. "I asked God to reveal His will to me. It had long been on my mind to…ah…to talk with your father. To request…that is, I had hoped that our affections were mutual…"

Garnet laid a hand on his arm, halting the stumbling flow. He gawked at it until, flushing scarlet, Garnet snatched her hand away. "I like you, Joshua," she said. "But it isn't going to work out between us.

I've known that for years. I believe what you came for today was to tell me that—finally—you agree with me."

He shrugged, his fingers rubbing over the chain of his watch fob, his gaze avoiding hers. "I prayed," he repeated after a while. "All these years, I've been praying for the Lord to change your heart. Your…ways."

Garnet rose, shook out Joshua's coat and handed it to him. "Did you ever ask the Lord to change yours?" Her throat ached, and her pulse reverberated through her eardrums at the finality of the circumstances. And yet a nascent feeling of peace drifted down, enveloping her in a gauze-thin cloak. "Good-bye, Joshua."

"Garnet…"

Garnet managed a wry smile. "I think I'll go on up the hill. I'd like to visit my mother's grave. Would you mind very much explaining to Miss Spindle for me? Don't worry. You'll be pleasantly surprised at her amenable disposition."

She turned without another word and headed up the rocky slope.

❦

ADLERVILLE

"You're a fine physician, Dr. MacAllister." Mrs. Jorvik's hands were busy as she talked, sewing infinitesimal stitches in the torn hem of a child's smock. "I was right sorry, I was, when I heard you weren't returning. But Amos's death—"

"Was my fault, I know. If I had stayed with him…"

Her hands stilled, and the worn plump face creased in a bittersweet smile. " 'Tis little use fretting over what might have been. He was bad off, was my husband, by the time he let me send for you in the first place." Eyes reddened from too many hours of work with too little light surveyed Sloan with placid acceptance. "To my way of thinking, he would have died that night, no matter whether you labored at his bedside or no."

"Mrs. Jorvik"—even the days and weeks of steadfast prayer could not diminish the agonizing confession—"I must tell you this. You deserve to know. My brother—the telegram said only that he was gravely injured. I didn't know"—the words emerged thick, sticking in his throat like wet sand—"I didn't know then that he was already dead."

Mrs. Jorvik went still. For several moments the only sound in the tiny neat-as-a-butler's-pantry room was the crackle of the fire and the contented patter of Gretchen, the Jorviks' youngest child. Absorbed, the baby was playing with a tattered rag doll on the floor by her mother's chair. Gretchen would be almost eighteen months now. And she would never know her father.

The guilt sucked at his conscience, tugging Sloan from behind the wall of grace God had erected in his behalf. He wanted to bury his head in his hands and weep. Instead he kept his gaze on the poignant tableau of widowed mother and fatherless child, and prayed for the strength to endure.

"That was a difficult admission for you to make," Mrs. Jorvik finally said. She followed the direction of Sloan's gaze and leaned over to pick Gretchen up. "Almost, I'm thinking, as difficult as it is for me to hear. Like me, you regret that Amos will not know his youngest daughter, that she will not know him."

"Yes. With every breath I draw. God has forgiven me, Mrs. Jorvik. I believe I've come to accept that much, at least. I'm struggling to forgive myself." He inhaled, held his breath until he could finish what he had to say, then slowly let it out. "What I need to know is…will *you* forgive me?"

Another bittersweet smile flickered across her face. Gretchen's chubby hands reached for one of the long braids pinned in a roll behind her mother's ear, but without ever taking her gaze from Sloan's, Mrs. Jorvik reached for a wooden spoon and handed it to the baby to play with instead. "Dr. MacAllister," she said, "I will say this to you. I have come to believe that whatever *right* choices we make are by the grace of God, or," she paused, lips pursed, then added with a shake of the head, " *'tur,'* my grandfather would say. Luck. Chance. You had to make a choice that day. I do not know whether your choice was the right one, but I do know that you did what you felt in your heart was the right thing."

"If I had known my brother was already dead—"

"But you did not. Nor do you know that you would have been able to save my husband." She set the squirming baby back on the floor, then leaned forward. "That knowledge must rest with God. You are a good man, Dr. MacAllister. I have clung to that, these months. Now I see that the time has not been easy for you either."

She laid her callused palm on top of Sloan's. "I can promise that I will forgive you, one day. My pain…is very deep. But to see you, to hear you ask me…I think this is a right choice, Dr. MacAllister. And I think it must be God's choice. So I wish you to return to your new home now. In peace."

She stood, and Sloan followed suit, feeling awkward, as uncertain as a yearling stepping into an unfamiliar meadow. "I appreciate your honesty," he said, his voice low.

" 'Tis who I am." She secured Gretchen against her ample hip. "Forgiveness sometimes comes easily, does it not? But sometimes…I think we must work a little harder at it, wait a little longer for it."

"Yes ma'am. But it's worth the effort." He tickled the baby's cheek, his heart twisting when she giggled in innocent delight. "Because without it, life is darker than the deepest mine shaft." He smiled. "Believe me, I've been in that mine shaft. I'll take your promise, Mrs. Jorvik, and thank you for it. I know I don't deserve anything."

"Dr. MacAllister, none of us deserves God's blessings, least of all myself. But 'tis your choice, and mine, to accept them when they come our way."

Choices, Lord. A double-edged sword You created within the human mind, this divine piece of Yourself. A moral conscience. Sloan mulled over his visit to Adlerville on the long trip home to Tom's Brook.

He prayed it was the right decision for him, to make his permanent home in the Shenandoah Valley. For months now, the progression of his feelings about the old rambling farmhouse had been solidifying from desperation to determination to devotion. He'd fallen in love with a place, with the same unexpectedness with which he'd fallen in love with a woman. He didn't want to leave either one.

For all of Sloan's adult life as a Christian he had, well, *chosen* to believe that God would somehow guide him in the decisions he made about the course of his life. This past year he had been forced to face an unpalatable truth: Regardless of that willed belief in the presence of God's Spirit within Sloan's mortal flesh, he was nonetheless still as prone to stumbling as a drunken reprobate promising never to lift another bottle to his lips.

The love of God, the grace of Jesus, the fellowship of the Holy Spirit…he would continue to enjoy them with only limited success for the duration of his earthly existence. He would doubtless make more wrong choices in the future, or at least not-so-right choices. And life would continue to bring occasional mud holes and stones across his path that were neither his own nor the Lord's doing. Thankfully, he could depend on the love of God to pick him up, the grace of Jesus to forgive him, and the Holy Spirit to nudge him back onto the right path again each time.

But God was never going to force His will on Sloan—or anyone, because over the course of the last year Sloan had also discovered how much the Almighty treasured the gift of free choice He had bequeathed His children.

I understand, Lord. Took awhile, but he finally understood. He wanted Garnet to love him, marry him, and move into his house in Tom's Brook because she chose to, not because Sloan had manipulated her feelings to achieve his own ends.

So he set his face to the south and prayed that the choice to settle there was God's as well as his own.

Twenty-Six

You're saying that this…outing…is a *test?*" Felicity stalked back and forth across the barn aisle. The deep flounces at the hem of her watered-silk skirt swirled the fresh straw Garnet had just strewn to keep down the dust.

Garnet hid a smile. Three days had passed since Joshua's visit, and for two of those Garnet had been mulling over her idea. Felicity, predictably, was not receiving it well. "In fact, yes. This is a test for both of us, since you'll have input on the final grade."

"Don't assume that dry tone with me, miss. Might I remind you that you already agreed to this trip? We've been making preparations for weeks—I've written countless letters in your behalf, arranged for you to interview with two instructors whom I hold in extremely high regard. Two!"

She stopped in the middle of her hand-waving tirade, then slowly turned to Garnet. "Why, you poor dear. I understand. Would have sooner except you caught me so completely off guard." Her gaze swept over Garnet's rumpled house gown and soiled pinafore. "Heavens, girl, you do look like a country bumpkin who wouldn't know a Whistler from a penny whistle. Almost gave me heart palpitations."

"Mm…well, I didn't want to clean the stalls in my Sunday-go-to-meeting clothes." Garnet stuck a straw between her teeth and hooked her thumbs inside the bib of her pinafore. "Miz Ward, what's a penny whistle?"

Felicity gave an appreciative peal of laughter. The fierce red spots staining her cheekbones faded. "Garnet, you've more facets than a Brazilian diamond. And you're the only person I know who can so neatly put me in my place."

She stepped closer, nose wrinkling, then gamely pressed a rose-scented cheek to Garnet's before backing away. "Very well. I accept your...challenge. We'll go to the site of your choice, you with your pens and me with my oils. We'll reproduce on paper what we each 'see.' Have I interpreted this correctly so far?"

Garnet nodded. "We'll give ourselves, oh...two hours, then compare each other's works. If I like what you have to say—and you like what *I* have to say, I'll accompany you without further objection."

"You really are the most peculiar person. But—very well. Does tomorrow suit you?"

"Tomorrow suits me just fine." Garnet removed the kerchief that had kept her hair out of her face and tossed it over the pitchfork. "I have the place all picked out."

The bridge at Cedar Creek. Where her life had changed forever. It seemed only fitting that she return and discover if after this visit, her life would be changed forever...again.

The autumn sky shimmered with such an intense blue it hurt to gaze at it. Mare's-tail clouds—white flowing strokes against the deep azure canvas—provided the only relief from that endless blue. Low humidity, little wind, temperature hovering in the midfifties according to the thermometer nailed next to the entrance of Cooper's, where Garnet and Felicity had stopped to purchase the makings of a picnic lunch.

"I don't know why," Felicity groused the entire thirty minutes, "you refused to let me have the chef from my hotel pack us a basket."

"Because we're doing this my way." Garnet watched Mrs. Cooper bring the lever of the cheese cutter down over a round of cheese, severing a nickel's worth from the block to add to Garnet's pile of apples, soda crackers, and some striped candy sticks.

When they left the store laden with two metal lunch pails, Felicity was still mumbling disgruntled remarks beneath her breath.

An hour later Felicity halted halfway up the incline of the sunlit meadow they had to cross to reach the creek. "Why haven't you brought me here before? This is lovely, Garnet. Look, see how that old boulder is jutting up through that clump of sumac? If I frame the bridge between that, and the stand of cedar to the right of the bridge, the contrast of colors will be truly remarkable."

Garnet's mind had been fixed on the bank of the creek, where she'd found Phineas. But she stopped, obediently studying the scene Felicity had described. Reluctant astonishment seeped inside. "You're right," she admitted slowly. "I was so focused on a different spot that I wasn't even thinking about other possibilities."

"Ha. One of the first lessons a good artist learns is to frame the entire world, whatever setting one happens to find herself in. See? By accompanying me on my lecture tour—"

"I'm conceding a battle, not the war. You have good vision. Today"—Garnet smiled a mischievous smile—"we'll see how our visions compare." She shrugged the cloth bag off her shoulder and dropped it at her feet. "There. I've marked the spot. After we fetch your easel and the rest of our supplies, we should have just enough time for our two hours before we have to start back. My father's more particular than ever, you see, about my being out after sunset."

"It won't take two hours." Felicity set off across the meadow, her stride brisk, spine straight as a paintbrush handle. "Within thirty minutes, I believe you'll concede."

At a little before 3:30—and she knew the time because Felicity in a fit of utter exasperation had unpinned her watch brooch so she could thrust it under Garnet's nose—they decided to continue the argument on the way back to Sinclair Run.

Garnet conceded the advantages of oil—easier to correct a mistake, greater texture, the challenge of replicating nature's colors. Felicity conceded that there was challenge to be found in the exquisite detail that pen-and-ink demanded, and that it was possible to create the illusion of reality without the use of color. She debated which medium demanded the most patient hand. Throughout their often spirited exchange, Goatsbeard with little guidance plodded along the Pike, so well-trained he didn't even stop to yank grass from the roadside.

On the outskirts of Tom's Brook, distant shouts and screams of pain terminated their debate with shocking abruptness.

"Whoa, there," Garnet automatically calmed a shying, tail-swishing Goatsbeard. She searched the countryside off to the right of the road.

A man on horseback appeared at the crest of a shallow slope, then plunged down toward the Pike at a full gallop. When he caught sight of the buggy, he sent his horse over the low stone wall with heart-stopping recklessness.

"Help!" He sawed the reins, struggling to control his lathered mount. The man was minus coat and hat; his hands and shirt, Garnet realized in horror, were smeared with blood. "Accident—other side of the hill. Logging wagon overturned—there's injuries, bad ones. A couple of men already...please! Can you go for help?"

"Dr. Sloan MacAllister—he lives in Tom's Brook?" Her father had mentioned in passing that Sloan had been in Pennsylvania. But he should have returned by now. The shock of his absence had bitten deep, but Garnet ignored it now. "Has someone sent for him?"

"Yes'm." The man glanced up and down the road. "I'm headed for Tom's Brook, hope to round up as many men as I can. If you—"

"We'll round up men. You get back to yours." Garnet jiggled the reins, lifting her hand to acknowledge the man's heartfelt thanks as he tore back off up the hill.

"Garnet, I have to be in Woodstock before six. I'm having dinner with the mayor, then catching a train to Washington." Felicity grabbed the arm rail with one hand and her hat with the other. "Could you please slow down? We'll be of no help to anybody if we ourselves suffer an accident."

"This stretch of the road's safe enough." Garnet urged Goatsbeard into a gallop. "Right now, speed is more important."

"Fine! Tell the sheriff or someone then!" She had to raise her voice to be heard. "Look, there's a house. You can have the people there dash off to—"

"I'm going to the mercantile by the railroad. More people there. And Felicity, I'll offer a ride to anyone who doesn't have transportation to the scene. You can either come along or stay at the store. It's by the depot." She slowed Goatsbeard to a trot, then turned right onto the road that led to the store.

"Oh, for heaven's sake. I'm no Florence Nightingale. Garnet, think, my dear. This will not be a fitting scene for either of us."

Garnet pulled the buggy to a rocking halt in front of the store. "I'm going to help if I can," she said and jumped down.

Less than five minutes later she led a procession of anxious, sober-faced men back to the Pike. Vernon Rawls, the store's proprietor, rode in the buggy with Garnet and a tight-lipped Felicity Ward, who for some unknown reason refused to stay behind.

"Hope whoever they sent after Doc MacAllister doesn't have trouble finding him," Mr. Rawls shouted over the clatter of hooves and spinning wheels. Garnet sensed his sideways regard. "This is mighty noble of you, miss. But it's best if you let me out before we're too close. This won't be a sight for ladies."

"Precisely what I said," Felicity snapped. "But…perhaps we can be of help. From a distance, of course."

"You do have a lot of underskirts that could be used for bandages," Garnet agreed.

After that, Felicity didn't speak again.

In spite of the men's warnings, the carnage that greeted them shocked Garnet to queasy immobility.

A jumbled pile of massive logs covered the narrow logging road that wound between two hills. The remains of a flatbed wagon lay on its side, one of the wheels crushed, the other dangling like a broken hand. One mule lay in a lifeless heap, still in its traces. Near the dead mule, a man lay in a puddle of blood. He wasn't moving.

The screams came from beneath the logs, where several men lay trapped, crushed, maniacal with fear and pain. Another man lay face-down, dangling arms and legs draped over one of the rough stubbled tree trunks. His head—

Garnet flinched, squeezed her eyes shut, and pressed a fist to her mouth to hold back the bile curdling in her throat. Roaring filled her head.

"God in heaven…" Mr. Rawls tried to take her arm, but Garnet shook him off.

"I'll be all right," she managed. "Go help. I'll…see about the others."

Behind her, one of the townsmen bent double and vomited. Felicity half screamed, then fled back toward the buggy. Garnet breathed deeply through her nose and gritted her teeth until her blurred vision stabilized. Then she lifted her skirts and ran toward the screams.

All about her men were shouting orders, swearing, calling for help, calling for bandages. Garnet scrambled around several logs, climbed over another, until she reached a couple of sweating men trying in vain to free one of the trapped loggers. Only his upper torso was visible. One arm strained upward toward a would-be rescuer, his hand curved claw-like, blindly grasping at the other man's shirt.

"Get me out!" he begged. Beneath the thick whiskers and beard his face glistened, pasty white and contorted with agony. "Get me out…" His other arm lay oddly motionless.

Garnet spotted a bloodied, jagged splinter protruding from just below his elbow, and with a barely suppressed gasp realized it was a bone. She chewed her inside lip until she tasted the coppery flavor of her own blood, but when one of the rescuers spied her and sharply ordered her away, she shook her head.

"I'll hold his hand. It might help calm him, until you can get him free."

"You're either an angel or a blamed fool."

Garnet squeezed around the two sweating men, her gaze fixed upon the wild-eyed logger. "Take my hand," she said. "What's your name? Tell me your name."

"Os—Oscar."

"All right, Oscar. Here, rest your head in my lap. No, I don't care about the blood. Now, take my hand…that's it. I know it hurts. Help will be here soon."

A hoarse sound, part sob and part groan, burst from his lips. His hand convulsed around hers with such force the pain streaked up her elbow, but Garnet smiled down into his glassy eyes. "Hold on," she whispered, and wiped the sweat-soaked hair off his forehead.

Her world was reduced to a two-foot circle, with Oscar the linch-pin. All around them a swarm of noise and activity buzzed—the sound of saws and shouting and snorting mules, chains clanking and booted feet thudding ceaselessly in the chewed-up earth. Movement on either side of her, the two men grunting with exertion, their gloved hands slipping on the branch-sheared surface of a log whose diameter spanned over two feet. The nauseous odors of oozing sap and spilled blood. The acrid smell of fear.

Abruptly Oscar screamed; his eyes rolled backward, and his head lolled sideways.

"Got it!" One of the rescuers shouted exultantly.

"Here, miss." A clean-shaven young man with a shock of white-blond hair dropped beside her. "We've freed him. Move away, now, so's we can carry him to safety." His admiring gaze caused a blush to suffuse Garnet's cheeks.

She sat without moving for a moment after they hefted the uncon-scious man from beneath the log and toted him away—broken arm dangling obscenely, lower body covered with blood. Her hand throbbed, and she realized in a sort of dim frustration that she was trem-bling. Shaking her head, she forced her numbed legs to move, though she had to brace herself against the log until the dancing black spots dis-appeared.

Farther down, she caught a glimpse of a black-and-yellow checked woolen shirt, and the back of a flapped cap. "There's someone else in here!" she called.

Nobody came. Heart thumping, Garnet scanned the scene. The narrow hollow swarmed with men, every last one of them frantically doing his best to aid the injured and to prevent the jumbled logs from shifting. There was nobody available. Nobody but Garnet in a position to help. *Lord? I don't know if I can.*

A strange feeling, like a soundless rushing wind, swirled around and through her. Calmness infused her, steadying her hands and imbuing her with fresh determination. Garnet kept her gaze on the bright shirt and thanked God in whispered wonder as she squirmed her way over to the trapped man.

Her courage faltered when she reached him and spied the blood gurgling from a deep wound in his chest. Something, perhaps a jagged stump of a branch, had torn through his shirt front, ripping it half away as it punctured skin…muscle… All Garnet could see was mangled flesh and blood. So much blood.

"Lord? Help me, please," she whispered. Feeling clumsy and stupid because she didn't know what to do, Garnet knelt beside the man. Her hands hovered uncertainly.

It was a small miracle of sorts that the logging cap he wore hadn't been knocked off. The flaps, she realized. The flaps could be used to help staunch the flow of blood. As carefully as she could, Garnet tugged the cap away, then slid her hands beneath his neck and turned his head.

The present shattered in an unvoiced scream, ripped away by a five-and-a-half-year-old nightmare.

She was looking into the face of a murderer.

Twenty-Seven

The man's eyelids fluttered, then lifted. He groaned and coughed, and a trickle of blood oozed from the corner of his mouth. Awareness dawned slowly. "You!" he struggled feebly against Garnet's hands before his body abruptly went slack. "Just let me die," he whispered. " 'Tis what I deserve."

Garnet tried to answer, her lips half parting in soundless denial.

A grimace deepened the pain-scored lines slashing the gaunt face. "Just...go away," he said. "You're safe. The man you saw...he was an...anarchist. Hired to—" He broke off, huge drops of sweat popping out on his brow. "We had...to stop him. We—"

"Don't talk," Garnet finally managed, but the words sounded as though a croaking stranger had spoken.

"Can't...die, not telling." He tried to take a breath, but fresh blood gushed from the wound, and his eyes rolled backward like Oscar's had.

Galvanized, Garnet jammed the earflap of his cap on top of the gaping hole. The man's body tautened like a bow. He groaned. Desperate, Garnet pressed, using the heel of one hand while with her other she tore at the long scarf fashioned in a bow around her neck.

She found herself praying, soft breathless snatches, inarticulate but breathed from the depths of her being. Her eyes stung, her arms began to quiver from the strain, her spine felt as though hot bricks were being piled one by one on top of her with crushing weight and searing heat.

Blood soaked through the cap. She tossed it aside, frantically used both hands to finish untying the stubborn scarf, then wadded it into a lump and pressed it against the still bleeding wound. How could a man still live and be losing blood like that?

"Hurts. God Almighty...hurts."

"I know it hurts. But I think I *have* to press. I'm sorry. You're still bleeding."

"Why?" He coughed again, groaned in pain. "I...stood by. That day."

Garnet forced her gaze away from his chest, and stared down into the cloudy confusion of his eyes. "You stopped the others, in the end. You didn't let them..." Hot color flooded her cheeks; it was idiotic of her to be squeamish, but she couldn't help it. "You prevented them from ruining me," she finished. "And you stopped them—they would have murdered me, after...along with that man."

"You were so young." His fingers twitched, but he was too weak now to lift his hand. "And...your hair. So beautiful. Sun caught it...the others...just wanted. But I—we had a daughter. Would have been your age back then." A single tear slid down, leaving a shiny trail in the dirt-smeared face. "She'd died, couple months before. I couldn't—couldn't let them..." His voice trailed away.

"Thank you," Garnet said.

The sense of wonder grew, filling her up, lending strength to her flagging muscles, cushioning her on a pillow of preternatural peace. She could do this, she thought. She could hang on, hang on until help arrived. The Lord had blessed her with a miracle, right here in the middle of death and destruction. He had heard her cry.

"What's your name?" she asked, hoping he was still conscious though his eyes had closed. "Mister? What's your name?"

"Critchley. Raymond...Critchley." His tongue passed over alarmingly blue-tinged lips. "Know you. Miss Sinclair. Known...for years."

"It's going to be all right, Mr. Critchley," Garnet promised. Perhaps later she would smile at God's sense of irony. "I'm not going to leave you. I promise."

"Angel," he whispered. His eyelids lifted, and he looked straight up into Garnet's face. "Red-haired angel." Beneath her hands his chest rose, fell. His eyes closed again.

"Mr. Critchley!"

There was no response. She wouldn't let go. *I'm not going to let him go, Lord.* Pressure. She had to stop the bleeding. That day, the day at the creek, she had helped to save Phineas, Sloan told her later, because she had staunched the flow of blood. God wouldn't save a fox but turn away a man…even if the man was a murderer… On the cross Jesus had forgiven a murderer, hadn't He? No…the man on the cross had been a thief. *Press, Garnet. Don't relax.* She ignored the pain, the cramps shooting up into her shoulders, her calves. She ignored the dizziness, the sickening swirl gathering momentum, the gleeful voices in her head telling her she couldn't hold on long enough, she was a doubter, God didn't help those who didn't trust Him…Mr. Critchley would die because of her. Justice, it was justice he deserved, not mercy.

Masculine hands appeared in front of her. Garnet blinked. The hands were attached to arms, stretched out on either side of her.

"Easy, Garnet. You're doing fine. Press here and here, just for a moment longer. You can do it, that's it."

Sloan's voice. Sloan's hands. Sloan's strength surrounding her, supporting her. *You can do it,* he'd said. So she did. And when more hands appeared, replacing her bloodied ones, when she was lifted up and away, she found herself gazing for a single second that spanned a river of demolished dreams into a pair of storm-cloud-gray eyes.

"Sloan…"

"I know." His index finger brushed her temple, her cheek. "I'll try not to hurt him. And I'll do my best to save his life. Don't worry." His smile was rich with memories. "I'm a doctor."

A sob spoiled her smile, but it was enough. Even as she allowed a burly man with muttonchop whiskers to steer her backward, out of the way, Sloan had dropped down beside Mr. Critchley. The man who had taken over for Garnet crawled onto the log, while a third man handed Sloan his medical bag.

Dr. MacAllister had returned.

For over an hour Sloan labored over Raymond Critchley. Ray Senior, father of the engaging Raymond who over the summer had spent hours between school and chores, helping Sloan with his home restoration. There were five other brothers and sisters, along with Mrs. Critchley. They needed their father; she needed her husband.

So he poured himself out, praying as he worked that Jesus' hands would take over, that the superior knowledge of the Great Physician would grant him skills beyond his own. Not because he was worthy—but because he had been restored. Because he was loved.

Not because Raymond Critchley—senior or junior—deserved it, but because God's love for all His children, the unregenerate as well as the restored, had no limits.

The afternoon light had deepened to autumn gold by the time a physician from Strasburg approached to offer assistance. Sloan finally drew a needed breath of relief. With devoted nursing care and God's continued mercy, Raymond Critchley should live. It would be safe now to relinquish him into another's doctor's care. But Sloan wouldn't. Couldn't, until he'd determined that he was turning Mr. Critchley over to a bona fide physician, not an incompetent hack who still believed in archaic rituals such as bleeding a patient who'd already lost a pint through no wish of his own.

He ran a swift look over the other doctor, who was making his way toward Sloan and the injured man through a narrow path that had been cleared in the past hour. The long black cutaway coat and striped gray trousers might be a tad affected under the circumstances, but Sloan was relieved by the intelligence he read in the bluff features. "He's unconscious but stable. I've closed the wound, administered two cc's of morphine borate via hypodermic injection for pain, also amyl nitrite to stabilize the heart. Set the broken leg—a simple fracture of the tibia fortunately."

"How's the breathing? Can he be moved?" As he spoke, the Strasburg doctor fixed a stethoscope to his ears. "May I?" Belatedly he paused, glanced at Sloan. "Ah, name's Hanover, by the way. Dr. Terence Hanover."

"Sloan MacAllister." A wry smile flickered at one corner of his mouth. "*Dr.* Sloan MacAllister. Pleased to meet you, Hanover."

"Likewise. Heard about you, you know." He knelt beside Sloan and leaned over Raymond Critchley. "This man was fortunate to have you nearby."

"He was more fortunate than you realize, and I had little to do with it."

Weariness descended, shackling his limbs in heavy chains. Sloan stood, staggered, and thanked the man who'd been helping him with Critchley—a bricklayer from town named Milt. Milt loped off to fetch help with loading Mr. Critchley onto a wagon with the other injured. After Hanover finished his examination, Sloan discussed various prognoses and courses of treatment while he cleaned up as best he could with the torn sleeve of someone's donated jacket.

"If you don't mind a fellow professional's opinion, you need to share the load, so to speak, Dr. MacAllister," Hanover observed finally. "You look as though a couple of these logs rolled over *you*. Go. Rest. I'll see to your patients. From what I've heard, there's a fair number of very lucky men here today." His gaze slid beyond Sloan, toward a large chestnut tree whose leaves were tipped with autumn gold. "What in blazes are two women doing here?"

"Don't know about one of them," Sloan replied. "But the redhaired lady saved this man's life. I'm on my way over there to thank her right now." Among other things.

"Hmm. You don't say. Must be an extraordinary woman…"

"Yes, she is."

Hanover rested a hand on Sloan's shoulder, giving it a friendly squeeze. "Go on, man. Quit hovering. Or haven't I convinced you yet that I won't kill the patients you labored so skillfully to save?"

They shook hands, and Sloan headed across the sweep of stubbled grasses. Behind him pink and orange smears of color stained the deep blue sky. His path to the chestnut tree led him into a bar of golden sunlight. It poured over the meadow, almost as though lighting his way…to Garnet.

Sloan's weariness lifted with every step. All he could see now was Garnet, all he could think about now was the look on her face when she'd seen him.

It was going to be all right, wasn't it?

He paid scant attention to the other woman, a robust brunette with blazing blue eyes and a greenish cast to her skin. From the look of her, doubtless she had spent the past hours cowering in a buggy. Probably the artist—he couldn't recall her name. She seemed to be trying to persuade Garnet to leave but turned when she heard Sloan's approach.

"Ah. At last, the famous Dr. MacAllister." She stepped forward, blocking his view of Garnet. "Since conditions couldn't be *less* proper, I'll introduce myself. Mrs. Felicity Ward. I've been longing for an introduction, Dr.—"

"Excuse me, Mrs. Ward." Sloan ignored the outstretched hand, stepped around her, and stopped directly in front of Garnet. "How are you doing?" he asked, his hands twitching with the need to hold her.

Over the past hour she'd made an attempt to pin her hair back into a neat roll, but several tangled strands hung limply about her face and neck. Her clothing, like his, was bloodied beyond repair. The blank, shattered expression in her eyes alarmed him.

"How is Mr. Critchley?"

Her soft voice sounded hollow, and she kept wiping her hands with a red-stained handkerchief, over and over as though she didn't realize what she was doing.

Sloan stepped closer, setting his bag on the ground. Very gently he lifted both her hands, tossed aside the crumpled linen square and captured her restless fingers in his own. "You saved his life. He's going to live, Garnet. Barring complications, of course," he added with a doctor's caution.

"For heaven's sake, can we spare the postmortems?" Mrs. Ward said. "Garnet, you see? The man's fine. I am not. I've never been so…so *revolted*, in my entire life." She glanced at the handkerchief Sloan had tossed to the ground. "All that blood…the screams—it's been unbearable."

Sloan put a firm arm around Garnet. Her slender form felt boneless, but she refused to lean against him. He frowned, grappling with the implications. "Mrs. Ward. I need to make sure Miss Sinclair is all right. Excuse us."

"Well, that's plain enough." The woman's lips thinned. She pressed two gloved fingers against her temple, then expelled her breath in an impatient sigh. "I'll wait in the buggy. But I will point out that I've *been* waiting. And in case you haven't noticed, it will be dark in an hour." She flounced off.

Sloan focused on Garnet. "I want you to sit down. Your pulse is a bit sluggish…" He studied her. "You're still a bit shocky, I'm thinking."

"Don't want to sit." She offered him a small smile. "Won't be able to rise."

"Then I'll help you." He got her down, propped her against the trunk of the tree, then carefully arranged her skirt over her stockinged feet. "I see you're still up to your favorite habit of removing your shoes," he murmured. He couldn't help it, his fingers reached with a mind of their own to brush a bright lock of hair away from her cheek. "Don't move. I'll be right back."

When he returned a few moments later, he brought along a canteen, a collapsible metal cup, and a clean rag from one of the other wagons that had arrived earlier to help. He'd taken time to thoroughly wash his own hands, but nothing else. He'd also requested that the swarm of curious bystanders maintain a respectful distance.

"Here we go. Let's clean you up a bit more, hmm? Don't worry. My back will provide a screen of sorts, and Mr. Rawls will keep the crowd away. Try to relax. Did you know everyone's calling you the red-haired angel of mercy?"

He kept up the rambling flow while he poured water into the cup and handed it to her. He wasn't surprised when she couldn't fold her fingers around it. Matter-of-factly he held the cup to her lips instead.

"Sorry," Garnet said after swallowing a few sips. "It's just that…" her voice trailed off.

"It's all right. You're worn out." As he spoke he poured more water onto the rag. Then he carefully wiped her face and hands, even folded back the blood-stiffened cuffs of her shirtwaist to bathe her wrists. "I wish I could find words to tell you how much I admire what you did. You saved Mr. Critchley's life, Garnet."

"Sloan…?"

"Feel a little better?" He smiled into her eyes, hiding his mounting concern at her lethargy. She'd battled so valiantly, with a heart-swelling gallantry and grace that brought a lump to his throat. He loved her more deeply than he had words to describe…yet she somehow seemed to be slipping away from him.

Was this—this lethargy a mental shield erected against *him* instead of her body's defense against the carnage she'd witnessed? The possibility burst over Sloan, rattling him so thoroughly he lost his composure. "Garnet, it's all right. Everything's all right. You've got to believe me. We need to have a talk, you and I. There are things I need to share, things—" He shut his mouth, wanting to bang his fool head against the tree trunk. He was behaving like an insensitive clod.

"Mr. Critchley's one of the men."

"Yes. The one whose life you saved." He kept his voice gentle, in stark contrast to his private self-denunciation. "I can't begin to tell you how proud—"

"He's one of the men I saw. That day. Five years ago."

If she'd fired a bullet into his gut, Sloan couldn't have been more surprised. "What?"

"Mr. Critchley…saved me." Suddenly her eyes were swimming. "He's the man who wouldn't let the others h-hurt me."

"God. God in heaven." *What have You done to me?* He couldn't take it in, couldn't grasp that he'd just battled to save the life of one of the gutter trash, conscienceless murderers who had almost destroyed Garnet's life. "I'm going after him." Pure rage catapulted him to his feet. "Whether he lives or dies, he's going to jail. I don't care if he bleeds to death, I don't care—"

"Don't, Sloan."

She was trying to rise. Sloan grabbed her and hauled her close. He didn't care who witnessed the embrace. "Sweetheart, don't be afraid. I won't let anything happen to you. You're safe. I'll protect you, I promise—"

Damp fingers pressed against his mustache and lips, stemming the heedless words. He had hardly realized it was her hand before she pulled it away.

"He never wanted to hurt me, Sloan."

"Never wanted to hurt you?" Shaken by his rage as much as Garnet's intimate gesture, Sloan shook his head. Denial. Disbelief. The overwhelming compulsion to protect. Yet Garnet was straining away from him, and he realized abruptly that his hold was too tight. He forced his fingers to relax their grip, but he couldn't release her. "Garnet, the fear of what he and those men threatened to do to you and your family has dominated your life since you were sixteen years old." The other men, he thought, his panic rising. *Where were the other men?*

A single tear slipped down her cheek. "I know. But you were right. That ridiculous bonnet never fooled anyone except me. Mr. Critchley knew all along. He never wanted to hurt me," she repeated. "He said…that day, I think I reminded him of his own daughter. Sloan… don't look like that. Please."

"I can't help it. I love you."

Beneath his hands he felt her stiffen. Sloan closed his eyes. *God, I'm sorry. Sorry.*

"You…love me? How can you love me? You left me, I haven't heard from you since the day we—" She stopped.

A muscle in his jaw jumped. It had been easier to face Kristen Jorvik, humbly confessing his sin, than it was to reopen his eyes and face Garnet. But he had no choice. "I shouldn't have said it—no! Don't struggle. Please. I didn't mean what you're thinking. I only meant I hadn't planned to tell you yet, not under these circumstances."

She stood there, stiff and still, eyes dark. He couldn't read their expression. This time, it was painfully obvious that she'd closed herself off to him. And he couldn't bear it. "Garnet, let me take you home. Let me explain. Please."

"I don't think—"

"I've remembered why your name is so familiar." Mrs. Ward blind-sided him, so focused had Sloan been on reaching Garnet that he hadn't noticed the other woman's return until it was too late. "You're from Baltimore, right? One of the Daniel MacAllister sons—the youngest, I believe?"

The chill of winter sleet iced Sloan's spine. Slowly he forced himself to drop Garnet's arm, to face Mrs. Ward. The purveyor of his destruction. "Yes. I'm Daniel MacAllister's youngest son."

Mrs. Ward nodded. Satisfaction, and a spark of sympathy, gleamed in the worldly blue eyes. "I have friends in Baltimore—stayed with them last winter. The town was full of gossip over the death of, I believe it was Thomas, your middle brother. He killed himself, didn't he? Over an illicit liaison with your…yes. It was your fiancée, wasn't it?"

Beside him, Garnet inhaled, a soft sharp sound. Sloan sensed more than saw her involuntary recoil, and there was nothing, nothing on earth or in heaven he could do to shield her from the awful truth. He'd planned to tell her, had spent the last days setting the stage in his mind. He'd explain everything—his past, his restoration. His love. He hadn't wanted to hide anything from her. But he had wanted to choose the time, the place.

It was inevitable that the sins of a man would ultimately be exposed to the light. Unfortunately, seldom were they exposed at the sinner's convenience.

His lips bared in a savage smile. "Yes. My brother Tom committed suicide." He speared Mrs. Ward with a look that dared her to drop her gaze. "He broke into my pharmacy, ingested a handful of every powder and pill he found. And after he went mad from the self-induced toxicosis, he finished the job with a scalpel."

There was little satisfaction in watching the artist turn pale. Little triumph when her gaze dropped, and a flush climbed into her cheeks. As though in a dream Sloan turned to Garnet. He watched his hand stretch toward her, drop. "I'm sorry," he whispered. "It wasn't supposed to happen like this…"

Then, still moving in the same dreamlike state, he walked away.

Twenty-Eight

*G*arnet watched Sloan's retreating figure, feeling as though her body didn't belong to her. Instead of the iciness, her blood churned, bubbling and hot, like a pot of Leah's soup boiling over. Instead of frozen immobility, she wanted to…to lash out. To physically *hurt* someone.

No, not just someone. Felicity Ward.

The powerful, strange feelings consumed her, all thoughts of Raymond Critchley momentarily banished. She turned the force of those feelings on her target. "How *could* you? You ought to be ashamed. Ashamed! Do you ever think of anyone but yourself, Felicity? Have you ever in your entire self-absorbed life considered that other people were not created for your benefit? You hurt Sloan." She pointed a shaking finger toward his diminishing figure. "You *hurt* him. Shamed him—"

"Enough. Goodness, Garnet. I can't believe my eyes! Look at you— oh, very well. I apologize, for my unwelcome intrusion as well as my insensitivity."

"I'm not the one who needs the apology."

"I can see that." She seemed to hesitate, and between one blink and the next, Garnet realized why: The confident, patronizing woman was… intimidated. By Garnet.

Well. Good.

"I'd begun to think you really didn't have the temper to match the hair," Felicity said.

"I didn't, until now. I'm tempted to get carried away by the novelty of it." Garnet swept a furious glance over Felicity's pristine appearance. "Tell me all the other tidbits of gossip about Sloan that you've withheld—the ones you savor in private until an occasion where you can inflict the most damage."

Felicity's chin angled. "You have no right to speak to me like that. Why do you want to know anyway? I'd think we both heard quite enough of the sordid details."

"My reasons are none of your concern." She folded her arms.

Felicity's mouth curved in a brittle smile. "Fine. It isn't much. And I didn't mention anything before because, until five minutes ago, I didn't make the connection." She paused. "I'm not sure I care overmuch for this…belligerent Garnet."

"She's becoming more so…"

"Oh, do calm down, girl. You're weaving on your feet, in case you haven't realized it. Losing one's temper tends to be very exhausting."

Sighing, Felicity lifted a pacifying hand and started talking. "The MacAllisters are a fine old family, roots go back to pre-Revolutionary days, according to my friends in Baltimore. Their estate is purported to be magnificent—dignified Georgian, all brick. Landscaping by Mr. Frederick Olmstead's firm, I believe. I'd love to paint it. I suppose I've ruined any chance of fulfilling that desire."

Garnet made a sound that reminded her of Phineas growling.

Felicity stepped back, a quick, satisfying retreat. "Yes, well…I don't know much else. Sloan's father is dead, and the eldest son lives in the family home with his wife and children and the widowed mother. My friends claim it is an unpleasant atmosphere. The eldest son's a stuffy, pompous sort, and it seems his wife despises him. The mother's become a recluse of sorts—the scandal of her son's death, you understand—"

Abruptly she stopped, and something like a wince passed across her face. "She blamed the youngest son"—her voice rose—"told him to his face he was a murderer, and she never wanted to see him again. It was Sloan…all this time, it was your Dr. MacAllister."

"Why would his mother blame *him?*" Stunned, Garnet tried and failed to imagine the trauma Sloan must have endured from the repudiation by his own family. "You said the brother killed himself. That's not Sloan's fault." Frantically she searched the hill behind Felicity. Her heart jumped, a hard painful twist against her ribs. There was no sign of Sloan. "He probably wasn't even there. Regardless, under the circumstances"—*betrayed by his fiancée*—"how could he be blamed?"

But whether or not he had been there, he would blame himself. His bottomless compassion, his vow before God to heal… Why couldn't his family see the wounded soul of this man? No wonder he was bitter. All these months he'd been carrying an intolerable load, and Garnet hadn't known. She'd foisted all her pain, her past onto his broad shoulders, and he hadn't complained. His own mother had denounced him, Jenna had betrayed him—but Sloan hadn't turned his back on Garnet. And that day, the day he'd kissed her, when he'd been trying to open his wounded heart to her, she'd been so afraid of her own feelings she hadn't considered how vulnerable Sloan had made himself.

She was no better than Felicity.

He'd told her that he loved her. And she'd stood there like a scarecrow.

"I've shared everything I know about it," Felicity said. "Can we please go now? The next time I see the poor man, I promise to deliver a fulsome apology."

Her facile remorse sparked Garnet's newfound temper. "Just a moment. I need to put on my shoes."

She stuffed her feet in the unlaced boots, fastened them, and stood up. She smiled at the other woman. Then she leaned down, swept up the canteen—still half full—and calmly upended it over Felicity's head. Felicity shrieked, hands flailing in useless protest. When the canteen was empty, Garnet slung the strap over Felicity's soaked shoulder. "I'm afraid you'll have to find another ride home. You seem to have gotten yourself all wet, and I don't want to ruin the fabric on the buggy seat. Besides…I have someone I need to see before I go home." She lifted her skirts and ran, her gaze on the brow of the hill. He was gone…but if she hurried, perhaps she could catch him before it was too late.

Goatsbeard, rested now and adept at cross-country excursions, leaped without protest into a canter the instant she jiggled the reins. The buggy jolted up the hill, its springs groaning in protest. Garnet gripped the reins firmly, her gaze trained on the lone rider headed for a patch of woods at the foot of the meadow. Shadows had lengthened, veiling the air. Sunset was only moments away. "Sloan!" Useless to call of course, he'd never hear. But she screamed his name anyway, over and over.

A wheel glanced off a large stone. The buggy lurched, bouncing so hard Garnet's head smacked the roof. She fought for control, though her fatigued muscles possessed the strength of wilted flower stalks. Goatsbeard stumbled, almost jerking the reins from her hands. Wind whipped through her hair, tearing the last of the pins until the mass unfurled, spilling into her face, over her shoulders, blinding her. She clutched the slippery reins with one hand while the other swiped at her hair. *"Sloan!"*

Just before the woods swallowed him, she saw Dulcie half rear and swivel around. The mare whinnied, and Garnet saw Goatsbeard's ears prick forward. With the last of her shredding strength she slowed the horse to a trot. Sloan started back up the hill toward her, emerging from the purple shadows into a fiery spear of sunlight that streamed across the earth. They met fifty yards from the woods. Behind them, the mountains swallowed the sun, shrouding the meadow in misty lavender.

Sloan leaped from the saddle and snatched her out of the buggy. Beneath his fading summer tan his face was pale, set in harsh lines. "You little idiot!" He wrapped his arms around her, smothering her against his chest. "You could have killed yourself!"

His heart thundered in her ear. Garnet tried to speak, but the words clogged in her throat, and all she could do was cling. Then his hand was burrowing beneath the wild mass of hair, closing over her neck. Hard fingers slid up her throat, cupped her chin, and lifted her head.

His mouth descended, and he kissed her with a wild fervor that turned her world to a sparking Catherine wheel.

Only when his lips softened, drifted to her cheeks, her temples, and finally her closed eyelids, did Garnet realize she was weeping.

"Shh…" He murmured to her, soothing words whose meaning was unintelligible but whose tone filled her with comfort. With peace.

Eventually she managed to worm one of her hands between them, pressing it against the warm spot between his beard-stubbled chin and neck, where a vein pumped strong and sure against her fingers. She could no more control the slow tears soaking her face than she could still the fine trembling that seized her limbs.

Without warning Sloan swept her up into his arms.

"Wh-what are you doing?"

"I'm carrying you." Some unsettling emotion seethed beneath the terse words. "Into the woods, before we're interrupted by anyone else."

Tremulous, Garnet laid her head against the bunched muscles of his shoulder. "That sounds ominous. What about the horses?"

Without pausing Sloan whistled, a low but melodious sound. Dulcie ambled over, following them just as Phineas followed Garnet across the yard. Goatsbeard plodded along behind them.

"Is there anything you can't do?" Garnet murmured into his neck, half to herself.

She wasn't too surprised when Sloan answered, "Arrange the circumstances of my life."

They entered the woods, and he gently set her down. His hands caged her shoulders in a deceptively light clasp—Garnet sensed his tension and held herself still.

"Papa's going to worry, you know. Especially now."

"I do know that. We won't be here but a moment." He pulled a long breath, his hands kneading her shoulders with restless fingers. "Why did you chase after me like that?" he finally asked. "You could have been injured, could have been killed. Garnet?" His voice roughened, and abruptly he stepped back and pressed his fists over his eyes.

"You were hurting. I couldn't bear it." She shivered in the gathering darkness. "Sloan, what Felicity said—I'm sorry. Not because of what she said, but because of how it affected you. That's why you came down here to the Valley, isn't it? You needed to escape. To heal."

"Forget it. It's not important right now."

"Yes, it is. Your brother's death wasn't your fault. Even if you were there—"

"I was in Adlerville. Someday, I'll tell you about it. Garnet, it doesn't matter." His hand lifted in a jerky motion, dropped back to his side. He still wouldn't look at her. "Did you risk your life chasing after me just because you felt sorry for me?"

The careful tonelessness of the question made her wince. Immersed in her own insecurities, she'd forgotten that—inconceivable as it seemed—Sloan was almost as vulnerable to her as she was to him.

"There's a difference," she told him quietly, "between pity, and…and hurting along with someone you…care about very much." Sloan went still, so still she couldn't even hear him breathing. She hurried on. "Beyond that, I was afraid if I didn't follow you immediately I might never have the chance to ask you a question. It's a selfish question, perhaps, under the circumstances, but it's important to me. Perhaps, to both of us, if you—" She was stammering, incoherent, but pride no longer mattered. "I wanted to ask you a question," she repeated.

His head lifted. "What question? If it's about what I said earlier, before that, that woman—"

"I wanted to ask why you think my father put a cardinal feather in the secret drawer of my heartwood chest," she interrupted before she lost her courage. "I've never understood. I-I love flowers, you see. Always have. And Papa told me…he told me," she had to moisten her lips, had to twine her hands together to keep them still, "that someday a man, a special man would discover that drawer. He'd understand, about the feather, because this man"—her voice broke—"would understand…me."

Shadows…too many shadows, in the forest, in her heart. She couldn't see Sloan's face and yet…and yet…was he *smiling* at her?

Doubt and fear swooped about her like barn swallows. *Lord? If You hear me, I need to understand.* "I know, the cardinal feather is red, just like my hair. But I hate my hair, and I don't even like birds. And after that summer, I was convinced that God was punishing me, that I'd never meet a man like that. A man who would…"

"Love you," Sloan finished. He combed his fingers through the tangled wildness of her hair, his touch tender. "This hair whose color you hate—remember when Jacob told me you dyed it once?"

She nodded, unable to speak.

"Even if you'd succeeded, when your hair grew out it would always be red. Wouldn't it?" He lifted a handful of strands and tickled her nose with the ends. Then he took her face in his hands. "Like a cardinal's feathers. Because that's how God created cardinals, and that's how God created you, my darling. Did you know that the deeper red a male cardinal's feather is, the easier it is to attract a mate? All part of the divine design. God cares about the cardinals as well as the sparrows, and He cares about you, Garnet Sinclair. In fact, He loves you far more than He does those birds."

"I know that," she whispered, but a blush heated her cheeks when Sloan's response was a soft laugh.

"You know it in your head." His thumbs brushed her temples, caressing circles that intensified the heat of her burning cheeks. "But you've had a little more trouble accepting it in your heart. That's what your father and I talked about, one memorable evening. But God loves you for who you are, red hair, freckles, doubts, and all."

Now his head dipped so he could brush a featherlike kiss across her trembling lips. "And God's nature is like that cardinal's red feather. Unchanging. Unchangeable. His love, His compassion—His forgiveness will never fail you, Garnet. What I believe Jacob has prayed for you, all these years, is that one day you'll stop fighting yourself. That you'll accept who you are, hair color, doubts, 'wild nature,' and all. I'm praying for that as well, you see."

His hands slid down to her wrists, and he held her a little ways back. Deepening shadows veiled his face to an indistinct blur, but the power of his words bathed her in radiance. "Because if you can accept with your heart as well as your head how very beautiful you are in God's eyes, I'm hoping that you'll be able to accept how very beautiful you are to me. And sweetheart, if you were bald and cross-eyed, you'd still be beautiful to me."

Garnet whispered his name, half in wonder, half a prayerful plea.

"I'm praying that you'll accept my love. Freely. Without conditions or reservations." Now his thumbs were stroking the insides of her wrists. Beneath his mustache she glimpsed a flash of white teeth. "God's been teaching me a few things as well. About timing, and choices. So I won't pressure you. I can wait for Him to help heal your heart, the way He healed mine."

His smile turned wry. "No doubt I'll never wait as patiently as the Lord, I'm sorry to say. But I will wait. Because I love you."

"I don't think," Garnet managed, lifting her arms to him, "that you'll have to wait for very long." She drew his head down and told him with her kiss what she wasn't able to tell him in words.

Twenty-Nine

*T*en days later, accompanied by gray drizzle and lowering clouds that obscured the mountains, Garnet and Sloan paid a visit to Raymond Critchley. His condition, according to the Strasburg doctor who had agreed to take over his care, was still critical, but the prognosis remained hopeful.

Garnet stayed in the hallway with Mrs. Critchley while Sloan and Dr. Hanover conferred over the patient's bedside. It was very strange, she thought while she waited without speaking beside the anxious woman, whose heavy moon-shaped face was haggard with exhaustion. Throughout the ride from Sinclair Run to the Critchleys' house on the edge of Tom's Brook, she had been twitchy with nerves, monosyllabic even with Sloan. He'd finally ceased his efforts to distract her with conversation and simply wrapped a bracing arm around her shoulders.

When they arrived at the big old frame house, six desperately grateful, desperately ashamed faces waited for them in stilted silence. One by one the younger children—prompted by their mother—mumbled strained thank-yous. Raymond Junior, however, looked her straight in the eye. After thanking her, he grabbed a coat and cap from the hall tree. "I have to work." He crammed the cap over his white-blond hair. "Right now, I'm the man of the family." He paused, then added slowly, "But I'm not wanting it to stay that way."

"You mind your manners, Ray Bob. This ain't your say-so."

Why…they were afraid that she might be bent on vengeance, Garnet realized in dawning amazement. The Critchleys needed her absolution as much as she needed to reconcile the present with the past. With that realization, the knot in her stomach at last began to unravel. Her twitching nerves calmed. And the nebulous peace that had first touched her the day she knelt over a blood-soaked Mr. Critchley drifted back inside.

Yes, it was strange how God's grace covered her even when she couldn't find the words to ask for it.

"Don't reckon I can ever repay what you done for my man," Mrs. Critchley said suddenly. Her fleshy hands twisted in the folds of her apron, and she kept her gaze glued to the closed door. "But I'm grateful for what you did, Miss Sinclair. Particularly when…what I mean to say is"—her mouth worked, and her hands crushed the apron—"Raymond's not a bad man. I got to tell you that. A hard man, some might say, but he's done the best he could by us. We ain't never gone hungry, even when the mine closed down all them years back."

The mine closed, Sloan had told Garnet and Jacob, after the union brought in thugs to settle grievances between workers and an intractable management. Raymond Critchley had apparently uncovered a plot to blow up the mine, but instead of going to the authorities, Critchley and his gang of cohorts—equally reprehensibly—took matters into their own hands. The rest of the details were sketchy. All Sloan had been able to dig up was that the murdered man was one of the union thugs. Garnet wondered if Mrs. Critchley herself could fill in missing details. But with her husband barely hanging on to life in the next room, she was unwilling to broach the subject.

Garnet smiled. "Dr. MacAllister's the one who deserves your thanks." She smiled. Part of grace, she was learning, was the urge to pass some of it along.

"I've said my piece to the doc. But all the same, he ain't the one I'm grateful to."

The door opened, and Dr. Hanover gestured for them to come in. Garnet went immediately to Sloan, who was waiting at the head of the iron bedstead. His level gaze warned her, but Garnet still barely stifled a shocked gasp. Though she had last seen him injured and helpless, she remembered more vividly the man from her nightmares—a big, robust man with a full beard and iron-gray hair. This Raymond Critchley resembled a corpse, with folds of sagging skin drooping about a gaunt face. His hair was more white than gray, and the beard had been shaved.

His hands lay motionless on top of the quilt. Eyes cloudy with pain and medication fluttered open when his wife leaned to speak in his ear.

"Just a few moments," Dr. Hanover warned.

"Got visitors," Mrs. Critchley spoke, raising her voice. She pulled up a wooden chair and sat, taking his hand and holding it in hers. " 'Tis Miss Sinclair, and Doc MacAllister, come to see how you're faring."

The cloudy gaze flickered, searched, and found Garnet. His cracked, colorless lips moved. A light breath seemed to shudder from his lungs. "Thought…you were an angel," he whispered.

"I'm not." Garnet felt Sloan's hand on her shoulder, gently squeezing. "I'm glad you're alive. Your family needs you, so you have to fight to recover your strength."

His head moved a little, and a grimace of pain deepened the harsh lines furrowing either side of his nose. "Reckon you came to—" He tried to take another breath, and droplets of sweat formed on his temples and brow.

"I'm afraid you'll have to leave," Dr. Hanover began, but Critchley's hoarse denial wrung a worried sound from his wife and a scowl from Dr. Hanover.

Sloan was trying to draw Garnet away, but she covered the hand pulling her shoulder with her own. "We'll leave as soon as I reassure Mr. Critchley." She glanced across the bed. "Don't worry. Your husband is safe. I promise you, Mrs. Critchley, I mean your husband no harm."

"But we must know about the other men," Sloan's quiet voice intruded, the inflexible iron tone so unusual Garnet swiveled her head to search his face. "Because I need to ensure that my fiancée is safe as well."

"Ah." The deep lines faded marginally, and Mr. Critchley's cracked lips peeled in the hint of a smile. "Understand…"

"MacAllister, I appreciate what you're going through, but as a physician, you must know that this man does not need to be talking."

"Then stop hindering him."

"Dr. Hanover, I believe Mr. Critchley's recovery will be accomplished more quickly if the two of us can reassure ourselves about a matter," Garnet said before Sloan's protectiveness swelled to downright bullying. She held the injured man's gaze. "I don't plan to press charges, and neither does Dr. MacAllister. It's all in the past, Mr. Critchley. Ever since last week, I've come to better understand what the Bible means when it counsels us to let the dead bury the dead."

She surreptitiously wiped her hands on her skirt. "We shouldn't live in the past. We definitely can't undo it. We might even have to pay for mistakes we made. But we can learn from those mistakes and apply those lessons to make the present better. What you do with your con-science is between you and God, Mr. Critchley. Same as me. If you turn yourself in, do it because you know it's the right thing to do—not because of me. All I need to know—all Dr. MacAllister and I need to know, " she amended with a quick backward glance—"is whether I'm in any danger from the men who helped you."

"No." Another grimace of pain crossed his face. "God as my wit-ness...no."

Dr. Hanover strode around to the other side of the bed, checked his patient's pulse, then patted the back of Mrs. Critchley's hand. With a silent look of censure he reached for a stoppered bottle of medicine on a bedside table.

"Two dead—Jack...Grubber. Mine cave-in. Four...years ago." He swallowed the spoonful of medicine, and for a few seconds his eyes closed. Then: "Shelley...left. Heard couple years ago...he was out west. Won't never...come back." His eyes opened again, fixed on Garnet with feverish intensity. "You're safe. I'll...turn myself in, when I can."

Mrs. Critchley paled, but there was no surprise in the red-rimmed eyes.

This time, when Dr. Hanover ordered them to leave, Garnet and Sloan obeyed. Sloan murmured a thank-you to the other doctor as they reached the bedroom door. Garnet turned, her hand lifting a farewell wave to Mrs. Critchley. But the woman's head was bowed, all her atten-tion on her husband.

The door shut behind them with a quiet click, and Garnet and Sloan descended the stairs in a reflective silence, unbroken even after Sloan joined her in his buggy. It was no longer raining, though the gray day hung cold and wet around them. The only sound was water drip-ping from the eaves of the roof.

For a long moment Sloan sat without speaking, his head turned toward the Critchleys' house. Garnet waited, content to float in the quiet, sunlit pool of God's enduring peace.

Then Sloan's shoulders lifted. He turned to face her. "Now that we've laid your past to rest"—smiling, he cupped her chin in one large hand—"I think it's time to settle the matter of your future."

"Well," Garnet replied, "I wonder if I need to warn you about my temper…"

"Can't be worse than mine."

Her heart was full because of what shone out of Sloan's eyes, because of the sunlight filling her up. "Then there's this lecture tour. I heard that Felicity left four days ago. I suppose I could telegraph her and ask—"

His mouth covered hers, and Garnet forgot about teasing, forgot about her surroundings…forgot about everything but the indescribable joy of being loved by this man.

A man who looked at her like her father used to look at her mother.

Part II

MEREDITH

Interlude

*R*ain clouds smothered Great North Mountain, tarnishing the late afternoon sky. His gaze indulgent, Jacob stood on the side porch, flat cap pushed to the back of his head, elbows propped up on the railing. A good autumn soaker, he thought as he savored the cedar-rich moistness of the air. That's what the valley needed to fill the runs and ponds again.

He glanced down, where the second heartwood chest—this one Meredith's—sat at his feet, waiting for him to clean it up and restore its luster. Since moving away, she brought it back home every couple of months, on his request. As Jacob feared, once again the chest was covered with dust, the wood dry. Ah, Merry-go-round…so busy chasing after life she hadn't learned how to live it.

Jacob's mouth quirked in a rueful smile. His eldest daughter's project was Garnet's wedding, the end of October. *Meredith does have the energy of the sun, doesn't she, Lord?* Unlike her father at the moment. He ought to be about his own work, not dreaming up on the porch.

" 'Tis my favorite spot in all the world," Mary used to say. Jacob straightened, resettled his cap. Mary, God rest her blessed soul, would have scolded him for sure, dawdling out here like a blatherskite.

The fragrance of fresh-from-the-oven bread drifted to the porch, tweaking his nose. Jacob's mouth began to water. When she wasn't wandering or drawing, Garnet was almost as dab a hand in the kitchen as Leah. And his Leah was the best cook 'twixt Winchester and Lexington, no matter that his youngest's heart was set on schooling and had been since she was old enough to scribble on a slate.

Jacob chuckled suddenly. He wondered how long it would be before Meredith decided that *she* needed to go to college. His eldest did want to be the best at everything. That competitive streak, along with her impetuous nature, tended to fling her into trouble. Like the time his soft heart and her misguided stubbornness landed him near death's door because she'd been that determined to have things her own way, no matter what her sisters—or her father—wanted or needed. She never meant to cause hurt—he well remembered that her desire had been to please her papa. Of course, for Meredith, if it was convenient to please herself at the same time, so much the better.

It had been while he was recovering from a bout with the ulcer, he remembered, that he'd settled on the special object to place in Meredith's heirloom chest. Shoulders propped against the corner column, his thoughts drifted again, back a score of years...*no*. She was, heaven help him, she was twenty-three now, well into spinsterhood. She'd been about nine then, already headstrong, determined as the oldest daughter to replace Mary in spite of her tender years.

All three girls had been baking that day, and like today it had been a damp autumn afternoon. But it hadn't been bread—it had been gingerbread...

❦

...cookies. Tension began to coil inside. So that's what had been keeping the girls out of his hair this gray September day.

Ah yes. His girls—they'd grown so fast. Great heaven above, Meredith was nine her last birthday, and Garnet not far behind. Even Leah at age six was losing the last of her baby fat. And they worked so hard to please him, all of them trying to make up for the loss of their mother, his wife.

Resolutely ignoring his worry over the gingerbread, he headed for his workshop.

An hour later high-pitched yells from inside the house interrupted his work, and Jacob clicked his tongue as he laid the chisel aside. What would they be fighting over now, the wee gilpeys? He swiped his hands on the stained apron, then stepped outside his workshop and whistled, an ear-piercing shriek audible a quarter-mile away.

Loud enough to capture even the attention of three quarreling girls.

As always, Meredith tumbled through the front door first, her pixy-ish form swathed in one of Mary's old aprons, her face dusted with flour. "I brought you your favorite cookies!" Hazel eyes dancing, she waved the plate stacked high with gingerbread girls beneath Jacob's nose.

"Meredith…"

"I promise, they're good—lots better than the ones we made over the summer." She plucked the top cookie and held it poised at his mouth. "They're good because I measured everything while Garnet stirred."

Jacob had to smile. "Ah. And Leah?"

"She's cleaning up. She hates a mess." Meredith shrugged. "Hurry and take a bite, Papa! I left a batch in the oven but Leah might forget, and Garnet's mad at me so she might let them burn on purpose."

"Slow down, Merry-go-round." Stalling, he tried for a stern look. "And why would Garnet be mad at you, hmm?"

She planted flour-coated fists on her matchstick waist, and gave Jacob one of her all-right-but-only-because-I-choose-to-answer glares. "Garnet says you'd rather have Powhatan Rolls. Leah wants both—well, I know she really wants cookies but Garnet says that doesn't count 'cause Leah's only six, so—"

She paused for breath, and Jacob laid his index finger across the rosebud lips. "You know Doc Porter warned me about my sweet tooth, the last time I had that bad tummy ache?"

Round green-gold eyes shimmered with uncertainty. "Dr. Porter said it was diz—dizpeppery—I heard him."

"Listening at the door again, were you?"

The tears slid down her flour-dusted cheeks. An easy weeper was his Meredith. "It was open." She threw herself into his arms. "They're your gingerbread cookies, with the special cookie cutter, the one Mama always—"

Jacob kissed the uneven part in her hair, hugged her tight. "I know…I know. Your mama used to treat that cookie cutter like it was made of silver instead of tin, didn't she?"

"I was careful. I treated it like it was silver too."

"Ah." He knelt down. "The proper name," he said, holding her spiky-lashed, defiant gaze, "is dyspepsia. Diz-pep-see-ah. Tonight after supper you will learn to spell it, and next week when we go to town we'll stop by Doc Porter's, and you will learn what it means."

"I already know."

"And you were making gingerbread cookies anyway?"

"They're your favorite. I wanted to do something for you."

Sighing, Jacob cupped the flushed cheeks, holding her still. "For me—or for you?"

"Garnet and Leah would have—"

"For me—or for you, Meredith Margaret Sinclair?"

She stiffened, and her mouth quivered. Thick black eyelashes fluttered down in a futile attempt to hide. "I wanted to make you some cookies," she whispered again, more tears slipping over.

Jacob shook his head, studying his oldest child. "Someday," he replied after a long time, "I'm afraid life is going to teach you a painful lesson, Merry-go-round. That stubborn heart of yours is going to end up bruised and battered, I'm thinking. But I want you to remember this."

He stopped, waiting until his eldest daughter looked at him. Jacob touched his lips to her forehead and her damp cheeks, then rubbed noses—the family's unspoken signal of love. "Remember that me and the Lord...well, we'll always love you, no matter what. You'll never be able to outstubborn either one of us."

❧❧❧

Ah yes, Jacob thought now, a bittersweet smile touching the corners of his mouth. That was when he knew what would go into the secret drawer of Meredith's heirloom chest, and he prayed that someday she would understand.

Thirty

*M*eredith steamed into the lobby, her footsteps marching in a drumroll across the parquet floor. Oblivious to the startled looks and puzzled good-mornings from the hotel staff, she banged her way through the door that led to the back, shoved open the second set of doors, stalked across the thick carpet to Mr. Walker's office, and pounded on the door.

"Come in, before you knock it down."

She was in no mood for Benjamin Walker's unruffled sense of humor. "Have you seen the letter to the editor in this week's edition of the *Winchester Leader*?" She slammed the rolled-up paper onto the desk in front of him. "That—that *fiend* Mr. Clarke called you an unprincipled carpetbagger. He accuses you, and by inference anyone under your employ, of—wait. I'll read it."

She stalked around the desk. "Right here. '…of bleeding our struggling economy from local citizens until they've either expired or have themselves been trapped into employment by the nefarious'—nefarious!—'Benjamin Walker.' " She glared. Her insides felt as though two tomcats were clawing each other in uncontrollable fury. "What are we going to do about it?"

"Well, I suppose my great-grandfather would have challenged Mr. J. Preston Clarke to a duel. Unfortunately those pistols—"

"Don't be ridiculous! This—"

"—were stolen back in '63. There's also the minor technicality that dueling is against the law."

"—is a gross insult, a-an underhanded pack of drivel designed to turn people against you so you won't be able to build the springs resort you've been planning for a year. A year!"

"Miss Sinclair—"

"Besides which, it's full of lies. You can't be a carpetbagger. Mrs. Biggs told me you were from Richmond. Your father fought with General Lee himself."

"Meredith, sit down, close your mouth, and take a deep breath. Better yet…take a dozen deep breaths." He rose, pointing to his huge leather office chair.

"Don't coddle me. I want to know, as your office manager, what you plan to do about this. I don't need to—" She broke off with a startled squeak when Mr. Walker's large hands closed over her shoulders and plonked her down into his vacated chair.

As always, the cyclone of emotion abruptly fizzled. She sat, now feeling chagrin instead of anger: She'd done it again. No matter how many times she promised herself that she'd be sweet tempered like Garnet, or at least as disciplined as Leah, somehow circumstances always tripped her up. And more often than not, in front of her employer.

If she were Benjamin Walker, she'd fire herself.

"Under control now?"

"I was never out of control." Defense was automatic. Meredith hated admitting she was wrong.

Benjamin Walker was the most annoying man she'd ever known. Just once, she'd like to see *him* lose the indefatigable control that surrounded him like a medieval suit of armor. He stood over her, arms folded, propped against the edge of his desk, looking as relaxed as if they'd just exchanged pleasantries about the weather. A look of polite amusement crinkled the corners of his eyes. It was a look he directed upon her a lot, and it never failed to irritate Meredith.

Irritate…and intimidate. Other than her father, she'd never met a man so comfortable with himself that he seldom raised his voice, seldom hurried—and never yielded an inch to anyone. Including Meredith.

"After working with you for almost a year, I've learned to value your astuteness about people," he said. "I also admire your integrity. But Miss

Sinclair," he said, leaning down until he was so close Meredith felt the warmth of his breath against her ear, "the concept of control has never been one you seem able to grasp."

He straightened, picked up the paper, and began to read as though he were alone in the room.

Strangely flustered, Meredith pushed the chair back and stood. Was that last remark a veiled censure or just one of those mild quips he was fond of tossing her way, almost as though he enjoyed watching her response? No, definitely not the latter, which implied flirtatious over-tones. Over the last months she'd noted the manner of woman that interested Mr. Walker, all of them beautiful, all of them cosmopolitan ladies with pedigrees that made plain ol' Meredith Sinclair more of a scruffy alley cat surrounded by pampered Persians. Her love of fashion did not include the resources to compete with such women, had she been so inclined. Which of course she wasn't. Neither was Benjamin Walker. After all, he was her employer.

"I think I'll invite Mr. J. Preston Clarke for dinner," Mr. Walker said.

"What?"

"Here, at my private table in the Shenandoah dining room." One eyebrow quirked. "Blink if you understand, Miss Sinclair."

Simmering, Meredith tugged the starched cuffs of her shirtwaist down over her wrists. "One of these days, Mr. Walker, your condescension is going to cost you the best office manager you ever hired." No longer uncertain, she whisked sideways around the other side of the desk. "I'll discuss appropriate menus with Gaspar—haggis, perhaps? An overstuffed sheep's bladder seems appropriate for both of you."

He chuckled and reached the door before Meredith, blocking her exit. For such a large man, he moved with surprising speed. "A novel concept. Unfortunately, Gaspar is likely to object to such a delicacy. To my knowledge he's never attempted haggis and therefore might be reluctant. So how about if you and Lowell make arrangements to pay a call on Mr. Clarke? Issue the invitation and find out *his* favorite choice for a meal. You've read your scriptures, I daresay. Let's try treating our enemy with kindness, hmm?"

"Yes, Mr. Walker."

"And Miss Sinclair?" He paused, and Meredith tensed, not trusting the smooth face and narrowed gaze. "Try not to gut and fillet the poor fellow until he's had a chance to defend himself, all right?"

"Certainly, Mr. Walker." She smiled. "I'll even extend the same courtesy to you."

She sailed through the door without looking back.

J. Preston Clarke lived on the outskirts of Winchester in an imposing stone mansion that resembled a castle, complete with a corner tower. His family had lived in the northern end of the Valley for over a hundred years, and their influence, Meredith knew, was powerful. She'd heard of them most of her life, of course, with Sinclair Run only an hour's buggy ride down the road, but until now they were just an old family who had somehow managed to survive the War with their wealth intact. According to her research over the past week, the present Mr. Clarke stirred a lot of pots with his very sticky fingers. Mining. Agriculture. Banking.

She'd come to visualize him as a miserly king, lording it over the starving peasants. Most folk in the Valley, at least where she had grown up, lived in simple clapboard houses and eked out a hand-to-mouth subsistence. On the other hand, perhaps the Clarke family boasted a man like Jacob Sinclair. Her father's financial stability resulted from a fortuitous combination of skill and Scottish savvy. Meredith supposed she and her sisters had grown up sheltered and a trifle spoiled: Life had not dealt so kindly with most other Southern mountain folk.

The railroads had helped some in recent years, and men like Benjamin Walker had contributed investments in local economies. But to Meredith's way of thinking, Mr. Clarke's penchant for buying whatever struck his fancy just because he had the money was the attitude of a covetous mercenary.

It would be interesting, this coming battle of the minds between her employer and a man who thought himself impervious to consequences.

An officious colored servant dressed in livery—ridiculous because this was Winchester, Virginia, not New York or Boston—ushered

Meredith and Lowell Kingston, Mr. Walker's secretary, into a dark room full of mounted trophy heads and leather furniture.

"Must not be a Mrs. Clarke," Lowell observed. "A lady would never have callers wait in here." He adjusted his spectacles over the bump in the middle of his nose. "I wonder if Mr. Clarke's a hunter or if these are for show."

"They're disgusting either way. I feel as though they're all staring at me. And there was a Mrs. Clarke. She died three years ago, giving birth. A son. The baby didn't survive either."

She tried to quash the instant swell of compassion that bit of research had produced. Meredith had no intention of feeling sorry for the man who had grossly maligned her employer. Instead she prowled the room, her fingers trailing over the slick surface of a carved ebony table, the chilly marble statue of a roaring lion. A stereopticon with a stack of scenes beside it caught her attention.

"Look at this, Lowell." She shuffled through the cardboard photographs. "All views of spas and hotel resorts, from White Sulfur Springs to some place in Colorado."

"That would be the Cliff House, in Manitou Springs," a smooth voice said behind her. "Excellent accommodations, first-rate amenities." J. Preston Clarke strolled across the room to Meredith. He stopped in front of her and bowed. "Welcome to my home." He ignored Lowell.

Her first impression was that J. Preston Clarke didn't look at all like the sort of man who would write a slanderous attack on a man he'd never met or furnish a room with animals' heads. He was fashionably slender, with thick, sandy hair parted in the middle and a neat mustache. Brown eyes studied Meredith with a flicker of interest.

Tiny pins danced along her nerves, but Meredith resisted the urge to make sure all the buttons on her basque were fastened. "I've not had the opportunity for much travel," she said. "But the Cliff House appears to exemplify the sort of establishment my employer plans to build. I take it from these photographs that you're interested in a similar pursuit?"

"Ah. You're a very forthright young woman, Miss—Sinclair, that was the name on the letter you wrote to me last week?"

She nodded. "And this is Mr. Walker's secretary, Mr. Kingston."

"May I offer you some refreshments?" He gestured toward a collection of decanters on a sideboard, but his gaze never wavered from Meredith. "A fine mineral water from one of my own companies. A nice little business in France. The water's one of my personal favorites." His voice assumed an amused tone. "No poisons added, I promise."

"No thank you. We won't be here long enough for refreshments, Mr. Clarke."

"A pity. I've never met a female office manager before. I've been looking forward to getting to know you." He paused. "My objections to Mr. Walker and his schemes do not extend to you, of course."

Lowell cleared his throat.

Meredith's chin lifted. "As I am Mr. Walker's office manager, I'm afraid I disagree. At any rate, my employer builds hotels. He does not 'scheme.' Now. The reason Mr. Kingston and I are here is to invite you personally to join Mr. Walker for dinner at his private table in the Excelsior Hotel."

"I see." Mr. Clarke rocked a little on his heels, hands pressed together beneath his chin as though contemplating the invitation. "I'm to be wined and dined—bribed, so to speak."

He laughed out loud when Meredith went rigid. Behind her, Lowell sputtered an incoherent objection. "Please, sheathe your swords," their host finished. "Merely a small joke—a play on words, as it were."

"You should be more careful with your words, Mr. Clarke."

"I'm very careful with things that matter the most to me, Miss Sinclair."

His head tipped sideways as his gaze roved over her in undisguised approval, and Meredith realized he was flirting with her. Intrigued she tried to decide how best to respond. This particular wrinkle had not occurred to her in spite of learning from Mrs. Biggs that J. Preston Clarke was a sought-after widower, only thirty-one years old. Certainly she was flattered, but she was not about to succumb to the smooth-voiced blandishments or appreciative glances of any man. Especially a man like J. Preston Clarke.

"Ah...Mr. Walker has instructed us to inquire as to your favorite dishes. His chef will prepare the menu of your choice." Deliberately she turned to Lowell. "Mr. Kingston will make careful notes to ensure that the meal meets your expectations."

"Thoughtful. Thorough. I'm impressed," Mr. Clarke said. "Excellent. I much prefer a challenge. Won't sway the inevitable outcome, of course." He waved a long-fingered hand. "However, I'd enjoy the opportunity to compare the culinary expertise of your hotel chef to my own. So long as your company at the table is included, Miss Sinclair, I'll accept the invitation with pleasure."

Lowell stepped to her side. "Sir, your brashness is offensive."

Mr. Clarke's head swiveled toward Lowell, whose complexion after a protracted moment turned a dusky rose. Only then did Mr. Clarke turn to Meredith. "Miss Sinclair doesn't agree with you. Do you?" he murmured.

Oh, he was a smooth one, all right. The challenge was irresistible. "Don't worry, Lowell." There wasn't a man alive she couldn't handle, when she put her mind to it, Meredith assured herself with a cool nod to J. Preston Clarke. "No," she told him, "I don't find your brashness offensive. Inappropriate, certainly. This is a business call, after all." She paused, then added, "But as long as you remain a gentleman instead of a boor, I wouldn't find your invitation...offensive."

"I'm relieved to hear it." He executed a shallow bow. Admiration shone from his warm brown eyes. "I promise to remain on my best gentlemanly behavior."

Meredith's heart skipped a beat. She had prepared herself for a difficult, unpleasant misanthrope, not this handsome charmer. His blatant disregard for propriety seemed so contradictory under the circumstances that Meredith wondered if he was actually telling the truth.

If so, perhaps her initial outrage had led her to make a monumental error about J. Preston Clarke. Perhaps the letter to the editor was based on a similar snap judgment, precipitated by hearsay and ignorance. Written out of righteous outrage instead of malice.

Meredith knew her Bible, had memorized whole passages when she was a child. She knew all too well that it would be a sin for her to judge the splinter in Mr. Clarke's eye, when there was a log in her own in need of extraction. Mr. Walker's instinct to respond with Christian charity had been more astute than she realized.

Was it possible? Instead of dueling pistols at dawn, so to speak, Mr. Clarke and her employer would reach some congenial arrangement, even form a working arrangement of some sort. Mr. Clarke had shown an interest in resort hotels—he might invest in Mr. Walker's newest venture.

Sparks of anticipation crackled through Meredith. What if…what if this was God's plan, arranging circumstances to bring her into contact with an intriguing, attractive man? Certainly the Lord wanted to teach her a lesson, reminding her not to jump to conclusions about someone she'd never met. But if Mr. Clarke chose to pursue her… Wouldn't it be an answer to prayer if he turned out to be for Meredith what Sloan MacAllister was for Garnet?

Stay calm, she reminded herself. *Cordial but aloof.* "The invitation was extended by Mr. Walker," she said. "It was my understanding that dinner would include only the two of you." She allowed the hint of a smile to reach her eyes. "I can inquire about modifications, if you like."

"Do so. Then I can look forward to seeing you again very soon. And meeting Mr. Walker, of course."

Was it wishful thinking, or was the responding gleam in Mr. Clarke's eye for her, instead of the coming battle of wills between two strong-minded men?

Thirty-One

A persistent bone-chilling wind buffeted Benjamin Walker as he prowled the edge of an airy glade, empty except for a few bare-branched trees. Absently Ben tucked the flapping end of his wool muffler into his coat, then stroked a slender beech's smooth bark before stuffing his hands back in his pockets. He didn't notice the cold. His mind was filled with images of leafy trees, clear blue skies, and summer sunshine.

Over there, under that tulip tree, the bandstand. This glade will be a park, with bridle paths and promenades… Main building needs to be centered halfway up that hill, with paved lanes leading to the men's and ladies' swimming pools…over there, off to the right where fewer trees will have to be sacrificed. Have to call Cade Beringer to handle the botanical details. And we'll definitely have to grade the earth a tad, make it more level for carriages. Now for the spring house I'll—

"Mr. Walker? Sir? Starting to snow. We need to be heading back, afore we end up food for a hungry bear."

"Be there in a moment, Hominy."

…cover it with a Grecian temple. No. Too pretentious. A pagoda? No. These ancient mountains simply don't lend themselves to pseudocultures. All right, shelve the design for right now. Picture the hotel. Porches, with doors to each room opening onto—

"Am I going to have to hoist you over my shoulder like a bale of cotton?"

Hominy's paw of a hand clamped over his shoulder and administered a mood-breaking shake. Resigned, only mildly annoyed, Ben let himself be herded back toward the brougham, whose gleaming navy panels and roof were dusted with white. "Hey, you should have told me it was snowing. We need to head back before we're lost and some hungry wild animal makes a meal of us. Not a bear though. They're still hibernating."

"If you'd listened to me hollerin' at you for the last five minutes, cast your eyes toward the sky—" Hominy stopped, the smooth ebony face cracking into laughter. He tugged on the cauliflower ear Ben had never been able to persuade him to have examined by a reputable physician. "You sorry scamp. Slicker than spit, aren't you, Mr. Ben?" He whacked his back hard enough to cause Ben to stumble. "Heard every word I hollered. Just couldn't be bothered."

"You know me so well." Ben twisted for a last look around the secluded valley, but the snow was falling thick and fast now, shrouding it in a swirling veil. "This is going to be a good hotel, Hominy. I can feel it, all the way in my bones."

"My bones is so cold they quit feeling half-hour ago." Hominy's crooked-tooth smile flashed white as the falling snow. "Now don't start fretting over me. I'm just funning you a bit, Mr. Ben. Got enough bulk to this old carcass of mine to warm the both of us."

"Good thing I sent Lowell along to chaperon Miss Sinclair. Sure to have ruffled his hidebound feathers some, hearing you speak so disrespectfully to the man who puts bacon in your larder so you can expand the bulk."

Hominy snorted. "That boy needs to have somebody roll him around in the dirt a time or two, take the starch out of his spine as well as his shirt."

"He's a good secretary." Unperturbed, Ben opened the carriage door before Hominy could. "Besides, he's supporting his mother and invalid brother. I can put up with a bit of posturing."

He'd put up with a lot more, if he had to. Ben knew firsthand the dry-as-ashes panic that hollowed a man's stomach when he was the sole barrier between his family and starvation. He also knew the soul-shriveling desolation of failing.

Hominy unfolded the lap robe and deftly draped it over Ben. Only then did he step back to shut the door and climb into the driver's seat. Suddenly the door yanked open again. "What time is it?" he asked Ben.

Ben obligingly dug beneath the folds of thick wool to tug out his watch. "Six minutes to four. We've plenty of time. Mind the horses if the track is slippery. I'd rather keep my dinner guests waiting than risk breaking one of the horse's legs. And, Hominy?"

"Sir?"

With an equally deft flick of his wrist he whipped off the lap robe and tossed it into Hominy's face. "You need that more than I do. No, don't bother arguing the matter. The longer you do, the later I'll be. Then we'll both have to listen to Julianna Frobisher and her simpering mother complain about my poor manners."

"Ain't proper."

"*Isn't* proper, my friend. Poor Miss Arbuckle would be mortified to hear her rigorous lessons haven't borne fruit." Chuckling, he yanked the door closed in Hominy's face, sat back, and closed his eyes. Through the small window above his head he could hear Hominy's grumbling. But it was all bark and no bite, and both of them knew it.

Hominy Hawes was the only person allowed to treat Ben with such familiarity—because nobody else remained alive who could claim that they'd changed Benjamin Daniel Walker's wet nappies. Hominy's mother had been a slave, one of their housemaids; her strapping son helped tend the horses, but from the beginning he and little Benjamin formed a strong, inexplicable bond. One of his earliest memories was of Hominy lifting him onto the back of a horse, holding him with such calm, capable hands that a tiny three-year-old boy had not been afraid.

He hadn't understood then that the color of their skin signified a chasm that would tear a country apart. Hominy's disappearance, along with most of the other servants, only intensified the agony he suffered over the disintegration and death of his entire family.

Just last spring, when his manservant confessed a yearning to clean up his rough edges, Ben had arranged for a private tutor in the evenings. A retired nanny with nothing to do but tend her garden, Miss Arbuckle gratefully seized the opportunity. Neither Ben nor Hominy was inclined to dissect the matter, though both of them knew that Hominy was determined to turn himself into a gentleman. A worthy goal for an ex-slave, one he'd never attained despite years of "freedom" up north. When he'd knocked on Ben's door late one night years earlier, Hominy had been starving, so severely beaten Ben wouldn't have recognized him except for the misshapen ear.

Their relationship with each other was unique, impossible to categorize. Friend as well as servant, companion as well as bodyguard, driver…nursemaid…over the past fifteen years Ben had given up trying to categorize. Hominy himself preferred the title "manservant."

"Honored to serve you, Mr. Ben," he'd once said. "Salary aside, you make me feel more of a man than anybody outside my pa."

Ben moodily contemplated his muddy boots. Hominy's father, like Ben's, had died in the War. Strange how even after a quarter-century both sons felt compelled to honor their dead families.

Family… Other than an aging cousin, the Walker family with its once impeccable lineage and vast wealth no longer existed except in the memories of other Southerners whose way of life had been destroyed thirty years earlier.

But by all he cherished, Benjamin Walker vowed to maintain the shield of wealth he'd earned over the past two decades. Never again would anyone under his care have to suffer the barbarous cruelties inflicted on the poor and downtrodden.

Ah, well. No point in torturing himself with ancient history. It was 1890, dawn of a new era, cusp of a new century, and Ben had plans. Lots of plans, foremost of which was the development of Poplar Springs Resort, some six miles southwest of Winchester. The tourist economy was booming, and Ben was determined to do his share to usher in a brighter future for the Blue Ridge Mountains that had healed his soul. As soon as this issue of Preston Clarke was resolved, his latest dream could commence building its way to reality.

Head propped against the seatback, body relaxed in spite of the frequent bumps that tested the double-suspension springs, Ben's mind returned to the placement of the main hotel building. His focus was legendary—Hominy once told him that when he was dreaming and scheming on site, birds could mistake him for a statue. But it was such a focus that ensured success.

And not just with his building projects.

Meredith Sinclair.

A slow smile spread over Ben's face. As though she sat opposite him, he could see the glowing freshness of her face, with the lively dancing eyes and obstinate mouth, all framed by thick chestnut hair in a style that altered by the week. Chignon, twists, a new one she'd told him was a pompadour—his office manager tried them all. She was also a clotheshorse. Despite her limited means, Meredith managed to appear each day dressed up neat and pretty as a picture in a lady's fashion magazine. And what Ben wanted more than he was willing to admit aloud was to thoroughly disarrange all that starched and coiffured perfection.

Wants, however, could be cudgeled into submission by a man's will.

By the time he was twelve years old, Benjamin Walker had learned the value of patient endurance. He'd also learned caution. Not even for a fascinating woman would he compromise the decisions about his life he'd made two decades earlier. If he let Meredith see his interest, she'd break his heart into confetti-sized scraps.

Meredith Sinclair was unlike any woman Ben had ever known. She wasn't calculating; in some nebulous way he couldn't put his finger on she wasn't even confident, despite the lethal combination of beauty, charm, and a quick mind. Yet his indomitable office manager was a world-class breaker of masculine hearts, because for some peculiar reason she *was* oblivious to the power of her charms.

Meredith, he acknowledged wryly as they reached the main road and Hominy urged the horses to a canter, promised to be more of a challenge than even the twenty years it had required to rebuild his family fortune. That he might fail never crossed his mind, because once he set his course he was unstoppable. He'd had to be.

In her own way, of course, Meredith was equally unstoppable, though if he compared their two wills, his would have the slow inevitability of a glacier, while Meredith's more resembled a—he couldn't decide whether a tornado or a volcano would be more accurate. The smile broadened to a grin. The girl had intrigued him from the moment she'd answered an advertisement for a dining room hostess.

"I'd make an outstanding hostess," she announced, her gaze candid, the gamine face bright with life. "But I'm more interested in the other position you advertised."

"Back office assistant?" He folded his arms across his chest. "Typing, filing papers? Why? I can tell by the look of you that you'd make a better hostess. You're well-dressed, attractive."

A look had flashed through her eyes then, one that blended bitterness, cynicism—and a flash of vulnerability. It was the vulnerability that had captivated him.

"I'm not flattering you." He kept his voice calm. "I'm analyzing your qualifications. Well-dressed and pleasing to the eye are two prerequisites for the position. You also enjoy people. I watched you through the door, chatting with the other applicants, trying to put everyone at ease. I watched the way you darted over to pick up the handkerchief that fell out of Mrs. Stuebens's reticule as she was leaving the dining room."

"Anybody would have done that."

"But not everyone would have been able to surprise a laugh out of a woman who recently lost her husband of fifty-two years."

"Oh." Her head dropped. Ben watched her swallow, watched the set of her shoulders square when she lifted her gaze again. "I do like people. But I'll never know how I feel about working in an office unless I'm given the opportunity." Her lips curved in a smile as her steady gaze threw down the gauntlet.

Because the novelty of hiring a woman for an office assistant appealed to his sense of omnipotence—he was wealthy and in charge, therefore he could hire anybody he pleased—Ben proceeded to interview her on the spot, instead of passing her along to the restaurant manager as he had done with the other women. He hired her as his office assistant three days later, after none of the other applicants met his expectations.

Outside, the snowflakes were hurtling past the window in a gray white blur. Dusk and speed transformed the passing scenery to pastel smears.

During the last months he'd come to rely on Meredith's off-the-cuff observations more than he'd ever intended when he hired her. So much so that he'd promoted her to office manager. Oh, she was impulsive, and ofttimes as unpredictable as a honeybee darting from flower to flower. But her insights showed a rare perception.

Except with him.

Ben continued to be very circumspect in his behavior. But Meredith was testing his control to a degree he found amusing as well as frustrating. For a woman who attracted men just by walking into a room and smiling, she seemed blind to Ben's attraction to her. He planned to keep it that way, until he was ready to make a move of his own.

＊

Meredith caught Mr. Walker as he crossed the lobby. He was wearing his gray frock coat and silk tie, with a single white rose attached to his lapel—which meant he must be entertaining guests for dinner. Meredith searched her memory, then hesitated, but the news she wanted to share would not wait. "Mr. Walker."

He turned. "Miss Sinclair. I'd be delighted to hear the outcome of your visit with Clarke, but I've dinner guests. Tomorrow's soon enough."

"Mrs. Frobisher won't mind waiting for a few moments. Gaspar's serving her the oyster soup she gushed about the last time."

"Mrs. Frobisher and her charming daughter have been waiting"— he glanced toward the huge grandfather clock standing next to the door to the gentlemen's parlor—"for twenty minutes, I'm sorry to say."

"I'll walk with you as far as their table. That way you can volunteer my services if Mrs. Frobisher pitches her twice-yearly entreaty for you to join the Preservation Society."

"I believe I can fight my own battles—oh, all right. Seeing as how you've latched yourself to my side. So tell me, will my next dinner guest be J. Preston Clarke?"

Meredith beamed at him. Mr. Walker was the most accommodating man, certainly one of the most even-tempered. No matter how much she blew and blustered, he never turned a hair. "Ten days, Thursday after next. I suggested seven-thirty. Lowell reminded me that you'll be at a meeting in Strasburg until late that afternoon."

She took a deep breath. "Mr. Walker, I'd like to tell you that I think your approach, over the matter of Mr. Clarke's letter, I mean, was certainly more insightful than my own."

"Oh?" The evening headwaiter approached, and Mr. Walker held him off with a slight wave. "I'll be through with Miss Sinclair in a moment, Henry. Tell Mrs. and Miss Frobisher I'll be there shortly. And—see if you can scrounge up some breads and a selection of cheeses, arrange them in a basket or whatever for them to take home. Sort of an apology for my tardiness?"

"Yes sir."

"You're practically doing a tap dance on my best patent leather shoes, Miss Sinclair." His mouth quirked in a half-smile. "Go ahead, spit it out instead of softening me up with flattery. What is it? He wants green turtle soup, French caviar? Breast of antelope from Wyoming Territory?"

"Mr. Clarke requested that I join the two of you. Actually, he refused to come until I agreed."

"I…see." For a moment that stretched uncomfortably Mr. Walker stood unmoving with his hands clasped behind his back, his head ducked as though he were contemplating the patent leather shoes to see if Meredith had scratched them after all.

"At first I tried to dissuade him. This is business, after all, and since the letter was a slur against you, I felt my presence would be inappropriate. The two of you needed to work through the matter on your own, I thought. But I changed my mind."

An indecipherable mumble issued from Mr. Walker's throat. Meredith slanted him a severe look before continuing.

"We may have misjudged Mr. Clarke, as he misjudged you. He's a most cordial gentleman and was pleased by your invitation. Since he did seem to indicate a—a desire for my presence as well, I took the liberty of agreeing. I didn't think you'd mind too much. I can be smiling and silent, or charming and chatty, whichever role suits the occasion."

She was talking too fast now and brought herself to an abrupt halt. "Mr. Walker?"

He had the most peculiar expression on his face, or rather the most…unnerving lack of expression. A wave of uncertainty smacked between Meredith's shoulder blades, an odious sensation. She lifted her chin. "If there's a problem, I apologize. Mr. Clarke was most insistent. If you're concerned that I might be waiting for a chance to—I believe 'gut and fillet' him was the phrase—then let me reassure you. I think I was grossly mistaken about his motivation. I'm convinced Mr. Clarke was simply guilty of a lack of understanding of the kind of man you are, and dinner is a perfect—"

"What kind of man am I, Miss Sinclair?"

Bewildered, Meredith stared up into the unsmiling face. "What do you mean? As a hotelier, you have a reputation second to none throughout the Valley. If the correspondence I've read from out-of-state guests is to be believed, that reputation has spread far beyond state borders. Your plan to allow the dining room here at the Excelsior to remain open year-round is not only profitable, but a boon to the local economy. When Mr. Clarke meets you, I'm confident he'll agree."

Mr. Walker arched one eyebrow. "That wasn't precisely what I asked, but we'll let it go." He studied her a moment. "We'll try this one. What kind of man do you think Mr. Clarke is?"

Ah. That must be it. Her employer was wondering if she'd been seduced into the enemy camp, so to speak. Meredith took a calming breath. "I told you I found him to be charming. He's willing to concede that his letter was a trifle inflammatory and that he should have investigated further before he wrote it. It's…um…possible that he found me attractive. Some gentlemen do, you know."

"From what I've observed, Miss Sinclair, most every man who meets you finds you attractive. Are you telling me that this attraction is mutual? Is that why you want to join us for dinner?"

His voice was mild, the tone pleasant…and yet for some reason a blush seeped into Meredith's cheeks. She searched his face, noticing for the first time how very dark blue his eyes were. "I'm sorry if you find my character displeasing. I wasn't aware that you thought of me as a— a hussy."

A faint smile softened the line of his mouth. "I don't. But if you're drawn to an unprincipled shark like J. Preston Clarke, I might have to change my mind about your powers of discernment."

"Apparently so. It never occurred to me that you would lower yourself to impugning the character of a man you've never met."

"What do you consider Mr. Clarke's letter?"

The flush deepened. "This is ridiculous. You have guests waiting. If you don't want me to join you and Mr. Clarke for dinner, just say so. But you'll have to meet him on some other ground. He was adamant that if I'm not included, he doesn't plan to accept."

"Miss Sinclair. As my office manager, it would have been appropriate for you to join us for the meal, had I so indicated. I don't like being countermanded." Something flashed in the blue eyes, like the glint of heat lightning in a cloudless sky. "On the other hand, it might be interesting. Very well. Go ahead. Primp yourself up with a fancy hair style and a new gown. Perhaps the distraction will keep Mr. Clarke so off balance he'll agree to anything I say."

He bowed, then sauntered into the dining room.

Thirty-Two

Swathed in one of her best friend FrannieBeth's aprons, Meredith lifted the wet, giggling toddler out of the tin washtub. "Oh, you sweet little sugarplum!" She kissed the chubby fingers splayed across her face. "Be still, now. Auntie Merry needs to dry you before you catch a chill."

"You're going to need to dry yourself as well," FrannieBeth commented from the fireplace, where she was sweeping up the cinders. "Oh, Meredith, no! Your lovely shirtwaist—here. Give me the squirmer."

Meredith wrapped Jessup in the rough towel and hugged him close. "Not a chance. Besides, you'll just make him sooty again. Stop fretting, FrannieBeth. I haven't enjoyed myself this much in a coon's age." It was amazing, for their lives shared little in common anymore. Still, they'd known each other forever, over twenty years, and in many ways FrannieBeth was like another sister.

"*Enjoyed* yourself? I find that hard to believe." Smiling and shaking her head, FrannieBeth finished at the fireplace and proceeded to attack the cookstove's ash pit.

Meredith played patty-cake with Jessup as she efficiently diapered and dressed his squirming form. It had been a long time since she'd been able to play with babies. "He's growing so fast," she said, finally depositing him on the floor with a collection of wooden spoons and empty thread spools to keep him occupied. "I can't believe he's walking now."

"More work for me," her friend grumbled with an indulgent smile. "I do appreciate your help today, Meredith. Though I still feel guilty, you coming over for a visit and spending more time taking care of my— Alice! What are you doing with Miss Merry's hat?"

"She said I could play with it." Alice's bottom lip pooched out. "I'm a fancy lady, just like Miss Merry."

Meredith swallowed a gasp of laughter. She snagged FrannieBeth's arm before the outraged mother swooped down on her hapless child. "It's all right, I did give her the hat. Let her be, Fran."

"But that hat's one of your favorites, Meredith. And it's expensive. There's one in the Sears catalog not half so nice, and it costs three dollars." Her gaze narrowed. "And I ought to wash her mouth with lye soap, talking like that."

The mirth bubbled out and over. Laughing, Meredith knelt on the floor by the bewildered Alice. "Here. Let me help you, darling. I'll teach you how to adjust the angle the next time I visit." She righted the black felt hat, perching it on Alice's flyaway curls, then retied the velvet bow at the back that Alice had tugged apart. "Alice," she whispered as she worked, "the reason your mama is upset is because 'fancy lady' isn't a proper term to use."

"Why not?" Alice whispered back. Her rounded eyes searched Meredith's.

Nonplussed, Meredith tweaked the soft little nose. "Ask your mama after I leave."

"But you're a lady, and Mama says you like to wear fancy clothes. Why aren't you a fancy lady?"

"Alice, I'll explain later," FrannieBeth told her daughter. "Now you go put Miss Merry's hat back where you found it. You can pick the eye-sprouts out of the potatoes I fetched from the cellar, so I can peel the skins."

Alice crossed her arms and planted her feet on the warped floor-boards of the Magruders' kitchen. "Don't want to. Want to go with Merry. She doesn't have to pick eye-sprouts from 'taters."

Meredith gestured to FrannieBeth, who from the look of her was inches away from tanning a truculent four-year-old's bottom. "Now that's where you're wrong, miss priss. Not only do I pick those sprouts, I know how to arrange the clean potatoes all exactly the same size. Used to have a contest with my sisters." She winked at Alice. "*I* always won. I bet if you and I clean your mama's potatoes, I'll beat you as well."

"Will not." Diverted, the girl scuttled across the floor and climbed on the stool in front of the worktable.

FrannieBeth mouthed a thank-you, rescued Jessup before he up-ended the slop bucket by the sink, and carried him off for a nap while Meredith and Alice engaged in a friendly but fierce battle over the potatoes.

An hour later FrannieBeth dropped onto a chair in the sitting room and lifted her feet onto a tapestry-covered footstool. "Whew...oh, this feels heavenly." She smiled blissfully at Meredith. "Thanks to you, I can enjoy thirty minutes like this. Such luxury...my best friend and thirty minutes of conversation without the two hooligans demanding my attention."

"Seems to me I should leave so you can take a nap along with them." Meredith studied her friend. She and FrannieBeth were the same age—twenty-three. Yet her friend looked more like a well-worn thirty.

"I'd rather talk. Don't have near enough opportunities, now that you've moved to Winchester. I envy you, you know."

To cover her embarrassment, Meredith picked up a pair of worsted stockings FrannieBeth had been repairing earlier in the day. "One of the reasons I needed to see you," she confessed, "is because I wanted to talk to you about...things." She worked two crooked stitches before FrannieBeth reached across and took stocking and needle away from her.

"You never could sew worth an unplucked chicken. From where I sit, your life looks mighty fine. A beautiful, independent gal working in town. Store-bought clothes, no babies tugging your skirts, whinin' and crying when they aren't getting into mischief. No husband tracking his muddy brogans across your freshly swept floor. Lots of people to talk to."

"There's a difference between having people around all the time and having someone you can open up with when you do talk."

Meredith's gaze wandered around the worn-looking room with its scarred furniture and faded rugs. The wainscoting still needed to be washed, but other than that the sitting room—like the rest of the house—was bandbox clean; the comfortable fragrance of cleaning soap permeated the air. Her friend had created a home, patched together with love and contentment along with the backbreaking labor. If she was honest with herself, the old farmhouse was more of a home than J. Preston Clarke's magnificent thirty-room mansion.

"Do you know," Meredith murmured into the silence, "for most of my life all I've ever wanted was a husband and a home of my own."

FrannieBeth looked startled, and Meredith laughed to cover the bitter taste left by her confession and her friend's reaction. "When I left Sinclair Run, I wasn't chasing after a career. I was chasing after Lamar Aikens. I thought I was in love with him."

"You've been chasing boys since you were six years old and gave Rowley Futch a black eye for stealing your apple."

"Hmph. So I did. Well, the next day he told me he loved me and wanted me to marry him." Meredith sighed. "Good thing I refused. Last time I saw Rowley he was the size of a cotton bale, with a mouth full of rotten teeth when he smiled. You're blessed to have Duncan. He's a good man."

"I know."

For a while they sat, Meredith watching FrannieBeth's quick hands mend the hole in the stocking, while her mind searched for a way to mend the holes in her heart. She felt hot and full, as though she'd swallowed a beehive.

"I don't mean to chase after men," she finally said. "I just"—she waved her hand jerkily—"well, God did create a man and a woman, remember? He designed us so man wouldn't be lonely. Is there anything wrong with thinking that God doesn't want woman to be lonely either?"

"I'd worry about you if I didn't know you better." FrannieBeth folded the mended stocking and laid it aside. "But I do know you, and I can tell that something is vexing you, Meredith. Something painful. I believe God wants us to be married and content. I thank Him for Duncan every day, no matter how much I might complain about his muddy shoes or his snoring when he sleeps."

She leaned forward a little, a curious expression in the tired face. "So why are you up in Winchester, hitched to a job instead of Lamar?"

Meredith stood and wandered across to the window, peering out through the panes to the dreary afternoon. The snow the previous week had melted, leaving behind an earth still colored by winter's chilly fingers, gray and brown and black. Even the evergreens seemed to have lost their rich green luster.

"Because the job offer I received was at least an honorable one," she said without turning around.

"What do you mean, Merry? You were so convinced that Lamar Aikens was the one. Even your father gave up trying to persuade you otherwise. Are you telling me that Lamar…that he…" She fumbled to a halt.

"Let's just say that Mr. Aikens's idea of commitment didn't include a wedding ring."

She spied a wagon turning onto the lane just before the hill hid it from view. She turned back around. "Duncan's home." Her discomfort eased at the outrage darkening FrannieBeth's face. "Don't waste your energy on Lamar. I got over him long ago. The thing is…I discovered that I *do* enjoy working. I enjoy the challenge, the satisfaction of accomplishing a difficult task, like coordinating excursions for hotel guests. Or reorganizing Mr. Walker's files. He promoted me to his manager after that one—I'd finally convinced Mrs. Biggs that lumping every piece of correspondence into drawers until the cabinet was full was not the most efficient—"

She broke off, finally noticing FrannieBeth's blank look. Frustrated, she tried to explain. "I enjoy being…stretched, I suppose describes it best. I'm not sure even now what I'm capable of. Certainly I've enjoyed my job as an office manager. Yet…" She hesitated, then confessed on a small laugh, "Sometimes I almost panic. I want to run home and crawl into Papa's arms like I was Alice's age. And now," she hesitated, "now I might have met someone. A man."

FrannieBeth leaped up and gave her a hug. "I *knew* you'd been holding back something all day. Hurry up and tell me before Duncan arrives. Who is it? Your boss—that good-looking Mr. Walker that Garnet told me about?"

"Benjamin Walker? Heavens, no." For some reason a flush crawled over her face. "In the first place, I work for him. In the second…he doesn't look at me that way. I don't even know if he's aware that I'm a woman."

The words caught in her throat as the memory surfaced. *"Most every man who meets you finds you attractive,"* he'd told her. "Most every man" plainly did not include Benjamin Walker. Not that she cared two pins about it one way or the other. "I'm not talking about my employer," she repeated firmly. "I'm talking about a Mr. Clarke. J. Preston Clarke. He's a widower, but he's only thirty—"

"The *Clarkes?* The family who practically owns the northern half of the Valley and east all the way to Front Royal?"

"Yes, but—"

"Meredith, you've gotten hold of some wild notions before, but this piece of foolishness is the wildest! People like you and me don't get noticed by people like the Clarkes. He's not just rich, he's…you may as well set your cap for one of them Vanderbilts as cast your eye on Mr. Clarke."

"He cast his eye on me first." Meredith pinned a bright smile on her face and marched past FrannieBeth toward the hall. "Mercysake, here I've been rattling on when I need to be going. Duncan's home. It's getting late, and I promised Papa I'd help with supper."

"Merry, I'm sorry. Please don't be hurt. I didn't mean it that way."

"I know you didn't." She grabbed her hat, indifferent to the crushed brim and limp velvet bow, hurriedly pinning it in place. "Besides, you're probably right. I've mistaken the situation. I do that a lot."

"Whooee, gal! Where'd you get to? I'm home! Sure does smell good in here." Duncan's head poked through the kitchen doorway. "Hey, there, Meredith. Thought that looked like Jacob's rig. You leaving? Too bad. You're a sight to behold, you are." He wrapped a lanky arm around FrannieBeth. "So's my missus. Brought you something from Cooper's." He grinned at her. "He was unloading bolts of cloth. I helped. 'Member that Simpson calico you told me you like so much? He sold me six yards at wholesale price, as a thank-you."

FrannieBeth's face lit up. Duncan's grin deepened. He doffed his cap toward Meredith, kissed his wife, then disappeared to clean up.

Still smiling, FrannieBeth walked Meredith to the front door. "Now that I think on it," she said, "I reckon I wouldn't trade places with you after all. Job might be nice—the income sure enough would make me feel like I was worth more than I do here, ofttimes. But I can't imagine not having a man to depend on. Who protects me, provides for me and the young uns, who"—she blushed, giggling—"keeps me warm at night. He's a lot of work, for sure. But we take care of each other."

"I can see that." Meredith hugged her tight and managed to keep the smile on her face and her eyes dry until she was safe inside the buggy.

I want that too, Lord. Oh, I want that too.

God had blessed FrannieBeth. He'd brought Sloan and Garnet together. What was wrong with her, that God denied her the deepest desire of her heart?

❧

Jacob fitted the tenon into the mortise, tapped the pieces firmly into place with a cloth-covered mallet, then clamped the joints of the three-legged table together until the glue dried. "You've been home the better part of two days, Merry-girl. Don't you think 'tis about time you told your father what's burning a hole in your soul?"

"I'm fine. Just tired from helping FrannieBeth all day. And I've been helping you since I returned. I've done more work on my off days than a week's work at the hotel."

She'd been sanding the board Jacob gave her an hour ago when she wandered into his workshop, restless, moody as a badger. He'd asked if she minded helping him out a spell, showed her what to do, and left her to it. Now Jacob walked over to his oldest daughter, plucked the sandpaper and board away, then took her sawdust-coated hands.

"Who's hurt you, lass?"

"Nobody." But she ducked her head. "I—it's been almost a month since I was home last. I missed you, is all. And Garnet. The train stopped for only a few moments in Tom's Brook, and I didn't have time to go out to their place. But I left word at the mercantile for them to come visit if they could. I'm just disappointed because it doesn't look as though they'll make it."

"Miss you girls myself." Jacob hung his work apron on a peg, then methodically began putting away tools, keeping his back to Meredith. "Leah writes every week, bless her, but 'tis not the same as a real conversation. She—"

"I'm sorry I don't write like I should."

Jacob flung a look over his shoulder. "Don't be putting meaning in my words that was never intended." He lifted his wooden tool chest, carried it to the shelf in the back corner. "What I was telling you is that Leah's at a time in her life where being home isn't near as important as becoming the woman God intended her to be. She might not have a clear vision of that yet, but we both know it won't include Sinclair Run."

"Papa…" She flung her arms around his waist and pressed her cheek between his shoulder blades.

"Now don't cloud up on me, there's a good girl." Jacob turned and held her until she drew in a shaky breath. "I'm making a point, Merry-go-round. Let me finish it, hmm?"

"Yes, Papa." She kissed his cheek and stepped back. "You've made it just fine. You're trying to tell me that life is full of changes, and that some of those are painful. But no matter where we go or what we do, this will always be home. And a place to come back to when we don't have any other place to go."

"Imp. 'Tis God's truth, though, so how about if you stop fretting because you might not see either sister this trip and let's go see what Clara left for our supper."

His Meredith was bright as a silver dollar, all right. But like Garnet, she couldn't be pushed into sharing her troubles. If Jacob played it light, didn't fret over her, likely she'd get around to telling him what had prompted her unannounced appearance in the entry of his workshop a little before noon the previous day. This morning, after fussing over him like an overzealous nurse, she'd flitted off to the Magruders'.

Jacob ushered her outside, then slid the heavy doors to his workshop closed. It was one of those capricious March days, a spring teaser, he called them. Morning had been mild, with a pastel blue sky and benevolent sunshine that beckoned buds on trees and the pink azaleas Garnet had planted on either side of the porch steps. By afternoon the sky had turned the color of hoarfrost. Likely a winter storm would blow over the mountains tomorrow, like the one that dumped three inches of wet snow the previous week.

More than either of his other daughters, Meredith reminded Jacob of the weather.

"Papa, listen!" Meredith grabbed his arm. "Do you hear? Hoofbeats, I hear hoofbeats! Maybe it's Garnet—yes. It is! Hope they brought Phineas…"

Like a yearling filly she scampered down the lane, heavy skirts hiked in her hands. Shaking his head Jacob continued toward the porch.

The pain struck suddenly, as was its habit, only this time the severity stopped him in his tracks. He pressed a hand against his side and breathed heavily through his nose to dispel the uprush of nausea. By the time Sloan's new rockaway rolled to a stop at the hitching post, Jacob managed to greet them with a smile.

Meredith jumped down from the long step, where she'd precariously perched with her hands clinging over the door. She waved to Jacob and laughed.

"You look about ten, instead of a respectable young woman with an important job," Jacob said. "One of these years, you'll pull that stunt and Sloan will be setting a broken limb or two run over by a buggy wheel."

"Better Sloan than old Doc Porter."

"Thanks, I think." Sloan winked at Jacob, then turned to lift Garnet down.

The utter devotion evident on his face when he looked at his new wife brought a lump to Jacob's throat. *Och, Lord, but 'tis such a rare gift You've blessed me with, to be able to see the lass glowing with the pure sweet light of love.*

He watched the two sisters embrace, both of them laughing and exclaiming. There was a faint note of desperation to Meredith's gaiety, more obvious to Jacob, juxtaposed as it was against Garnet's deeper joy.

"Yes, of course Phineas came along for the ride," she was assuring Meredith now. "But you'll have to give him a little while. He's shy with strangers, and he only met you a couple of times, remember. Here…"

Indifferent to the dirt, she crouched on the floor of the buggy, stretching out one arm. "It's all right, baby. If you'd just look, you'd see that everything is familiar. You'll even remember Meredith, if you'll just poke your pointy little nose out here, quit hiding under the seat."

"Sweetheart, let him come at his own pace." Sloan wrapped an arm around his wife and tugged her toward the porch. "Sometimes, it's better not to force it."

Humor danced through Garnet's eyes. "Can't resist an object lesson, can you?" She glanced over his shoulder to Jacob. "No wonder the two of you hit it off from the beginning." Her hand lifted to rest against Sloan's cheek. "And I thank God for it every day."

Never a man to abide by societal rules, Sloan turned his head and pressed a kiss to Garnet's palm. "I'll fetch our supper. That might be the primary reason Phineas is hanging back."

"Supper?" Jacob stepped closer. "You brought along a meal, did you? Don't trust the cook you hired for me?"

"From what I saw when I rummaged in the kitchen earlier, I for one am not going to complain," Meredith said. She gave Garnet a shove. "I'll help Sloan. Go on, go talk to Papa. I've had him all afternoon. Are you staying the night?"

"Not this trip," Sloan answered. "Got a couple of ladies due to begin their labor any moment, and a case of influenza I promised to check in on, first thing in the morning."

Meredith's jaw set. "Oh. Well, I'm glad someone brought you my note, so I can at least enjoy an evening with you."

Sloan met Jacob's gaze. "We didn't receive a note," he said after a moment's pause. "We just…knew we needed to come. Jacob, are you feeling all right?"

Both girls froze, and Jacob wanted to kick his too-observant son-in-law. "Right as rain," he promised and made a show of clasping Garnet's shoulders and rubbing noses.

"Papa?" Meredith's anxious face appeared next to Garnet's. "Are you hiding something?" She turned to her brother-in-law. "Sloan, why did you ask how he felt?"

"Quit your fretting," Jacob said. "I've got all but one of my family around me, we're going to have a bonny evening, and I'll hear no more queries as to my health." He started up the steps. "Come along then," he ordered Garnet, "tell me about your drawings while I clean up. We'll let those two take care of dinner preparations."

He opened the door for Garnet and stood back to let her enter the darkened hallway first. Only after a surreptitious backward peek toward Meredith and Sloan did Jacob hurriedly mop the perspiration from his brow. He popped a tablet into his mouth before following Garnet inside.

Thirty-Three

"Can I ask you something, before we go inside?" Meredith ventured after she helped Sloan carry two picnic baskets and a smaller cloth-covered basket of mouth-watering yeast rolls up onto the porch.

"Of course, Meredith. What's wrong?"

"It's not medical," she blurted, then wished she'd bitten her tongue before opening her mouth at all. "Never mind, it's not important. Mercysake, but everything smells heavenly. What's in here anyway?" She set her basket down next to Sloan's.

"Food. Meredith, relax. If you don't need me as a physician, then remember that I'm your brother-in-law. Family. You can ask anything you like."

She tapped the ends of her fingers together—a nervous habit she'd tried for years to break without success. Sloan waited, not speaking, a half-smile showing beneath the thick mustache. His stance was relaxed, shoulders propped against a post, his expression peaceful. He looked very different from the dark, brooding man Leah had described the previous summer.

"Garnet's very lucky. I've never seen her look so…radiant. And happy."

"Not lucky. Blessed by God. Both of us." He paused, then added with a gentle smile, "And not because of anything either of us did, you know. It's called grace."

"I used to think you were hard as petrified oak. I was afraid Garnet was going to have her heart broken in tiny pieces because of it." Meredith finally hugged her elbows to still the betraying flutter of her fingers. "She came to see me last summer. Did she ever tell you? I'm afraid I recommended that she go on that lecture tour with Mrs. Ward. I'm glad Garnet made a wiser choice. I wish—"

With a forced laugh she turned to search the yard. "I wish Phineas would hurry up and come out from his hiding place. It's still such an amazement, a fox for a pet."

"I've thought the same thing, many times." His hand closed over her elbow and turned her back around. "How about if you come out from yours, hmm?"

"My what?"

"Wherever it is you're hiding." His hand dropped away. "In most ways, you and Garnet are very different, personalities as well as looks. But there's something about the expression in your eyes, Meredith. I've seen it in Garnet's, not as much as I used to, thank the Lord. But I've learned to recognize it."

"Oh?" This had been a mistake. She should have known better, should have kept her flapping gums sewed together. They hadn't come to hear about her problems, didn't need their ears filled with her secret insecurities. Her...her *whining*. Her father didn't need the burden either. No matter how he tried to disguise it, Jacob was still coping with loneliness.

Meredith tossed her head and injected a bright note in her voice. "What have you learned to recognize?"

"A troubled heart," Sloan said.

Traitorous tears welled up, making a mockery of her forced insouciance. "Sorry." She swiped them away, blinking furiously. "Leah never cries. Garnet seldom cries. I cry all the time. I hate it. I'm sorry."

"I have a clean handkerchief and two shoulders. You're welcome to them all." He handed her the folded cloth from his pocket. "Garnet used to hate her hair," he commented while Meredith blew her nose. "I'm sure you knew that."

"She was teased all through our childhood. I was too, about the tears. At least until the boys learned I could give them bloody noses and make them cry as well." Incredibly she felt lighter inside. "You're trying to tell me that I should just accept the way I am, right?"

"Mm. You hide it well, I'm beginning to realize." His gaze roved over her. "Even windblown and covered with sawdust, you still project an aura of sophistication, Miss Meredith Sinclair. Part of it's style—the clothing, the way you wear your hair. But it's all a facade, isn't it?" He balled his hand and tapped her uplifted chin. "Inside, I'm beginning to see that your heart is as tender as your sister's."

"According to my employer, my heart's too busy falling at men's feet or chasing after them until they trip over their own. I imagine Mr. Walker's of a mind that my heart is about as tender as the sole of an old boot." She searched Sloan's face. "You're a man. Which makes this awkward because…well, because I don't want you to think…" She blew out a frustrated breath.

"Think what, Meredith?" Sloan asked finally.

She never should have yielded to the impulse to talk about this. Meredith ignored the prickles of discomfort tickling the back of her throat and plunged forward. "Think that I'm a—a flirt. A tease. The sort of woman men might enjoy but never respect."

"I've known a woman like that. You're nothing like her at all." His mouth thinned, a flicker of deep anger licking through the words. "Has someone made you feel that way?"

Meredith regarded him warily. "Garnet's told me about your temper and your control. I'm finally beginning to understand both."

"Quit dodging the subject." He smiled to soften the order, but Meredith decided not to test his patience further. Sometimes medicine was best swallowed quickly.

"There are two gentlemen. One of them, I have reason to believe, finds my company pleasing. It's possible that we could form an attachment. The other gentleman"—she had to stop a moment to swallow against the unpleasant taste—"has no interest in forming any kind of personal attachment."

She paused again, briefly considered the attraction of dashing toward the barn to hide in the hayloft, felt disgust with herself at the thought, and fixed her gaze on her brother-in-law. "I don't understand why the gentleman who is not attracted to me would belittle my feelings toward the other man who has given every indication that the feelings are mutual."

"I can't speak for all men," Sloan said. "But it might help me to advise you better if you tell me their names."

"What difference would that make?"

"None. Unless you want my advice." Head tilted sideways, he stroked the ends of his mustache. "Would your employer, Benjamin Walker, happen to be one of those men?"

"Yes. The latter." She had to look away then. "He more or less implied that I was behaving like a shallow flirt, or a woman of loose morals, because of my regard for a gentleman who may or may not turn out to be a business associate."

Meredith tried to choose her words carefully. Tried to remain as rational as Leah...or at least as calm as Garnet. "There was a misunderstanding between Mr. Walker and J. Preston Clarke. I'm convinced it was—"

"J. Preston Clarke? He's the man for whom you've developed this...attraction?"

His incredulity made her bristle and banished much of her uncertainty. "Not you, too." Meredith planted her hands on her hips and plunged into battle. "I know he's the richest man in this part of the state— even more wealthy than Mr. Walker. I know I'm just a cabinetmaker's daughter, whose only claim to kinship with that sort is"—she punched the middle of Sloan's chest—"my well-heeled Yankee brother-in-law."

"Meredith, that's beside the point. You—"

"And for your information, I didn't pursue Mr. Clarke. This...this whatever has happened between us...it just *happened*." She was making a hopeless botch of everything. "Never mind. Just...never mind. I'm sorry I brought it up."

She picked up a heavy basket of food, opened the door, then turned to glare at Sloan. "I'll get supper on the table. You and Garnet probably want to start home before too late." Pain leaked through in spite of her resolve. "Thank you for putting me in my place. You do it almost as well as Mr. Walker."

Cloud cover obscured the night sky, leaving only the diffused glow from the twin lamps mounted on either side of their carriage to light the way. Sloan drove slowly, with one arm looped around Garnet's shoulders. Phineas sat between them with pricked ears, plainly enjoying the damp chilly air.

Garnet burrowed her gloved fingers into the fox's thick fur. "Do you want to tell me what happened between you and Meredith? She went out of her way to avoid talking to you at supper." In fact, her sister had all but acted as though Sloan didn't exist. "She's unhappy, I know that. Whenever she talks too much about nothing, we know something's wrong. Leah used to hide in the spring house, she got so weary of what she called Meredith's 'chirpy chatter.'"

Sloan laughed. "An apt description."

"Papa and I were sort of hoping she talked to you when the two of you were on the porch. Every time I tried to pry anything out of her, she changed the subject."

"I'm probably not her favorite person right now." His hand rose from her shoulder, and his fingers softly stroked her cheek. "Truth to tell, I'm not real proud of myself."

"Sloan...what happened? No—it's all right, baby." She patted Phineas, who relaxed back against her side with a tail-wagging whine.

"Spoiled rotten, old man, that's what you are." In the fitful lantern glow Garnet saw him smile. "And I know you're shy, but you didn't help the situation with Meredith, my pet. She just wanted to play with you, you know, not skin you for a stole."

"Sloan..."

The stroking fingers tugged the hair at the nape of her neck, then returned to the reins while he negotiated a rough patch of road. "If I had to venture a diagnosis, I'd say Meredith's struggling with some aspects of her life right now. I should have addressed that underlying issue, when she and I were out on the porch. Instead I came across like a heavy-handed older brother." He heaved a sigh. "Your sister's quite taken with J. Preston Clarke, I'm afraid."

"What? J. Preston Clarke? *The* Preston Clarke? Where could she have met him—oh. Through Mr. Walker, of course."

Dismayed, Garnet lifted Phineas onto her lap so she could snuggle closer to Sloan. "Well, the attraction must be mutual. Meredith has too much pride to chase after a man who hasn't expressed an interest." She rubbed her cheek against Sloan's sturdy shoulder. "I was afraid it was something like this, though I never expected it to be Preston Clarke. Oh, Sloan...she's lonely. She hides it well, but I know my sister. She wants someone to love, someone to love her. Like us. And with Meredith, I'm afraid discretion has always taken second place to impulse. Buttercups and bitterweed. Why did she have to fall for Mr. Clarke?"

"From the little bit I gleaned from her, you're right. The interest was initiated by him."

"And why not? Meredith's beautiful, charming. She's been the belle of Shenandoah County since we were in pinafores." *But J. Preston Clarke?* Garnet shivered a little, remembering one of her conversations with Felicity the previous summer. "Felicity Ward met Mr. Clarke. She told me he reminded her of some Italian man she'd read about in a book— Casanova, I believe was the name. I'd never heard of him. She also said Mr. Clarke enjoyed his power a bit too much."

"Mm. She said that, did she?"

Garnet nudged him. "Don't think you can adopt that lofty physician's tone with me. What haven't you told me, Dr. MacAllister? Dire consequences await arrogant husbands."

"Is that a threat, Mrs. MacAllister?"

"It might be."

His teeth flashed in a pirate's smile. Before she could blink, he pulled the horses to a halt, set the brake, and captured her mouth in a passionate kiss. "What's the penalty?" he whispered after a while. His mouth nibbled a warm trail from the line of her jaw to the sensitive spot just behind her ear. "Hmm?"

"I love you." Garnet wrapped her hands around his wrists and tugged. "But you can't divert me with seduction this time." She kissed the corner of his smiling mouth. "What do you know about Preston Clarke?"

"Smart as a fox, isn't she, fella? Very well. I can restrain myself until we're home." Sloan released her and straightened, patting an offended Phineas, who had had to leap onto the floor to avoid being squashed by his amorous demonstration. "I don't like repeating rumors, sweetheart."

"Nor do I. But Meredith is my sister. Is that what upset her? You told her something about Mr. Clarke she didn't want to hear?"

"Not exactly. She's under the impression that I object to…how shall I put it? To the differences in their stations, I suppose. She's partly correct. From what I've heard about the Clarkes, the family makes my mother sound like a patron saint of the common folk. I'm afraid Meredith will be hurt, even if the attraction is serious on both their parts."

"I daresay your family's wealth surpasses even the Clarkes'. Yet you still married me." She hesitated. "Sloan? When *are* we going to go visit your mother? I know you were hurt when she didn't attend our wedding, but—"

"Leave it, sweetheart. When the time is right, I promise we'll go. But I have patients who need me. If something happened because we were visiting…"

"All right." Garnet brought his clenched hand to her mouth and pressed a kiss to his knuckles. "I understand. We'll wait until God finishes healing all those old wounds inside your soul."

"I love you more than I have words to describe, Mrs. MacAllister." He cupped her face, then released her to pick up the reins. "Preston Clarke's rumored to keep a mistress in Front Royal," he said as the carriage wheels began to turn.

"Oh. Oh, dear."

"I didn't tell your sister. She didn't give me the opportunity, and I frankly don't know how I would have approached the matter if she had."

"Meredith wouldn't have believed you, if she truly cares for Mr. Clarke," Garnet said. "She'd claim it was nothing but nasty rumors, designed to smear his reputation out of jealousy or something. She's loyal to a fault. But there's still that impulsiveness…" She sighed. "Papa's fretted over her for years, you know. Well, not fretted, precisely. Papa doesn't fret, he just talks to God more. But you're right. If Mr. Clarke has taken an interest in Meredith, I'm afraid that's our only recourse. A whole lot of prayer. And a whole lot of patience."

Without warning, Phineas leaped onto the seat. He barked, several short, high-pitched yaps, his front paws pressed against the glass Sloan had fixed in place before they left Sinclair Run.

"What's up, fella? What do you hear out there?"

"I hear it too." Garnet twisted on the seat, struggling to open her window. "Sloan, someone's yelling. Behind us."

Without further comment her husband pulled the carriage to the side of the road again. "Stay here." He opened the door and jumped lightly to the ground.

"Sloan! Garnet! Wait! *Stop!*"

Bareback astride a horse, her skirts and petticoats shockingly hiked, Meredith galloped out of the darkness. She hauled back on the reins, bringing her mount to a half-rearing halt. "Oh, thank God!" She released her grip on the horse's mane to thrust tangled strands of unbound hair from her face. "Please. H-hurry."

Sloan caught her as she half fell, half hurled herself to the ground. "Steady. What's wrong? Is it Jacob?"

Teeth chattering, Meredith nodded, her wild-eyed gaze swinging to Garnet. "P-papa. Please…he's so sick. Sloan…he's so sick. I'm afraid he's going to—that he might—"

"Sweetheart, help your sister into the carriage while I tie her horse to the boot. Swiftly now. That's it. Hold on."

Hold on. Garnet grabbed Meredith's arm and shoved her inside. "Don't step on Phineas." Her lips felt numb, and the words sounded as though they'd been strained through a cider press. She climbed in after her sister.

"H-he was lifting my heartwood chest down. He wanted to—I was going to take it back…he doubled over. I grabbed the chest, put it on the floor. And Papa…Papa—" Her hands covered her face as she began to sob, great wrenching cries that soaked her face.

Phineas whined, his small body quivering against her ankles. Garnet lifted him to her lap, and he licked her face. She couldn't breathe, couldn't think, but Phineas calmed her. The unconditional love visible in the unblinking eyes reminded her that God knew when a sparrow fell from its nest—or a cruelly injured fox needed help. Phineas reassured her that she wasn't alone. That their father wasn't alone, not even now. *Thank You, Lord.*

"Here." She lifted Phineas and dumped him in Meredith's lap. "H-hold him. It helps."

"He doesn't like me. He won't want me to—oh." The tear-thickened words ceased when Phineas burrowed his cold nose against her neck and emitted another low whine. Meredith choked and buried her face in the soft fur.

Sloan climbed inside, slamming the door. "Hang on. We'll be back there as fast as we can." His hand closed around Garnet's and squeezed.

Then he lifted the reins. Seconds later the carriage was racing through the night.

Thirty-Four

*H*ands clasped behind his back, Ben strolled along the deserted piazza of the Jeffersonian Hotel in Luray. The hotel wouldn't officially open until May, but Ben had received permission to look around because the consortium of Northern speculators who had invested in the place six years earlier were hoping he would buy it. After two days of detailed investigation, however, Ben had increasing qualms about fulfilling their hope.

Yes, the Luray Caverns brought in tourists, enough to fill hotels to capacity as soon as they were built. With mind-numbing swiftness factories and businesses had swelled the small town's population, though nowhere near the forty thousand people that the Shenandoah Valley Railroad president had predicted.

Luray was a boom town, and yet…

Ben stepped into the street, frowning as he studied the three-story hotel. Someone touched his arm. "Excuse me, Mr. Walker?" The hotel manager's son stepped back, smiling nervously.

"Yes?"

"You have a call on the telephone, sir. If you'll follow me?"

A telephone call? Concern mounting, Ben hurried after the boy, into the deserted hotel.

An hour later he and Hominy were on the way to the depot, where he made arrangements to catch a southbound train out of Strasburg to Woodstock. Mrs. Biggs couldn't provide as much information as he would have liked, so Ben had decided to pay a visit to the Sinclair home in person. Find out for himself the gravity of Jacob Sinclair's illness.

"You sure you don't need me to come along with you, Mr. Ben?" Hominy asked again after the ticket transactions.

"I'm a big boy now, Hominy. I reckon I can find my way around without getting lost."

"Still don't look right, you not having a driver, or a—"

"If you say 'servant' I'll have to fire you."

"Don't get uppity with me, Mr. Ben." They exchanged mock glares. "A man in your station ought to have himself a valet. Miss Arbuckle said so."

"Perhaps I'll fire Miss Arbuckle instead."

Ben hefted his traveling case onto the loaded cart, waving aside the overworked station agent. "There. See how efficiently I took care of my bag? I don't need a valet, and 'station' has nothing to do with it. Be that as it may"—he clasped Hominy's massive shoulder—"I'm still going to Sinclair Run. Don't worry. I have something in mind to keep you occupied, so you won't go to worrying about me."

"Ah." The deep chocolate face relaxed. "You want me to find out more 'bout why folks is leaving here? Why the county poorhouses are busting at the seams?"

"No. What you've unearthed was enough. I've made my decision." Ben gestured toward the end of the platform, where fewer people milled about. "I need you to do something back in Winchester."

He explained in careful detail. When the train pulled up moments later, a determined glint had replaced the doubt in Hominy's eyes.

Once the train was in motion, Ben set aside the matter he had discussed with Hominy, along with the Jeffersonian Hotel in Luray, and focused his thoughts on Meredith Sinclair's latest difficulty. Sometimes he wondered if his office manager's middle name was Drama.

Last summer it had been the sister, he remembered. Some kind of an accident. The family had suffered its fair share of trials, right enough. But at least they were still a family, able to pull together for support even though the mother had died years earlier, Meredith once told him. Ben hoped they wouldn't have to pull together for another funeral, this one for their father.

He debarked in Woodstock, which was only a few miles from Sinclair Run, and rented a hack. The owner of the livery provided directions to Sinclair Run.

"But this ain't a good time, if you're after ordering furniture." He cast an experienced eye over Ben's well-cut three-piece tweed suit and stylish fedora. "Ah…Jacob's feelin' right poorly, from what I hear."

"I know. I'm paying a call to find out how he's doing." But the man had given him an idea. "He makes good furniture, does he?"

"The best. Couldn't afford any myself, but I seen a sideboard he built for Judge Milstead, some years back. I hear tell Jacob's new son-in-law's got him fashioning a whole bedroom suite. Keep Jacob in clover the rest of his life." The loquacious fellow spat a stream of tobacco juice in a spittoon and rubbed the expanse of his belly. "Assuming the doc can keep him alive, so's he don't end up pushing daisies instead of living in the clover."

Ben thanked him for the information and climbed into the two-seater road wagon. Several miles later he turned left onto a winding lane that disappeared behind a hill crowded with cedar and hardwood trees.

His first impression of the Sinclair home was a surprise. He hadn't expected anything this large, nor so finely crafted. Wood siding, with steeply pitched roofs and a dormer that provided whimsical asymmetry. Beautifully turned ornamentation. Ben wondered when it had been built—sometime after the War, no doubt, except where had Sinclair procured the funds?

Meredith and her family were fast becoming an obsession, but Ben shied away from the implications. He did, however, make a mental note to inquire about the builder at some appropriate time in the future. The man would definitely be worth pursuing as an addition to Ben's cadre of highly skilled professionals.

After securing the reins, he pulled out his watch: 4:27. Without warning, memories swelled, clamoring against the tightly locked door of the past. *His mother's quiet voice murmured in his ear, her frail fingers pointing to a large brick house that to Ben's seven-year-old eyes was the size of a castle. "That was your heritage, Benjamin. If God had willed it, we would be inside now, entertaining callers for afternoon tea." She'd patted his head.* Even now he could almost feel the boneless pressure of her cold fingers. *"I tried...I lost it. Perhaps...it was never meant to be. But I want you to see it. Remember it because it is your heritage, whether or not you ever run up and down the stairs again."*

Ben crammed the watch back in his pocket and mounted the porch steps. He knocked, but after several moments with no response, he turned away, vaguely uneasy about the depth of his disappointment. Then the door opened behind him, and Ben swiveled back around.

"Mr. Walker?" Meredith's incredulous gaze scanned him from head to toe, as though afraid her eyes were playing tricks on her.

"Good afternoon, Miss Sinclair."

He schooled his face to remain expressionless, wondering if *his* eyes were playing tricks. In all the time he'd known her, Meredith Sinclair's appearance had been a point of pride to her. Never a hair out of place, shirtwaists always starched and pressed, accessories always appropriate. Her costumes, though not expensive, were always elegant, always the height of fashion.

The woman who faced him now more resembled the laundress after a hard day. The contrast delighted Ben, but all he said was, "Mrs. Biggs told me that your father was very ill and that you had taken emergency sick leave."

"But...why are you here?" Faint color climbed into her cheeks, and her hand patted ineffectually at her disheveled hair, behind her in a long braid. "I beg your pardon. I don't mean to be rude. It's just...I'm...I know I look—"

"You look like a devoted daughter," Ben interrupted. He stepped forward, forcing Meredith to make way for him to come inside. "How is your father? Don't fret—I won't stay long. But I wanted to know."

"Sloan—Dr. MacAllister, my sister Garnet's husband, says Papa's passed through the crisis stage." Her red-rimmed eyes glistened with fresh tears, and she waved an apology. "Sorry. It's just...for the past five days we haven't known if..." She took the handkerchief Ben handed her. "But he's going to be fine. Fine."

Her head went back, and she took a deep breath. Ben watched

while she composed herself, trying, he knew, to distance herself from the unexpected intimacy of her employer's presence in her home. "I'm very relieved to hear that," he said. "Are you taking care of him all by yourself?"

"I'm as good a nurse as either of my sisters."

"I'm sure you are. Calm your ruffled feathers. The question wasn't intended as a criticism. Candidly, I admire you, whether or not you had help."

"Meredith?" a low musical voice softly called. "Who was—oh." The middle sister, the one with red hair and haunting eyes Ben remembered from the previous summer, descended the stairs. "Aren't you—?"

"Benjamin Walker. Yes." He smiled. "Sorry to drop in. Obviously you're not receiving callers. But you don't own a telephone, and I wanted to find out how Mr. Sinclair was doing."

"That was thoughtful of you." The redhead—what was her name?—smiled. Her gaze slid sideways to Meredith. "Please. Come into the parlor. Unlike us, it's quite tidy. Thanks to our younger sister, Leah, it received a thorough cleaning before she had to go back to school. Meredith, Papa's asleep, so you can entertain Mr. Walker while I fetch some refreshments."

Ben watched her give Meredith's hand a squeeze, a look of understanding deepening her fine gray green eyes. Then she whisked through a doorway.

"In spite of what she thinks, Garnet's the beautiful sister," Meredith said, making Ben wonder what mistaken interpretation she'd applied to his expression. "Leah got all the brains." She gestured to a comfortably worn sofa covered with finely crafted throw pillows. "As you've learned, I got all the brass. It's a bit tarnished right now, but I promise to polish myself back up before I return to work." She hesitated. "I...do I still have a job, Mr. Walker?"

"Don't be absurd. Of course you do. Mrs. Biggs and Lowell can muddle along for a while, but we all look forward to the return of my office manager."

Some of the gray fatigue lifted from her face. Ben stood by a parlor chair next to the sofa until Meredith sat down, and for a moment he rested his hand on her shoulder. A tremor rippled through her deter-minedly erect frame. Ben stepped back, though not before his fingers tucked a limp strand of chestnut hair behind her ear.

"Mr. Walker!"

Unrepentant, he dropped onto the sofa. "Stop fretting about your appearance when it's irrelevant to the circumstances. How you look is important only when you're on the job, not when you've spent the past five days fighting off death in your father's behalf."

"I wasn't fretting." He quirked a brow, waiting without comment until she made a face. "Oh, very well. I was. I suppose you're right. Over the past week I haven't cared a straw what I threw on, so I shouldn't now. I should thank God that death has been banished from the door, so to speak. Actually, most of the credit goes to Sloan. We just did what he told us to do."

"Here we go." Garnet Sinclair returned with a tray. "It's only tea and day-old biscuits, I'm afraid. The cook we hired for our father quit, which was more of a blessing than a burden. Because she couldn't cook." She and Meredith exchanged wry glances. "Leah made these before she went back to school yesterday." After everyone was served, she told them she needed to pack, that when her husband returned to check on his patient that evening she planned to go back home with him to Tom's Brook. She would have her tea while she worked, and keep an eye on their father.

After she vanished up the stairs, Ben and Meredith sat quietly, drinking their hot tea. For a few moments he chewed over Garnet's behavior. Discretion, or indifference to propriety? Finally he shrugged and focused his attention on Meredith, debating whether to broach a potentially volatile issue, or just wait for events to unfold.

Meredith, not for the first time, took the decision out of his hands.

"I plan to be back by tomorrow, at the latest, since the dinner with Mr. Clarke is Thursday. What have you been up to?"

"Been in Luray for three days." He didn't elaborate. "I'll return to Winchester this evening, since my office manager hasn't been there to mop up any spills. No, Miss Sinclair. Don't apologize." He laid aside the cup and leaned forward. "You're a vital member of my staff. But I don't want you to return until you're satisfied about your father's condition, even if it takes another week."

"You'd like that, wouldn't you? If I'm not present for dinner Thursday evening, Mr. Clarke will be placed in an awkward position."

Impudent baggage. Unfortunately, Ben couldn't deny a degree of truth, even if it wasn't the whole truth. "What makes you think my motives are completely impure, Miss Sinclair? Your family, not your job, should be the most important part of your life."

"I haven't noticed much evidence of that noble sentiment on your part. In the almost three years I've known you, you haven't even mentioned your family, much less paid them a visit."

"I don't have any family. They're all dead." He waited until her horrified gaze met his. "My father and my three oldest brothers died in the War. My mother lingered two years after that before dying herself, her health as well as her heart broken. My only sister contracted pneumonia while I was searching for work in a burned-down city. Since I was all of nine years old at the time, I didn't fare too well. There was no money for a doctor. My sister died in my arms. She was six."

Silence filled the parlor.

"I'm so sorry," Meredith said, her voice stifled. She leaned forward, her fingers skimming his clenched knuckles. "Mr. Walker...I'm sorry. I had no right. What I said—I was rude. Insensitive."

Ben scraped up a smile. "It was a long time ago. Hominy's the closest thing to family I have left. He...used to help take care of me, when I was a toddler."

"I know. He told me some months ago."

"So you see, it has nothing to do with J. Preston Clarke." Of course, some of it did. He'd do everything in his power to keep his naive office manager out of the clutches of the man. But his next words came straight from the darkest corner of his soul. "Jobs can be lost, Miss Sinclair, new ones secured. But if you lose your family, it's forever."

Thirty-Five

$\mathcal{F}$or the first time since she was a gawky thirteen-year-old, Meredith didn't know what to say. Not even in her most impractical dreams had she ever conjured up Benjamin Walker in the family parlor. Even if she had been so foolish, certainly she would have imagined far different circumstances.

Yet there he lounged, relaxed and at ease. The upholstered sofa, accustomed to slighter feminine bodies, seemed made to accommodate his broad shoulders and six foot-plus frame. His large hands handled the plain stoneware mug with the same delicacy with which he'd sipped Brazilian coffee from a translucent Haviland cup in the posh surroundings of Excelsior's dining room. He looked around the room as though he had nothing on his mind beyond a congenial social visit.

Yet the words about his family still burned Meredith's ears. She couldn't wrap her mind around it, couldn't find the words to tell him how ashamed she was of her impetuous accusation.

In the space of two heartbeats, Benjamin Walker had turned from a sophisticated, imperturbable employer to a vulnerable, flesh-and-blood man. And Meredith wasn't quite sure how to reconcile the two.

"My mother died when I was seven." Restless, she gathered the empty mugs and stood. "Until this past week when I thought I would lose my father, I've never felt so alone and scared in my entire life. Um...I'll just take these to the kitchen."

"Leave it." The quiet words were spoken with his usual half-smile, but the order was unmistakable. "Relax. Sit back down, why don't you?"

"It won't take—all right."

His smile deepened. Meredith's mouth twitched in response because, for some reason, she was able to relax.

"Tell me about your father," he said. "He really is out of danger?"

She nodded. "For years he's suffered from what I understand is called a duodenal ulcer. Sloan said this particular episode was so dangerous because it was complicated by some condition whose name I can't begin to pronounce. I have a feeling our old family doctor wouldn't have even heard of it." She picked up her half-eaten biscuit and nibbled, talking between bites. "Not that it matters. Sloan's the most amazing doctor I've ever known. I'm convinced he has God's ear, twenty-four hours a day. My brother-in-law is half-physician, half-priest, the way he talks to the Lord all the time."

"Regardless of who was responsible, I'm very glad your father's better." He regarded her with a peculiar twist of his lips. "I can't remember the last time I talked to God about anything."

"Oh." She blinked, uncertain how to respond.

Mr. Walker shrugged. "You needn't worry over my immortal soul. I accept all the childhood tenets of my Christian faith and yes, I'm grateful for Jesus' sacrifice. But as far as I'm concerned, what I accomplish with my life is my responsibility. Not God's. So why talk to Him?"

For a moment there was silence, not quite comfortable. "I'd better go," he said.

"You...you're welcome to stay for supper, if you like. It's not much —Papa's diet is very restrictive right now, and for simplicity's sake Garnet and I eat pretty much the same thing. But you'd be welcome."

She was talking too fast. When she caught sight of her steepling fingers, she thrust them into her lap.

"Thank you, but I think company's the last thing you need, especially when it's a man who makes you as nervous as I seem to."

"I am not uncomfortable." *At least, not any longer,* she promised herself. "This is my home, for goodness' sake. Besides, you've seen me looking my worst and haven't run screaming back down the lane."

"It was close." His gaze fell on her heartwood chest, sitting forgotten beside the chair. "That's an interesting piece. What is it—a legless footstool?"

Annoyed, Meredith leaned over and picked up her chest, hugging it close. Her nose caught a whiff of the fresh coat of shellac her father had applied a week earlier. He'd looked so disappointed the day she'd brought it home covered with dust and sheepishly handed it to him. He hadn't uttered a word of reproach, just cleaned it up until the wood shone like glistening satin again.

She glanced at Benjamin Walker, her fingers curling protectively around the edges. "It's my heartwood chest. Papa made it for me when I was a girl. He made one for each of us…"

The words trailed into awkward silence when Mr. Walker reached for the chest and sat back down with it balanced on his knees. "Nice work. Finish is as soft and smooth as"—he looked across at Meredith—"as your hands."

"Mr. Walker!"

"What's this?"

Unbelievably, his fingers had located the secret drawer. Without thought Meredith snatched the chest back, then retreated behind the back of the sofa. "I thought you had to leave."

"So I do."

He stood easily, then swiveled on his heel and reached her in two long strides. The chest was plucked from her grasp again, and Benjamin Walker returned to his seat.

Belated indignation sputtered forth. "That was rude. It's none of your concern. I don't want you to see—"

It was too late. She watched with her hands digging into the sofa's tufted velvet back, while the man she had catalogued as congenial and easygoing opened the drawer nobody but her family had ever seen.

"A cookie cutter?" He held it in strong-looking, blunt fingers, a look of intense concentration on his face. "There's a story here, isn't there?" He paused. "I'd like to hear it, Meredith."

For the first time in her life, Meredith couldn't think of a single thing to say. The emotions jumping inside her were both too volatile and too fragile. "My father put it in there. I don't know why."

She tried to swallow, then moistened her lips. Temper building, she rounded the chair and thrust out her hand. "Give it to me. I might work for you, but that doesn't give you the right to pry into my personal life. To take advantage when I'm worn out from worrying about my father."

"You're right." But he didn't hand over the dented tin gingerbread girl. Instead, he carefully laid it back in its nest inside the secret drawer. "There." He closed it up and placed the chest in her hands, his fingers brushing against hers.

Meredith jerked, then turned and laid the chest back on the floor. When she straightened, Mr. Walker was in the hallway, removing his fedora from the hall tree.

"Thank you for stopping by. It was…very thoughtful."

"You're welcome."

"If our old housekeeper Mrs. Willowby arrives in the morning as planned, I should be back by tomorrow afternoon. Assuming my father is completely out of danger."

"Of course."

"Mr. Walker…" She wished she weren't so tired, wished she could organize her jumbled thoughts.

"Miss Sinclair…"

Suddenly he was right in front of her, and he was lifting her right hand, bringing it—*was he going to kiss her hand?* Transfixed, Meredith's breath wedged in her throat while she watched his head dip and warm lips brushed the back of her hand. Her gaze jerked up to his face. "Why did you do that?"

He released her hand and stepped back. "Because I wanted to, Miss Sinclair." He picked his hat back up. "And because you looked both defenseless and imperious. A captivating combination."

He opened the front door, and Meredith trailed after him like an automaton.

Just before he climbed into the buggy seat he turned around. "By the way…one of these days I'd like to meet your father. I have a theory or two about your cookie cutter, and I'd like to discuss them with him. Good afternoon," he paused, then added very softly, "Meredith."

She peeked inside her father's room thirty minutes later, relieved when his head turned toward her and he gestured with his hand.

Meredith sat down in the chair they'd stationed beside the bed. "Mr. Walker was just here, inquiring after you."

"Oh, aye?" The bones of his skull stood out prominently, and the lines in his beloved face were deeper. But love burned unabated from his eyes. "Most considerate of him."

"Papa…" She wanted to bury her face in her hands and weep, she wanted God to make him well, to restore his health…more than anything, she wanted—no, *needed*—to talk.

Instead she leaned over and gently smoothed back his thinning hair. "Sloan should be here soon, and Mrs. Willowby arrives tomorrow. I'd rather stay here myself—"

"We've been all through that, Merry-go-round. 'Tis best this way. You girls worry too much, instead of trusting the Lord. Mrs. Willowby's one of His angels, don't you know, and I'm looking forward to renewing our acquaintance." A faint smile drifted over his face. "Remember what you did when she came to be our housekeeper right after your dear mother died?"

Resigned, she folded her hands. "How could I forget, with you reminding me at least once a season?"

"Standing at the door, rolling pin clutched in both hands and the light of battle in your eye, informing the poor lady she was neither welcome nor needed. You were the new mistress of the house, and you could care for everyone just fine."

"And all the while I'm scorching the soup I'd made for dinner, Leah's screaming at the top of her lungs, and Garnet's tugging my arm to try and keep me from braining Mrs. Willowby with the rolling pin. Yes, Papa, I remember. I also remember that Mrs. Willowby was wise enough to tell you that we'd all recover best if we were left alone, with our papa, and to call her again in six months."

"And we managed just fine until she did return, didn't we, lass?" His hand fumbled across the counterpane. "As we'll manage now. Mrs. Willowby was a dear blessing for all of us, those few years we needed her the most. But before and after, we still managed just fine. Never forget that, Merry-girl. Sometimes a board has to suffer an extra sanding or two, perhaps even the bite of the chisel. But the final result is a thing of beauty. Trust the Lord's purpose, lass. Everything will be all right."

For a while they sat, hands linked, Meredith every now and then dabbing the corner of her eyes, grateful when her father pretended not to notice.

"Papa?"

"Mm?"

"Am I a selfish person? Someone who thinks more highly of her own wants than she does everyone else's?"

"Now why would you be asking is what I'd like to know." He dragged her hand up over his chest, tightening his grip when Meredith would have freed herself. "You've been brooding for days. I've noticed, aye, even when the pain was gnawing at my vitals."

"Papa, that wasn't why—I mean, your condition…did I cause it?"

"No. *No*. Meredith, look at me. Don't do this to yourself, lass." He grimaced, and Meredith leaped to snatch up the sodium bicarbonate, her fingers trembling. "Stop it. I'm all right." He grabbed her wrist. "Meredith Margaret Sinclair! I'm all right."

Garnet rushed into the room. "Papa, Meredith! What is it?"

"He's in pain. He needs—"

"What I need is for the two of you to stop leaping like fleas every time I twitch." Jacob glowered at them. "Lord save me, but you'd think after a week you'd allow your poor father the luxury of a painful belch or two."

Garnet laughed and hugged Meredith. "He must be better, to be fussing at us."

Ashamed of her outburst, Meredith rose, pretending to straighten the bottles and the assortment of spoons on the rolling teacart Leah had turned into a bedside table. "It will be a relief to leave him to Mrs. Willowby. Someone new he can scold."

"You are going back in the morning then?" Garnet's gray green eyes assessed her with a shrewdness that caused Meredith to bristle.

"What of it? Papa himself is insisting. Besides, you're going home tonight."

"Only if Sloan convinces me that Papa's out of danger and needs nothing but a few more weeks of bed rest."

"Won't do it," Jacob interrupted. "Too much to do."

"No, you don't," Meredith said. "Leah and I took care of that. We found the list of your orders out in the workshop, compared those to the ledger in your desk, and wrote to everyone, explaining the delay."

" 'Tis a sorry day when a father loses control of his own daughters." He stirred, and Garnet moved to the other side of the bed, straightening covers, bending down to kiss his perspiring forehead.

Within moments he'd drifted back to sleep.

Meredith and Garnet tiptoed out, waiting until they were in the kitchen to speak.

"Are you sure you shouldn't wait another day or two?" Garnet asked.

"Are you sure?" Meredith countered. "Mr. Walker has been more understanding than most employers"—far more than she deserved—"but it's not right to take advantage of the situation when we all know that Mrs. Willowby is coming."

Garnet busied herself washing the cups and saucers, keeping her back to Meredith. "You're right," she said. "I was being selfish. I miss Sloan, I even miss Phineas. But that's not the same as your not being able to honor your job commitment."

She glanced over her shoulder, and guilt crawled through Meredith at the sweetness of her sister's smile. "So I'll tell Sloan that I've decided to stay here another few days, at least until Mrs. Willowby is more familiar with Papa's care."

"I detest it when you're a martyr." Meredith moved to the sink and wrapped an arm fiercely around her sister. "Especially when you're better at it than I am." They exchanged a laugh. "We're being silly. Let's wait for Sloan. If he pronounces Papa well along the road to recovery, there's absolutely no reason why we both can't leave him to Mrs. Willowby's 'angelic' care, and our worries at the door." She picked up a drying cloth.

"Meredith?"

"What?"

"Be careful, Thursday night."

Meredith made a production out of drying a mug and hanging it on the spindle in the huge open-faced cupboard Jacob had made the winter she was twelve. One of the spindles was crudely finished, lacking in symmetry. She first rubbed its rough surface with her fingers, then the smooth one next to it, which was almost indistinguishable from all the others.

Full of confidence, Meredith had insisted on helping her father, but she had refused to listen to his patient instructions. Jacob fastened that first attempt in place on the cupboard in spite of Meredith's pleading.

For her second attempt, she had carefully listened, carefully followed instructions. To this day those two spindles offered encouragement—and warning—whenever she entered the kitchen.

Meredith clung to the second spindle now, feeling as though she were somehow clinging to her father's hand. "You're trying to warn me away from Mr. Clarke, aren't you?" she asked Garnet at last. "Why? I thought you of all people would understand."

"I do. More than you've ever given me credit for."

"Then why—Sorry." Meredith lifted her hands, let them drop. "Let's not quarrel. I wish you would believe that I'm trying as hard as I can not to make the same mistake I did with Lamar. But what if...what if Mr. Clarke is the man God has picked out for me? How will I know if I don't take advantage of these opportunities?"

Garnet opened her mouth, closed it. Then: "I don't know. I'm still learning how to listen myself. Just...be careful. I understand that you're trying to free God's hand. Until you know for sure, all I ask is that you remember to guard your heart."

"I'll try. Unfortunately, redbird, that's always been one of your strengths, not mine."

Thirty-Six

On Thursday gusts of wind buffeted the Valley throughout the day, and a March squall blew over the western mountains after lunch. But by sunset the sky shone a clear ice blue, washed with pink and lavender on the horizon.

"…and make sure the waiters don't bring out the salmon until Mr. Clarke has finished his soup." Meredith scanned her sheet of notes. "About the hothouse melon from California. You are quite satisfied with its quality?"

"Mademoiselle, I am quite satisfied with *everything*."

Gaspar turned, issuing terse instructions to a servant hovering in the background. The young girl bobbed her head and scurried off. Muttering to himself, Gaspar lifted the lid from a large pot and sniffed the contents before fixing an indulgent eye on Meredith. "I am satisfied with everything," he said with a smile, "except my ability to be ready by the hour of eight o'clock if you persist in demanding an accounting of the preparations, *non?*"

Meredith blushed. Gaspar ruled his domain with a firm hand. Yet for some reason she'd never understood, the austere Frenchman had taken a liking to her. "Mr. Clarke plans to compare your culinary skills to those of his personal chef. Did I tell you?"

Gaspar furiously chewed the corners of his walrus mustache. "There is no comparison. I am…incomparable."

"Of course you are. Mr. Walker wouldn't employ you otherwise."

They exchanged satisfied nods. Then Meredith whisked out of the kitchen, snatching a carrot stick from a stack of washed vegetables on her way. The laborer busily slicing turnips on a massive butcher's block winked at her, and she waved in response.

A quick foray with the restaurant manager was next. "A word, Mr. Dayton?"

"Miss Sinclair, we've spoken four times since noon. What do you wish to know now?" Mr. Dayton's narrow face—he reminded Meredith of a starving basset hound—was resigned.

Despite months of showering him with sunny charm, Meredith had never coaxed the poor fellow from beneath his shell of perpetual gloom. Today she was too nervous to try.

"I just wanted to remind you to make sure the napkins are folded in the Calais Douvres design. Mr. Walker told me it's a new one, very popular in fashionable New York hotels. I'd hate for him to dash in from Strasburg at the last moment and find everything less than perfect. This dinner with Mr. Clarke is very important, you know."

"I have had the privilege of managing this restaurant for many important meals, Miss Sinclair. Most of them before you arrived on the scene."

"I know that. And of course you're right. This is just the first one where I'll be a guest as well as an office manager." She offered a contrite smile. "Don't worry. I won't bother you again. I promise."

Mr. Dayton stiffly inclined his head. "Has Mr. Walker returned yet?"

"Hominy told me his train's due to arrive at 6:30. That won't give him much time, which is why I'm trying to ensure that everything is under control."

The mournful eyes studied her without expression. "Miss Sinclair, I believe everyone and everything is under control...but you."

He was right, but Meredith wasn't about to admit it. "It's an important meeting," she repeated. "J. Preston Clarke wields a lot of influence hereabouts. It's vital to persuade him that Mr. Walker's new venture is a worthy one that will boost the local economy instead of drain it. The ambiance of the meal can help to achieve the desired effect."

"Mr. Walker doesn't need the patronage of J. Preston Clarke."

"Perhaps you think so. But it can't hurt."

Over the next several hours, while she prepared herself for the dinner, Meredith fumed over the hotel staff's attitude toward Preston Clarke.

She could appreciate their loyalty to Benjamin Walker. After all, he was the kind of man who inspired loyalty in everyone, from a scullery maid to the president of the Shenandoah Valley Railroad.

But Meredith recognized the advantage to be gained through establishing a favorable connection with Mr. Clarke, whose influence extended far beyond the Shenandoah Valley, perhaps even as far as the nation's capitol. One of his uncles was reputed to be a lawyer with the ears of several congressmen. Why couldn't everyone else comprehend the potential as well?

By 7:30, after thanking a parlor maid for fastening her corset stays and the buttons on her dinner gown, Meredith's nerves were wound more tightly than corkscrew curls. After the admiring maid left, Meredith studied herself more critically in a cheval mirror. Good. The deep mauve color flattered without shouting. While the gown might not be from Paris, it was the best she could muster with less than three weeks to prepare—and half her monthly salary. Her share of Leah's tuition, at Leah's insistence, had been sacrificed.

For the past two weeks Meredith had struggled with the guilt. Now, faced with the daunting prospect of dinner with two wealthy gentlemen used to the company of equally wealthy society ladies, Meredith silently thanked her youngest sister. Next month she would live on bread and water so she could send Leah twice as much.

Chin lifted, she turned sideways, twisting her neck to view the back of her gown. The smaller bustle—one of the fashion statements of the season—was much easier to manage, so hopefully she wouldn't make an idiot of herself when she sat down. And the grumbling seamstress had yielded to Meredith's insistence, raising the neckline an additional two inches. Enjoying the company of gentlemen was one thing. "Advertising one's wares" was an accusation Meredith was determined never to risk.

She fastened the necklace Garnet had given her for Christmas around her neck. It wasn't expensive, but the simple locket reminded her of her family and helped counteract the jittery state of her insides.

For her hair, she'd settled on the classic elegance of a Roman knot, thankful that her naturally thick hair had never needed artificial switches.

The style suited circumstances perfectly, she decided, since this was after all a business as well as a social occasion. As she studied the result—still neatly in place because she hadn't faced the six-block walk from her boardinghouse—she reminded herself to thank Mr. Walker. Before he left that morning, due to the inclement weather he had insisted that one of the ground-floor rooms be readied for her use. The night might have turned fair, but Meredith appreciated his gesture nonetheless.

After the meal, of course, she planned to return to her room at the boardinghouse.

Wouldn't it be a divine sign of sorts, if Mr. Clarke offered to drive her home?

You're stalling, Meredith, not to mention presuming on the Lord again. On the other hand, perhaps she was merely exercising her faith. A sort of Ruth, gleaning Boaz's wheat, though Meredith had no intention of curling up at any man's feet to sleep. A ride home in his carriage would suffice quite—

Impatient with herself, Meredith turned her back on the mirror, pulled on her long white gloves, and sailed out the door.

She pressed a hand to her fluttering stomach as she promenaded down the long hall to the lobby. Wouldn't do to keel over into the salad from lightheadedness. *All right then, focus on something else, say a prayer—no. Too easily distracted.* She had to keep it something concrete, something she could see or touch or hear like…like the gentle sway of the lighter bustle. The elegant weight of its train.

For weeks Meredith had been preparing for this evening. Yet now that the moment had arrived at last, deep-seated insecurity assailed her along with excitement. What if she'd been mistaken about Mr. Clarke's intentions? His regard? The hall narrowed, darkened to a tunnel that led not toward the hopeful answer to a prayer, but the inescapable dungeon of her most secret fear. *God? I'm so lonely…so tired of pretending that I'm content being a professional spinster. I don't want to spend the rest of my life alone.*

Mr. Walker met her in the lobby. "Dressed for the kill, are we?" he murmured, bowing over her extended hand.

"Of course." Dry-mouthed, she watched his lips brush her gloved knuckles before tucking her hand inside his arm. He cut a dashing figure in his formal blacks and blinding white shirtfront. Dashing…yet dangerous. Dangerous? "So are you."

"Lots of shades of meaning in that expression, aren't there? Too bad our perspectives are in opposite corners."

Meredith stopped. "What is that supposed to mean?"

"You can think about it, while Mr. Clarke and I…discourse…over the meal." He continued walking, forcing her to join him or trip over the hem of her gown.

"I take it you prefer that I play the part of a charming but silent fixture? Something to soften the atmosphere?"

His quiet chuckle raised goose bumps along with her hackles. "You don't need to play at the charm. Silence, on the other hand, might be too big a stretch. Tell you what, Miss Sinclair. I'll let you decide. Use your womanly instincts, and we'll see what happens."

"Use my 'womanly' instincts? How…ungentlemanly of you, Mr. Walker. Especially when I've spent the last hours making sure my appearance evokes the soul of professional discretion."

Meredith looked up into the freshly shaved face, to the firm line of his jaw and the unyielding slant of cheekbone. A shiver danced down her spine. Three days earlier, his unexpected visit to Sinclair Run had forced her to see Benjamin Walker as a man, not merely her employer. In the ensuing days, however, she had convinced herself that fundamentally nothing had changed: Over the last year she'd enjoyed working for Mr. Walker, enjoyed his easygoing smile and affable charm. Their relationship was based on nothing beyond mutual respect. Meredith saw no reason to alter her perception just because he'd been clever enough to locate the secret compartment in her heartwood chest.

Anybody who examined it closely enough could locate it—she'd never understood why her father placed such significance in a childhood keepsake. Mr. Walker's behavior that day was just a momentary aberration. The kiss he'd brushed against her knuckles had been nothing beyond a courtly gesture, in keeping with his sophistication.

He'd never given her cause to regard him in any other way.

Until now.

Meredith squared her shoulders. Fluttering her eyelashes, she curved her lips in what an effusive suitor once dubbed the "alluring smile of DaVinci's *Mona Lisa*." "If I understand you correctly, you're wanting me to play the part of coquette."

Off to their right, a doorman opened the massive oak door. J. Preston Clarke swept in, his black evening cloak swirling, then settling about his shoulders. He removed his top hat and handed it and the cloak to the doorman. Light from the crystal chandelier overhead gleamed on the neat part of his hair. Like Benjamin Walker, he was dressed to the nines in formal dinner attire.

Mr. Walker leaned down, forcing Meredith's attention. "Will you merely be playing the part, Miss Sinclair?"

Then he straightened, leading her across the lobby toward Mr. Clarke, whose rapt gaze fastened on to Meredith as though the man beside her were invisible. Such unconcealed admiration dispelled much of the queer sensation of hurt weighing Meredith's limbs and allowed her to pull her arm free. She smiled.

"Mr. Clarke! It's a pleasure to see you again. I've been looking forward to this occasion. Allow me to present my employer, Mr. Benjamin Walker."

Ben lifted the crystal goblet, sipping sparkling water while he watched Preston Clarke and Meredith. A cigar-store Indian could see that Meredith was smitten; what young woman wouldn't be, with the man drowning her in deference intensified by a charisma women no doubt found irresistible. Ben wondered cynically how much Clarke's money and pedigreed background added to the allure.

The deference seemed patronizing, the charisma calculated...but Ben gave the fellow full marks for the consistency of his performance. By the end of the evening, Ben himself was almost convinced that Preston Clarke might prove to be a useful professional asset. Almost.

"I confess to amazement that your chef was able to procure my favorite bottled water." Clarke lifted his own goblet. "Since it's imported from France and frightfully expensive, I'm left to conclude that you and I enjoy not only similar tastes, but the ability to indulge them." He drained the goblet. "A surprise for both of us, hmm? Hopefully, a pleasant one. Might be an indication of other similar tastes."

Egotistical peacock. If Preston ever demanded an exact inventory of his private cellars, one of those surprises would be the absence of a case of his favorite mineral water. Two days earlier, Hominy had persuaded Clarke's butler to donate the case "for the sake of comparison of local mineral waters." Hominy had declined to tell the butler precisely *how* the comparison would be achieved or by whom. Ben's and Hominy's subterfuge was perhaps less than honorable, but Ben decided the mild astonishment on Clarke's face upon taking his first sip was worth the momentary discomfort of a tweaking conscience.

"Life is full of surprises," he replied with a bland smile. He glanced at Meredith. "Wouldn't you agree, Miss Sinclair?"

"Life would be boring without the occasional surprise."

She launched into a lighthearted tale to illustrate the point, her lively face tinted a delectable apricot color. Clarke responded with a gallant riposte. They both laughed, then Clarke regaled her with a story of his own.

"And of course I couldn't refuse," he eventually concluded with a wry smile. "One simply can't afford to offend one's relatives, especially when it's a charming elderly aunt. Do you agree, Mr. Walker?"

From the corner of his eye Ben caught Meredith's tiny flinch. "I certainly do," he said. "As I recently told Miss Sinclair, jobs can always be replaced. Family members cannot."

"Ah. I detect an undercurrent here. You've lost family then?"

Ben dropped his napkin on the table and leaned back. "I'm sure you've had me investigated as thoroughly as I've had you investigated. You know I have no close family members left."

A sore point, he admitted to himself, since somehow the bulk of Preston's family had survived the War intact. Clarkes proliferated from Winchester to Washington, secure as sultans in the profits that followed the war.

"Of course," Preston said. "You're quite right. Forgive me." Ben grudgingly gave him credit for aplomb. "My family has lived here for over a hundred years, and I tend toward—I admit it—a rather feudal cast of mind. People look to us for support, for economic stability. You may have discovered that for yourself, in your own investigation. When an outsider attains a certain level of influence…" He smiled and shrugged.

"Ah yes. The letter to the editor." Ben quirked a brow, returning his guest's bland smile.

"Let's just say that letter was the first move in a chess game. A game, I confess, that I've begun to thoroughly enjoy."

"Some might question your tactics, though Miss Sinclair assures me that your motives were pure."

Preston threw his head back and laughed. "Hardly that. Where did you find this gem, Mr. Walker? I might have to steal her away from you." He bestowed upon Meredith a smile that had every one of Ben's muscles clenching in protest.

The apricot tint deepened in Meredith's cheeks. Her worried gaze darted between Ben and his dinner guest.

"Shall we adjourn?" Ben kept his voice carefully neutral as he signaled to his headwaiter, Henry. "I've always considered it poor manners to discuss business over a meal."

"Were we discussing business?" Preston inquired, his expression as congenial as Ben's. "If so, I'm intrigued by your inclusion of Miss Sinclair. Women and business shouldn't mix, my father always told me. Not only is it rude, but women are much smarter than men. If we ever invited them into our domain, we'd lose control altogether."

This time all three of them laughed, though doubtless only Ben's was forced. Meredith rose, and the men followed suit. She looked incredibly fetching in her mauve gown. Incredibly…tempting. He wanted to crush the puffy, flirtatious short sleeves beneath his hands, caress the strip of bare skin between sleeve and gloves with his fingertips.

The inexpensive locket around her white throat caged his sensual impulses, however—a poignant reminder that Meredith was not like most of the women with whom he'd associated over the last decade.

Or was she?

Now, as he watched Preston offer her his arm and Meredith's graceful acceptance, Ben found himself wondering which of the two was the cat and which the helpless mouse.

Thirty-Seven

through subsequent meetings, a business association developed between Benjamin Walker and J. Preston Clarke, though Meredith was not privy to many of the details. At first she was confused, because she had received the strong impression that—regardless of her own personal feelings—Mr. Walker neither liked nor trusted J. Preston Clarke. Eventually, however, she concluded that her first impression was faulty, based no doubt on her own emotional vulnerabilities.

As the weeks passed, her office duties grew to include the role of liaison between the two, delivering papers, messages, and bulging reports when Mr. Walker's secretary Lowell was occupied with other tasks. Delighted with any opportunity for contact with Preston Clarke, Meredith decided to consider this new role an indication of God's blessing.

One afternoon Mr. Walker called her into his office to ask if she minded running some more papers over to Mr. Clarke's lawyer. When she arrived, Mr. Clarke himself was just leaving. He insisted on accompanying her inside to introduce her to Ellis York, his lawyer, then giving her a lift back to the hotel in his carriage.

On the way to the hotel he invited her to dinner. Meredith refused.

"Are you worried about my reputation or your own?" he asked.

"Both." Meredith watched the buildings flash past in a blur. "It's a bit awkward with you and Mr. Walker discussing a partnership venture. I do work for him."

"It would only be awkward if you worked for me." He leaned forward, hands stacked on the ivory handle of his walking stick, which he began tapping on the floor of the carriage. "Then of course, I'd have to dismiss you in order to invite you to dinner. Are you in need of a chaperone? My aunt is visiting. Did I mention that?"

"Mr. Clarke, I'll join you for dinner—if you tell me why you're inviting me."

"Why, Miss Sinclair, for the pleasure of your company, of course. Beyond that, a gentleman must be careful never to commit himself." He sat back, smiling. "Say yes. It's only dinner—my driver will pick you up and return you home early enough that you won't be yawning at work the next day."

Meredith was unable to resist.

At first she did try to convince herself that she could keep her distance, that the vast social differences between them prohibited the development of a serious relationship. She didn't want to jeopardize her job, of course, but when she queried Mr. Walker about the matter, his indifferent response was that what she did with her personal life was none of his affair. It was as though his visit to Sinclair Run had never happened.

Nonplussed, Meredith obliged by treating him with the same detachment, which wasn't difficult as the weeks passed and Preston Clarke dominated both her spare time as well as her thoughts. Unlike Benjamin Walker, Preston was attentive yet...courtly. He made her feel cherished, as though she were the most important person in his life.

Once, as she readied herself for bed after an evening with Preston at a garden party, Meredith found herself reaching for her heartwood chest and extracting the cookie cutter. But the impulse disturbed her, and she hastily shoved the cookie cutter back inside when the memory of Benjamin Walker's face intruded itself over Preston's.

After that she ignored the chest.

Garnet and Sloan disapproved of Preston of course, but since they confined their disapproval to the occasional letter, Meredith was able to ignore the tone, dismissing it as the natural overprotectiveness of family. Leah's only comment, in the one letter she'd dashed off, was that she'd given up counseling her oldest sister in matters of the heart.

It was harder to ignore her father, so Meredith avoided returning home. In truth, she was kept so busy she had little spare time. Thankfully he had recovered completely from his bout with the ulcer, though Mrs. Willowby was firmly ensconced as housekeeper now. Meredith soothed her guilty conscience by reminding herself that her father was no longer alone, and that Leah would return from Mary Baldwin in May. Meredith contented herself with writing cheerful weekly epistles that didn't mention Preston at all.

"You're looking mighty pretty today, Miss Sinclair."

With a start Meredith looked up from the stack of reservation requests she'd been going through. "Morning, Hominy. You're looking mighty—" she thought for a moment—"*elegant* yourself."

"Elegant," he quoted in stentorian dignity, "is an adjective vulgarized by misuse."

They beamed at each other, enjoying the opportunity to banter about some of Miss Arbuckle's choices in etiquette books for her pupil. "Actually," Meredith said, "you do look very elegant. Is that a new suit?"

Hominy smoothed the lapels of his brown-and-tan tweed suit. "Bought it last week when Mr. Walker and I were in Washington."

Some of Meredith's good mood faded. The trip to Washington was a sore point with her, because she had no idea why it had taken place. Mr. Walker had refused to divulge any details, except that he and Hominy would be gone the entire week. They had returned only the previous night; this morning Mr. Walker was already in his office when Meredith arrived, with the Do Not Disturb sign posted on the doorknob.

Nobody—including Hominy—knocked on Mr. Walker's door when that sign was displayed. Ignoring the order had cost Meredith's predecessor his job. Meredith did not plan to repeat his mistake.

"Well," she observed brightly to Hominy, "I'm glad to see your trip was productive. I hope Mr. Walker enjoyed an equal measure of success."

Hominy's round face sobered, and the coffee-colored eyes flickered. "Depends on your notion of success, Miss Meredith. Mr. Ben, now, he's got a lot—"

"I'm ready to go if you are, Hominy." Mr. Walker's lazy drawl had an edge to it, but when Meredith twisted to look at him, nothing showed on his face. "It's already ten. I'd like to be back by this afternoon."

"Where—" Meredith started to ask, then hesitated.

"The site of the new hotel."

He crossed from the door of his office to stand beside Hominy. "You find something amusing about that, Miss Sinclair?"

"Of course not." She pressed her lips together to try and contain the smile. "It's just that when Hominy's not around, you seem much larger, Mr. Walker. But standing side by side…" Belatedly she buried her nose in the stack of correspondence. "I beg your pardon."

"Mine, Hominy's—or both?" Mr. Walker's ungloved hand suddenly planted itself on top of the letters.

Meredith's head jerked up, relieved to note the twinkle in his eye even as his proximity disconcerted her. She edged back in her chair. "Perhaps I should come along with you," she said. "As penance, I'll take whatever notes you require."

"That would be more like punishment for me. The last time you filled in for Lowell, I spent more time answering your questions about what I wanted you to write down than I did on what I needed for you to write down."

Relieved, Meredith's smile broadened to a grin. "I know. I was incorrigible. But I'd never been to an architect's office. It was fascinating."

For a moment their gazes held, and a strange tightness began to wrap her in its coils.

"When does Mr. Kingston return?" Hominy's rumbling voice broke the spell. "Mrs. Biggs told me the extra work's causing her eyes to cross."

"She only says that because you sympathize with her. You're too soft-hearted, Hominy. Sometimes a soft heart doesn't get the job done." He stepped back, and Meredith blinked, wondering if she'd imagined the undertone of bitterness. "Let's go. Time's a precious commodity, and it seems as though I never have enough of it."

Long after they left and Meredith returned to her work, she found her concentration fractured because her mind kept playing over the expression on Benjamin Walker's face just before he turned away.

The regulator clock had just struck the half-hour when Hominy's massive form filled the doorway. "Miss Meredith," the deep bass rumble echoed in the quiet room, "you's to come with me at once."

Meredith had been helping Mrs. Biggs search the files on previous guests who had made reservations for the coming summer season, to see if any special arrangements needed to be made. She and the older woman exchanged concerned glances over Hominy's grammatical lapse—an infallible barometer of ill tidings.

"What's the matter?" Meredith asked.

"Come with me. Bring your wrap and hat. You won't be returning." He folded his arms, looking stolid and unmovable.

"I'll come," Meredith promised, and took a quick calming breath. "But not until you tell me where I'm going. Is it—has something happened to Mr. Walker?"

Hominy's chest swelled to the point that Meredith wondered if the buttons would pop off his new suit. It was only then that she noticed his rumpled appearance. Smudges of dirt marred one sleeve, dust and pollen coated his shoulders. His boots were coated with drying mud.

"Hominy, what has happened?" Meredith rushed to his side. "You're frightening me. Please, I'll go with you, but I need to know—"

"Mr. Walker ordered me to fetch you," he finally said. "It is his place to explain."

"Go along, dear." Mrs. Biggs had come up beside Meredith, her matronly bulk reassuring. She patted Meredith, then handed her her shawl and hat. "Mustn't keep Mr. Walker waiting, after all. Whatever it is, 'tis his place to handle, not ours. Here"—she rummaged around the waist of her basque and produced several of the lemon drops she loved—"take along a few of these. Settles your nerves."

"Mrs. Biggs, my nerves would be fine if I were given some explanation, no matter how meager."

"I can appreciate that, dear, but I've worked for Mr. Walker longer than you have." She slid a look upward at Hominy's impassive face. "If he sent Mr. Hominy to fetch you instead of coming himself, it must be important enough for you to obey without question. Have a little faith, and scat. I can finish up here."

Outflanked, Meredith hurriedly pinned on her hat, threw the shawl over her shoulders, and followed Hominy into the bright May sunshine. Mr. Walker's carriage waited at the curb.

"Hominy…"

"Mr. Walker will tell you." He opened the door and waited.

A shiver darted along her spine. The antagonism she thought she had glimpsed before he shuttered his eyes was mirrored in his voice. What was wrong? Meredith climbed into the carriage, wincing a little when the door shut behind her with an ominous *thud*. In moments she deduced that the carriage was heading out of town, roughly southwest. *Oh.* For some reason, Mr. Walker must have changed his mind and needed her presence at the site where he planned to build the Poplar Springs Resort. It didn't explain Hominy's inexplicable antagonism however. Meredith settled back against the seat, unwrapped a lemon drop, and spent the next half-hour trying to fortify her wits.

She told herself there was nothing wrong with her nerves.

Several gigs were scattered about the small clearing at the end of the grassy lane. Wooden stakes marking construction sites had sprouted along with spring flowers. Meredith stuck her head through the window but couldn't see anyone. Hominy swung the horses around, the carriage came to a halt, and Mr. Walker stepped forward to open the door.

Meredith automatically started to give him her hand, chastising words on her lips. Then she caught sight of his face, and snatched her hand back. The jesting reproof died unspoken. "Mr. Walker?"

"Miss Sinclair." He backed up, proffering a sweeping bow rife with mockery as she descended to the trampled meadow grass. "I trust you enjoyed a pleasant trip…"

"It was fine. If you wanted me to accompany you, it would have saved Hominy a—"

"…because the way I feel right now, I can't vouch for the return."

Meredith's mouth dropped open then snapped shut. She clutched her shawl and spared a quick sideways glance at Hominy. But he turned his back and went to do something with the horses. "All right," she said, anger flicking to life. "If you're trying to confuse and intimidate me, you've succeeded. But you're also annoying me. I don't like it, and I want an explanation. Who do the other buggies belong to? Where are they?"

"I imagine they're staying out of my way right now." His voice frosted the mild spring air. "But to answer your question, two of the buggies belong to a couple of surveyors. One of them hired by me. The other…" He stepped closer to Meredith, and though she instinctively wanted to retreat, she stiffened her spine and tilted her head, "…was hired by your dear suitor."

"My suitor? Are you referring by any chance to Preston?"

The pupils of Mr. Walker's eyes seemed to contract to needle points. "First name basis now, are we?" he said, very softly. "In that case—Meredith—yes. I'm referring to Preston."

"What does that have to do with his hiring a surveyor? Perhaps you forgot to tell him that you'd already hired one." She glared back. "I never thought you could be such a bully. Stop this, for mercysake, and just tell me what's got you in a snit. Surely you're not changing your mind about working with Pre—with Mr. Clarke. He told me…that is to say, I was given to understand that he wanted to be a—a partner, in the Poplar Springs venture."

His silence was far more ominous than her own blustering. This time, when he took another step toward her, Meredith did retreat, until her spine bumped into the side of the carriage. Before she could dart sideways, his palms slammed against the lacquered surface on either side of her head. Muscled forearms trapped her between an unyielding object—his carriage, and an immovable forceful male—himself.

"What promises did Clarke make to you to purchase your silence? Your compliance?"

"I don't know what you're talking about." She'd never been afraid of a man in her life, and she wasn't about to admit to fear right now. But if Mr. Walker's chest moved one inch closer, Meredith was going to make her father proud. "Mr. Walker…stop this."

"Call me Ben. When you stab someone in the back, you may as well call him by name. Just to make sure you don't forget."

"I'll call you a lot more if you don't stop trying to frighten me."

The corner of his mouth curled in a sinister smile that tripled Meredith's heartbeat. "My dear Meredith, I don't have to try. You're already frightened out of your pretty little hat." His gaze flicked over the red silk poppies mounted to the crown, then speared into Meredith's faltering gaze. "So…tell me, when exactly did you find out that J. Preston Clarke purchased all the land adjacent to Poplar Springs Resort so that he could build a resort of his own?"

Thirty-Eight

*H*ominy's stolid face appeared over Mr. Walker's shoulder. "The two surveyors and Mr. York are headed this way. You want me to...delay their approach?"

"Not at all. In fact, I'd like the two-faced, unprincipled pettifogger Ellis York to deliver a message to his equally unprincipled client." His gaze remained on Meredith's. "He can deliver Miss Sinclair along with it."

"Stop talking as though I'm deaf!" Meredith lifted her hands to shove against Mr. Walker's forearms. She might as well have tried to shift the stone pilings of a railroad bridge. "Mr. Walker, if you don't move, I'm going to hurt you." Shocked confusion swept all caution aside. "My father taught all of us how to defend ourselves against mashers, brigands, and bullies. I never thought that would include you."

"I never thought my office manager, a young woman whom I respected, an employee I trusted"—he hurled the words with arctic softness—"would betray me."

"What? I don't understand. Betray you? I *told* you I don't know—"

"Keep your voice down, unless you enjoy making a spectacle of yourself."

"You're the only one making a spectacle," Meredith flung back, but she lowered her voice.

"I'll...ah...persuade the three gentlemen to remain where they're at," Hominy murmured. He walked off.

A stark sense of abandonment quelled Meredith's outrage, until Hominy turned back around after only a few paces. Relief caused her knees to tremble. Hominy after all was coming to her defense. She wasn't alone...

"Remember that whatever you say she'll likely as not report back to Mr. Clarke," he said.

Hot tears burned the backs of Meredith's eyes. For some reason, this terse condemnation hurt almost as much as Mr. Walker's irrational claims of betrayal. Over the months she had come to value Hominy's friendship as much as his respect. His quest for self-improvement taught her much about dignity; the hilarious exchanges they'd dubbed politeness practices helped her understand why Hominy was more friend than manservant to Mr. Walker.

This monumental misunderstanding loomed over her like Mr. Walker, with the same unnerving aura of threat.

It must be her deepening attachment to Preston. Despite Meredith's scrupulous attempts to keep her personal life separated from her job, Mr. Walker and Hominy must have been nurturing a growing ill will. Instead of openly confronting her, however, they had chosen to confuse and humiliate her with trumped-up charges directed at both her and Preston.

But—why?

"Your tears are crocodile tears," Mr. Walker said. "I'm not moved. You knew this morning, before Hominy and I drove out here. Didn't you?" A muscle in his jaw twitched. "You were smiling—*laughing*. And I thought you'd finally—" He stopped, and the banked emotion radiating from him caused Meredith to press back against the carriage. "Yet all the time you were lying."

Abruptly his hands fell away, and he swiveled on his heel. "If you hadn't laughed, I might have been able to forgive you."

Laughed at what? She vaguely remembered smiling at him… He wasn't making any sense. "I haven't done anything. And the tears," which she despised, "are because I-I'm angry."

Warm sunshine poured over them, but Meredith shivered, hugging her arms against the feeble lie. She stared at Benjamin Walker's broad back. His icy rage was all the more potent for its control. Until this moment, she would have vowed his deepest emotion was aggravation. "Mr. Walker…I've been very candid with you about my feelings for Preston Clarke. But they have nothing to do with my position as your office manager. I even asked you, remember? Your—contempt, or whatever it is, is completely irrational."

Her voice was rising again. She took several calming breaths. "You told me that whatever I chose to do in my private—"

"Spare me." He turned back around. "I asked you a question. You still haven't answered it. That's all I'm interested in hearing right now." His hand rose, and in spite of herself Meredith flinched.

A strange expression flashed across Mr. Walker's face. He ran his hand around his crumpled collar, drawing Meredith's attention to his equally untidy appearance. Like Hominy, Mr. Walker looked as though he'd spent hours tramping about the woods. When he spoke again, his voice was shorn of any emotion at all. "I apologize for scaring you. I wasn't going to strike you. I've never hit a woman in my life, and I won't—no matter how great the provocation."

He glanced toward the meadow to their right. "After you tell me what I need to know, you're free to leave with Mr. York."

"I certainly don't want to ride back with you."

"The feeling is mutual. Just tell me two things. I want to know when Clarke first brought you in on the scheme. And…tell me why. If you did it because you're in love with him, well, you wouldn't be the first person blinded by the emotion. But if you did it for money, or"—his chest rose and fell—"because you feel as though I've wronged you some-how, tell me. I deserve that much, Meredith."

A thick silence descended. For the first time Meredith looked fully into his face without the screen of her temper or the shield of their respective roles. His naked contempt struck her more painfully than a blow. The rage shocked her.

But it was the hurt lurking beneath those darker emotions that stole all the breath from her lungs. The imperturbable Benjamin Walker was…hurt. Hurt because he actually believed that Meredith was privy to some supposed plan of Preston's. It was a misunderstanding, of course, one that she would untangle as soon as possible. She thrust aside her own emotional pain. The depth of Benjamin Walker's reaction told Meredith more graphically than words that she had been equally mis-taken in her perceptions about this man.

Meredith wasn't the only one hiding behind a facade.

"I haven't betrayed you." Her throat felt as though sand had been poured into it. "Mr. Walker—Benjamin. There's been some kind of monstrous misunderstanding. But you must believe me. I haven't betrayed—"

"Stop lying to me!"

He might as well have slapped her. "I'm not lying!" Meredith shouted back. Her hand lifted as though with a mind of its own and pummeled his chest. "Don't you ever call me a liar again!"

He captured her fist and held it away. "I could call you a lot of names." Abruptly he turned, fingers vising around her wrist. "Since you insist on playing games, we'll do it the hard way. Gentlemanly fool that I am, I was trying to spare you added humiliation." He hauled her away from the concealing bulk of the carriage and marched her across the grass toward the cluster of men.

Meredith's choices were unpalatable: allow him to manhandle her or kick his shins and bolt for the carriage, an equally immature solution. Or she could shore up her pride and—bluff.

His hand cupped her elbow, preventing any escape while maintaining the illusion of courtesy. "Miss Sinclair, allow me to introduce Mr. Desmond Hill and Mr. Oliver Johnson. You're of course well acquainted with Mr. York." At last, the burning pressure of his hand fell away, releasing her.

Meredith aimed a polite smile between the two surveyors, but her attention was riveted on Preston's lawyer. She focused on the red dianthus he always wore fastened to the lapel of his suits. "Mr. York, I'd appreciate it if you could explain to Mr. Walker that he has misunderstood."

"Certainly, Miss Sinclair." He tucked his chin, his light gray eyes chilly. "Pray enlighten me as to the nature of Mr. Walker's misunderstanding."

"He seems to think that Mr. Clarke is guilty of some scheme, undercutting Poplar Springs by purchasing the adjacent property to build his own resort."

Mr. York exchanged glances with Desmond Hill, a spindly man with a dripping nose, then turned to Benjamin Walker. "Ah…Miss Sinclair.

Your completely erroneous allegations against my client are both inflammatory and egregious. I am a trifle confused by them myself." He removed his narrow spectacles and made a production of cleaning the lenses. "This is highly unorthodox. Most inappropriate."

"I agree," Benjamin said. "Regrettably the circumstances are unorthodox and the timing inappropriate. But an explanation from you would be helpful—with all appropriate discretion, of course."

A hard-edged smile bared his teeth. When he looked down at Meredith, it was as though he'd politely skewered her with an ice pick.

Mr. York replaced his glasses and looked at her with equal distaste. "Very well. As you know, for the past two weeks, Mr. Clarke has been heavily involved in final negotiations involving the construction of a venture he plans to call Healing Springs Hotel. He told me himself that you had encouraged the development, that you were the one who brought him the results of the water analyses, which indicated the salutary qualities of the alkaline-calci-chalybeate springs."

"What are you talking about?" The sky seemed to be pressing down upon her back, its weight buckling her knees. "I don't know about any analyses, or…a healing springs hotel. I did encourage him, yes. But I thought he was talking about h-his joint venture with—" She couldn't say Mr. Walker's name. Her lips felt numb. Rubbery. "I thought he was referring to Poplar Springs," she finally managed. "Mr. York…you're mistaken."

A curious buzzing revolved in her head. She shook it, then forced herself to turn toward Benjamin. "I don't know what he's talking about."

The dripping-nosed surveyor wiped the back of his hand across his mouth. "She must've been in the sun too long. She's the one who showed me that report. She was in the room with Mr. Clarke when he hired me to do the survey. He was most specific that I note the location of every one of those springs. All but one of them is on the properties he's purchasing."

Benjamin Walker was staring at her. Everyone was staring. She backed up a step, tried to speak, but the thoughts refused to form themselves into words. Tried to move, but she couldn't feel her feet inside her shoes. The others were talking, but she wasn't sure whether they were speaking to her or among themselves. She heard Mr. Walker's name, and Preston's.

Preston. That was the solution. She must go to Preston. He needed to know that for some reason his lawyer and surveyor were conspiring to slander—no. That couldn't be right. She lifted her hand to her forehead.

"Are you all right?" Benjamin asked, the words spoken close to her ear so that Meredith understood they had been addressed specifically to her.

"No. I'm not all right."

What a hypocrite he was, asking the question when his tone of voice indicated nothing but grudging reluctance. Meredith refused to look at him again.

Only when his hand tightened did she realize he had taken hold of her arm, and she was all but leaning against him. Every movement stiff, she pulled herself free and twined her numb fingers together. "Mr. York, may I have a lift back to town, please? I'm going to see Pres"—she caught herself—"Mr. Clarke. He'll straighten everything out. This has all been an appalling lack of proper communication."

"I will drive you into town, Miss Sinclair, but I must warn you that I'm not inclined to discuss this matter any further until I myself have had a conference with Mr. Clarke." He cleared his throat. "Shall we go?"

It took the last of her shattered dignity to risk one final glance into Benjamin Walker's stone-cast features. "I'll save us both the awkwardness of your firing me. You'll have my letter of resignation in the morning. I cannot work for a man who"—her voice broke, and she swallowed repeatedly before regaining control—"a man who thinks I'm a liar and a traitor."

Thirty-Nine

*B*en watched the buggies until they disappeared, swallowed up by afternoon shadows and forest.

"I'm going for a walk," he told Hominy, hovering at his shoulder like a brooding guardian angel. "Don't worry, I'm all right. I just want to look around."

"Mr. Ben—"

"Leave it be, Hominy." He pinched the bridge of his nose and scraped up a semblance of a smile. "Give me"—*a month, a year, the rest of my life*—"an hour. If I haven't returned, then you can fetch me."

"I know what you're thinking. Don't do it, Mr. Ben. She's not worth it."

"Possibly." He glanced over his shoulder. "An hour," he repeated as he strolled across the meadow.

It was a perfect spring day. Enamel blue sky, thickets of creamy mountain laurel, a soft breeze that bore the intoxicating scent of moist woodlands. Birds warbling. Ben's hands fisted as he walked, because right now the beauty of the afternoon jarred his raw senses. His mind seethed with storm clouds instead of sunshine, and the only scent filling his nostrils was the fading aroma of lemon drop candy.

The betrayal struck afresh, brutal as fists pounding his unprotected flesh. Ben focused on a large flat boulder halfway up a gentle hill covered with wild rhododendron. Over the months he'd sat on that boulder and dreamed, picturing the resort in exquisite detail, down to the rows of tulips he'd planned to import from Holland, which would line the driveway every spring.

Why? He thought about hurling the question at heaven, but he hadn't prayed since he was a boy, so the gesture seemed futile. God seldom provided answers. The Lord made provisions for people's ultimate reconciliation, then left them to flounder their way through a wretched mortal existence. Jesus' resurrected presence offered scant consolation, limited as it was to a noncorporeal Spirit more arcane than His controversial walk on earth as a man. It seemed pointless to depend on the naive faith of his mother or on the teachings of the elderly cousin who had raised Ben.

Ben sat on the rock, leaning back with his palms braced against its rough granite surface. He wished he could harden his heart like the boulder. A bitter laugh escaped, the sound obscene in this sylvan cathedral. After all these years—years when he would have sworn he'd learned every lesson there was to learn about human greed…depravity…selfishness—he'd still been caught off guard.

He closed his eyes, hearing his mother's gentle voice as though she were sitting beside him. *"Don't ever swallow bitterness, Benjy-love. Spit it out, and let the water of life fill you with hope. With acceptance. People do evil things, sometimes for causes they believe with all their hearts,"* she'd reminded him over and over, all of them red-eyed from grief after the news of his father's death. *"And God's people suffer alongside unbelievers. But God is faithful, Benjamin. His love makes us able to bear the rest. Promise me that you'll remember. All pain is bearable, if we remember how much God loves His children. Promise you'll be faithful too. You're not just Horace Walker's only son now—you're a child of God as well. Don't let either of them down."*

It had been a weighty burden for a small boy, but Ben never questioned the responsibility, even when he held the dead body of his little sister in his arms. He'd learned honor from the cradle, been weaned on respecting and protecting women as a God-ordained dictate. And until an hour ago, he'd never said or done anything to shame his parents' memories.

Groaning aloud, he jackknifed forward and buried his face in his hands. He wished he could bury the memory of Meredith's fragile, frozen face, all her color and glorious temper vanquished. Because of him. He was thirty-three years old, and for most of those years he'd lived a life of quiet resilience and nonaggressive determination.

He kept his emotions ruthlessly suppressed, because excessive emotion led to rash decisions. Rash decisions led to measures that could never be undone, like the actions by his father and brothers that had taken their lives, and ultimately his mother's in grieving herself to death.

He had known from the first time he laid eyes on her that Meredith's nature would lead her into trouble; her feelings spilled over everyone around her, as uncontainable as soap bubbles in a playful wind. He shouldn't blame her for responding to Clarke—especially when Ben's insane concept of chivalry precluded making his own interest more obvious.

That's right, Benjamin. Blame it on someone else—salves your pride a bit, right? If he'd given in to his baser needs, perhaps Meredith wouldn't have succumbed to a man who had led her down a sunlit path straight into quicksand.

"Mr. Ben, it's been an hour. Come along with me. No sense grieving out here all alone."

Ben patted the rock. "Then grieve with me a spell. I'm not ready to go back." His gaze shifted to rove over the spring-colored meadow. A cottontail rabbit loped across the fresh carpet of grass and clover. White and pink confections of dogwood blossoms peeked from between stately trunks of pine and budding hardwoods, vying with the riotous purple of the rhododendrons. "It's hard…letting go."

Admitting it out loud helped cement the necessity in his mind. But it didn't stop the pain from searing his insides.

"You could still fight him in court. We found enough evidence of coercion and intimidation in his acquisition of the properties, 'specially that patch of land with the mineral springs owned by Mrs. Oppenheimer."

"Remember what we discovered in Washington? Money will buy anything but a good night's sleep. If Clarke's willing to stoop to lying and intimidation to achieve his ends, it means he'd employ similar tactics to keep the truth from coming to light. He's got that fine, upstanding reputation to maintain. You and I, now, we might have bent a commandment or two over the years, but I learned a long time ago that I'm not willing to use power or money—whatever the reason—if I can't go to bed at night with a clean conscience. That means Preston would win any court battles."

He ran his fingertips over the rough surface of the stone, a wry smile weaving through his words, "Besides, Mrs. Oppenheimer's a widow. She doesn't have much left but her dignity. If word gets out that she was gulled, or worse—bullied, into selling her property to a man revered throughout the northern Valley, who do you think will suffer?"

" 'Tisn't fair."

Ben eschewed correcting his old friend. "Life isn't." He turned sideways, drawing up a leg and propping his elbow on the bent knee. "In all the years we've been together, we've never talked about religion. What do you think about God, Hominy?"

"Not much, I reckon. Your mama and daddy set a lot of store by their faith. My mama did too, but all it ever got her was a cross made out of sticks propped over her grave. My pa now, before he was a slave, he was a Chickahominy brave, remember. For whatever reason, reckon I tend to place more stock in the faith of my father's Chickahominy ancestors." He regarded Ben soberly. "Why are you asking?"

Ben pulled a wry face. "Trying to make sense of it all. If God has some grand scheme in mind, He hasn't shared it with me. Not that I've asked," he added after a moment.

For a while they sat, listening to the birds, soaking up the majestic silence that nonetheless brought little peace.

"Meredith believes in God," Ben finally said. "I overheard her talking to Mrs. Biggs a couple of weeks ago, sharing that she believes God brought Preston Clarke into her life."

"Then let him have her."

"I…" he closed his eyes but still couldn't banish the sight of Meredith's defeated expression when she at last accepted the uselessness of pleading her innocence. "Hominy…what if we're wrong about her?"

His companion snorted. "I was waiting for this. You want me to find out, don't you? You refuse to believe the evidence in front of your eyes. You heard same as me the testimony of two men, one of 'em a—what'd you jump for?"

"That phrase." Ben stood, restless, a nagging unease pushing its way to the surface. "It's from the Bible. Elrod—the cousin who took me in—read passages of Scripture to me every morning for the three years I lived with him. There's a scene. Jesus was defending himself to the religious leaders, claiming God as one of his witnesses, himself as the other. I didn't understand, since our legal system nowadays wouldn't allow such a tactic. There's no way Jesus could 'prove' God's testimony. Elrod and I used to debate about it."

"Didn't work for Jesus, did it? They killed him anyway. Be that as it may, old Mr. York and the surveyor Mr. Clarke hired, they're the ones proving Miss Sinclair's guilt."

"I know. I also know this whole setup bothers me the same way. I don't trust Ellis York or that snot-nosed surveyor who claimed Meredith knew what was going on. How credible were the 'witnesses' who testified *against* Jesus at His trial?"

He smacked his fist against his palm. "It's just that every time I think about her cozying up to Preston Clarke, it makes me want to smash this boulder over somebody's head."

Hominy's deep brown eyes regarded him quizzically. "Mr. Ben, I might be mad as fire over what Miss Sinclair done, but I draw the line at murder."

"You saphead! If you think—"

The blaze of fury ignited so swiftly and burned so brightly that it wasn't until Hominy stood up to wait, his own arms dangling loosely, that Ben's sanity clicked back into place. Appalled, he realized that he, too, was standing. He stared at the handful of Hominy's starched shirt crumpled inside his fist, then up into his friend's unflinching eyes.

With a hoarse apology he opened his hand, tottered backward two steps and dropped down to the boulder again. "I can't believe I did that," he said, and shuddered. "God in heaven…I can't believe I did that."

"Don't worry about it, Mr. Ben. You didn't do anything."

Ben lifted his head. "Didn't do anything? Hominy, I almost *hit* you!"

" 'Almost' don't matter. Fact is, you caught yourself." The leathery black palm descended on his shoulder and briefly squeezed. "Trust me,

Mr. Ben. I've seen a lot in my years—a sight more than you even. Known a lot of sorry men. Fewer I'd tip my hat to. But you're one of them. You're a good man, and you know I call it as I sees it, with you."

Hominy hesitated, then added softly, "And I'd have let you take a swipe to help the pain. That's all it is, Mr. Ben. You're fighting soul-pain. It doesn't get much more hurtful than that."

"I've never felt like this before."

"Well, now, as to that, even with all those pretty ladies hankering after you over the years…I never saw one of them bring the gleam to your eye I saw when you looked at Miss Sinclair. Take a spell to get over it." He pursed his lips, scowling as he tugged his ear. "Get over it faster, I'm thinking, if you build here anyway. You've poured your heart into the plans. Won't matter what kind of fancy hotel Preston Clarke puts up next to yours. No matter how many pockets he lines or officials he bribes, he'll never be able to create what you could, Mr. Ben."

"He's got something I want even more." Ben rose and headed back down the slope. "But there's nothing I can do about that, other than what I'm going to do."

And when that matter was taken care of, he was going to pay a visit to Jacob Sinclair. Meredith might be lost to him now, but in all his life Ben had never been able to let go of anything or anyone for whom he had assumed responsibility. Only after talking with Meredith's father and testing a few truths of his own would he eventually be able to relinquish the woman with whom he had fallen in love.

Forty

$\mathcal{P}$reston owned a four-story brick building on Piccadilly Street, with a suite of offices for himself on the main level. Mr. York's law office occupied two rooms on the third floor. Disapproval radiating from the stiff set of his shoulders, after a clipped farewell he left Meredith with Preston's secretary.

Equally stiff, Meredith stood in front of Luther Platt's desk, her fingers clutching the fringe of her shawl. She was unable to summon a coherent sentence.

"Mr. Clarke is in a conference," Luther finally said. He meticulously capped his fountain pen and laid it aside. "I don't believe he was expecting you?"

"I'll wait."

"Mr. Clarke is not to be interrupted, and this conference might last until six. After that he has a dinner engagement. Why don't you leave a note? I'll see that he receives it."

After he'd read it himself, Meredith knew. "I'll wait, however long."

Without conscious thought she wandered over to the alcove where she and Preston had enjoyed tea four days earlier. The memory mocked her. Meredith sank down on the posh French sofa before her legs betrayed her. Luther was an obsequious toad, resentful of her not only because of her relationship with Preston—but because she was Benjamin Walker's office manager, a position that placed her above Luther.

No longer was she Benjamin Walker's office manager.

A chill from her bones spread outward. She pressed the soles of her muddied Oxford tie shoes together, concentrating on lining up the toes as though precision mattered. The same sense of unreality had enabled her to sustain her poise for the endless five-mile carriage ride back to town with a frigidly silent Ellis York.

He had treated her like a criminal—*Don't think about Mr. York. Think about*—an image of Benjamin Walker surfaced in her mind, brutal in its clarity: the contempt that darkened his eyes to indigo; the power of the arms that had trapped her inside an angry cage.

All Meredith's muscles clenched in a spasm of denial.

In the space of an hour she had lost her job, Mr. Walker's respect, and a lot of her confidence. A show of righteous anger might help, yet even that avenue offered scant consolation. After the anger was spent, she'd still be unemployed and shattered.

Her wrists ached. She stared dully at her clenched hands. *Preston.* All she had to do was hold herself together for Preston. Somehow he would resolve everything. The charges against him were absurd. Mr. Walker must have misunderstood. It must be the lawyer's fault; that was the answer. Mr. York was withholding information for some reason. He had bribed that surveyor, the one with the drippy nose. Yes, that must be it…

All that property. Surely Preston had purchased it as part of his and Mr. Walker's joint venture. Meredith vaguely remembered hearing Preston talk about a land purchase, but she'd no idea where the acreage had been located.

Still, she should have confronted Benjamin Walker, instead of allowing him to badger her into a state of near insensibility. And she should have defended Preston, as well as herself.

Benjamin had called her a liar.

He didn't believe in her innocence. He'd questioned her integrity, shamed her not only in front of Hominy, but three other men, two of them utter strangers. Long ago, Lamar Aikens had shamed her when he suggested that she become his mistress, because he claimed that marriage was unnecessary for two independent minds such as theirs. Yet Benjamin Walker's allegations hurt Meredith far more cruelly than Lamar's tawdry proposal.

It was one thing to have been perceived as a naive country girl. It was entirely another to be wrongfully accused of a perfidious act.

Her stomach twisted like a pretzel, nausea roiling greasily. Meredith held herself still, breathing in shallow, unsteady puffs. She felt as though she'd been plunged inside a thick cloud, unable to see and with nothing to grab on to, to find her way.

Outside, late afternoon light deepened to luminous amber. Pedestrians strolled past the large window, oblivious to her turmoil. Gentlemen in dark suits and bowlers, farmers in overalls…a mother wheeling her baby in a perambulator. A couple, the woman's hand resting on the arm of her escort. They stopped a little beyond Meredith when a breeze knocked her hat askew. His expression tender, the man solicitously restored it to the proper angle, while the woman blushed and laughed.

The icy knot that had lodged beneath Meredith's breastbone bristled with needle-sharp spikes. All of them felt as though they'd pierced her heart. *Preston, please hurry,* she thought, watching the couple until they vanished from her line of sight. She needed his devotion, the admiring gleam of his warm brown eyes. More than anything, she needed his reassurance—and an explanation.

Wrapped in misery, Meredith waited for the time to pass. Waited for the pain to diminish. Waited…

"My dear…what on earth? It's going on seven o'clock. Mr. Platt, I trust you have an explanation for this."

"Your instructions specifically forbade interruption, Mr. Clarke. Miss Sinclair, however, insisted on waiting."

"Preston," she was vaguely astonished at the scratchy sound of her voice, "I must talk with you." She glanced around. "Your conference… where…"

"They left through the side entrance. My dear, you're trembling. Has something happened? Platt, a glass of sherry—"

"No. Nothing. Thank you." Meredith clung to Preston's hand a moment. "I—can we talk? In private?"

A flicker of something indecipherable came and went in his expression. "Of course. But I'm afraid I don't have very long, my dear. I have a dinner engagement which regrettably does not include you."

"I'm hardly in any shape for company, so it's just as well." She watched his mouth curve in a smile. He lifted her hands and pressed a light kiss to her knuckles. "Preston—" Her throat clogged, and she stifled the sob of relief that struggled to escape.

"Ah. Obviously something has upset you. A family crisis? No? Then it must be—Mr. Walker."

Meredith shuddered. "Preston, this needs to be discussed in private."

"You're dismissed, Platt," Preston ordered without looking away from Meredith. "In the morning, we'll discuss your shabby treatment of Miss Sinclair."

"Yes, Mr. Clarke." Voice and face wooden, the secretary lifted his hat off the rack and left without another word.

Preston steered Meredith inside his office, which reeked of cigar smoke and liquor. Seemingly indifferent to the impropriety of it, he led her to a leather chair. "Sit here. I'll pour you a drink. Yes, yes—of water. I know how you feel about strong spirits. I trust you'll refrain from preaching while I imbibe."

He was pouring liquid into crystal tumblers while he spoke, the light sting of his words jarring. Vaguely alarmed, Meredith took the glass he offered and thanked him. A sensation of plunging off a craggy mountain cliff made her lightheaded.

Something was wrong.

Preston tossed back a mouthful of amber liquid. "What has Walker done to you, hmm? No, let me guess." He stood over her, sipping his drink and watching her through hooded eyes. "You're covered with road dust, which tells me you've been traveling. Out to the Poplar Springs site?"

"Yes." She wrapped her hands around the cool glass, pressing the surface with her fingers. It felt real, tangible. *God? Help me.* "Preston, what I was told"—she raised her head and forced the condemnatory sentence out—"is true, isn't it?"

It was all there, no longer disguised. The aura of triumph in his face, the glittering malice in brown eyes that for weeks had bathed her in nothing but admiration. Respect. How could she have been deceived so completely? Why would God put her through this humiliation again?

"Truth, my dear, comes dressed to suit many occasions. Take yourself, for instance."

"Let's not." All Meredith wanted to do now was to escape. She started to rise, but Preston's hand landed heavily on her shoulder, keeping her still. Astonished by the casual force of it, Meredith uttered no protest.

"What a novel picture," Preston said. "I like you, sitting before me like a vanquished maiden. I give you full marks, my dear. You've proven to be more of a challenge than I originally planned. It hasn't been easy, using you."

"I…see. You used me to—to get to Mr. Walker."

"Yes." His voice was almost gentle. "He couldn't be bought off or blackmailed, an annoying inconvenience for me. His reputation—well, let's just say if he'd kept his enterprises out of my corner of the world, I would have wished him well. I haven't decided about the hotel here in town. Perhaps I'll let him keep it as a consolation prize." His gaze swept over her, turning almost dreamy. "I can see you in the lobby, on my arm. Wearing a Worth evening gown, one I'd order especially for you. You deserve more than gowns purchased from a Montgomery Ward's catalog, my dear."

"Preston…" She took a swallow of water to ease the burning in her throat. She didn't think he even realized how deeply he'd insulted her. "What you did to Mr. Walker, what you're doing to me—it's monstrous. Despicable."

"All depends on your point of view. For me, the actions were expedient. I'm sorry that you…" Before she realized his intent, his fingers were brushing the line of her chin.

Thought followed action. She knocked his hand away and rose, clumsy with anger, to her feet. "Don't you ever touch me again, you— you *profligate!*"

"Ah. The maiden has claws. I'd wondered." He tugged out his handkerchief and touched it to his forehead, then jammed it back inside his waistcoat. "Didn't your father ever warn you about men, pet? You and I are alone. It wouldn't be wise to provoke me too far." The dreamy expression had vanished, replaced by one of subtle cruelty.

His erratic displays of conflicting moods were almost as frightening as his revelations. "It would be equally unwise to provoke me," Meredith managed to retort. Her heart thumped against her ribs as she gauged the distance to the doorway.

Beneath the mustache Preston's lips thinned to an unpleasant line. "It's almost a temptation to send you back to your employer...somewhat the worse for wear. Be careful, my—"

"He's not my employer. I quit after he accused me of lying." At least she now understood his accusations.

For some reason the terse declaration seemed to lighten Preston's mood again. "Must have been an interesting confrontation. I only heard Ellis's rather dry version, of course. The one where you deny any role in my 'scheme to undercut Poplar Springs'—was that the gist of it? You played your part to perfection."

"I was *not* playing a part!"

"Forgive me. Of course you're right. You weren't playing a part. The image tantalizes." His malicious chuckle grated, and Meredith's hands clenched in impotent fists. "Mr. Hill—my surveyor?—added a nice touch of authenticity, don't you think? Even Ellis was almost convinced that you had no knowledge of my plans before Hill stepped in."

"I didn't. I don't. And you know it." Now the pain arrived, fresh as a wound, bleeding away the bravado. *Again. Again.* She'd been duped and betrayed again and had nobody to blame but herself. Not God. This wasn't God's will. Just Meredith's. She was impulsive. She was...stupid.

But she was also the daughter of Jacob Sinclair.

"You've known about Poplar Springs for almost a year," she said. "Why wait until now to—to do what you did?"

Preston picked up one of the smoldering cigars and considered the tip for a moment. "It took that long to...arrange...the purchase of all the adjoining land," he admitted. "After Mr. Walker was obliging enough to show me the plans for Poplar Springs, I realized it would have been a top-of-the-line resort spa." He took a puff on the cigar and blew the smoke upward. "I couldn't allow that to happen."

"Couldn't *allow* it? You can't stop it," Meredith said, her voice suddenly fierce. No matter how badly Benjamin had treated her, defense of him was automatic, as instinctive as breathing. "Even if you build your own health spa, it won't stop Mr. Walker. He knows what he's doing, has planned for every detail."

The resort was his dream. He'd called in all manner of experts, from architects to engineers to a botanist to plan the grounds. The threat of competition, even with adjoining properties, would not cause Benjamin to fold his tent and steal meekly away in defeat. "He'll find a way, he'll build it in spite of your detestable conniving."

"An interesting response for a former employee whose employer believes her to be a lying and a faithless Jezebel." Cigar clamped between his teeth, Preston strolled over to a sideboard and poured himself another drink. "I find your loyalty commendable, if wasted. Nonetheless, he won't be building Poplar Springs." Turning, he lifted the filled glass. "Congratulate yourself, my dear. Thanks to you—unwittingly of course—Benjamin Walker has finally tasted defeat."

"I'll explain. Make him understand. I won't let you use me to destroy a man's dreams." As Preston had just destroyed hers.

"Empty words, futile effort, my dear." He ran his thumb around the lip of the glass before adding lightly, "And…unwise, shall we say? I'm afraid a lot of people wouldn't take too kindly to even a hint of scurrilous gossip. About myself, of course." His voice deepened. "You must understand. Powerful men of my stature have to guard their reputations, regardless of the cost. Meredith, my dear—please. I wouldn't want you to be…hurt. You're very vulnerable, aren't you?"

"I—what do you mean?" Stunned, not wanting to comprehend, she searched his face. "Preston, are you *threatening* me?"

"I'm only helping you curb your impulsive nature."

"How generous. How may I help you curb your villainous nature?"

A faint smile curved his lips. "Like I said, impulsive. Let it go, Meredith. There's nothing you can say or do to alter the inevitable."

"Preston, none of this makes sense. Threatening me is ludicrous— I have no influence over Mr. Walker. Especially now."

Preston swallowed the drink in three gulps. "Ludicrous as you find it, you can trust me in this, Meredith."

After stubbing out the cigar he strolled back across the room to stand in front of her, hands tucked inside his pockets in a subtle insult. "Benjamin Walker is through in Winchester."

"You'd like to think so." Her movements brittle, Meredith edged around him toward the door.

"Meredith?"

She tensed, not trusting the regretful tone of his voice. Warily she turned around.

"Earlier I told you that it hasn't been easy, using you," he said. His hands spread in an almost helpless gesture. "I need you to believe that."

"You—need me to believe that? You charmed me. You cultivated a false image of someone I could admire, someone I could"—her chin lifted—"I thought you were the man God arranged...I *trusted* you." She hurled the words at him. "I trusted you, and you threw that trust back in my face. I never really knew you at all, and you want to be absolved?"

"Try to understand. It was the only way. I regret having to hurt you, but—"

"Spare me your pretense at remorse. You don't know the meaning of the word." Meredith stalked toward the door. "Benjamin Walker's worth a dozen of you. There's more integrity in his littlest toe than you possess in your entire frame! I'm ashamed of myself for not realizing it sooner."

Choking, she wrapped her slippery palm over the brass doorknob. "I'm ashamed of myself. But all I feel for you is pity. You might own a fortune in gold, Preston, but you're nothing but dross."

It was very satisfying to slam the door in his face.

Forty-One

$\mathcal{P}$apa? It's late. What are you doing standing on the porch in the dark?"

Jacob reached backward, drawing Leah against his side. It still astonished him, this youngest daughter a woman grown instead of his baby, no bigger than a whittling stick. "Thinking. Praying. It's a soft night, and the Big Dipper up there looks like it's about to spill a drop or two of God's grace over us."

"More likely the Lord's going to spill a bit of ague, you out here in the chilly spring night in your shirtsleeves." She dropped her head on his shoulder.

Jacob inhaled the scents of cleaning soap and vanilla, Leah's favorite scent, the only fragrance of toilet water she would wear. Love vibrated all the way to his fingertips. Love and—uneasiness, though not about Leah. " 'Tis a joy to have you back home, lass. I've missed your bullying." He searched for a lock of fine silky hair and gave it a tug. "But don't be thinking I'm expecting you to stay beyond the summer. When September comes round again, I'll put you back on the train."

Leah wriggled from beneath his arm. With nothing beyond a quarter-moon hanging, Jacob was able to discern only the pale oval of her face and the blurred impression of her light blue gown.

"I just returned home two days ago. What on earth possessed you to brood about something that won't happen for months?"

"I do not brood," Jacob protested. Leah made a scoffing sound. "Och, you always were a pert one, weren't you? Very well then, I'll enjoy my little wren for now and leave tomorrow where it belongs, in the Lord's hands." He found her nose and gave it an affectionate tweak. "And I was not brooding."

"Yes, Papa." The smile in her voice made Jacob's lips twitch in response. "Just like you didn't brood when Meredith went haring off after—Papa? What is it? What's wrong?" she asked, all lightheartedness gone. "You're not in pain, are you?

"No, lass." Jacob propped a hip on the porch rail and crossed his ankles. "In fact I—"

"Oh. Well, remember to watch your diet. And Sloan told me that undue agitation would—"

"The only agitation in my life," Jacob interrupted dryly, "comes from a gaggle of women treating me like a wee babe. Took most of this past month to convince Mrs. Willowby not to check on me every hour of the day. Only time I had a moment's privacy was bedtime." And even then, more often than not those first weeks after Garnet and Meredith left, Effie's footsteps creaked the floorboards outside the door, though she never knocked or intruded.

"Mrs. Willowby was acting on Sloan's instructions. Take your protests to him. Papa,"—the light voice took on a hint of steel—"if it's not the ulcer, tell me what's bothering you. Something is, and I want to know."

Jacob heaved a sigh and gave in. With Leah, there'd never been any use to prevaricate. "Can't stop thinking about Meredith. She's been gnawing at my mind most of this day. I figure the Lord's laid her on my heart for a reason. So I came out here to talk a bit to Him about her before going to bed."

"Oh. I'm sorry I intruded."

He heard the scrape of her footsteps retreating across the porch. "Don't go. You can pray with me if you like."

"Papa, if God knows everything, then what do you hope to accomplish by nagging Him with your worries?"

"A bit of peace." Jacob smiled sadly. "The comfort of knowing that He's there, willing to listen to those worries. Sort of like my girls come to me at times, needing a hug, needing to know how much they're loved, no matter where they are or what they do."

Leah scampered back across the porch and burrowed inside his waiting arms. "Papa," the whisper drifted into his ear, "if I could feel God like I can feel you, I'd pray with you."

How well he knew that. Jacob tightened his arms, rocking her while his gaze returned to the starlit night. Leah's lack of understanding made his heart ache, but at least when he was holding her he could rest assured that, for this brief moment at least, she was safe.

He wasn't so sure about Meredith.

Lord? Keep her close inside Your arms, since I can't have her in mine.

❧❀❧

"Sloan?" Roused from sleep by the creaking bedsprings, Garnet yawned, her hand blindly patting the empty space beside her.

"Over here by the window, sweetheart. It's all right. Go back to sleep."

"Someone knocked? You have to go?" She struggled to rise, but before she was fully upright in the bed Sloan was leaning over her, gently laying her back down while his mouth brushed soothing kisses over her face.

"Nobody knocked on the door." His hand lifted her nighttime braid, his fingers sifting through the tuft of hair at the end. "I was praying."

An uprush of love spilled through Garnet along with a prickle of uncertainty. She wrapped her hands around his wrist, hugging his arm to her chest. "Why didn't you wake me?" she whispered. "Who for this time?"

When he didn't immediately answer, the last of Garnet's sleep-lulled security fled. Her nails dug into his wrist. "Sloan? Is it Papa? Do we need to—"

His kiss stemmed the flow of panicked words. "Hush, sweetheart. Not your father…so far as I know, he's still basking in Leah's homecoming. And he's welcome to bask away, long as he finishes the armoire he promised to have done for us by the end of the month. It'll be nice, won't it, to finally have our bedroom suite completed—a legacy for our children to cherish. Furniture made by their grandfather, the famous Jacob Sinclair."

"Sloan…" She pressed her fingers against his lips. "You may as well tell me. Let me pray too." In the sliver of pale moonlight drifting through the window, his silhouette loomed above her, a dark guardian angel whose love for Garnet humbled her.

She watched his shoulders shift, then he was sliding back under the quilt and tucking her against his side. Garnet settled in her spot, head nestled between his chin and shoulder, her left hand over the comforting beat of his heart.

Sloan pressed a last kiss to her temple. "It's Meredith," he admitted then and held her still. "For some reason, we need to be praying for Meredith. I don't know why, so I was just…praying."

Garnet quelled the lurch of panic. Then, because she had learned to trust God's all-loving Presence as much as she trusted her husband, she closed her eyes and prayed for her older sister.

⌖

Somewhere along the lonely walk back to her boardinghouse, Meredith decided to pack her belongings and in the morning leave Winchester in the dust. Any spiritual insight to be derived from the debacle of the last eighteen months could be absorbed just as thoroughly somewhere else.

There was precedent in a retreat. King David had cowered in a cave once. And she thought it was Elijah who crept under a rock or something. With those noble heroes of the Bible as her models, Meredith managed to deflect the crushing shame, ignore the corrosive loneliness.

Two blocks from her boardinghouse, she decided she was angry with Benjamin Walker, almost as angry as she was over Preston's perfidy. The notion transformed her. With each step ringing hollowly into the spring night, Meredith fed her anger another incendiary thought to fan the flames. Benjamin had no right to treat her as he had, especially when she'd defended his honor so valiantly. Yes, even in the midst of her own destroyed dreams, *she* hadn't betrayed *him*. Benjamin hadn't given her the benefit of the doubt. Hadn't even had the courtesy to confront her quietly, in the privacy of his office. Instead he'd sent Hominy as his lackey. And to think she'd been helping the dignified servant to become a gentleman. *Gentleman, ha!*

The pair of them deserved a hiding with a willow switch. No, a railroad tie.

As for J. Preston Clarke, well, if she weren't a God-fearing young woman she knew just what she would wish for that snake.

Meredith decided that she thoroughly despised the entire male species.

A block from her boardinghouse, she decided she was angry at God after all, for putting her in this humiliating predicament. Why shove Preston in her path in the first place, when as the omniscient Creator of the universe, the Lord knew all along what would happen? What use was there in spending all your life obeying the tenets of His word, when God let you down without a lick of warning? He knew the desires of her heart, yet He thwarted her at every turn. It wasn't fair...

By the time she reached the gate in front of the boardinghouse, her anger and outrage had flared into self-righteous fury, an emotion far more satisfying than shame.

She stubbornly ignored a tiny flicker of caution.

It was quite dark now and very still. Only a single light shone through the parlor window of the boardinghouse. The good citizens of Winchester were all cozily ensconced in their homes; Meredith might have been the only soul on the planet. A ghost-white quarter-moon filtered through the newly leafed trees lining the streets, but other than the low-pitched hum of insects serenading one another in a hedge next door, the night wrapped her in a smothering shroud of silence.

She hated the silence, and when she thought about her room—a dark cell devoid of company—every nerve rebelled. She'd be alone with her thoughts, with an anger she couldn't sustain on her own. She needed to vent her wrath, preferably upon one of the people who deserved it the most. Not Preston—she never wanted to see that man again, never wanted to speak his name.

Fine. She couldn't satisfy her thirst for vengeance with a deceitful snake, so she would seek satisfaction from the man whose lack of faith in her wounded far more deeply than Meredith was prepared to admit. At least Benjamin should be easy to find. He lived in a suite of rooms on the top floor of the Excelsior. Meredith knew his schedule, and he had nothing planned this evening—unless he and Hominy had scuttled off somewhere like the cowards they were. But she would find the witless Mr. Walker if it took the entire night. If necessary she'd hunt him down in his private domain—hammer down the door, hang propriety and dignity and respectability.

It didn't matter anymore. She was doomed to a spinster's life and no longer cared a fig for her reputation. Virtuous Christian ladies gained nothing for their trouble but misery, so perhaps it was time to sample some of that fruit from the tree of knowledge.

Decision made, Meredith marched back down the street, her heels drumming out a furious rhythm in counterpoint to the blood throbbing in her ears.

The tiny voice nibbled the corner of her conscience, urging calm.

Meredith ignored the voice. Ignored as well the seeds of uncertainty sprouting, springing to life when she shoved through the front entrance to the Excelsior. "Where's Mr. Walker?" she demanded of Clyde Henckle, the night porter.

"Miss Sinclair?" Well-trained, after a single incredulous glance Clyde snapped to attention. "Um…I believe he's still in his offices."

"Alone?"

"I couldn't say. Shall I inquire for you?"

"That won't be necessary." She steamed across the lobby without another word.

The outer office was dark and empty, but a thin strip of light showed beneath Benjamin's door. Head tilted for battle, Meredith pounded her fist on the panel, then threw it open without waiting for permission to enter. What could he do to her, after all? She'd already resigned.

Benjamin was seated behind his desk. He was coatless, shirtsleeves rolled up his forearms, tie and collar dangling over the back of his chair. For once, the sartorial image was lacking. Good. It was easier to deliver a scorching denunciation to a tired-looking, rumpled man.

Meredith sucked in a deep breath and started across the room.

Benjamin hadn't risen, but his dark blue eyes slowly studied her from the top of her head downward, finally returning to her face. "Where have you been?" The mildness of his question belied the rigid set of his jaw. The lines scoring his forehead deepened. "Meredith, where have you been for"—he glanced at the clock sitting in front of him—"the last four hours?"

"Why? What possible difference could it make to you?" She reached the desk and stood, shaking in her outrage, heated words straining to spew forth.

"Hominy's out looking for you."

"Oh? How nice, setting your faithful bodyguard after me. Wanted to make sure I hadn't pilfered through your desk? Stolen papers out of your safe?"

He stood slowly, never taking his gaze away from her. "I wanted to make sure you were all right. In spite of what you've done, I needed to—"

"I haven't done anything to you!" Meredith yelled, her hands fisting. "It was all a scheme. I was nothing but a pawn in a contemptible game. And you're as blind and *stupid* as I was. He wants to ruin you, he wanted to keep you from building Poplar Springs. He used me, and he lied to me. And you fell for the lies, you didn't even try to believe me. He— I—"

"Where's your shawl? Your hat? Meredith, tell me where you've been for the past four hours."

Meredith blinked, disoriented. Her shawl? Her hat? The trivial questions and Benjamin's steely calm seemed a bewilderingly inappropriate response. "I-I must have left them. At Pre—at his office. I had to wait for—" She stopped, then banged her fist on top of his desk, knocking over the clock. "How dare you question me! It's a ruse, you're trying to maneuver the conversation. You're nothing but a bully, Benjamin Walker."

When he rounded the desk she met him halfway, quivering with the need to strike. To hurt him as he had hurt her. "I can't believe I defended you to Preston. I wish I hadn't. You didn't even try to defend me, listen to my side. You're no better than Preston!"

"No?" Quicker than a pouncing tomcat his hands closed over her arms and jerked her against his chest. "At least I don't leave a lady alone in my office while I whistle off to dine with my mistress."

"Take your hands off— Mistress?" She stilled. "His mistress?"

"They're enjoying supper in my dining room as we speak." Raw violence leapt from his eyes to the hands gripping her upper arms. As quickly as the dangerous flicker appeared, it was gone. His hold gentled. "Everyone knows about her. Everyone, apparently, but you."

"Let me go."

"Only if you promise not to bolt or slap my face."

Choking on humiliation, for once Meredith couldn't summon an answer. When his hands fell away she didn't move. If she tried, she would crumple at his feet.

"I should have listened to my instincts," Benjamin murmured after a prolonged silence. "Told you weeks ago, when I saw what you were doing. Of course, I'd told myself your affairs of the heart were none of my business, as long as they didn't interfere with your work. I did think you'd have more pride than to throw yourself at a man like Preston Clarke, however."

"Pride," she whispered. "It does go before destruction."

"Oh?" His head tilted sideways. "In your case, I'd have said pig-headedness rather than pride. Or perhaps impulse. What do you think, Meredith? I know what I'm thinking. I'm relieved that you resigned." He stroked under his chin, where beard stubble shadowed his face and neck. "I'm a little disappointed in myself for missing these defects in your character when I hired you. I'm afraid under the circumstances a letter of reference would—"

A gurgling half-shriek erupted from Meredith's lips. She flew at him, hands fisted, blinded by a geyser of wrath. In all her twenty-three years she'd never known such consuming rage, not even when she discovered that Preston had played her for a Judas goat.

She was no match for Benjamin Walker, landing only a single glancing blow against a granite-muscled shoulder because he jerked his head back with blinding speed. Then she was locked in an unbreakable embrace.

"That's more like it." He manacled her fists in one large hand while his other arm circled her ribs, keeping her smashed against his torso so she was unable to even kick or stomp his instep, or—

"I was afraid I was going to have to start insulting your family next, to provoke a reaction."

The words, spoken with such calm authority, arrested the spiraling rage. Dazed, Meredith gaped at the face scant inches away from hers. "You were—all those words, you didn't mean…you were only…"

His head lowered until his breath fanned her heated cheeks. "Yes. I was only provoking you. I know you're innocent, and there's nothing wrong with your character. I've grown…quite fond…of all your quirks, including the pigheadedness." The arm holding her against him shifted. "So I provoked you. Because I didn't want to do this, to a drooping, defeated woman."

And his mouth covered hers.

Forty-Two

For a first kiss, his timing showed deplorable judgment, Ben thought in the walled-off portion of his mind still capable of analysis. On the other hand, considering the day he'd suffered through —and what he'd just heard—Meredith was fortunate that he maintained enough scruples not to carry her off to his upstairs suite like a marauding warrior. *She hadn't betrayed him.* And she must care, more than she realized, or she never would have hunted him down.

He forced himself to lift his head, dragging air into his lungs. Meredith was gazing at him in such bewilderment Ben almost kissed her again. Instead he lifted a hand to her cheek, brushing a stray teardrop aside with his fingertips. "I won't apologize. Been wanting to do that for"—his thumb skimmed the line of her jaw, up to the soft skin just behind her ear—"well, it feels like forever."

Her throat muscles quivered, and she passed her tongue around her lips. "I didn't know."

A smile twitched the corner of his lips. "I made sure you didn't. You were seeing another man, after all. I also wasn't about to take advantage of an employee who might fear for her position if she spurned any advances." He couldn't help it. He dropped a light kiss on the tip of her nose. "That's the real reason I've accepted your resignation."

Disillusionment muddied the green gold eyes. "You just want to seduce me like Lamar Aikens. You're no better than Preston."

Still swimming in relief and the memory of their kiss, the verbal thrust caught Ben off guard. He lifted his hands at once and took two steps backward. She might as well have slapped his face. "If that's all I wanted, I wouldn't have waited this long. And just now... I didn't want to stop with a kiss, Meredith."

He waited until comprehension filled her eyes. "If you need to fling a few accusations at my head, go ahead. I probably deserve some of them. But bridle your tongue until you make sure they *are* deserved." His voice softened to a knife-edged whisper. "And don't ever compare me to J. Preston Clarke again."

"No. All right. I—you're not. I won't..." She looked down. Ben watched her fingers flutter in a tattoo against each other until she twined her hands together. She shuddered before she lifted her head. "It's just that I don't understand how you could want to kiss me, when you"—she cleared her throat several times—"behaved the way you did this afternoon."

Well, he probably deserved that. Ben knew he would carry the memory of that afternoon for the rest of his worthless life. She'd stood before him, chin lifted, eyes like wounds in a face the color of bleached bone. And she'd done her best to crack his jaw with her fist, all the while looking the way he felt: as though he'd stabbed her through the heart. She'd looked that way when he flung out the information about Preston Clarke's mistress, until he goaded her into losing her temper.

The kiss had been inevitable for several reasons. Relief. Exultation. Desire. Perhaps, most of all, because he couldn't bear to see her defeated and empty-eyed. An angered Meredith Sinclair was a magnificent creature, incandescent with unleashed passion. And he'd wanted her with a force that rocked him to his toes. Yet Meredith hadn't known the depth of his feelings, still didn't because all he had done since she burst into his office was to react, bombarding her with unleashed emotions of his own. Emotions he was still trying to comprehend himself.

What a mess they'd made of things.

"When I sent Hominy to fetch you this afternoon, at the time I thought you had betrayed me," he said. "I was angry, yes. And I was hurt. But hurt and anger don't always kill desire." A corner of his mouth curled in a wry smile. "You really don't know much about men, do you?"

Her head snapped back. "I know everything about men I need to know. All of you are lower than the belly of a garter snake."

Now there was vintage Meredith. Ben rubbed the back of his neck, reining in a defensive retort. He'd confused her, and he'd frightened her;

with Meredith, belligerence masked an ocean of insecurities, not true antagonism. "I've had similar thoughts about the female of the species myself," he said, his voice mild.

He reached behind her to right the quaint kettledrum-shaped clock, setting it back on its onyx base. The task allowed his arm to graze her side. Meredith scrambled backward, tripping over the hem of her gown. Ben grabbed her arm. "Steady there. You're skittish, for someone who knows everything about men."

She jerked her arm free. "I've reason enough to be skittish, the way you're staring at me."

"Ah. How am I staring at you?"

A fiery blush suffused her face, delighting him. "Never mind." She shook out the rumpled folds of her skirt, smoothed the tucks of her shirtwaist. "Mr. Walker, if you know now that I didn't betray—"

"Call me Benjamin or Ben. After the kiss we shared, 'Mr. Walker' is a trifle overdone, don't you think?" Because he knew she was more nervous than she would ever admit, Ben strolled back behind his desk. "I'll walk you home." He picked up his collar and buttoned it back in place.

"I walked myself here, I'm perfectly capable of walking myself back. Besides, I don't want… I don't understand—" She stopped.

Ben finished fastening the collar, but paused as he reached for the tie. "Meredith…" The name emerged in a long sigh. Her back was turned, shoulders bowed.

Ben rummaged in his pockets, eventually locating his handkerchief. "Here. I have plenty more, in the bottom drawer of my desk. I've started keeping a supply there, just for you, since on an average of three times a week you—no, shh. It's all right. Don't turn away. It's all right."

He kept up the soothing patter while he pulled her into his embrace. At first she resisted, but Ben had known enough women over the years to recognize the difference between a rebuff and embarrassed reluctance. Firmly he pressed her damp cheek to his breast. His other hand kneaded her taut neck muscles. Ben closed his eyes, savoring the feel of her safe in his arms. That she was weeping mattered not at all. For a little while, he thought, just for a little while.

"I hate being like this," she finally choked out, her nose still buried in his shirtfront. "Hate it… Tears are weak. The mark of a sn-sniveling ninny."

"For some, perhaps. My mother used to tell me that tears watered the soul. She said the saddest people on earth are the ones who refuse to cry."

"Then I should be the happiest woman on earth," Meredith responded in a thick voice. In a convulsive movement she gathered handfuls of his shirt in her fists, ground her face back into his shoulder, and released the desolate tears of a soul at the end of her resources. Ben held her, rocked her—and wished he could join her.

But all the tears in all the world would not restore circumstances or right the injustices both of them had suffered.

He loved her, but he was still raw *because* he loved her. Though he now understood that Meredith hadn't betrayed him, it would take a long time to heal the pain of this afternoon. She had, after all, clung to her belief in Clarke's innocence until the bounder himself told her otherwise.

The kiss had relieved Ben greatly; Meredith would never have responded to him had her heart still belonged solely to J. Preston Clarke. But despite the brief explosion of passion, and their present closeness, Ben remained wary of confessing his feelings, let alone asking Meredith about hers. He was too scared of what her answer might be.

A step scraped across the parquet floor of the outside offices. He glanced across the room just as Hominy materialized in the doorway. The big man stopped dead, a thunderous scowl replacing the lines of concern.

"Should have known better than to leave you alone."

Meredith jumped and tried to pull away, but Ben ignored her efforts, gathering her closer instead. "We both leaped to conclusions earlier." He gestured Hominy over with a quick jerk of his chin. "Don't make the same mistake. She's innocent, Hominy. Meredith's only sin is gullibility. She believed Preston Clarke was an honorable man." Meredith made a muffled sound, and he rubbed the back of her shoulders, feeling the tension rebuilding. "Clarke saw an easy mark and took advantage."

"Wouldn't have, if you'd listened to me. Ain't got the sense God gave a billy goat."

Meddling old coot, Ben thought, smiling in spite of his irritation. Meredith squirmed more forcefully, and he let her go. Then he lifted her hand and curled her fingers around his handkerchief. "Mop up, you'll feel better."

"Thank you."

Her voice was hoarse, her hand not quite steady. Some women could cry and maintain their looks. Meredith was not one of them. Yet Ben watched with pride filling his heart, as with a sort of stubborn grace she nonetheless gathered dignity back around her like an ermine stole.

When she finished with his handkerchief, she folded it into a neat square, looked across at Hominy, and cleared her throat. "I tend to agree, about his lack of sense. But I'd like to know why you said it," she said, edging away from Ben. "What didn't Mr. Walker listen to you about?"

"Never mind that now." Ben stepped in front of her, blocking her path. "It's not important. We can discuss everything another time. It's late. You're exhausted. Let me take you home."

The light of battle glinted from her swollen, red-rimmed eyes. "Let's discuss this now." She peered around him. "Hominy? What doesn't he want to tell me?"

"Not my place to tell you, Miss Sinclair." The deep voice softened, though his left hand rose defensively to his ear. "Mr. Ben's my employer, see. But he's also a friend. Now from the looks of things, the two of you—"

Ben hastily interrupted. "Why don't you fetch her some water? And have Clyde rummage around the cloak room for a shawl or cape or something, hmm?"

Instead of obeying, Hominy folded his arms across his chest and planted his feet on the carpet. "Might be a better idea for me to stay here."

Meredith laid a hand on Ben's arm, startling him. He glanced down. Incredibly, Meredith was smiling. "You're a wonderful friend," she told Ben's overprotective watchdog. When she turned that sweet smile on Ben he felt as though he'd taken a punch straight to the gut. "I'm all right now. My sisters would tell you that these bouts tend to wear everyone out. Fortunately, once they're over I'm usually docile as a spring lamb."

"I doubt that." Ben brushed the corner of her cheekbone, then the tip of her nose with his index finger. "You look terrible," he said, his voice tender.

"Please. Don't cater to my sensibilities," she grumbled. "I might say the same about yourself…except it wouldn't be true." She muttered the last phrase beneath her breath, but when she realized Ben had heard, a deep blush converged over her already reddened nose and eyes until her entire face glowed. "Never mind. Don't you say another word."

Chin jutted forward, she marched across the carpet to Hominy. "You should know that Preston Clarke is doing everything in his power to prohibit Mr. Walker from building Poplar Springs. But I only discovered that an hour ago, when he told me himself. Hominy, Preston betrayed all of us. But please believe that I want Mr. Walker to build his dream every bit as much as you."

" 'Preciate that, Miss Sinclair," Hominy replied with grave dignity. " 'Preciate it more, if you'd convince him of that."

"Hominy—" Ben warned, but the black man shook his head.

"She ought to know, Mr. Ben. It's only right, and if you don't tell her, I figure I have to."

"What do I need to know?" Ben watched fresh panic leap through her, stripping the life and color he'd spent the last moments doing his best to restore. "What's happened? Has Preston—has he already threatened you?"

Ben clenched his hands and contemplated the satisfaction of firing his manservant. He was cornered, and he knew it. Expelling his breath in a long sigh, Ben gave in.

"About three hours ago, I sold the Poplar Springs acreage to the Baltimore and Ohio Railroad. Preston Clarke can play all the nasty power games with them he cares to." He stopped, waited until he could continue in the same light tone. "If God's in a mood for granting justice, Preston will learn what it feels like to be the chewed-up bone of contention."

Meredith was staring at him as though he'd turned into a horned toad. "You sold the land? Y-you're letting Preston win? You won't even try to fight him?"

"He would if—"

"That's enough, Hominy."

Hominy's nostrils flared, but he inclined his head and didn't finish the sentence. Three long strides brought Ben to Meredith's side. "No.

I'm not going to fight." He held her gaze. "The man's corrupt, bent upon achieving his ends regardless of the means. I'd be a fool to stand in the way of a man like that."

"Poplar Springs…all your plans. I can't believe you'd throw everything away. You could fight him. Why won't you even try?" She searched his face, and something in Ben shriveled at her expression. "I never thought you'd be a—" She reached toward him, then let her hand drop to her side. "Somehow even when I was so angry I wanted to hurl bricks at you, I still believed you'd build Poplar Springs."

"Go ahead and say it." Ben tried to look away from her, but some sick lunacy prevented the simple movement. "I can see it in your face. Go ahead and say it."

God help him, he'd thought he couldn't feel any worse pain than the agony he'd endured when he believed Meredith had betrayed him. He'd been wrong. Wrong because her lack of faith now was an even worse betrayal. Obviously the kiss had meant little to her. He loved, but Meredith… Muscles clenched, Ben curled his lips into a taunting sneer. "Why show control now? Discretion? You never have before. After all, I accused you of being Clarke's pet chippy. Well, darling, here's your chance to get even. So have at it. You're really good with words when you're mad. Say it, Meredith. Spit it out."

Her eyes darkened with an indefinable stew of emotions. Ben willed her to hurry up and deliver the killing blow, so he could crawl off to the isolated comfort of his upstairs rooms. And wait for the pain to kill him.

"You want me to call you a coward," she said at last, but instead of slamming him like bullets, her words fell at his feet like tears. "I don't want to. I can't bear to think of you that way, not after—" She pressed shaking fingers against her mouth and turned away. "Excuse me," she said after a moment, "you're right. It's time for me to go home. Hominy, a buggy? I don't believe I feel up to the walk right now."

Without waiting for an answer she fled from the room. Ben watched her retreat and wondered vaguely why he was still upright. There was no feeling in his knees, and he knew that if he had the strength to press his hand against the left side of his chest, he wouldn't detect even a flutter of life.

Forty-Three

*L*ike a wounded animal Meredith crept through the dark outer offices, toward a small cloakroom in the back. It was the only place where she could be alone, away from bright lights and curious faces and the inevitable questions sure to arise over her appearance. *Just for a few moments,* she promised herself over and over. She would hide there for just a few moments, until she could make sense of what had happened in Benjamin's office.

Benjamin...

She was so confused. Didn't know what to think, how to feel. Should she pray for forgiveness? Scream for mercy? She'd lost all confidence in her own judgment. She didn't trust herself, she didn't trust God, she didn't trust anyone or anything. Preston had only feigned interest in her, Benjamin indifference. Yet over the past hours each had gone to great lengths to demonstrate that the opposite was true. Blurred images of their faces swirled before her, their expressions fluid as creek water pouring over stones.

Meredith's fingers fumbled upward, touching her lips. She could still feel the imprint of Benjamin's lips and the strength of his arms, filling her with sensations for which she knew no words. With tremulous longings that were tangled with despair.

Preston had kissed her once or twice, light brushes of his lips against her cheek or temple. A tepid effort, which she now realized had elicited an equally tepid response on her part. At the time Meredith assumed his restraint a gesture of respect. Now she wasn't sure, since Benjamin's behavior, and her response, suggested a different interpretation altogether.

Nothing, not her first schoolgirl crush nor her infatuation with

Lamar Aikens, nor even her obsession with Preston—nothing in Meredith's life had prepared her for this—this raw longing inside her. She had never perceived herself as anything but a competent office manager for Benjamin. And she'd thought that Preston was an answer to prayer.

Benjamin was right. Her knowledge of men was false, based on self-deception. And she knew even less about herself. It had been humiliatingly simple for both Preston and Benjamin to dupe her, because she wasn't a confident, worldly woman at all. She was nothing but a green country girl.

There, of course, was the answer. It was her own self-deception which had opened wide the barn door, allowing all of her common sense to stampede into the night. Hard on the heels of common sense followed every lesson in life, every spiritual truth she had resisted because of her stubbornness. Now she was well and truly alone inside that barn, vulnerable as a motherless foal.

Meredith knew she needed to examine the magnitude of her misconceptions, but right now she was too emotionally battered to do more than—hide in the cloakroom.

"Miss Sinclair?"

"Hominy, no more. Not right now." The effort to speak exhausted her. She hoped he would take the hint and leave her alone.

"I might be sorry about disturbing you," the deep drawl pushed its way past her stupor, " 'cept for Mr. Ben. He doesn't deserve what's happened. He surely doesn't deserve what you're thinking, no matter that you didn't say the word to his face."

She hadn't deserved everything that had been heaped upon her head either. "You have no idea what I'm thinking." Her voice was leaden. "What I thought."

But Hominy had reached her now and looked as though he would plant himself there until he'd spoken his piece.

"Very well," she said. "Say whatever you need to say. I'm listening."

"Thank you, Miss Sinclair." The whites of his coffee-colored eyes gleamed in the darkened room, shifting from Meredith to Benjamin's office door, now closed. "Um…Mr. Ben, he didn't want you to know this."

"Then why are you telling me?"

"Because only one of them gentlemen in your life's a coward, Miss Sinclair. And it isn't Benjamin Walker. The real reason Mr. Ben sold that land isn't 'cause he don't have the gumption to face that sorry piece of trash, Mr. Clarke." He hesitated, then added in a low voice, "Mr. Ben sold it to protect you, Miss Sinclair."

The revelation felled her with a single swipe. "To—protect me? He's *protecting* me?" Guilt rose, hot and thick as bile. She pressed a fist against her mouth. "Preston did threaten him, didn't he?"

Hominy nodded. "Swore he'd see to it that your good name would be forever smirched. If you wanted another job, no one would hire you. No man would take you to wife, no decent folk would invite you into their homes. Naught but a pack of lies, and Mr. Clarke knowing it. But he told Mr. Ben it wouldn't matter. Your reputation would be ruined all the same, and not even Mr. Ben could stop tongues from wagging."

"But I'm leaving. I resigned. Preston can't use me as leverage, there was no need to—to sell Poplar Springs." Practically stuttering, she grabbed Hominy's arm. "Hominy, you have to make him understand— no." She tossed her head. "*I'll* make him understand. Tell me, was any money exchanged this afternoon?"

"I…don't reckon I know, Miss Sinclair."

"Do you know if contracts were actually signed? Have you or Lowell or Mrs. Biggs carried any documents to the courthouse? Was his lawyer present—no." Benjamin's lawyer, Douglass X. Hackett, was in Roanoke this week. "We can undo the damage, Hominy."

"Miss Sinclair—"

"Not this evening, it's too late. But first thing in the morning." In a half-dozen steps she reached her desk and fumbled for the lamp. "I'll need my writing pad. I'm too rattled to remember names. Oh, why didn't he *tell* me? The noble, crackbrained idiot…I don't understand. Doesn't make a lick of sense. Hominy, what did you—"

"Miss Sinclair? What you're doing—it won't do no good. Wasn't just your reputation Mr. Ben's wantin' to—"

"Your grammar's slipping. Don't worry, Hominy. I'm not as

discomposed as I look. It's all right. I'm not going to—*oh!*...I resigned!" She stared blankly at Hominy. "I'm no longer office manager."

"Don't matter. He won't change his mind about the land," Hominy said. The dark eyes reflected the hopelessness Meredith heard in his voice. "I tried, near got my own self booted out over it. But you know Mr. Ben. Once his mind's made up, might as well try to stop a sunset."

"He'd made up his mind to build Poplar Springs."

"Yes, he had. But that was before—" The full lips pressed together as though he wanted to say more but wasn't going to.

"I won't let him do this." She pressed the heels of her hands over her burning eyes.

For once she would control her emotions. She refused to be at the mercy of those particular innermost parts God had created in secret twenty-three years ago. It was time the Lord made good on some of the promises she'd heard all her life and showed her and Benjamin a way to escape this infernal coil. *You allowed this, do You hear? The least You can do is help me to clean it up.*

An eerie prickling sensation skimmed across her skin, as though a warm breeze had blown through an opened window. Meredith froze, trying to grasp an elusive thought that danced at the periphery of her conscience.

"I didn't mean to cause you more pain." Hominy spoke into the strained silence. "I just had to tell you." He shifted, not meeting her gaze. "Mr. Ben, he's, well, I don't reckon there's a finer man."

The strange prickling sensation dimmed. Meredith dismissed it with an impatient shrug, because one overriding conviction demanded her attention: She must talk to Benjamin. "I have to talk to him. Is he still in there?" She nodded toward his office.

"Don't know. I'm afraid he might have used the back door. I shouldn't have stayed away this long. No telling where he might roam, the way he's hurting right now." Even as he spoke Hominy was retracing his steps.

"Wait." Garnet darted in front of him. "Hominy..." Abruptly the words dried up in a spasm of uncertainty. "I...um...let me go in there. Alone, I mean. By myself." Embarrassment glued her tongue to the roof of her mouth, but she stood her ground. "I wouldn't do this under normal circumstances. You do know me, Hominy. It's just that…there's things I need to say to him, things I can't…say with an audience."

A jumbled prayer arrowed straight from the depths of her being. *God? Help me. Please.*

She didn't know what Hominy saw reflected in her face. But in an unprecedented gesture—one he never would have proffered under normal circumstances—he reached out his hand, and gently squeezed her shoulder.

"I'll fetch the buggy," he said. "I'll wait there. You're not to go home by yourself, Miss Sinclair."

"No, I won't." The lump in her throat swelled. She touched the back of his hand. "Thank you," she whispered.

"Reckon I'm the one to be thanking you," Hominy said. He touched his forehead and silently departed through the outer door.

Benjamin hadn't left. Meredith breathed a silent thanks as she slipped inside his office. Her mouth was dry, her hands trembling, her heart so full of emotion it hurt to take a breath. For a moment she stood just over the threshold, watching the motionless figure across the room.

Still coatless, he stood with his back to Meredith, staring out into the night, his hands tucked inside his pockets. The only light in the silent room glowed softly from a banquet lamp on a cluttered book table next to his left elbow.

Suddenly shy, Meredith took one tentative step, then another, until she was only a step or two from him. Benjamin gave no sign he was aware of her presence.

Mr. Walker, she started to say, but caught herself. In her heart, he'd never be "Mr. Walker" again. "B-Benjamin?"

His shoulders stiffened, but he didn't turn. "Did Hominy send you? I wish he'd take his meddling elsewhere. Go away, Meredith. I'm not fit company right now."

"That's how I felt, but Hominy wouldn't leave me alone either." She'd have given her right leg for a glass of water. "I thank God he didn't." With difficulty she managed to clear her throat.

"You have a peculiar relationship with the Almighty. From what I understand, you also thanked God for sending Preston Clarke into your path."

If he'd sounded sarcastic, or even affected the light indifference that wounded more deeply than a heated tirade, Meredith might have lost her courage. But his voice betrayed only exhaustion. A soul battered like Meredith's within and without.

"I'm beginning to realize," she said very quietly, "that what *I* understand about God is that…I understand very little at all. But I think for the first time in my life, I'm ready to learn. Benjamin, please turn around. I need to say something"—she tried to take a deep breath—"and you deserve to have it said to your face."

A visible shudder snaked down his spine. When he turned around, the opaline glow from the lamp illuminated his set face. He looked, she realized, as though he were facing his executioner.

"I'm sorry, so sorry," she blurted, the words tumbling forth in her need to heal his pain. "About everything. Hominy told me, you see. I didn't understand. I don't. It's just that it never would have occurred to me, that you'd sell your dream to protect me. I still don't understand…"

The words began to wobble. Desperate, she plowed ahead, because nothing mattered in this moment but that Benjamin's hurt be assuaged. "I was wrong to think what I did, Benjamin. And it was only that one instant, truly. Even when you wanted me to call you a coward, I didn't. I couldn't, because no matter what you read in my reaction, I never really believed it. Please, will you forgive me?"

"I thought," he replied after the longest pause of Meredith's life, "you'd expect me to ask *your* forgiveness."

"For—what happened this afternoon? I don't care about that anymore. It's done, finished. We were both played for fools by an insignificant toad who tries to pretend he's a prince."

The ghost of a smile appeared. "I've always loved your gift for description. Meredith, tell me. Does this reversal of devotion to Clarke have anything to do with the fact that I kissed you like I did earlier? It was a mistake, I know. And you do deserve an apology in spite of what I—"

"I never thought you were a coward, but if you try to apologize for that kiss, I will decide you're a-a—" Abruptly she launched herself forward, threw her arms around Benjamin's neck, and planted a clumsy kiss on the corner of his mouth. The dizzying sensation that her bones were dissolving poured through her once more.

Meredith gasped and wrenched herself away—no great feat because throughout the entire impulsive embrace Benjamin stood rigid as an iron post.

"I-I'm not going to apologize." She pressed one hand hard over her heart, the other on the corner of the table. "I've…been wanting to do that for"—she bit her lip, then finished with a broken laugh—"a half-hour, at least."

"Meredith—"

"But it seemed like forever." She kept her gaze glued to his, where she could vaguely discern tiny sparks of light starting to glitter in the night darkness of his eyes. Their expression gave her the courage to continue. "Benjamin, you were right. I don't know anything at all about men, not really. I…well, I do enjoy their company. I've even foolishly chased one or two. I know now I was self-centered and ignorant. You were right. I made it easy for Preston."

"You don't need to—"

"Because until you, nobody, including Preston, ever made me feel so…alive. This afternoon, I was angry enough to hit you. Which of course I shouldn't have because Papa told us over and over never to hit unless it was for self-defense. He told us a woman has no right to strike a man just because she's angry, because a man who is any kind of man at all would never dream of hitting back. Just like you said, remember? And then, you hurt me so deeply that I could barely stand upright, and I didn't realize at the time that only someone you care about—a lot— could cause that intensity of hurt. But it was when you held me in your arms that—"

"That you realized why I'm thanking God that I'm longer your employer and you're no longer my employee. Is that what you were going to say?" Benjamin asked in a husky undertone, his hands now lightly cupping her shoulders.

He drew her toward him, his thumbs tracing the line of her collarbones in a gesture that turned her knees to water. "You do have a way with words, my love. But right now you're using too many of them." His head dipped until his breath caressed her face. "I need this more than I've needed anything in my life," he whispered just before his mouth closed over hers again.

Meredith clung to the broad shoulders and allowed her heart and soul and mind to take flight.

And it was very strange… Even with her entire being focused on the man kissing her so passionately, somewhere deep inside was a kind of *knowing*. An awareness that Benjamin's arms weren't the only ones wrapped around her, holding her as though they would never let go.

Forty-Four

"You've the constitution of an ox." Ben groaned up the last few feet of the mountainside and collapsed alongside his old friend Cade Beringer. "What do you feed yourself these days? Steel shavings?"

"Nothing so exotic." Laughing at him, Cade leaned back on his elbows and breathed in the hot June air as though it was as cool and clear as a mountain spring. "Just years of tramping about. If you'd enjoy a bit more of God's creation in the raw, instead of looking once a day through a window in one of your hotel offices, you wouldn't be wheezing like a broken-down plug of a horse." He easily avoided Ben's tired swipe. "How many hotels you own now anyway?"

"Six." The seventh would have been Poplar Springs, but Ben closed his mind against the residual grief. "If I didn't spend my time slaving in my offices, there wouldn't be any money to build more hotels with grounds to landscape. I'd have no reason to hire you then, would I? You wouldn't be able to enjoy all the comforts of a new hotel for a couple of months while you created beautiful surroundings. You'd just spend years tramping through these mountains without a breath of luxury. Could you survive on nuts and berries, my friend?"

"Indefinitely. Take a look around. See that dead elm over there with the cluster of mushrooms? Those are morels—'merkles' to some folk. Good eating. Then there's jack-in-the-pulpit. *Arisaema triphyllum* if you want the Latin classification. Plant itself is poisonous, but the bulb's not bad if you boil it. That's what the Indians did. And did you know that—"

"All right. I concede!" Ben studied the relaxed man beside him. He hadn't seen Cade for almost two years, but his friend hadn't changed much. In some ways it was as though they'd seen each other yesterday.

Cade Beringer was an easy man to like. "If I didn't know better—and you weren't sporting that tawny lion's mane of yours—I'd swear you were an Indian yourself, your skin's so brown."

"Except for my eyes. Last time I read up on it, indigenous North American tribes suffered from a dearth of green eyes."

"Ah yes. How could I forget your eyes? 'Greener than her favorite pair of jade earrings'—wasn't that how the sweet young lady described them two years ago? You remember, don't you? She tracked you down all over the resort grounds, no matter how hard you tried to hide." Ben chuckled when Cade groaned and covered his face with his arm. "Too bad it was my hotel, instead of a forest, hmm? You might have succeeded in losing her."

"She was a regular little Delilah, wasn't she?" Cade shifted, lying back to study the sky. "Never did understand what she saw in a man like me. No matter how many times I explained that I was only interested in the landscape, she seemed to think I could be persuaded…otherwise."

Ben glanced at him. "I always wondered how you finally fended her off."

"I invited her to spend the day with me. It, ah, happened to be the day I spent hauling two dozen loads of manure in to prepare the ground for all those flower beds you wanted." A sheepish smile flashed across the sun-browned face. "I hadn't known genteel ladies knew those kinds of words. Last thing I saw of Miss Genevieve Mayfield was her back. Her bustle was twitching like the tail of a wet cat."

They both laughed, then settled into the sun-baked meadow grass, hands behind their heads. Bees droned among the purple clover, and a pair of jays in the trees below filled the air with rusty-hinge warbles. Heat rose in grass-scented waves, imbuing the air with a soporific potion more seductive than a narcotic.

For the first time in weeks, Ben felt his muscles softening, his nerves unraveling one at the time, until the sharp-edged memories dissolved from his brain like hot wax. Until this moment, he hadn't realized how badly he'd needed to get away. To…heal.

"Thanks, Cade," he murmured after a while, his voice drowsy.

"My pleasure." Cade stretched like the sleeping lion Ben had compared him to, his own voice sounding as drugged as Ben's. "To my way of thinking, nothing refreshes the soul quite like being still and resting in God's presence."

"Don't know about God's presence, but I have needed the quiet." His hand combed through the prickly grass. "These past weeks have been pretty bad."

"I thought you looked a bit drawn when you picked me up at the train station yesterday. Want to talk about it?"

"No."

"No problem." There was a short pause. "Want to talk to the Lord about it?"

Restless suddenly, Ben jackknifed to a sitting position and wrapped his arms around his knees. Cade had strolled into the Excelsior early that morning. The summer season was in full swing, every room booked through September. Guests filled the lobby, the hallways, the dining room; their carriages and curricles and roadsters choked the once peaceful streets.

Normally Ben thrived in the crackling busyness of tourist season. Yet Cade had appraised him in a single look, and before Ben quite figured out that he'd been outmaneuvered, they were headed south on the Valley Pike. Cade turned the buggy westward at Round Hill, not stopping until they reached the base of Little North Mountain. Then they'd hiked to this grassy knob overlooking the hazy Valley below.

No human sounds other than their voices stirred the air. No clattering typewriters, no ringing bells. No steam whistles or factory whistles, no constant interruptions by streams of guests, no staff members watching him. Waiting.

"Someone asked me a couple of months ago if I ever prayed." Ben turned his head sideways, measuring Cade's expression. "I told her I hadn't talked to God in years. But I'll confess to you, Cade…lately I've been wondering about it."

"Wondering's good. Do a lot of it myself."

Ben emitted a rude sound. "I've known a fair amount of religious folks in my thirty-odd years, from pious ministers praying pontifical blessings over meals to"—Meredith's image blasted away his state of somnolence—"a woman who, near as I can figure it, first decides what she wants, then asks God to arrange it."

"A common human mistake." Cade's voice was peaceful. "Jesus did tell us, after all, to ask whatever we would, and He promised to grant it. Trouble is, what Jesus was talking about, and what His disciples heard— what we hear nineteen hundred years later—are two different things."

"Not in the mood for preaching, Cade."

"Sorry. Sometimes I can't help myself."

Ben plucked a nearby flower and began tearing the petals off, one by one. He'd known Cade for going on six years now. Had known from their first meeting that this man was the most devout Christian he had ever met, in spite of the fact that Cade seldom attended a formal church service. Yet Cade never put a fellow's teeth on edge about his faith. He sprinkled references to God and Jesus through his conversations so naturally it was impossible to take offense—mainly, Ben realized as he chewed on it, because Cade was simply sharing from his heart. Not trying to badger or grandstand.

If Ben were ever inclined to have a serious conversation about God with anyone besides Hominy, he reckoned it would be with Cade Beringer.

He found himself wondering why. They had little in common other than their mutual love for the mountains and the pleasure of occasionally working together. Baffled, he studied Cade. With minimal effort this seemingly easygoing man had been able to entice Ben to abandon a mound of paperwork and a day's worth of appointments and accompany him on a vigorous hike.

How had it happened?

Might be prudent, Ben decided, to remember that Cade's easygoing personality also housed an indomitable will.

"I don't know what I'm doing up here," he admitted out loud. "I'll be up half the night, catching up on all the work I left behind. I was supposed to dine with the New York Steubens." If Cade could be persuaded not to linger up here, Ben might still return in time to attend a musicale in the park at ten with a party of guests from—was it North Carolina or New Jersey? He was having difficulty keeping up these days without an office manager. "I must be crazy," he said. "Why did I let you talk me into this?"

"Oh, I imagine if you'd be honest with yourself, you'd figure it out." Cade rose to his feet. "Think about it a bit, why don't you? I spotted a stand of timber a little way back down the hillside that I'd like to check out. I'll see you in a bit."

He gathered up his knapsack and loped off.

Ben shook his head in disbelief. Cade Beringer was almost as much of a contradiction as Meredith. With his lean-muscled body and inexhaustible stamina, the man looked like he could go a dozen rounds in the ring with a prizefighter and win. But Cade Beringer was—a botanist. A botanist, a biologist, and a landscape designer. He was also a woodsman as at home in these mountains as Ben was hosting a formal dinner for two hundred or addressing the chamber of commerce in Richmond.

People. Any man who claimed to have insight into their convoluted behavior was destined for humiliation. Human beings were nothing but a mass of contradictions. How in blue blazes was one supposed to understand God, when it was impossible to fathom the quirks of the *human* condition?

Meredith, for instance. Ben rolled to his feet as well and began prowling the rocky, tree-choked hillside. He hadn't seen her in two weeks. She'd fled to Sinclair Run, needing, Ben knew, to sort things through. He'd let her go. If Meredith wouldn't return his love freely, there was little to be gained by forcing her to stay. She might have stolen his heart. He was fighting not to lose what remained of his mind.

But he would like to have had that talk with Jacob Sinclair. That old tin cookie cutter in her jewelry chest continued to tantalize his thoughts. What had Meredith called it, her heartwood chest? Whatever, the cookie cutter's incongruous presence in a chest designed to house heirloom jewelry spoke of a puzzle, one Ben would risk a lifetime trying to solve. If Meredith ever allowed him the opportunity.

She had written him twice, short notes that said little but revealed a lot. She was driving her sister Leah to distraction and her teetotaler father to drink. She'd paid a couple of visits to friends, driven up to

Tom's Brook to her sister Garnet's, but she missed her job. The excitement of the season. She missed the hotel and Lowell and Mrs. Biggs. Gaspar's cooking. The staff.

She missed Ben. He knew it, simply by the conspicuous absence of any mention of his name in those letters. But she was either too uncertain, or too contrary, to admit it. Ben gave a derisive snort. How many times over these two weeks had he himself risked the words? The letters he'd composed in reply reeked of avuncular affection. Friendly banter. Sprinkled with a word here and there of honest feeling, enough to blunt the jab of his conscience. In spite of admitting to himself months earlier that he was in love with her, he'd never given Meredith the words.

Why should he risk a declaration when Meredith couldn't even confess that she missed him?

Ever since he'd met her, she had displayed a propensity for hurling herself into affairs of the heart. Despite the undeniable passion between them, and a renewed sense of loyalty, complete trust was proving to be as elusive as a will-o'-the-wisp.

She might never trust him enough to give him her heart.

That's it, Walker. Why not at least admit it to yourself, up here all alone in the sanctity of this unspoiled mountain, where you've nobody to face but yourself.

And God.

Cade's soft suggestion insinuated itself into his mind, like a soft breeze whispering past his ear. *"Want to talk to the Lord about it?"*

All right. Certainly, by all means… God, I know You're up here, and I suppose I even know You're listening. But since I don't have a hair of a notion what it is I'm supposed to talk to You about, You're going to have to be a little more obvious about communicating Your efforts in my behalf.

For his first truly honest prayer, it wasn't much. But the elusive uncertainties mired deep inside his spirit seemed to lift, along with his mood.

Ben kicked a stone, idly following its path as it sailed into a clump of boulders rising from the side of the mountain. *Pretty fair kick,* he thought with a self-satisfied tickle of pleasure.

Far away he heard the stone rattling and rolling among the boulders. Then he heard the faint sound of a resonant splash. Water? Cade hadn't mentioned any runs, and they certainly hadn't passed any on the hike up.

Ben was moving before the thought completed itself in his head. He scrambled through underbrush and over boulders, scraping his hands, his hiking boots slipping on moss and lichen.

What he discovered was—a miracle.

"Cade! Hey, Cade! Get up here, man!"

Gurgling sluggishly, a spring of water bubbled to the surface of a small pool scarcely two feet in diameter. Ben dropped to his haunches and scooped up a handful of the cool liquid. No odor—wasn't a sulfur spring then. He took a cautious sip, and the sweet-tart bite of it ran through him like a lightning bolt.

"Ben! Where are you?" Cade called. Then, "Never mind, I see the tracks."

A moment later his lithe form dropped down next to Ben. "A spring." A satisfied smile filled his face. "Thank You, Lord. 'There shall come water out of it, that the people may drink.' "

He stretched out along the slab of rock that formed a natural stone enclosure and ducked his face into the gently stirring surface of the pool. When he lifted his head, then turned dripping to Ben, the unfettered joy radiated from him like the glow of a hundred suns. "Mineral, not a hot spring," he said. "Think it's alum, but it could be chalybeate. You'll need to have it professionally analyzed." He swiped dripping hair away from his forehead. "The land's for sale, in case you're interested."

Ben barely heard. He rolled up the sleeve of his shirt, then plunged his arm into the pool all the way up to his armpit. "It's deep, but there's enough movement against my fingers…Cade, do you think there's more than one? I mean, most of the spa resorts have as many as four spring houses, some of them with four different types of water." Like the land Preston Clarke had gobbled up.

"Let's explore a bit, all right? See what other pearls of great price we can unearth."

"You're mixing your metaphors, if I recall my—wait a moment. You knew, didn't you?" Ben watched Cade's deep green eyes crinkle at the corners. "That's why you brought me up here."

"Passed through here last summer. There were signs, yes. I found an old Indian trail that at times veered off in erratic directions. Could have been to the site of a spring. I didn't have time to pursue it but thought it worth a return trip." He drank some of the water, then bounded to his feet. "I camped in that meadow halfway up the mountain, and one evening noticed a buck pawing a spot of earth, then licking it. Like I said, I didn't have time to pursue it, but I made a note of the spot."

"Why'd you wait to tell me? Where's the spot?"

"On the edge of the meadow, near that stand of timber. You could build a springhouse without having to cut down any trees, I imagine."

Like the tiny spring bubbling at his feet, a sense of wonder gushed upward through Ben, leaving him shaken. "My God," he whispered, reverently. "He…I never actually expected Him to answer. Not like this. Not—with this." His wet fingers curled into a fist, and he pressed it against his head. "Cade, I—" The words stuck in his throat.

"It's all right. I understand." Cade wrapped an arm about Ben's shoulder in an unselfconscious hug. "You had that talk with the Lord, didn't you?"

"Uh, well, yes, I suppose I did." He stared down at the tiny pool of water.

"Enjoy the moment. They don't always occur this dramatically." After giving him an affectionate whack between his shoulder blades, Cade stepped back. "You hold on to the memory, my friend. It will sustain you through the times when you'd swear you were talking to nothing but thin air. Come on now. Let's go see what other gifts the Lord wants to delight you with today."

By the time the sun was easing toward the ragged tops of the mountains, Cade and Ben—mostly Cade, Ben cheerfully admitted—discovered a total of four springs. Head spinning with plans, he would have spent the night camping under the stars, except he knew Hominy would set out with a search party if Ben didn't return before long.

"You said you know the owner?" he asked Cade as they hiked back down to the base of the mountain.

"I do," Cade said without turning. He was leading the way through a precipitous stretch of steep trail, where both men needed to watch their step.

"And they're willing to sell?" Ben stepped on a rock that rolled beneath his boot. He wobbled sideways, caught himself, and decided he needed to concentrate more on his footing than the plans whirling through his head. "I'll meet their price. Won't even try to negotiate. Do they know about the springs?"

"Not until this afternoon. And thanks for being willing to meet my price. It isn't inflated, I promise."

"What? *You* own it?"

Without thinking Ben lengthened his stride, determined to reach the man some dozen paces below him. He leaped with careless haste onto a flat boulder, his intent to waylay Cade with a shortcut. Instead his weight threw the unstable boulder off balance. It tilted, pitching Ben sideways. His leg buckled beneath him, and he fell in an ungainly welter of flailing arms. His left ankle slid beneath the protruding lip of the boulder.

The last thing Ben felt was a sword thrust of pain. The last thing he heard was the sickening crunch of his ankle bone as it snapped.

Then he passed out.

Forty-Five

SINCLAIR RUN

*F*ireflies danced about the edges of the front yard, delighting the neighborhood children who raced to capture them in empty canning jars. It was a perfect evening for a picnic, a welcome distraction from the endless hours between dusk and dawn.

Every now and then a persistent June bug pinged in a suicidal bent into one of the Japanese lanterns Meredith and Leah had strung along the porch. No matter how many times Meredith captured the prickly-legged insects and carried them to the edge of the yard, they seemed determined to rush headlong into disaster.

A demoralizing exercise, comparing oneself to an insect.

"This was a lovely idea, Meredith." FrannieBeth materialized from the crowd of neighbors gathered around the long tables set up in the yard. She waved a chicken leg. "Mrs. Tweedie's fried chicken is still the best in the Valley. Duncan's helped himself to six pieces, last time I noticed."

"Did you try some of Garnet's Victoria Buns? The recipe is one from Sloan's side of the family, and Garnet's determined to carry on tradition."

"Oh? I thought they'd washed their hands of his side of the family, seeing as how the family had washed their hands of Dr. MacAllister."

"There's some strain," Meredith allowed with a sigh, "but Garnet and Sloan aren't giving up. They're determined to 'pray their way to a reconciliation,' was the way Garnet put it, I believe."

FrannieBeth shook her head. "Garnet's looking beautiful, isn't she? I'd practically forgotten her hair because of that bonnet she used to wear all the time. Have you noticed how Alice follows her around like a puppy dog? She and JosieMae Whalen were about to exchange blows over who got to sit by her at the table."

"I saw. Looks like I've been replaced by my sister in Alice's affections." Meredith waved away FrannieBeth's anxious protests. "Mercysake, I'm not that sensitive, Frannie." She slapped at a mosquito. "Children have always loved Garnet."

"They love you just as much. You saw Jessup when we arrived—practically leaped out of my arms. He wanted his Auntie Merry." She paused. "Meredith? Are you doing better these days?"

"Only if I don't think," Meredith admitted.

"I still don't understand why you don't go back to Winchester, talk to him."

Because I'm terrified that I'll make the biggest mistake of my life. "Because I'm enjoying being at home, being…domestic." It wasn't a lie, and she wasn't hiding, she was enjoying the slower pace of a household routine. And her relationship with Leah had deepened, though her younger sister offered little in the way of counsel, on either matters of the heart or the spiritual questions that haunted Meredith. "I plan to go back, Frannie. I'm just…not ready yet."

"It's too lovely a night for long faces." Garnet joined them, her gaze on Meredith. She jostled her arm. "Why don't y'all come on over with us? I believe we're about to be treated to a concert. Mr. Whalen's brought his banjo, and Mr. Mueller brought the wooden flute Papa made for his seventieth birthday last year."

A high-pitched squall interrupted the flow of congenial conversations behind the three women. FrannieBeth shook her head. "That's Jessup. I'd recognize his train-whistle screech in a room full of little screamers. I'll go rescue whoever's holding him so we can enjoy the concert."

"I need to ask Papa if we have any more citronella candles," Meredith said. "The mosquitoes are bad this year."

Garnet blocked her retreat. "Meredith, please. Wait here for a few moments and talk to me. The whole evening you've been hanging on the fringes instead of being the center of the picnic. Everyone's noticed, but they're all too nice to put you on the spot about it."

"Then why are you?"

Unoffended, Garnet tugged her handkerchief out of her sleeve and dabbed the perspiration from Meredith's temples with the tenderness of a mother. "Because you're my sister, and I love you." She tucked the handkerchief away, then folded her arms across her middle. "And because one night a little over two weeks ago, I woke up in the middle of the night. Sloan was over at the window. He was praying. For you."

Meredith refused to look at her. "Well, I probably need all the prayers anyone offers in my behalf."

"I found out later that Papa was doing the same thing, at almost the same time. Meredith, the very next afternoon you turned up here looking, Papa said, like a bleached rag." She paused, wanting to reach out to her. "I don't understand, but I've learned to accept. Sloan and Papa have this—this extraordinary communication with the Lord. Somehow they can hear Him speaking to them."

"Garnet, this isn't the time or place to—"

"I used to think it was because they were special," her sister plowed on, taking Meredith's arm. "But Sloan has helped me see otherwise."

She led Meredith away from the lantern light, away from the children now playing hide-and-seek among the tables spread under the trees; led her away from the men clearing tables and the women carrying dishes inside the house with Leah; led her all the way to the far corner of the side yard.

Darkness enfolded them, offering a cocoonlike privacy.

"Garnet, I don't want to talk about this right now."

"You don't want to talk about it at all. Either about what God's trying to do in your life or about Benjamin Walker. Do you think I can't understand?" Garnet dropped her arm and stepped back. Only the bright flame of her hair glimmered in the matte black night. "Because I do. I do understand," she repeated quietly. "Did you know that, a year ago, I was afraid to talk to the Lord?"

"What? Why?"

"Because for years I'd labored under the weight of guilt. Of doubts and incomplete understanding. I thought I had to be a...a perfect Christian in order for God to listen to my prayers."

"That's absurd. You know better than that."

"Mm. In my mind, perhaps. But my heart wasn't listening. I think you've something of the same dilemma."

Meredith's laugh was short and bitter. "I think, with me, it's the other way around. I think my head isn't listening to my heart." She took a couple of steps, hands outstretched until she felt the cool-rough bark of the sugar maple that shaded the side of the house. "Remember the year lightning struck this tree, killed that huge limb that shaded our bedroom window?"

"That's not an occurrence any of us is likely to forget," Garnet murmured. She paused, a question poised in the silence.

"I thought the whole tree would die." Meredith leaned her back against the trunk and closed her eyes. "I was so upset…you know how dramatic I can be. I remember telling Papa that the lightning had killed part of me as well, because it killed my favorite tree."

"I remember."

"Papa told me to wait and see. That within the order of God's creation, sometimes nature has a way of healing itself."

"And of course he was right." Garnet reached to pluck a single leaf, twirling it between her fingers. "In the summer now the leaves are so thick on the rest of the tree you can't see where Papa cut away the dead branch."

"Garnet." Meredith opened her eyes and peered through the velvety night toward her sister. "What I feel—it's the same way I felt when lightning killed that limb. I-I still don't know whether I'll be able to heal myself."

"You won't have to." The gentle confidence flowed over Meredith like a bracing massage. "God's grace will heal you, if you allow it. You're in love with Benjamin Walker, aren't you?"

The exaltation of it burned. The pain of it froze her tongue to the roof of her mouth. All Meredith could do was to stand, mute and taut as barbed wire, while Garnet's quiet pronouncement faded into the night.

Then two slender arms were holding her close, and the fragrance of violets saturated her nose. "God will work this out for you, just as He worked things out for Sloan and me," Garnet said. She gave Meredith a reassuring shake. "And sometimes, sister dear, He works best without our input."

"You had to bring that up, didn't you?"

"I was kinder about it than Leah."

Meredith groaned, but the sensation of relief that loosened her muscles also helped restore her sense of humor. "Her latest effort included a logical tirade along the lines of 'You didn't think twice before chasing after that two-legged varmint Lamar so why aren't you collaring Benjamin Walker and telling *him* how it's going to be?'"

"One of these years, God's going to present her with a gentleman of her own, and Leah won't stand a chance."

"Garnet, I think you should prepare yourself for the possibility that Leah will spend the rest of her life in the pursuit of knowledge. One of the reasons she's having such a time with me is because she simply doesn't understand. I don't know if she can."

A light breeze stirred the tree branches above their heads, carrying with it the faint drumroll of hoofbeats.

"A late guest? Who are we missing?" Meredith wondered aloud.

"I hope it's not someone needing Sloan. Since I married a doctor, I confess I've come to be wary of the sound of hoofbeats in the night."

"Then let's go see who it is." Now it was Meredith who wrapped a bracing arm about Garnet. "Try not to worry before you have cause."

"You're a fine one to talk. Ever since you returned home, you've—"

"Garnet? Meredith?" Sloan's deep voice interrupted their determined banter. "You ladies hiding back here?"

"Under the maple," Meredith called, adding under her breath, "I'm sorry, redbird. Looks as though you were right."

Sloan's silhouette loomed over them. "Both of you need to come with me."

"Who is it?" Garnet asked, going to her husband at once.

Meredith lagged behind, unwilling to intrude. But Sloan turned back, waiting until she joined them.

"Meredith…" He hesitated.

"What is it?" Without warning, a shiver skated down her spine.

Sloan laid a warm hand over her forearm. "There's been an accident. Benjamin fell and broke his ankle."

"Benjamin? Broke his ankle?" Heart racing, she glared at Sloan.

"That was a silly thing for him to do. When? How will he run the hotel? Lowell's an efficient secretary, but he's dreadful with people, and Mrs. Biggs leaves at four every afternoon so—" Meredith jammed a fist over her mouth. "Sorry. I-I shouldn't carry on over a broken ankle. I mean, it could have been much worse, couldn't it? Garnet, remember the year Otis Teasel broke his leg and his arm?"

"Meredith, I'm sure Mr. Walker will be fine," Garnet began.

"Who brought the news? Hominy? And why? I mean, I don't know what I can do, what I sh-should do…"

"Take it easy, Meredith." Sloan squeezed her arm. "Let's go find out, hmm?"

Meredith abruptly threw off his arm and dashed toward the front of the house where a cluster of neighbors were gathered around a lathered horse. She shoved her way through, hardly aware of the commiserating pats and murmurs that followed her. Her father stood in the center, talking to a man in the rumpled, incredibly dusty uniform worn by the hotel staff.

"Clyde?" She stared at the aging night porter.

He was breathing in ragged pants, but his eyes lit with relief when he caught sight of Meredith. "Miz Sinclair…you's got to come. Mr. Ben—he needs you." He lifted a trembling hand in a fruitless effort to smooth windblown locks of gray hair from his dust-caked face.

"Where's Hominy? Why didn't he come?"

"Ease up a bit, lass. Give the man a chance to catch his breath."

Meredith ignored her father. "Clyde, did you ride all the way from Winchester?" She glanced around, relieved to see Leah threading her way through the crowd. "You shouldn't have done that. What would Mr. Walker do if something happened to you?"

"I owe…Mr. Ben…my life. Ah…thank you kindly, miss." He grabbed the glass Leah thrust out, downing the contents in four noisy gulps. "Beg pardon, Miss Sinclair."

"Why don't you come over here, sit down a bit?" Jacob suggested. "We'll take care of your horse."

"No, thank you kindly." Clyde straightened his shoulders. "I'll manage fine. Only rode from Tom's Brook, you see." He fastened his gaze on Meredith. "Mr. Beringer's there, going after a Dr. MacAllister in Mr. Walker's carriage. Hominy, he said you might be visiting there. I was to come along here, and wait, if you weren't. The doc's kin to you, ain't he, Miss Sinclair?"

"Dr. MacAllister is my brother-in-law. And he's here, Clyde." Fear numbed her fingers, caused her scalp to prickle.

"Ah. Reckon Mr. Beringer'll be here directly then." Clyde's gaze flickered over the crowd, now herded back under the trees. "Ah…can I speak plainly?"

"Of course."

"Mr. Ben's asking for you, miss."

"What?" Meredith felt her face flame even as her throat dried up in a spasm of fearful confusion.

"He don't know he's asking for you," Clyde hurriedly continued, fiddling with the brass buttons of his uniform coat. "See, the medicine they gave him, it's put him in some sort of state. But Hominy says to tell you"—he darted her a glance—"ah, says to tell you that Mr. Ben keeps calling your name. And Mr. Beringer fetched me, said we'd take Mr. Ben's carriage. He ought to be here real soon, Miss Sinclair."

Leah had come up behind her. "Well," she said practically, "Meredith, why don't you and Garnet go pack a valise, while I feed Mr.—?"

"Henckle, ma'am. Clyde Henckle. But if it's all the same, I'd best—"

"While I feed Mr. Henckle." Leah pushed Meredith into Garnet's arms. "Here. Go along now, Merry. It's going to be all right." She shook her head and concluded with mock sternness, "If you'd listened to me, you would already have been on the spot to play nurse to your beau."

"He's not my…" Meredith's voice trailed away. Docile, emotionally hamstrung, she allowed Garnet to guide her toward the house. She couldn't think. Mercysake, she couldn't even weep. All she seemed capable of right now was placing herself in the hands of people she loved and trusted.

As she climbed the porch steps, a peculiar *awareness* washed into her with the gentle insistence of a summer creek's gentle murmuring. A scrap of Scripture bobbed in the lapping tidewater: "He shall gather the lambs with His arm…carry them…"

"Garnet?" she whispered, half afraid she was on the verge of succumbing to some delusional expression of latent hysteria.

"I'm here. It's all right, Benjamin's going to be just fine."

"I know. It's not that." Halfway across the porch she stopped, took a deep breath, and peered into Garnet's concerned face. "I think…I think the Lord spoke to me just now."

With that hesitant pronouncement, like life returning to frostbitten limbs, emotion prickled through her. And her eyes swam with tears. Tears of humility, reverence—and joy. Tears of which for the first time in her life, Meredith was unashamed. "It feels so good, I'm afraid to talk about it."

"Then don't. Just be still." Garnet blinked moisture from her own eyes. "Be still and know, Meredith. Sometimes, words are even less necessary than actions. Trust me. I—"

"Miss Sinclair!"

Clyde came panting to the foot of the steps, but stopped uncertainly at the bottom. Meredith walked back across the porch.

"What is it, Clyde?"

"Forgot to mention that Hominy's wanting me to make sure you bring along some kind of box or chest. There's something inside of it, Hominy thinks. Something that's real important to Mr. Ben." He pulled out a handkerchief and blew his nose. "Hominy was hoping you'd know something about it."

"I do." Meredith dashed down the steps and pressed a kiss against the astonished doorman's cotton-wool beard. Inside, her heart whirled in a kaleidoscope of love. Fear. Hope. "Don't worry, Clyde. I'll bring it."

Over the doorman's head her gaze met her father's. Stunned joy had erased the weeks of strain from his beloved face. She smiled. "That 'box' is equally important to me."

Forty-Six

$\mathcal{B}$enjamin Walker's carriage rolled up the lane shortly after Garnet and Meredith disappeared inside the house. Leah watched a man pull the two horses to a neat halt beside the hitching rail and jump with lithe grace to the ground beside Jacob. *Efficient,* Leah decided as she turned away, her mind busy with all the tasks necessary for her to oversee Meredith's departure. In all the commotion her older sisters were sure to forget something.

Leah scanned the knot of people milling uncertainly about. She also needed to help the ladies clean up; it was obvious that the evening had come to an abrupt close. FrannieBeth and Mrs. Whalen had packed away a basket or two, but like everyone else their attention was focused on Mr. Henckle and the man Leah assumed was the unknown Mr. Beringer.

All right, then. First she'd make sure the cleaning up was under control, then she'd check on Meredith's progress. Couldn't depend on Garnet. All afternoon, her middle sister, though helpful as always, had seemed distracted, ofttimes staring off into the distance, a soft silly smile curving her lips. Leah clicked her tongue, then started for the tables just as her father called her name. Her foot tapped a restless beat in the packed dirt. "Yes, Papa?"

"Mr. Beringer, this is my youngest daughter, Leah. Leah, this is Mr. Cade Beringer, a friend of Mr. Walker's."

Leah nodded. "Mr. Beringer." Her gaze slid beyond him to the knot of curious neighbors.

"Could you take Mr. Beringer inside?" Jacob asked, forcing her attention. "He's wanting to return to Winchester as soon as possible of course, but I've persuaded him to clean up a bit, perhaps eat a bite while your sisters finish Meredith's packing."

Mr. Beringer was a tallish man—but thanks to Leah's pint-sized stature, most any man looked tall—with a shock of startling golden hair noticeable even in the soft lanterns' glow. He also looked exhausted, but she could have done without the extra chore. After a frank examination of his grime-encrusted face and clothing, Leah gave a cursory nod. "Certainly, I'll show you to the kitchen. You can freshen up in the washroom built into the side porch, and I'll fix you a plate."

"Thank you. Appreciate the sustenance, I admit." His shoulders lifted, and he rubbed a hand around the back of his neck before nodding to Jacob. "Mr. Sinclair, I can see you've a family blessed by the Lord. May He return your generosity to you a hundredfold. Shall we, Miss Sinclair?"

"Call me Leah," she snapped as she headed for the house. "With three sisters, it's ridiculous to stand on ceremony." His effusiveness annoyed her, yet she couldn't escape the niggling suspicion that she was being subtly reprimanded.

He caught up with her, moving with a fluid, unhurried stride which he shortened to match hers. "Very well then. Leah," he said. "Lovely name, despite its original meaning."

The top of her head scarcely reached his shoulder, making her feel more than ever like a chastened child. By now, Leah was almost as irritated with herself as she was with Cade Beringer. Their respective statures should be a matter of utter indifference; after all, body sizes were ordained by God, and she had trained herself years ago to ignore her diminutive frame with its unremarkable features. What mattered was her iron determination and thirst for knowledge, because with those she was capable of conquering any mountain she chose to climb. The only reason she was a trifle bothered right now was because—and she would never admit it to anyone but herself—she was as tired as Cade Beringer looked.

When they reached the porch, his hand grasped her elbow.

Startled, Leah freed herself firmly. "I'm not likely to trip over steps I've been climbing up and down for twenty years."

"Accidents happen," was the equable response, though he didn't try to take her arm again. But when Leah reached the door, blunt masculine fingers closed over the knob just as her hand lifted.

"I'm sure you also know how to open the door," Mr. Beringer

murmured in her ear. "On the other hand, it's both privilege and pleasure for a gentleman to extend that courtesy to ladies." He opened the door with another of those gleaming smiles. "It's a gesture of respect. Allow me."

Without a word Leah sailed past him into the house, leaving him to follow her down the hall to the kitchen. "Here's a cloth and towel." She handed him the items as she retrieved them from the linen closet. "The washroom's through there. Take your time." Hands on her hips, she stared him straight in the eye. "Looks like you rolled down the side of a mountain and collected half of it along the way."

"I might have," he said. "You're a very blunt young lady, Leah Sinclair."

Leah shrugged, turning away to rummage through the mounds of food gathered on every available surface. His quiet tolerance of her shrewish behavior disconcerted her, more so than the ribbings her sisters flung her way when they thought her manner too overbearing. She was ashamed of herself, yet didn't know how to rectify the situation.

"Leah."

"Yes?" She stacked soiled tin plates and carried them to the sink, deliberately refusing to face Mr. Beringer.

"Your father didn't realize how busy you were. Or how exhausted. I'll wait outside and explain to him."

"I'm not that busy," Leah managed, her face hot. She half turned. "Mr. Beringer, I—"

He was gone.

Leah dashed from the kitchen and raced down the hall, catching up with him just before he stepped onto the porch. "Mr. Beringer! Stop— please."

When he obliged, Leah found she still couldn't meet his gaze. "I... apologize. I don't know what possessed me, to treat a perfect stranger so rudely. If you'll—" She finally darted a glance upward, and his look of warm understanding so flummoxed her she forgot what she'd intended to say.

"If I'll—?" He took a step toward her.

Leah tensed. "If you'll return to the kitchen, I'll fix you that plate while you clean up. I've apologized for my...brusqueness. But as you observed, I've a lot to do, and standing here in the hall is wasting time." She stood aside, gesturing toward the kitchen. "Shall we?"

"Certainly. As soon as you tell me what it is about me that makes you so uncomfortable. Other than my filthy appearance."

"I don't know what you're talking about."

A smile softened the ruggedness of his features as he drew abreast and paused, studying her. "You're very young. I hadn't realized."

"I'm twenty years old, not that it's any of your concern. Could you please step back? I don't like being crowded." She edged away.

"I...see. Sorry."

He leaned back against the wall and folded his arms across his chest. Leah would have to practically brush up against him in order to return to the kitchen. She eyed him in growing consternation.

"You haven't answered my question," he said.

"Mr. Beringer, I'm 'uncomfortable,' as you phrased it, because I was rude to you. But I was rude to you, if you must know, because I don't appreciate fatuous demonstrations of faith designed to impress people you know nothing about."

"You know equally little about me, Leah. What made you conclude that I was a hypocrite?"

"I didn't say—"

"Yes," he interrupted firmly, "you did. Have you run across so many hypocrites that every stranger who speaks of the Lord becomes suspect?"

Leah's biology professor at Mary Baldwin would challenge her by using the same formidable logic, using her own words to try and twist her into a knot of contradictory conclusions. Within the classroom the experience was exhilarating. Nobody at home had ever been able to meet Leah on equal intellectual grounds, and the intense love she felt for her family precluded a ruthless dissection of their faith.

Cade Beringer was not family.

"The answer to your question is yes," she said. "Every person I meet who spouts pious phrases about God's goodness is suspect in my mind. Most of the time, they use their faith as a shield against their fears of a world they can neither control nor understand. Or they use it to inspire guilt in those who do not share their views."

"I don't, Leah. My faith in God defines who I am as a man. For me, Jesus is friend as well as Savior. Do you have friends?"

"Flesh and blood friends, yes. If you insist on a religious debate—proving, by the by, the truth of my statement—you'll have to follow me back to the kitchen. I'll fix you something to eat, but it's your choice whether or not to clean up."

Leah retreated toward the kitchen, uncomfortably aware of the man close on her heels. Close enough to make her feel…herded. *Mr. Beringer,* she told him in silent declaration, *you've made a serious miscalculation.*

"Do you prefer ham, turkey? Some cold fried chicken? Do you make it a habit of forcing your faith on everyone with whom you come in contact?" She whisked about the room, gathering food and utensils as she hurled a barrage of questions. "What would you like to drink? We have iced tea, limeade? There's some buttermilk in the springhouse out back. Can you prove that your 'salvation' experience provides you with greater insight into spiritual truths than my own?"

"Leah." He halted her by the effective method of stepping between her and the worktable where she was preparing his plate. "If there were more time, I'd find out why a twenty-year-old young lady on the springboard of life possesses the mind of a cynic."

In a move that silenced her completely he grasped her wrist, pried free the knife she'd planned to slice some ham with and laid it on the worktable. Then he cupped her hand in between both of his and held it against his chest. "I'll eat and drink whatever you offer," he said, his voice calm as the air before a thunderstorm. "As for the rest…I don't have to prove the reality of my relationship with the Lord to you or anyone else. And you"—he squeezed her hand, then gently released it—"will never be able to prove that it isn't as tangible as the relationship you share with your father and sisters."

Stepping back, he crossed toward the back washroom with the smooth, soundless power of a man of utter authority. Leah stared after him, dumbfounded for the first time in her life, the hand Cade had clasped still suspended in midair.

Throughout the journey back to Winchester Meredith held her heart-wood chest on her lap. She was grateful Clyde had insisted on riding up top with Mr. Beringer, affording Meredith privacy along with time to collect her thoughts.

The time to pray.

She sat in the corner of the plush goatskin cushion, her body swaying with the motion of the carriage, hands folded across the sturdy lid of her chest, her heart straining to recapture that elusive sensation she'd experienced on the porch. *Lord? I don't know how to listen very well.*

For most of Meredith's life, if she were brutally candid—and since she was trying to talk to God she knew absolute honesty before Him was not only unavoidable but required—she had talked to Him without ever waiting to hear what He might have to say. *I do that a lot, don't I, Lord?* And she knew in her heart that her stubborn nature would never change, that her only hope lay in making a continued effort to…to wait. To cultivate a listening ear, as her father would say.

She didn't like waiting.

The carriage dipped suddenly, and Meredith braced herself against the forward pitch, relaxing her death grip enough to push aside the curtain. They were descending the hill to Cedar Creek; they should arrive at the hotel within the hour. The wheels rattled across the covered bridge, then emerged on the other side for the climb to the top of the hill. Through the glass she heard Mr. Beringer's melodious baritone, coaxing the laboring horses along much in the same manner he had coaxed a babbling, uncertain Meredith into the carriage.

Above her the jet black sky was peppered with stars, tiny points of light thicker than the sugar sprinkles Leah dusted over the tops of her snickerdoodles. Garnet, she remembered with a lonely pang, used to lie outside on starry evenings and count stars until she fell asleep. Leah, on the other hand, pestered Jacob until he hauled home every book on astronomy he could lay his hands on. Stars, Leah informed her family when she was eleven years old, were nothing but balls of gas in the heavens.

As for Meredith…until this moment, she'd considered the stars about like she considered God—always there, but taken for granted.

She'd never paused to contemplate the mystery or majesty of this facet of creation, any more than she'd noticed the air she breathed.

Now, heedless of wind and road dust, she opened the window and craned her head outside, soaking in those sparkling points of light. Their incalculable number infused Meredith with a peculiar emotion that both humbled and exalted. Placed within the context of the universe, her own insignificance struck her with an intensity that made her want to weep.

Yet she also felt safe somehow, secure in the knowledge that she was…loved. By her family and friends. By—*please, God?*—by Benjamin.

But most of all, by the almighty Creator of the heavens and the earth. Oh yes…there it came, dispersing warmth and affirmation like perfume. Meredith closed her eyes. Come what may with Benjamin, she was God's beloved child, just as she was the eldest beloved daughter of Jacob Sinclair.

Finger by finger she relaxed her grip, allowing the peace to filter deep inside even with wind stinging her eyes and dust filming her throat and nostrils. In this moment, nothing could separate her from this reverent communion with her Lord.

Nothing, that is, until the carriage rounded a curve, throwing her off balance. Meredith grabbed the strap, then regretfully opened her eyes and closed the window. Almost at random, her attention wandered to her heartwood chest, coated courtesy of the open window with a fresh layer of dust. Her lips curved in a wry smile. *Sorry, Papa.*

Each motion tentative, she opened the secret drawer and withdrew the cookie cutter. "Why did you choose this, Papa?" she wondered aloud, picturing his lined face and work-scarred hands, hearing his oft-repeated answer.

That's between me and the Lord, Merry-go-round. You'll figure it out, one of these days.

Perhaps that day had arrived. Perhaps the answer waited in Winchester with the man who had called her name from the depths of his pain and his need.

She wanted to heed the reawakened awareness of God's Spirit, with its faint but irresistible urging. Prayed that she could listen. *Please, Lord. Don't let me make another mistake.*

Forty-Seven

*B*en surfaced from a drugged sleep with a sensation akin to fighting his way out of the airless hold of the sinking merchant clipper that had tried to take his life when he was sixteen. When something snagged his arm he fought back, twisting to free himself. The relentless pressure never wavered.

Only gradually did the jumbled noises separate themselves into recognizable sounds—words. The same ones. Spoken over and over in a ceaseless cadence that gradually penetrated his brain.

"…all right. You're all right, Mr. Ben. I've got you. Easy, Mr. Ben. It's all right, you're all right. I've got you."

The panic dissipated. Ben ceased struggling, his muscles going slack in relief. Hominy. It was Hominy's voice, Hominy's hand holding him still. He wasn't trapped in that stinking hold, wasn't going to drown. He was in his bed, and instead of seawater his body was soaked with sweat, torpid from medicine the infernal doctor had insisted he take.

But where was Meredith? He needed her desperately, yet retained no memory of her presence at any time over the last…the last…Ben groped in his mind for an accounting of the time lapsed since he'd broken his fool ankle. Gave up the exercise because his brain was a rock. Couldn't even force his eyes open, and his mouth was dry as a parched cotton field.

"Water?"

The pressure on his arm vanished. He felt his head being lifted, and the rim of a glass pressed against his bottom lip.

"Thanks." At last he was able to open his eyes, as though the water had moistened his eyelids along with his tongue.

Above him Hominy's gleaming black countenance blurred for a

moment then cleared. Ben had never seen his manservant look so worn, showing every one of his almost fifty years. When had the wiry hair sported all that gray? "Hominy...feel like—" No. Better not confess how he felt. His mother might have been dead for over a quarter of a century, but he'd never been able to get out from under her lessons in gentlemanly conduct.

"Mr. Ben? Sure is good to hear you, talking like you's who you is again."

Incredibly the urge to smile twitched the muscles on either side of Ben's mouth. "Must have been bad, to hear you talk like that."

Hominy's face split in a grin the size of a half-moon, and about as brilliant. "Don't you go to badgering me about my grammar. I might be tempted to break your other ankle."

"You'd just have to play nursemaid for me twice as long." He shifted, then stilled when a bolt of pain arched up from his ankle. "By the way, how long *have* I been out of it?"

"Ah, let's see. It's going on midnight, Wednesday. Mr. Beringer toted you in here early this afternoon. I swan, Mr. Ben, he looked near about as bad as you."

"He carried me down the mountain. We spent the night..."

"I reckon I know that. Don't want to pass another night like that ever again, Mr. Ben."

"I don't reckon I do either," Ben drawled back. "Though I don't remember a lot—I was pretty much out of my head, I'm afraid."

"Mr. Kingston and Miz Biggs, they were ready to call out the militia." Hominy paused. "I even had a look-see about Mr. Clarke's place, to make sure you, ah, weren't there."

"I am sorry, Hominy. For all of this. But it was worth it—I'll tell you why when I'm not so muzzy-brained. As for Preston Clarke, let the undercover private detectives we've hired for the season do their job. They're here not only to protect the hotel, Hominy. I don't want anything to happen to you or to the rest of my staff."

His voice gruff, Hominy leaned over to adjust the twisted covers and plump the pillow. "Well, next time you hare off with Mr. Beringer, I'm coming along so nothing else can happen to *you*."

Ben grimaced. "Sometimes, my friend, all the care in all the world can't prevent life's unpleasantries from intruding." Especially when there were compensations. No—treasure more precious than a pirate's horde. "Frankly, I'm relieved it's nothing worse than my ankle. Better that than my ribs. At least I can breathe." His entire body ached dully, but he'd break his own ribs before he complained. Hominy had suffered enough.

Yet despite Ben's present physical misery, there were snippets of peace, patches of utter contentment to cling to, together with an anticipation bubbling inside like the springs he and Cade had discovered.

The faint sound of voices drifted into the quiet room. Ben turned his head toward the doorway. Hope leaped inside his chest, because in spite of their hushed tones, one of those voices was female. *Meredith...* He tried to speak her name, but the longing was too intense. He waited in an agony of suspense until Cade's golden head appeared.

"I don't care if he's asleep," that light feminine voice whispered behind Cade, its vehemence zinging across to the bed, straight into Ben's heart. "I want to see him..."

In a flurry of rustling skirts Meredith shimmied past Cade's arm. She took two quick steps toward Ben then stopped. He drank in her anxious expression, the tremulous mouth. The endless weeks of separation evaporated as though they'd never occurred. Ben didn't notice Hominy's silent retreat, didn't hear the quiet closing of the door behind Meredith. His gaze locked on her face, and he managed to lift an unsteady hand in a beckoning gesture.

"B-Benjamin?" She flew across the room and sank to her knees on the floor. Their faces almost touched. "Benjamin?"

"I'm all right." And he was, finally. "Thank God. I'm all right." His trembling fingers tangled with hers. "Give me a couple of weeks, and I'll be right as rain. Nothing but a broken ankle, some assorted bumps and scrapes. Meredith," he breathed her name in a grateful prayer, "I needed you so much."

"I didn't know. Until Clyde rode up to the house, Benjamin, I didn't know." The pulse in her throat fluttered like hummingbird wings. "I should have been here. I should have known."

"You're here now." He couldn't stop touching her, didn't want to even try. His hand moved up her arm, reveling in the reality of flesh and bone beneath the soft cotton sleeve. "You look…"

"I look like the inside of a dustpan." She took a deep breath, coloring a little. "But I don't care. Someone told me once that appearances didn't matter when it's irrelevant to the circumstances."

The tips of his fingers brushed strands of dusty chestnut hair at her temples. "Beautiful," he said. "You look…beautiful."

Quick tears sheened her luminous green gold eyes. "That fall must have blinded you as well."

"I've heard before—love is blind." He watched her eyes widen, her mouth open in a soundless exclamation. "Meredith? Tell me you can feel it. Tell me you're not here out of pity or concern." Iron bands encased his ribs. Breath wedged in his parched throat, stalling the open declaration. For Benjamin, the words would be a commitment, one he'd shied away from his entire adult life.

He needed Meredith to admit she loved him, before he could afford to take the risk himself.

"I'm not here out of pity," she said, her voice strained. "But I am concerned. And I'm concerned, because I…because I—" She shoved away from the bed, rose clumsily to pace back and forth beside it.

Suddenly she stopped, whirling to face him, the action almost violent in its intensity. "Benjamin, I know what you need to hear. I don't know if I can say it. I'm terrified, you see." Her voice broke. "Terrified of making another mistake. I've made so many, because I don't listen to God. I don't know if you can understand—I'm not even certain myself."

Then, because she was Meredith and perhaps because the Lord was still in a miracle-granting mood, she threw her hands in the air. "I'm in love with you!" She yelled the words, and her belligerent expression challenged Ben. "There. I've told you. Think whatever you like about it. And for your information, I may have thought I was in love before, but this is different. Different, do you hear?"

"I hear. Meredith—" he began, tenderness in every syllable.

"It's different because of God," Meredith chugged right along, ignoring Ben. He wasn't sure she'd even heard. "I can't explain, and you're in no condition to listen. You look worse than I do, and you have a broken ankle. But I'm telling you, Benjamin Walker, that you'd better have something more than friendship in mind when you respond to me come morning."

"If you'll hush up your pretty little mouth and listen, I'll try to respond now."

"Don't you talk to me like—what? I mean—Benjamin, wait! You're hurt."

He'd risen onto an elbow, because he refused to lie there limp as a beached trout while he spoke the words aloud. His head was pounding, his ankle throbbed, and when he moved, the blasted medicine turned everything in the room the consistency of cheesecloth.

"Benjamin, please lie down." He felt her hands against his shoulders. "You're weak. You'll hurt yourself. You'll—"

"I love you."

The hands pressing against him fell away. Grinning like a fool, Ben collapsed back against the pillows. "Now give me a kiss to seal the declarations, so I can go to sleep. In the morning, I promise to tell you anything else you need to hear."

"You love me? Truly?"

"More than all the hotels in all the world. More than my life."

She looked dazed, as if he'd punched her diaphragm instead of making an avowal of love. Instead of a magnificent woman, Ben gazed up at an uncertain girl. He patted the bed. "Come here, sweetheart."

Obediently Meredith sat, still staring at him with unblinking eyes. "Lean down."

Again she obeyed, each motion tentative.

With the last of his waning strength, Ben curved his hand around the back of her neck and brought her mouth to his. "I love you, Meredith Sinclair," he whispered against her lips. He kissed her again. "And for your information, I've never told that to another woman, never felt for another woman what I feel for you."

With his thumbs he wiped away the welling tears. "It's a gift. From God, given to both of us. Let's accept it, and each other, hmm? Forget about the past, Meredith. It doesn't matter anymore. Can you do that, for me?"

"I can do that. Now." She leaned forward and laid her mouth almost reverently against his. "Go to sleep, Benjamin. I'll be here in the morning."

"Did you…bring the chest? Meredith…bring your heartwood chest?"

"Yes, I brought it with me. Go to sleep."

He drifted off, Meredith's hand curled tightly with his, her voice whispering into his ear.

≈•≈

Meredith fell back into the hotel routine as though she'd never left—with one significant alteration. Two days after she arrived, Benjamin closed the doors to the dining room, gathered the entire staff there, and announced his and Meredith's formal engagement. Even on crutches, her fiancé dominated the room with his self-assured presence.

Meredith floated through the days with newfound confidence, reveling in the unabashed approval of everyone in the hotel. Didn't matter to the staff that her position was now that of Mr. Walker's affianced instead of his office manager. She performed the same duties, more vital now than ever with Benjamin recovering from the broken ankle. And since the summer season was in full swing, the hotel crammed to the rafters with guests all hours of the day and far into the night…well, Meredith was in her element. And she loved every moment of it.

One afternoon a week later she tracked Benjamin down in the dining room, where he'd been having a discussion with Mr. Dayton. It was a little past two, and the large room was deserted except for waiters setting the tables for afternoon tea. From the restaurant manager's defeated slump, Meredith gleaned that Mr. Dayton was not happy with whatever Benjamin had told him.

After nodding to Meredith, he turned back to Benjamin. "Since you insist, I'll take care of the matter, Mr. Walker." After another nod, he left.

"You really are a bully underneath that lazy smile of yours. A charming one, I'll admit. But still a bully."

Benjamin leaned against the back of the rolling invalid chair he'd conceded to for better mobility and turned the smile on her full force.

"Oh? What have I done this time? No—come over here. Sit beside me so I can hold your hand."

"I will not." Meredith clutched her writing tablet against her chest. "If I come over there, you'll want more than holding my hand. Then my mind will turn to mush, and I'll forget what I was going to say."

"Precisely."

"Like I said—a bully."

"Like I've said for months—a tigress of an office manager. A kitten when—"

Meredith leaped across the room to press her palm against his lips. Frantically she glanced around. "Benjamin!"

He kissed the palm of her hand. "Sorry, love. Teasing you is irresistible when you're playing your office manager role. Now," his voice altered, "tell me what's the matter."

"How did you—never mind." She debated for only a moment, loath to disturb the idyll of this past week. Then: "A letter arrived in this morning's mail."

"What is it? Here now, your hand's trembling." Frowning, Benjamin wrapped his fingers around her wrist and tugged. "Sit down. Do you have the letter? Is it from one of your sisters? Your father?"

Meredith turned a dining room chair so she could be close beside him. "It's from Preston, Benjamin."

A stillness descended. The air seemed charged, as though lightning were about to strike. Meredith felt perspiration dampen her palms, and she had to suppress the cowardly impulse to tell Benjamin she'd left the letter in the office. It was amazing that she used to think of this man as a benign soul completely lacking in temper.

"Give it to me, sweetheart."

"Only if you promise to talk with me about how best to respond." She stared him down. "He betrayed both of us, Benjamin."

"Meredith." The blue eyes crackled with heat, but it was the softness of his voice that lifted the hairs on the back of her neck. "Give me the letter."

She plucked it from the back of her writing pad and slapped it against his chest. "Here."

Benjamin unfolded the single sheet of cream vellum, scanned the words, then tore the paper into confetti and let it fall to the floor. "Mr. Walker and his fiancée Miss Sinclair regretfully decline the invitation to attend his groundbreaking ceremony at the site of Healing Springs Hotel."

"I sort of thought burning it would have been more satisfying." Meredith attempted a smile, though the latent violence of Benjamin's action had rattled her.

It was still something of a revelation, both the intensity of his emotions and the control he was able to exert over them. She watched his hands clenching and unclenching on the invalid chair arms. After a moment she laid her palm over his.

"It still hurts, doesn't it? Losing Poplar Springs?"

"Yes. Not as much, of course, because—well, you know the reason."

Nobody but Meredith, Benjamin, Hominy, and Benjamin's lawyer, Mr. Hackett, knew that Benjamin was in the process of purchasing a thousand acres of land on Little North Mountain, let alone why. The information would remain a zealously guarded secret until the last legal loophole was secured.

"Benjamin?"

She wasn't sure what he saw in her face, but the lines creasing his forehead and cheeks vanished. "Don't, sweetheart. You're not to blame, for anything."

"I know that." This time she managed a smile. "Most of the time, I don't even think about it anymore, especially now." She leaned and kissed the top of his head. "It's just that earlier…for a moment when I first read that letter? Like you, I wanted to destroy it. Burn it, rip it up—didn't matter. But I wanted to do it in Preston's office. In front of Preston."

Meredith watched the last of the pain vanish from her beloved's face, watched the tension drain from his muscles. "Now why didn't I think of that?"

"Benjamin? Is that an awful sin? I mean, God does warn us that we're supposed to forgive, not entertain vengeful thoughts."

"We're human. I reckon as long as the thoughts don't extend to action, the Lord's willing to smile and look the other way, so to speak."

"That's irreverent, Mr. Walker. And if memory serves correctly, in God's eyes, sinful thoughts are no less so than sinful actions." Meredith pretended to pout. "Trust you to force me to answer my own question…"

He grinned. "And it worked, too, didn't it? Though I wasn't trying to be irreverent. It's just"—he looked sheepish and elated all at the same time—"I'm in love with the most wonderful woman in the world. I've learned that Cade and my mother were right. I like the way I feel, when I pray, as though I'm talking to a friend. For some reason, God's decided to fill my life with everything I've ever wanted. Right now, even lamed up with this ankle, I feel like I could do anything I set my mind to."

The momentary qualms vanished. "Why, Mr. Walker, there's absolutely no doubt in my mind of that," Meredith said. "And with both of us working together, we're…unstoppable!"

Forty-Eight

*G*arnet trailed her fingers over a cherry bureau in Meredith's ground-floor suite at the Excelsior Hotel. Not as fine as a Jacob Sinclair piece, she mused. But for all its splendor, these were still rooms in a hotel. She smiled to herself, thinking of Meredith's reaction were she to make that observation out loud. Meredith never broached life tentatively. When she finally realized she was in love with Benjamin Walker, that once impossible, undecipherable, annoyingly inflexible man metamorphosed into a masculine paragon of irreproachable character.

It would be entertaining to witness one of their inevitable altercations.

"What are you smiling about?" Meredith asked around a mouthful of hairpins.

Garnet glanced across the room where her sister sat at the dressing table, her hands busily pinning up her hair. "Your room. It's very elegant. A far cry from our childhood bedrooms at home. The bathroom is positively decadent."

Until Meredith moved in, the first-floor suite for the most part had been reserved for Benjamin Walker's most distinguished guests. The bathroom was half again the size of the parlored bedroom, with Italian tile floors, marble sink, and a soaking tub Garnet would have traded both her aching feet for.

"Ah yes. My very own private bathroom. When I saw it, I stopped protesting about moving into the hotel." Meredith's eyes crinkled. "I thank the Lord every day for saving me from the likes of Lamar Aikens."

"And Preston Clarke?" Garnet kept her voice casual.

A scowl clouded Meredith's sunny countenance. She jammed the last pin into her hair and twisted around on the vanity bench. "You're about as subtle as your hair, sister dear. I'll go to the grave with that particular reminder of my defective nature. I thank God for rescuing me from Preston Clarke as well, but Benjamin does a fine job of keeping me safe now"—her arm lifted in a sweeping gesture—"as you see. It would ease my mind considerably if my family would stop worrying about that… that wealthy weasel."

"He's a powerful man, and he threatened you." The prickling heat spread from her unstable stomach outwards; Garnet hoped her face wasn't turning green. Even in their comfortable carriage, the trip from Tom's Brook had not been pleasant. "You know Papa would prefer you to live at home until the wedding. He's"—*careful, Garnet*—"ambivalent about your living in the hotel."

"I know. But it's the height of the season, and Benjamin has a broken ankle." Meredith reached for a faux pearl hair comb that, Garnet knew, she wore to complement the real pearls in her betrothal ring. "If it eases your mind, I let Papa lecture me for the first quarter of an hour after you all arrived. Then I asked him how this was different from the boardinghouse, where two gentlemen clerks lived on the floor below me. At least three stories separate me from Benjamin's apartments, along with almost three hundred guests. And Hominy functions as my maiden auntie. I can count on one hand the number of moments Benjamin and I have been alone together."

"You don't have to convince me. I'm on your side." Without warning a wave of vertigo swept over Garnet.

She eased down onto an elegant lounge, swallowing hard against the upsurge of nausea as her hand instinctively slid over her flat abdomen. She ached to share her news, but after much discussion with Sloan the previous evening they had decided to wait a little longer. Tomorrow evening after all was Meredith's and Benjamin's formal engagement dinner. The entire family would be present—along with half the population of three counties, to hear Meredith tell it.

This moment belonged to her sister. Time enough later, to share her own joyful tidings.

"Are you all right? You're pale." Meredith bustled over, dropping down to kneel by the lounge. "Garnet? Shall I fetch Sloan, or would you like to try some of the crackers I stole from the kitchen?"

Garnet blinked twice, couldn't summon a response that didn't sound either stupid or hopelessly false. "Some crackers would be nice," she finally managed, avoiding Meredith's eye.

Without another word, her elder sister whisked away, returning shortly with a tray of soda crackers, a cold cloth, and a carafe of mineral water. "FrannieBeth, by the way, swears that if you nibble a couple of these even before you rise in the morning, it helps," she began conversationally as she handed Garnet a cracker before pouring her a glass of water. "And she ought to know, since she's been through this twice—no, three times. She lost the one in between Alice and Jessup, you know."

"Meredith…" Garnet said, but had to concentrate on chewing small bits of cracker for several moments. Sitting back, she gave in and allowed Meredith to dab her forehead with the cool cloth. After a while, when the worst of the queasiness passed, she slanted her sister a look. "How did you know?"

Meredith shrugged. "I wasn't sure, but a time or two at the picnic, I saw the way you reacted when certain foods passed under your nose. And Sloan hovered, more than usual. I'll be interested to see how Phineas reacts to a baby, seeing as how he's been your only 'child' for so long."

Garnet surprised them both by bursting into tears. "I'm sorry…don't know what's come over me. It's just that…I wanted to tell you, but we didn't want to detract from your engagement party."

Meredith emitted an inelegant snort. "Now that I'd never allow, not after all the planning and preparation invested to celebrate my particular…*ahem*…'momentous event.' Gaspar is determined to outshine even the lavish meals served at the huge resort hotels like Saratoga and the Greenbrier. Mr. Dayton is planning gigantic floral arrangements for every table—I asked him how we were supposed to find our plates. Poor man, he took me seriously, and it took ten minutes to convince him I'd been teasing."

She continued to feed Garnet crackers, talking all the while. "The wait staff, Benjamin told me this morning, decided among themselves that they wanted to dress in formal livery, in honor of the occasion. Only—they don't have formal livery. Benjamin's always felt it was pretentious, here in the mountains. But when Mr. Dayton mentioned it,

Benjamin was so touched he arranged express delivery from New York. The order arrived two days ago, and now the laundry room has had to hire extra—oh." Her hand clapped over her mouth. She made a face at Garnet. "I'm doing it again, rattling like my tongue's tied in the middle and loose at both ends, when we need to be talking about *you*."

"I don't mind. You're so full of life, Merry-go-round. If we have a daughter, I hope she's just like you." Garnet reached for Meredith's hand, and for precious seconds they clung to each other.

"Does everyone else know?" Meredith asked.

"No. We would have told Papa on the ride up here, but I didn't want to tell Leah before you knew. You're the oldest. I—I wanted you to be the first. It seemed right somehow."

She mopped her face with the cloth and sat up, feeling amazingly better. Sloan had warned her that she would experience wild mood swings but—since all she'd endured for the past several weeks until now had been sleepiness and increasing nausea—she hadn't really believed him.

"Well." Meredith studied her for a bright-eyed moment, then leaned down and hugged her, very gently. "Thanks, redbird. And congratulations. I've been wondering when it would happen, I confess. You didn't really think you could hide something like this from your big sister now, did you?"

"Yes. I did. Especially when Leah didn't suspect, and we're around her and Papa at least once a week. We don't see you very much these days, after all." Likely she'd see Meredith even less frequently in the future. Feeling weepy-eyed again, Garnet pressed the cloth to her hot cheeks until the urge passed.

"Meredith?"

"Hmm?"

"I—I'm not quite sure how to say this, actually." Carefully Garnet sat up, relieved when neither dizziness nor nausea assailed her anew. She drew in a deep breath. "I've been debating with myself ever since I knocked on your door. Actually…I've been praying. I…" She stopped, then finished in a rush, prompted by that inner urging that wouldn't leave her alone, "Please be careful, Meredith. Not just about Preston, but—your thoughts. Your attitude…"

"What's wrong with my attitude?"

Garnet sighed. "I knew no matter how I phrased this, you'd be defensive."

"I'm not defensive. Mercysake, but you're sensitive. Oh, never mind."

Meredith folded the cloth, placed it on the tray, then began stacking the remaining soda crackers in a neat pile. She wouldn't look at Garnet. "You can't help your sensitivity, any more than I can help the, ah, the defensiveness. Especially now, when you're in the family way."

"It's not just me," Garnet said. "Sloan feels the same way. You and Benjamin are so happy, and it's an answer to prayer to see the two of you, full of love and confidence about the future. But for some reason I can't explain—"

"Obviously."

"I think you need to be careful." Garnet swatted her sister's arm. The tension that had sprung up between them faded. "Just stay close to the Lord, Meredith. I can't explain it better than that, because I don't understand any better than you, the workings of God's mind. Just stay close to Him."

"You're sounding vaguely dramatic. Too much like me for comfort. Don't worry. I'll be careful about everything. But sometimes, don't you think God wants us to just bask in all the wonderful things He's done for us?"

Bask, but take nothing for granted, Garnet wanted to say. Instead, she smiled and hugged her sister, then left to hunt down her husband. Perhaps Meredith was right, and Garnet had fallen back into her old habit of doubting.

One more matter to pray over, Lord…

❧❧❧

Benjamin and Jacob were sitting on a bench inside the gazebo, which was situated in the center of a swath of green behind the hotel. Through the tall windows of the hotel filtered the not unpleasant sounds of the string orchestra tuning their instruments. Voices rose and fell in desultory conversations, but for the most part it was possible to sink into the peaceful silence of a late summer afternoon.

Much preferable, Ben decided when he and Jacob met in the lobby, to the constant noise and interruptions if they remained inside. He could also see the relief on Jacob's face when Ben suggested a walk. So they'd indulged in a stroll, or at least Jacob strolled while Hominy pushed Ben's rolling chair—he refused to have it referred to as an "invalid" chair—content with idle remarks between themselves and other tourists strolling the green or lounging on blankets spread over the grass. Several guests spoke to Ben, but most of them merely nodded as they passed, allowing him and Jacob at least a semblance of privacy. Eventually they ended up at the gazebo. After a murmured word with Ben, the manservant left, promising to return in an hour.

"Wish you hadn't gone to so much trouble," Jacob commented after Fred Vance, president of a local bank, told Ben how much he and his wife were looking forward to the engagement dinner. "Not necessary. Why not just give the girl a betrothal ring and be done with it?"

"No trouble at all, Mr. Sinclair. Fact is, the staff would have insisted. They love your daughter almost as much as I do, you see."

Besides, Meredith was in her element. She darted through the hotel like a gaily colored dragonfly, conferring with everyone from Charlie, the orphaned lad Ben had hired as a bootblack, to Gaspar, his autocratic head chef. Meredith of course enjoyed Ben's lack of easy mobility and tried to take shameless advantage of it. Occasionally, when she thought he wasn't aware of it, his affianced would add her own embellishments to some of Ben's orders. Life with Meredith, Ben had decided long ago, would never be pedestrian.

"Mm," Jacob said, a speculative gleam in his eye. "Well, as I told Garnet last year, there's more to a good marriage than a man and woman deciding betwixt themselves that they can't live without each other. Now I may spend most of my time with wood, but that doesn't make me a blockhead. I know you didn't bring me out here for a spot of idle chitchat." Methodically he pulled out his watch, checked the time, then snapped the lid shut. "What was it you wanted to talk about? I'd say you've perhaps a quarter of an hour before your Mr. Hominy returns, possibly less if Leah tracks me down to make sure I'm not indulging in sinful culinary delights."

He scratched his chin, then slanted Ben a thoughtful look. "Sloan's a delightful son-in-law. There when the occasion calls for it—but not one for poking his nose in a man's private affairs, don't you know."

"I promise to have a talk with Sloan to glean a few pointers," Ben promised solemnly. "As for the other, yes, I do want to talk to you." His ankle ached a little, and he eased his leg to a more comfortable position. "I'll try to keep it brief."

"Tell me what's on your mind, son. Something about my daughter's heartwood chest, wasn't it?"

"Yes sir." He contemplated the father of his future bride. Almost as much as he needed Meredith's love and respect did he long for the same from Jacob Sinclair. "My father died in the War," he said. "He left when I was six, after all my older brothers were killed. He was killed himself when I was seven."

"I'm sorry, lad. 'Twas a bad thing, the War. I was not called to the battleground—they needed my skills to make and repair wagons, mostly for General Jackson's troops." Jacob's gaze turned inward, and the gnarled fingers flexed around his upraised knee. "Lost all my tools and our first home, in '64 in the Burning."

"After the Battle of Fisher's Hill? When Sheridan defeated General Early, then set the Valley ablaze?"

"You've a long memory, for a lad scarce old enough at the time to be out of short pants."

"I was old enough to suffer grief," Ben returned quietly. "And old enough to vow that, come what may, I would take care of my own." Abruptly he changed the subject. "When I stopped by your house this past spring, I greatly admired its architecture. You built it, didn't you?"

Jacob nodded. "Mary, my wife, saw the house plan in a magazine. I purchased the plan, but I built it myself. Took two years. She did love that house…"

"You did a nice job." Ben contemplated the timbers that supported the gazebo's ceiling. "I've always wanted to build. But seems as though I do better with the planning and leaving the construction to others." But he had dreams, oh yes he had dreams the size of Massanutten Mountain, and Jacob Sinclair figured in a large part of them.

"God gives us different gifts, each of them designed with a particular purpose, don't you ken, for our ultimate good and His glory. I might have a way with a block of wood, lad, but without plans I never could have built that house my wife loved and you admired." He paused. "You're something of a dreamer as well as a planner, aren't you," he said then, and Ben almost tumbled off the bench in surprise. "Meredith used to talk about your resort hotels, when I was laid up with my blamed innards. Says you own six of 'em. She's still upset over the one you lost."

"I'm sorry for that. She understands me, you see." An understanding born of love, along with a perceptiveness apparently inherited from her father. "I suppose it was almost like losing a child."

Jacob straightened, leaning forward. "Now there I must disagree with you. There's no comparison, in losing a bit o' land, even all your material goods—and losing a loved one."

"I do know that." Bristling, Ben returned the level look with one of his own. "Are you worried that your daughter is marrying a man who covets his possessions more than his wife?"

"Should I be?"

"No."

Forget perceptiveness. Jacob Sinclair was sounding more like a meddling old man, with the sensitivity of an anvil. Ben stifled the urge to tell him to keep his worries as well as his opinions to himself. What was Jacob expecting him to do, for the love of heaven? "Prove" himself like some ancient Greek hero? He glowered at the other man, wondering if Sloan MacAllister had faced the same hurdle.

The answer, when it came to him, was ridiculously simple. "You know, I have a theory about that old cookie cutter you placed in Meredith's heartwood chest," he said. "Why don't I let you hear it?"

"I'd like that very much," Jacob replied.

The two men regarded each other solemnly. Then Benjamin began to talk.

Forty-Nine

For two days after their extravagant engagement dinner, Meredith floated in a golden haze of happiness. A meal fit for royalty, she assured Gaspar at least twice a day. Served in surroundings worthy of the fanciest restaurants in New York, she promised Mr. Dayton, corroborated by Mrs. Vance, whose husband was president of the First National Bank. Best of all, her entire family had been present, wrapping her and Benjamin in their support and love.

As for Benjamin...well, despite being confined to his rolling chair, or balanced on crutches when he presented his former office manager as his wife-to-be...her beloved fiancé had dominated the crowded room. The two-hundred-year-old, diamond-and-pearl betrothal ring that had belonged to his mother could not compare to the expression on his face as he slid the ring onto her finger. He had, Hominy told her, spent years tracking down the ring, which his mother had sold after the War to buy food for Benjamin and his little sister.

When Benjamin finally traced it to a New Jersey banker's wife, the woman had been so moved by the story that she had given the ring back to Benjamin, refusing to accept any payment. Benjamin stored it in a vault. "Sometimes," he told Meredith, "I was afraid it would stay there. Then God brought you to me."

He hadn't been consciously aware of it, yet God's unfailing love had shadowed her fiancé throughout his life.

For Meredith, the ring symbolized more than Benjamin's public claim of the woman he'd asked to be his wife: Imbued in it as well were Benjamin's honor, his determination—and love for his mother, whose faith had built a foundation on which Benjamin himself was finally able to stand.

Even when he was clinging to a pair of crutches.

It was amazing, Meredith thought on that blistering late July morning, the difference God made in her life as well, now that she had learned how to look for His hand in it.

"Morning, Miss Sinclair. You're looking mighty fine this day, if you don't mind my saying so."

Meredith smiled at Theo Kirculdy, the daytime manager of the hotel. "I don't mind at all, Mr. Kirculdy. Isn't it a beautiful morning?"

An answering smile flitted across the manager's blunt-featured face. "Yes, miss."

Full of her delight, Meredith promenaded across the crowded lobby, dispensing sunny greetings on staff and guests alike. Smiles and whispers followed in her wake, but she ignored them as a lady should, though a secret part would have enjoyed overhearing one or two of the whispers.

"Morning, Mrs. Biggs, Lowell." She bustled across the suite of offices to her desk, retrieved her writing pad, and scanned the reminder notes she'd penned the previous evening. "Let's see, Mrs. Biggs, looks like the first order of business is to check with the livery stable. There was some question about the availability of mounts."

"I'll mention it to Mr. Kingston. Ah, Miss Sinclair—?"

"If he's too busy with Mr. Walker, I'll run over there myself." Meredith placed a check mark by her notation. "What about the other complaints…um, the laundress pressed creases in Mrs. Fenway's dinner gown…strange odor emanating from the corner of the sitting room of the Royal Suite…several queries on specialty menu items—I'll pass those along to Gaspar and Mr. Day. "

"Miss Sinclair, Mr. Walker has requested—"

"Could you tell him I'll be along in a moment, Mrs. Biggs? As soon as we go over these items, all right?

She scuttled across to Lowell's desk. "Mr. Kingston, that letter from the Association of Architects in Philadelphia—they asked if Mr. Walker could be the keynote speaker?"

"Yes. The second week in September. He'll be off the crutches by then. Miss Sinclair, Mr. Walker's waiting for—"

"The *second* week in September?" Meredith glanced up from the pad. "That's the week after the hotel closes for the season. He usually stays here for the kitchen cleaning and repairs before the dining room reopens, because—"

"Miss Sinclair." Benjamin's deep voice interrupted, its tone faintly ironic. "Drop your infernal writing pad and come into my office, before you cause Lowell and Mrs. Biggs acute heart palpitations."

Meredith turned but refused to relinquish her hold on the writing tablet. "I—beg your pardon?"

Benjamin stood balanced on his crutches at the entrance to his private office. He was smiling the enigmatic smile, the one that instantly put Meredith on alert. For the sake of appearances, during working hours they kept their relationship scrupulously professional, not an easy task for Meredith when she wore a betrothal ring on her finger and her heart on her sleeve.

"What's going on?" She scanned the uncomfortable faces of her fellow workers. "This is what we do every morning. Why would it cause…um…was it heart palpitations?"

Lowell's neck and ears turned a dull red, and even Mrs. Biggs looked uncomfortable. "Well, now, my dear," she said, patting Meredith's hand, "I expect if you'll accompany Mr. Walker back into his office, he'll explain."

Oh my, yes. Mr. Walker would most definitely have some explaining to do. Meredith barely restrained herself until the door closed behind them before she launched into a vigorous tirade rife with hand waving. Benjamin waited, hip propped against his desk, the crutches stacked at his side, his face inscrutable.

Realization seeped in after a while. "Leah's had a talk with you, hasn't she?" she demanded. "Primed you with suggestions along the lines of 'how to quell Meredith on a rampage,' or something? Both of my sisters do that—stand there smirking, not saying a word until I run down." She folded her arms across her waist. Her lips twitched. "It's very effective, isn't it?"

"Yes. Are you finished?"

He was regarding her with a seriousness the occasion didn't warrant, transforming her temper into alarm as wild possibilities crashed together in her mind. "Preston? You discovered something. That's what this is all about."

"No. Not entirely." She watched Benjamin's chest rise and fall, and his hands gripped the desk with enough force to whiten his knuckles. "Meredith, I want you to move back to Sinclair Run."

"What? Move back home?" She gaped at him. "But—why?"

"Because your living here distresses your father."

"Of all the ridiculous...mercysake, Benjamin. He understands, he told me so himself. Nobody in the entire family objects. In fact, they all agreed it made perfect sense, particularly in light of Preston's threats."

Incensed, panicked, she began pacing. "Benjamin, you're making me very nervous. Please tell me why you've manufactured this—this outrageous ploy. I love being your office manager; I love helping you; I love being here with you. I thought you felt the same."

Abruptly an even more monstrous thought squeezed all the breath from her lungs. "You...Benjamin?" She swallowed hard, her heartbeat thumping in slow, painful thuds. Her right hand closed protectively over her left. "Are you saying that you...that you've changed your—"

Quick as a lightning stroke his arm flashed out. A single tug hauled her against his chest. One large hand cupped her chin, lifting her face. "Meredith." He shook her chin gently. "Always the dramatist. But I don't want to hear any more talk like that. Nor any thoughts, hmm? We'll have a lot of disagreements over a lot of issues, you and I. But my love for you will not be one of those issues."

Still holding her gaze, he released her chin to lift her left hand, his fingers brushing the ring. "With this ring," he repeated, his voice low, "I have pledged myself to you, before man and before God. We'll have a ceremony in your family church, come November. But Meredith, in my heart, you are already my wife. Don't doubt my love, ever again."

Meredith nodded, her throat too swollen with emotion to speak.

His face softened. He drew her up, unresisting, for a tender kiss, then held her at arm's length, his gaze intent on her face. "Would you do something for me? Right now?" he asked almost whimsically.

Contrite, Meredith nodded. Then: "Well. Perhaps. Do I have to go pack my bags?"

Benjamin chucked her under her chin and let her go. "I want you to go look inside the bottom cabinet of that rosewood secretary, behind my desk. No—don't ask any more questions. You'll understand when you do it."

Her heart was back to thumping in that slow hard rhythm that hurt her ribs and made it difficult to breathe, but Meredith walked over to the secretary, knelt down, and pulled open the doors.

"My heartwood chest?" She surged to her feet and whirled around.

"I had Hominy fetch it from your room for me." His face remained bland. "Could you bring it over here?" He gestured to the desktop.

Silently Meredith lifted her heartwood chest from its hiding place, carried it across to the desk, and set it down. Still without speaking, she watched Benjamin position the crutches and hobble around until they stood side by side.

"You didn't even notice it was gone, did you?"

"No." She refused to weep, absolutely refused. "I've been a bit pre-occupied the past several days." Her gaze flicked to the magnificent diamond-and-pearl ring, then returned to Benjamin.

"So you have." He nodded toward the chest. "I think it's time to discuss what's inside the secret drawer."

"You did talk with Papa then? I'd wondered." Meredith retrieved the gingerbread girl cutter, holding it in the palm of her hand. "Will you tell me about it?" she ventured when Benjamin continued to stand silently beside her. "You understand its significance. I can see it in your face."

It was difficult to force the words out, but she needed to know more than she needed to cling to her pride. "You called me the dramatist, yet you're the one making such a production over it." She flashed a brittle smile. "Go ahead. I promise not to have hysterics, no matter how awful a revelation you...you..."

It was no use. Nerves twined the words, tripping her tongue and making her sound depressingly childish. She pressed her lips together.

"Not awful." His voice gentled. "Not awful, sweetheart. Just...a part of you your father saw a long time ago, that he hoped one day you would see as well." His fingers traced around the dented cookie cutter, then burrowed beneath the soft cambric cuff of her shirtwaist to press the inside of her wrist. "Don't look so undone. I love you. Here…how about if we sit down? My hands get tired, balancing on these crutches…"

The brief interruption steadied her. They moved to the comfortable settee, and Meredith held up the cookie cutter, turning it around. "This was my mother's favorite, so of course it was mine, too. Garnet and I used to fight over it, after Mama died—is that it?" She searched Benjamin's face. "A reminder about the importance of family relationships?"

"Not quite." He flexed his hands in relief, then laced his fingers behind his head. "Jacob told me gingerbread cookies were his favorite. That until after Leah was born, apparently not a week passed but your mother made him some."

Memories began to stir, making her smile. Making her—weepy. "I tried to continue the tradition after she died. I was the oldest, and I thought it was my responsibility. They never tasted as good as Mama's…I guess that's why I stopped making them."

"You stopped making them, my love, because your father was too soft-hearted to refuse them even though they irritated his stomach. When you were about nine, he told me, he almost died because—"

"Because I wouldn't listen to Garnet, and I made him those gingerbread cookies. I remember." *Jesus. Help me…I remember.* Mrs. Willowby had gently explained to three terrified little girls that their father mustn't eat a lot of cookies or spicy foods. Meredith, unable to handle her feelings of guilt, had buried the entire episode—until now. If she hadn't already been seated, her knees would have buckled beneath her.

Blinking rapidly, Meredith laid the tin cookie cutter in her lap. "He was so sick…Mrs. Willowby came back then, to care for us. And it was my fault. Mine"—she lifted her swimming gaze to Benjamin's—"because I was too stubborn to admit I'd made the cookies because I wanted to. I knew better, knew they weren't good for Papa. But I was determined n-not to listen to my sisters. God forgive me…" She jammed a fist over her mouth and tried to turn away. She'd almost killed her father.

Benjamin's hands stilled the movement, holding her shoulders in a firm grip. "Do you remember what he told you that day?"

Meredith shook her head. "I made myself forget the entire episode, because I didn't like the way it made me feel. All these years, Papa has been waiting. Hoping… Why didn't I remember until now?" she choked out. Was she truly that blind to her shortcomings, so stiff-necked in her pride and stubbornness that not once in all the years of wondering had the significance reached her?

Matter-of-factly Benjamin stuffed a handkerchief in her hand. "Might be because you're a human being. Try to remember the point of the lesson, not the pain, sweetheart. That's what your father is hoping for."

The insightful observation calmed her more effectively than a comforting embrace. "Not much doubt of my human failings, is there?" She pressed her fingers against her temples, blew her nose into Benjamin's handkerchief, then stretched to plant a kiss on the corner of his mouth. "Your timing is…impeccable. I may be more stubborn than red clay, but I'm not stupid. When I was nine I more or less forced my father to eat cookies that might have killed him. Now you need for me to understand that staying here until the wedding might engender a similar response. Papa would never say anything, because he knows how much I love you. How much I love working as your office manager."

Benjamin stretched a long arm across the back of the settee, behind her head. His fingers stroked the taut tendons in her neck. "Well…did I mention that I hired you for your brains not your beauty?"

Meredith dug her elbow into his ribs. "Now you'll be without them until November, won't you?"

"I'm trying not to think about it." His fingers tightened, turning her face upward. "We both know it's the right thing to do. Merry-my-love, it's not just your father who's struggling with our present arrangements. Like you said, he would never have verbalized those concerns. However, Lowell's warned me that some of the guests are making remarks. While the gossip is nothing but the workings of petty minds, I'd rather not create a ruckus, ejecting guests for impugning my wife-to-be's reputation."

"Why hasn't someone told me?"

Two warm fingers touched her mouth. "I'm telling you now. This may or may not be Preston Clarke's work. Regardless of the initial source, you will need to pack your bags. We're leaving first thing in the morning. Mrs. Biggs has already arranged for a maid to help you."

His deep blue eyes darkened, and in spite of their surroundings, he pulled her into a hard embrace. "I don't know how I'll bear up without you."

"I don't know how I'll bear up without you."

They exchanged a kiss before Meredith tore free and stumbled to her feet. "We have to stop," she managed, though she longed to throw herself back into his arms and let the rest of the world hang. Especially the part inhabited by gossiping guests. "I want to"—she groped for the words, fumbling because her emotions were raw—"honor my father. I want to show him I've learned the lesson he's needed for me to learn all these years. I want to honor my heavenly Father as well. I just don't understand. Why does it have to be so painful?"

Benjamin struggled to his feet. Meredith automatically handed him the crutches. "Life usually is," he said as he positioned them under his arms. "As I recall, Jesus could have elected a dramatic—and painless—escape for Himself. But He didn't, which to my way of thinking sort of provides impetus as well as inspiration, for us to follow."

"How did you come to be so wise, Mr. Walker?" Meredith said, searching the rugged features, memorizing the sheen of his bronze-tipped hair, the thick dark lashes framing those incredible eyes that could see straight into her soul. "You've always been smart. But until lately, you haven't looked at life from a spiritual perspective." She paused, then admitted in a quiet voice, "Nor have I."

"I'd say God's been busy, cutting out all the stubborn knotholes in both our lives, hmm?"

"I love you." She bit her lip, trying to keep her voice steady. "Let's leave as early as we can in the morning, please. I'm afraid if I think about this too much, I might forget the lesson I just learned."

She glanced across the room, to the heartwood chest on top of Benjamin's desk. "Will you keep my heartwood chest for me? I can't explain it, but knowing that it's with you will help somehow."

"You don't have to explain." His voice was deeper, rougher than usual. "I understand very well."

For several moments after Meredith left, Ben sat deep in thought, behind his desk. One hand rested on top of the heartwood chest. Then, his mood pensive, he slowly opened a drawer and withdrew a slip of paper with a single sentence type written across the middle of the page: THERE ARE MORE DANGEROUS FLAMES THAN THOSE FANNED BY WAGGING TONGUES.

The private detectives did not know who had slipped the note under his door. Molly, who cleaned his rooms, had merely placed the folded paper unread on Ben's bureau; she had not noticed any strangers lurking about when she had arrived that morning at her usual time.

The chief of police had regretfully admitted that the threat was too vague for him to open an investigation, though he promised to have a couple of men patrol the grounds for a day or two.

"Got any enemies, Mr. Walker?" he'd asked, half joking.

Only one, Ben wanted to say. But he shrugged, shook his head, and thanked the chief for his time.

When Hominy arrived, Ben gestured him over to the desk. "I've made the arrangements for Meredith to leave," he said. "She thinks it's because of the gossip. I'd like to keep it that way. When we return from Sinclair Run"—he paused and inhaled, hands clenching the arms of his rolling chair—"I reckon you'll need to do a little quiet sleuthing. Just, don't get caught at it, my friend."

"It's Mr. Clarke who needs to be caught, Mr. Ben. I'll see what I can do."

"Keep within the law. I've broken a commandment or two over the years, but things are different now. I've changed." His gaze touched on the sheet of paper. "Regardless of what happens, I want to do what's right, not what's right for me."

Hominy tugged his ear, his gaze brooding. "Even if he goes scot-free? Even if that note's a threat, not just a taunt?"

Gently Ben lifted the heartwood chest onto his lap. "A few moments ago, Meredith agreed to leave—even though it was painful, she told me—because she wants to honor not only her father, but God." He looked up at his faithful manservant. "How can I do any less, Hominy?"

Fifty

he plaintive calls of Canada geese echoed somewhere in the late afternoon sky. J. Preston Clarke paused in his stroll, tipping his head back to search for the birds. *Early yet for them to be migrating,* he thought. *Must be a cold winter coming.* He spied the distinctive long-necked silhouettes as they skimmed the western horizon, above the copse of hardwoods that screened his house from the main road. Two of them—a pair. Canada geese mated for life. They seldom flew alone…unless one of the pair failed to evade a skilled hunter's weapon.

Preston resumed his stroll, the sound of his walking stick on the brick path now a peppering of staccato jabs. When he reached the bench almost hidden in the shade of an immense yellow poplar, he sat down, pulled a cigar from his vest pocket, and struck a match on the sole of his shoe. After lighting the cigar, he watched the flame twist and twirl as it devoured the flimsy matchstick. Dry wood burned rapidly, he knew.

For a long time he sat and smoked, while around him the shadows lengthened. Just before twilight faded completely, he reached inside his coat pocket and slowly withdrew a lady's white kid glove. His thumb traced over the tiny buttons. He closed his eyes and wondered if there was anything he could have done to achieve a different ending from the one about to transpire at the Excelsior Hotel.

❧❦❧

It was a little past 8:30 in the evening, and the Excelsior's dining room was almost empty except for Benjamin and Meredith and a few lingering guests scattered among the other tables. Waiters moved more leisurely, the conversational din had softened to murmurs, and the pianist Benjamin had hired for the past week switched from a Chopin étude to a melancholy Stephen Foster melody that made Meredith's eyes sting.

She glanced through the window beside her, where dusk had deepened the surroundings to a soft ebonized matte. Golden haloes of lamplight illuminated a stream of hotel guests, many of them doubtless headed for the open-air concert in front of the courthouse. Others might be on their way to enjoy a traveling production of *The Taming of the Shrew* or a lecture at one of the local churches—a variety of summertime entertainment was available this particular evening, Meredith remembered. After all, she had compiled and posted the list on the activities board that morning.

None of them appealed to her or Benjamin, and Benjamin's ankle provided a handy excuse to spend their last evening alone for almost two months quietly here at a largely deserted hotel. Only…Meredith picked at the lima beans cooling on her plate. It had been difficult to enjoy her final evening meal. Gaspar had outdone himself to make all her favorites—chicken pot pie, stewed tomatoes, the baby limas. Fresh Georgia peaches. For dessert, Edward, their waiter, told her that Gaspar had baked an apple dumpling bursting with caramel and nuts, just for Meredith.

"With cream sauce," he ended now as he removed her plate, his freckled face struggling to maintain its aloofness.

After he left, Benjamin leaned over the table. "Sweetheart, promise me you'll eat better while you're at home," he said, "or I'll find myself marrying a willow switch instead of a bride."

"I've agreed to go, but my appetite is protesting even if the rest of me isn't." She tried for a smile. "Perhaps it's also the weather. It's miserably hot."

"Hominy's joints have been aching all day, he told me. Probably be a storm tonight, clear the air a bit. Hopefully our trip tomorrow morning will be more pleasant." His expression belied the words.

Pleasant was not the word Meredith would have chosen, but for Benjamin's sake she launched into a spate of cheerful conversation. "The house will be nice and cool regardless. Papa built it with the best exposure to catch the breezes. I remember a night like this when I was eleven. My sisters and I sneaked outside after Papa had gone to bed. We went skinny-dipping in the run." Absently she arranged her napkin into the fan shape one of the waiters had taught her, months earlier. "At that time of the year it was shallow, no danger of us drowning, and we enjoyed a glorious half-hour of forbidden fun. When we sneaked back to the house, Papa was waiting on the top step of the porch."

Benjamin reached across to remove the napkin and toss it aside. His warm fingers, so much larger than hers, stroked the back of her hand. "What did your father do?"

"Tanned our hides, as we deserved. But tears were pouring down his face the whole time, which sobered the three of us more than the spanking. My sisters seldom disobeyed after that."

"I notice you don't include yourself."

"Every family needs a rebel. But I've learned my lesson. My father's a wonderful example of how I think God treats His children." She chewed her lower lip, realizing too late that she should have reminisced about a different topic. "I wish I were a more tractable child for them both. But at least I have a visual reminder now, since you helped me to understand why Papa put that cookie cutter in my heartwood chest."

"Want to change your mind, bring it with you?"

"Not really. Like I tried to explain, it helps me—makes our separation less painful, knowing that the most precious part of my past is being watched over by the man God has provided to go with me into the future."

A half-hour later, while Meredith did her best to appease Gaspar's wounded feelings by eating almost half of the apple dumpling, Benjamin suggested a walk around the grounds. "I'll be fine if we stick to the path," he promised. "And I'll even stay in this infernal chair, so you won't fret about how the crutches chafe the palms of my hands." He glanced around. "Let's check whether we can sneak out before Hominy returns to see if we're through with our meal."

The possibility of a small insurrection appealed, and Meredith perked up. "I need to make a quick stop by my room. Go ahead, I'll meet you in ten minutes…at the side entrance? Under the elm?"

He winked at her. "Done."

But Mr. Dayton stopped her at the entrance to the dining room, his basset-hound face even more mournful than usual. "Miss Sinclair?"

Meredith glanced over at the grandfather clock. "Yes? What is it, Mr. Dayton?"

He cleared his throat, and she was amazed when a tide of red crept across the restaurant manager's gaunt cheeks. "Since, ah, you are leaving us first thing in the morning, I wanted to...that is—this might be the last opportunity for me to wish you well. I wanted you to know—I've never seen Mr. Walker look happier."

"Oh..." Impulsively Meredith threw her arms around the shocked man in a brief but fierce hug. "It won't be your last opportunity." She stepped back, swiping at her eyes with the back of her hand. "Please. You must promise to attend the wedding in November. We would both be honored by your presence."

He cleared his throat again, looking awkward as well as stunned. For the first time since Meredith had met him, a smile crept across his face. Even more incredible, a suspicious dampness gathered at the corners of *his* eyes. "Well. I...um...the honor is entirely mine."

"Good. Then I'll expect to see you in church, come November."

She waved a cheerful farewell, then escaped before they further embarrassed themselves.

Eight minutes later, humming beneath her breath, Meredith started back across the sitting area of her suite. She was two steps away from the door when she heard a faint muffled noise, emanating from somewhere down the hall—no. Behind her? Outside, toward the dining room wing? It sounded, she mused with a little laugh as she reached for the doorknob, sort of like a soft explosion of feathers. Oh. Now she remembered. There was a fireworks display somewhere in town, and—

The door wouldn't open. Frowning, she twisted and tugged, growing more annoyed with each passing second.

Then she smelled the smoke.

And through the window heard a woman scream.

Revelation followed by instant denial froze Meredith where she stood, paralyzing her body as though she'd been propelled headfirst into an ice block. She stared at the shiny brass doorknob, at the intricate design of the rectangular escutcheon surrounding it, at her hands wrapped around the knob. The words pushed their way back into her brain, but it was not until a gossamer strand of smoke floated up from beneath the door panel and drifted past her nose that the paralysis shattered.

Fire! The hotel's on fire! She had to escape, had to open the door, had to find Benjamin, had to sound the alarm, had to make sure nobody was trapped, had to *open the door.* She was pounding, kicking, finally yelling at the top of her lungs, but the panel wouldn't yield, and she could feel the heat, hear the crackling, rustling roar of flames rushing down the hall, and she knew that she could not escape through the door, that she would have to find another way.

Whirling, she dashed across to the window, which overlooked the back lawns. Fingers clumsy with terror, she struggled to raise the sash high enough to shimmy herself and her long heavy skirts through, fumbled to unhook the wire screen and knock it away. A sob escaped when she heard a whooshing roar behind her. Flames licked beneath the door, igniting the carpeting. Dingy gray smoke thickened, billowed across the room toward her searching for air. Like Meredith. With a last agonized glance, she gathered handfuls of slippery crepe de Chine and lace-edged cotton as she ducked down to the opened window. In an inelegant tumble of limbs she clambered to freedom, landing beside a bushy shrub whose branches clutched at her skirts and stockings. Breathless, her heart skittering with panic, Meredith scrambled to her feet.

The hotel was designed as a central block with two wings on either side, the main lobby and dining room comprising the central block. Stunned, her breath squeezing out in shallow pants, she watched smoke leak through the row of windows to her immediate right, watched flames as well as smoke fill the dining room windows across the lawn.

Benjamin. Where was Benjamin? Meredith knew as surely as she could see those orange-and-yellow flames that he would not wait beneath the elm tree. He would come after Meredith, broken ankle, rolling chair or not. He would—with an anguished sob Meredith hiked her skirts and ran, screaming his name as loudly as she could, praying that God would be merciful, that Benjamin would hear her and know that she was no longer in her room. That Hominy would have found and restrained him before he threw his life away to save her.

Vaguely she registered the sound of other screams, the sound of breaking glass, and the sounds of the fire as it gathered strength. From far away she heard the clanging of a bell.

By the time she fought her way through a mob of hysterical guests and staff pouring out through the front entrance, the entire hotel was engulfed in flames. How could it happen so fast? Clawing and shoving, Meredith burst around the corner of the opposite wing—and spied Hominy wrestling a maniacal Benjamin to the ground. The rolling chair had fallen onto its side. With one arm Hominy held Benjamin in a headlock, while the other stretched like an iron bar across his heaving chest.

"Benjamin! Hominy! I'm here—I'm safe!"

She dropped to her knees beside Benjamin's head, tears blinding her as she placed her palms on either side of his bone-white face. "I'm all right," she said. "Benjamin, I'm all right."

He stared, blinked, and the crazed look filming his eyes gave way to relief. "Meredith, my love. I thought—"

"Mr. Ben, Miss Sinclair, we need to move away. The fire!" Without wasting time on words, Hominy hefted Benjamin to his feet, holding him steady while Meredith righted the wheelchair.

"I need to see if everyone's out. The dining room…I heard an explosion. I—"

"No sir. Too late. It's too late, Mr. Ben." For just a moment, Hominy's massive hand rested on Benjamin's shoulder. "Happened too fast. This was no accident, Mr. Ben."

Meredith thought about her mysteriously jammed door, but for once kept her thoughts to herself. Instead she lifted Benjamin's hand and held it tightly in her own. "Benjamin." She couldn't hear herself over the inferno and leaned over to press her mouth by his ear. "There's nothing you can do. I'll try—"

His head lifted; in the blistering heat and orange-streaked night their gazes met.

Meredith bit her lip until she drew blood but didn't volunteer to leave his side again. Hominy muscled the rolling chair across the lawn, and Meredith clung to Benjamin's hand as they joined the throng of people fleeing the doomed hotel.

By the time they traversed the length of the block to a safe distance, the crowd was six-deep. Hemmed in by the crush of onlookers, Meredith pressed against the rubber-tired wheels of Benjamin's chair and maintained her lifeline to his hand. Hominy's unyielding bulk sheltered their backs.

Nobody spoke. There was nothing to be said. Like the rest of the crowd, all they could do was to watch.

Twisted columns of smoke boiled upward into the night, chased by writhing fingers of fire. The stench of burning wood stung their nostrils. Sounds roared into their ears like a hundred waterfalls—the out-of-control flames, the shrieks of panicked guests, the desperate shouts from desperate men still fighting a losing battle against impossible odds. Hoses from several fire wagons soon lay in flaccid tangles along the ground. Winded firemen stood helplessly by empty hand pumpers, empty buckets scattered at their feet. The fire had proven to be too much even for the Rouss Fire Company's new steam pumper. Somewhere a bell still clanged without ceasing. A horse squealed in terror. Hot. It was so hot. Whenever Meredith remembered to breathe, her lungs writhed like the flames, protesting air the consistency of scorched sorghum.

Had someone wanted her to be trapped inside? The possibility was unthinkable. Meredith thrust it away.

In a cannonade of fire bursts, the glass in a score of windows exploded, hurling thousands of shards outward in a deadly shower. Fed afresh, red and orange pennants of flame unfurled through a hundred new openings. A woman nearby shrieked, and a man behind Meredith muttered an oath.

Through it all Benjamin sat unspeaking beside her, rigid as an iron statue. But his fingers dug into Meredith's with enough force to grind the bones of her hand together.

The guests... Slowly her reeling senses picked out the incongruous sight of clusters of the doomed hotel's guests, most of them dressed in their silk and satin evening finery, standing shoulder to shoulder with townsfolk dressed in homespun and calico. A few of the guests clutched a handful of possessions; most stood like everyone else with dangling hands and horror-dulled gazes.

Her heartwood chest...

Meredith's heart twisted in a spasm of denial. A half-formed prayer whispered upward. When she could no longer bear the sight, she closed her eyes, her only contact with the surroundings Benjamin's corpselike hand.

A breeze kissed her heat-seared cheek, and Meredith opened her eyes, blinking against the stinging ash. Another gust, this time strong enough to ruffle her sleeves, blew through the crowd. Across the way, rising wind hurled flames and sparks higher into the boiling night sky.

Suddenly a thunderclap shook the earth, its cavernous boom resounding over even the fire's incredible fury.

And rain poured forth from heaven. A drenching, pounding deluge.

Around them people scattered in all directions for shelter.

But Meredith, Benjamin, and Hominy remained rooted to the spot watching nature finally win the battle against the fire.

Fifty-One

*D*awn bathed the world in quiet tones of luminous pink. The air was clear, cool. Rain puddles dotted the sidewalks.

On the corner of the street where Meredith stood, however, a blackened ruin defied the crystalline promise of the new day. There was nothing left of the Excelsior Hotel but a pile of stinking rubble.

Meredith picked her way across the charred remains to where the veranda used to be. Overhead, instead of smoke and flames, a fading pearl moon glistened in the pastel blue sky. She was alone except for a milk wagon pulled by a sleepy mule. It clip-clopped behind her down the deserted street, and a roused bird warbled a greeting from the branches of a scarlet-tipped maple.

It might have been any other morning, after any other night.

Meredith's gaze drifted to the charred tree trunk a hand's span from where she stood, all that remained of the graceful elm where she and Benjamin were to have met. This time yesterday, she thought, the words repeating themselves in a tiresome cant, this time yesterday the hotel was teeming with life and color. With people. Now…Meredith tried not to dwell on what lay buried in that rubble. The fiery grave for ten people—eight guests and two hotel employees.

Grief was a dull spike, crushing her ribs. Clyde Henkle would never greet her at the door again, never gallantly compliment her latest hairstyle, never be able to take pride over his part in bringing Benjamin and Meredith together. And Mr. Dayton—

Meredith pressed her fingers over her heart and counted until the swell of emotion receded. Just hours ago, she had watched the stiffly reserved man wipe away a tear after she'd told him that she hoped he would make it to the wedding, come November.

The two men had died along with six of the guests they tried in vain to save; a couple from Roanoke perished after they fled from their flaming third-story room to the roof, then in panic, leaped to the burning shrubbery below.

But thanks to a merciful God, the remaining eighty-seven guests and staff inside when the fire broke out had all made it to safety. The other two hundred or so guests had already left the hotel for their sundry evening activities. If arson was the cause of the fire, at least the instigators had chosen their time for the least risk to human lives. It was difficult, however, to feel gratitude toward them…or him.

Rage and grief spiraled upward again, as consuming as the fire. Eventually Meredith managed to turn away from the ruins. From death. Morning sunlight poured into her, warm and insistent. Comforting. A gentle reminder that daylight always followed darkness. Meredith held on to that nascent hope on her solitary walk to the Taylor Hotel, where Benjamin was ensconced along with as many of Excelsior's guests as the proprietor could accommodate.

The entire community had pitched in to help; when every room in every hotel and boardinghouse was filled, stranded guests were welcomed into homes. At some point during the scarlet-and-black nightmare of the past twelve hours, Hominy steered Meredith into Mrs. Biggs's trembling arms. Equally traumatized but ever stoic, the office assistant urged a protesting Meredith to spend the remainder of the night with her and her husband, in their neat two-story bungalow four blocks away.

Meredith had protested until Benjamin uttered his first and only words since she found him wrestling with Hominy on the ground beneath the elm. "Please go with her. I need to know you're safe." He pressed his forehead against his fist, his shoulders bowed. "Please, Meredith."

Meredith went. She lay sleepless on a narrow bed in a tiny room filled with family photographs, lithographs, and a collection of Stafford-shire ceramic figurines. At dawn she gave up, rising with the sun to make her way to the Taylor Hotel.

She found Benjamin in a deserted alcove. He was sitting in a large upholstered chair, his ankle propped on a matching tasseled hassock.

Sunlight streamed through the window, outlining his profile with a soft golden hue which nonetheless could not hide his gray fatigue. His gaze was focused toward the window.

As Meredith watched he swallowed. A deep sigh shuddered up from his chest.

"Benjamin." She flew across the room, watching the naked flash of relief, of welcome, burn the dullness from his eyes. He held out his hand. The strong supple fingers were trembling. Meredith knelt at his side and pressed her cheek against his hand. "I couldn't sleep. I had to come. I left Mrs. Biggs a note—Benjamin?" She lifted her head. "We'll make it through this. Somehow, we'll survive."

"Yes. We will survive. Don't look at me like that, love. I'll be all right." He stroked her cheek, then cupped her chin. "I've had a lot of practice, remember."

"I know. I know you have." She tried to smile. "Trouble is, I haven't. I want to help you. I want to give you strength—I want to be your strength when you give out. Only I can't seem to think. Focus. I need my writing pad."

For some reason that inane remark sparked a burst of laughter from both of them.

"I need my desk clock."

"Oh? Well, I need my button boots with the round toes. These things pinch my feet. I almost walked over here barefoot."

"I need a fresh cravat."

"A clean hankie."

Abruptly Benjamin leaned forward in the chair, resting his forehead against hers. "Meredith, I love you so much." He lifted his head to look at her. "Your heartwood chest…" His voice thickened, and the dark blue gaze filled with agony. "We need to talk about it, face it. I-I can't deal with the rest, until we reconcile the loss of your heartwood chest."

"I don't want to. I'm too—" She took a hard, short breath. Felt as though she were inhaling embers. "Too ashamed of even thinking about it when you've lost so much more. And ten people lost their lives. Clyde. Mr. Dayton."

She rose, pacing the floor with restless steps. "I keep begging God to fill me with all that strength He promises us. Yet all I feel inside is panic." Almost defiantly she swiveled to face him. "And denial. Always the denial. I'd much rather focus on making a list of everything we need to do than think about Clyde and Mr. Dayton or my heartwood chest."

"Panic is natural. Denial won't make it—or reality—go away." He reached for a crutch lying on the floor and with remarkable ease hefted himself to his feet. "Trust me. I've experienced them both." He maneuvered himself forward, wielding the crutches with such skill they functioned almost as a part of his body. "Until recently, I was convinced that I was capable of managing whatever came my way. Relied on my own strength, my own wits." He paused, then admitted in a low voice, "Last night I learned I was wrong about that."

Watching him Meredith was struck anew by the return of the natural power Benjamin had always manifested. Regardless of his confession—no, she instantly corrected herself. *Because* of his confession, mentally as well as physically he was the strongest man she had ever known. Yet only now could she appreciate the depth of his character, because twice over the past weeks she had met the helpless little boy still hidden inside the quietly powerful man.

"You might not think so at the moment," she told him, "but you are the most estimable man I have ever known."

Looking uncomfortable, Benjamin shook his head. "Right now I'm as confused as you are," he said. His lips twisted in a bitter smile. "After years of relying on self, I finally learn to trust the Lord's wisdom over my own. Accept that I need His Presence in my daily life. And for what? Why did God allow this to happen when I've been trying to be obedient? Trying for the first time since I was a child to live my life in a manner that would honor Him?"

"I don't know. I know what I'm supposed to feel, I can even quote passages of Scripture, but—" Meredith spread her hands in a helpless gesture.

"Anything but that."

"Oh? Well, perhaps I should preach a sermon. I could probably expound for let's see, at least an hour. No? All right." She eyed him innocently. "How about if I steal your crutches? Then you'd have to listen."

Some of the bitterness shadowing his face lightened. "I've known people who use verses of Scripture as though they were crutches," he said. "But you're right. Since I can't stand on my own two feet without these, I consider myself reprimanded. Quote away, my love. Let's see if some verses will help both of us to hobble through the day."

"Benjamin…" She wrapped her arms around his waist and leaned her head against his chest. "You've forced me to admit that not a single one of them comes to mind at the moment."

She heard a quiet chuckle rumble beneath her ear.

That was when she decided not to burden him about the jammed door. What purpose would it serve? In her heart, Meredith knew the reason: She would certainly have perished had she completed her panicked exit through that door into the hallway. The window had offered her best hope of escape, so the door had been blocked to ensure that she had no other choice. *Preston.* It had to be Preston.

But neither she—nor even Benjamin with all his resources—would be able to prove anything, including the true explanation for that locked door. Perhaps Benjamin had been right all along, about the futility of fighting a man like J. Preston Clarke. Instead her fiancé had chosen a nobler path: protecting the woman he loved rather than pursuing vengeance, even in the name of justice. So Meredith would thank God for her life and leave the rest behind in the cooling ashes. She would depend on God's promises and trust Him to provide the discipline to carry the secret to her grave.

Yes, there was a time to speak, as Garnet had learned the previous year. But there was also a time for silence, as Meredith had discovered this morning. Some things *were* better left unrevealed.

She hugged Benjamin hard. "I love you."

For a precious span of time they stood, gathering strength from togetherness until another thought settled softly inside Meredith's heart. The spiritual manifestation of God's love *was* real—as real as the love she and Benjamin shared. She might not see Him as she could see Benjamin, and she might not be able to hold Him as she was holding Benjamin. But…perhaps it was the Lord's very Presence in their lives that imbued their human love with a touch of the divine.

"Benjamin?"

"Hmm?"

She felt his lips brush her hair. "I don't understand much about the workings of God's ways. But I think I'm beginning to grasp that it isn't necessary for me to understand."

Benjamin murmured an unintelligible sound of encouragement.

Meredith lifted her fingers to trace the deep lines scoring his face from nose to mouth, lines that hadn't been there yesterday. "It's life that delivers pain and tragedy. But it's God who gives us pieces of Himself, all of it wonderful, all of it designed to help us through the pain and tragedy of life. Not run from it."

Not deny the problems, until now her cowardly response. "He gives us the love. The peace. The joy, patience—all of it. I can't explain very well." She shook her head, frustrated. "I still have all this awful pain—so vast it hurts to breathe. I'll miss Clyde and Mr. Dayton. But I know, from being with you, that time really does heal. I know that, in time, you can rebuild the hotel. It's just that"—she forced herself not to lower her gaze—"I'm afraid there's always going to be a part of me that... I do know my heartwood chest was just a-a material object, like my mother's cookie cutter. Yet for me they were...they were..."

It was no use. Her throat closed, her brain refused to cooperate with her emotions. How was it possible to be so aware of God's Presence while at the same time be so full of heartache? Of confusion.

One of Benjamin's crutches fell clattering to the floor. His arm wrapped around her shoulders. "We'll get through, Merry-my-love." A gentle kiss warmed her temple. "I'll hold on to you. And you"—he staggered slightly, and Meredith tightened her own hold until her arms ached—"hold on to me. That way neither of us will fall. And together we'll try to both take hold as well of some of those...pieces of God."

Fifty-Two

$\mathcal{D}$earest Merry-my-love,

Words are hopelessly inadequate to convey how much
I miss you. Although it's only been four days since we
parted, it feels like four years. All that keeps me going is
the assurance of your love for me—and God's love for us
both. That blessed assurance and something that happened today, something that for me will provide precisely
the distraction I need to survive these coming weeks. As I
write these words I am smiling because, my love, I am
not going to tell you the nature of this distraction. Not
yet. I will tell you only that miracles of all sorts still occur
in our lives.

Well. Perhaps instead of waxing like a lovelorn
suitor (or more accurately—a lonely husband-to-be…)
I should apprise you of the circumstances. I know you
think you should be here, but in spite of missing you desperately I am relieved that you're not. Eighteen-hour
days…all of them blurring together until the only way I
know whether or not it's day or night is to look up at
the sky.

Stop fretting. Remember that we vowed to be as
honest in our letters as we would be if we were
together, because the mental closeness renders our physical separation less incapacitating (though your letter

of yesterday concerned me deeply). I wish you would weep with the easy frequency of your past. Don't allow this present loneliness to deprive you of a segment of your nature that I love every bit as much as I do the rest. And try not to be hurt by your sister Leah's inability to fathom your moods. She is after all still very young. I am sorry however that she has accepted the invitation to return to Mary Baldwin early to train as a teaching assistant. I know in spite of your differences that you will miss her.

But God willing, in a short span of weeks you and I will be together again, this time forever. Focus on the hope of the future, love, which will arrive sooner than you realize.

Enough lecturing, hmm? Normally I try to restrain myself, as I know how it annoys you. However, it is a little past one o'clock in the morning so I am exhausted physically (though, reference my first paragraph, exalted spiritually), tired enough that as you see not only am I rambling, I'm having trouble holding this pen correctly (forgive the blobs of ink, by the way). But like you, writing these letters keeps me sane, because no matter how bleary-eyed I might be, when I'm writing them I always feel closer to you. I can close my eyes right now and see you. When you read this letter, unless it's raining you'll be sitting in "our spot" beneath the shade of that tree under your bedroom window, in one of the two chairs we carried there last week. You shared the story of the lightning…

By the way, did I tell you that I had a talk with your father that last evening while you were helping Mrs. Willowby wash the supper dishes, about starting up a subcontracting business of sorts? He provides a prototype—like those lawn chairs—and I'll scour the countryside for skilled craftsmen in need of extra income. One day, love, your father's chairs will grace the porches and lawns of all my hotels.

I have a few other plans for him as well. But I digress. I was—now that I've glanced back at what I wrote—going to apprise you of what's happened here. You might be able to perceive that I'm stalling.

Yes, Meredith smiled up into the thick branches of the scarlet maple, she could see that he was stalling. Over the past ten minutes he had tantalized her curiosity, teased her temper, and tugged at her emotions—but she knew he'd been stalling. Her gaze dropped back to the letter. An audible gasp startled a pair of noisy purple finches.

...when I left the lawyer's office and J. Preston Clarke was waiting. He offered his condolences, his relief at the loss of "so few lives." He also made a point of informing me that he was on his way to France for an extended stay. I'd planned to have Hominy check on Mr. Clarke, of course, when there was time. But my mama didn't raise up a fool. If Preston had a part in the fire, I doubt we'll ever know it. He's been contacting guests behind my back, you see, and inviting them to spend the rest of their stay—gratis—at a hotel in Front Royal he recently purchased. In front of many witnesses, he proclaimed himself to be at my disposal, for any assistance. As Hominy and I discussed it later, it's evident that suggesting a police investigation of Preston Clarke would do nothing but invite trouble. Since I've enough of that already, as you have advised I have determined to forget what is past. Truthfully, I no longer care who or what caused the fire. When all is said and done, I was spared the loss of the most important part of my life—you. And I want to focus my energies on our future.

And our future, my love, will not be here in Winchester.

Meredith wasn't surprised. Lonely as she was without Benjamin, she faced the fact that she had dreaded returning to Winchester and a host of painful memories. Part of her might chafe at agreeing to spend the next few months preparing for the wedding instead of remaining at Benjamin's side, but she was shamefully relieved to be spared the logistical nightmare of the fire's aftermath.

She dropped the letter in her lap and tapped her fingers together for a moment. She would have stayed regardless, yielded to the pleas of the beleaguered hotel staff who relied on her organizational skills. But Benjamin's attention would have been divided. He loved her, and he needed her. He would, Meredith knew, have come to rely on her, possibly more than he should at this particular time. Benjamin needed to recover his self-confidence. And both of them needed to nurture their growing relationship with the Lord, independent of their relationship with each other. Their marriage ultimately would be the stronger for this painful time apart.

Though they had vowed complete honesty, she had nonetheless refrained from confessing these sentiments to Benjamin. Instinctively she sensed it was something that was better known yet unacknowledged. For Meredith that jammed hotel door was turning out to function as a symbol of the gift of sacrificial silence. When honesty was used merely to relieve one's private guilt, it became selfishness.

Is this another facet of love, Lord? Learning the difference?

The delicious prickling affirmation spread through her like a benediction. Meredith's fingers stilled, and with a contented hum she picked the letter up again.

"Meredith?"

She waved to her father, perched on the seat of the wagon out in the front yard. "You off to Woodstock?"

"Aye. How's the lad?"

"He's holding his own, Papa. Just as you said. But he isn't going to rebuild the Excelsior."

"Well, now, that doesn't surprise me. We talked, don't you know, the two nights he stayed here when he brought you home. He's a rain barrel full of plans and dreams, for that mineral springs resort he means to build with Mr. Beringer." He pushed back the brim of his cap. Even from across the patch of drying summer grass that separated them, Meredith detected the assessment gleaming in her father's eyes. "Has he told you that he's pestering me to help design the buildings?"

There was a funny tickle in the back of her throat. "I think," she replied when she knew her voice would be steady, "that he was working his way around to it. It's a wonderful idea, Papa. And so like Benjamin."

"Aye. The Lord's blessed you with a good man, lass. Just like He provided Sloan for Garnet. 'Tis enough to make one shout for joy." He jiggled the reins, and the wagon rolled forward. "Which I just might do along the road to Woodstock. And while I'm about it, I just might be after reminding Him that I've one more daughter…"

On a mild afternoon the second week of October, Benjamin returned to Sinclair Run.

Meredith had been up since dawn. Nerves jumpy as six cats in a roomful of rocking chairs, she'd driven her father to hide in his workshop, and Mrs. Willowby had escaped to do the weekly shopping at Cooper's. But the silence of an empty house soon drove Meredith herself outside. It was a glorious autumn day bursting with color, so why not wait for Benjamin on the porch?

She donned an apron to spare her new forest-green morning gown, chosen because Benjamin loved the color, and spent an energetic hour sweeping the wide plank floor and clipping dead blooms from the baskets of fall chrysanthemums Garnet had brought over two weeks earlier. She read two back issues of *American Monthly* and *Harper's*. Sat for endless moments gazing first at the sunlight sparkling off the diamond in her betrothal ring then down the tree-lined lane.

At a little past two, she decided that waiting was torturous, so she would simply walk along the road until Benjamin's carriage—

Rolled into view, Hominy's face gleaming in the sunshine like a crow's wing. He shifted the reins to one hand and waved.

Without warning, a massive ball of uncertainty swirled in Meredith's chest. Cotton-mouthed, heart slamming against her ribs, she stood at the top of the porch. Her feet refused to budge. Her eyes refused to blink, her breath remained wedged in her throat.

The carriage rolled to a halt. Hominy leaped down and opened the door. Benjamin descended, his gaze fixed on Meredith. She'd forgotten the intensity of those deep blue eyes, forgotten how tall he was, the breadth of his shoulders. The crutches were gone, his ankle healed.

He took two steps toward her and stopped. Slowly he lifted his hand. "What are you afraid of? I love you, and this time when I leave, you'll be coming with me."

"I wasn't afraid." Ah, but she hadn't forgotten the smoothness of his voice, the lazy drawl that turned her locked knees to water. Her own voice emerged in a wispy croak. She cleared her throat, lifting her chin. "I love you. And this time, when you leave, I wasn't going to give you the choice of leaving alone."

Benjamin threw back his head in a booming laugh. By the time Meredith flew down the steps, he was waiting for her, his arms lifting her high off the ground, twirling her completely around.

"Reckon I'll go water the horses," Hominy said cheerfully behind them. "Say hello to Mr. Sinclair who's over yonder being tactful."

Neither Meredith nor Benjamin responded. Her hands wrapped around the back of his neck as he lowered his head.

"I have something for you," he murmured a long time later, the words not quite steady. "Close your eyes."

"I don't want to close my eyes. I've been starved for the sight of you for two months. I don't want you out of my sight for two min—"

He kissed her again, a devastatingly tender kiss. "I'm nervous," he told her and gave her a sheepish smile. "And you only have to keep them closed for fifteen seconds. Your surprise is inside the carriage, but it isn't wrapped."

What on earth? Meredith covered her face with her hands. "There. But I'm counting. One, two, three…"

He returned before she reached "twelve" and, in an increasingly nervous voice, ordered her to open her eyes. When Meredith complied, all she could do was to stare. Finally, as though in a dream, she lifted her hand toward the small wooden chest Benjamin was holding out to her.

"It's…" She swallowed hard and tried again. "It's a-a jewelry chest?"

"Not quite." His fingers trembled a little as they stroked over the crudely finished surface. "I made it. You might, ah, see that I'm not the craftsman your father is. But I—"

"You made me a new heartwood chest." Her eyes swimming, she lifted it from Benjamin's hands and hugged it. "Benjamin, you made a new heartwood chest for me."

"Open it, love. There's no secret drawer—I sort of thought one wasn't necessary."

Meredith fumbled with the crooked brass clasp, her gaze never leaving Benjamin's. He stood there, big and fit as the well-muscled horses Hominy was leading toward the barn, yet shining out of his rugged face was the anxiety—and the anticipation—of that small boy. She had never loved him more, until she lifted the lid to her new heartwood chest.

Misshapen and darker in color now but recognizable all the same, her mother's gingerbread girl cookie cutter lay nestled in the middle of a clumsily attached blue satin-lined bed.

"I searched for it," Benjamin said. "Everyone told me it was no use. But I had to try. Had to hang on to the hope. I don't know how it survived the heat."

He stopped. "I probably wouldn't have found it, if I hadn't been on the crutches. I'd been crawling, you see—digging in the area where my office had been. The handle of one of the crutches caught on something. When I yanked it free, the cookie cutter tumbled out of a pile of ash and debris."

Tears flowed unchecked as Meredith lifted the cookie cutter out and cradled it in her palm. "You never know," she managed after a while in a voice thick with emotion, "what God's going to provide when you hang on to hope and keep trying."

Benjamin gently removed the cookie cutter, set it back in the chest, then laid the chest on the ground. His own eyes were wet. "It will make an interesting heirloom, won't it? I was thinking though, that between now and our wedding your father might be willing to help me make you a new heartwood chest."

Meredith reached up to press a kiss against his warm mouth. "Don't be ridiculous. I love this one, almost as much as I love the man who made it for me." With a resigned grin she accepted the handkerchief Benjamin gave her. "Yes. It's a relief to learn that I'm still a watering pot. Now"—she thrust the damp cloth away, picked up the chest, and grabbed Benjamin's hand—"let's go show Papa and give him the chance to welcome home his new son-in-law-to-be."

"Home…" Benjamin said. His fingers gripped hers. "Has a nice ring to it, doesn't it?"

Hand in hand they strolled across the yard.

The following is an excerpt from Sara Mitchell's
Virginia Autumn
Book 2 in the Sinclair Legacy series
Available in stores April 2002

❧❀❧

*H*is gaze dropped to her ringless left hand, then returned to her face. She resembled her two sisters neither in looks nor personality. What had it been like for her, he wondered, growing up in Meredith's and Garnet's shadow? "You're a teacher now, I believe?"

Unattractive red stained the bridge of her nose and forehead, while the rest of her complexion paled. "Yes. And I'll save you further speculations by stating that I am not, and have never been, married." She hesitated. "I apologize for more or less accusing you of collusion. For some reason Meredith refuses to accept my circumstances, and I'm afraid I made an erroneous assumption." A flicker of humor brightened eyes the color of bitter chocolate. "I seem to remember having to apologize to you the very first time we met."

"You were tired that day," Cade murmured. "Yes, I do remember. You're tired now, aren't you?"

"Of course not, I have excellent stamina. I—"

"I wasn't referring to physical fatigue." He leaned forward to maintain an aura of privacy in the depot's crowded waiting room. "I think you're tired on every other level of your being. Mental, emotional—and spiritual. Why don't we talk about it, while we wait for the train." Hands relaxed on his knees, he kept his voice soft, nonthreatening, as if he were gentling a suspicious wild animal. "It's been a long time, but I think we can consider each other old friends, don't you?"

"You're impertinent, Mr. Beringer."

"Yes, I admit it…Leah. But I'm also interested."

And he was, somewhat to his surprise. Intrigued by this touchy little martinet whose manner failed to disguise a deep loneliness Cade had sensed from all the way across the room. "Besides, the least I can do since we're headed to the same place"—he hid a smile when she all but gnashed her teeth at him—"is to ensure that you arrive safely."

"I'm quite capable of taking care of myself. Furthermore, I'm not inclined to engage in either casual or intimate conversation with you, regardless of our past association."

"I've a notion you're used to taking care not only of yourself, but everyone else around you. No wonder you're weary." He shifted back, noting the slight relaxation of her shoulders. "I promise to be a good traveling companion. If you don't feel like talking about yourself, we can talk about Ben and Meredith. We have an hour before our train arrives. And—we have the rest of the summer."

Each motion precise, Leah picked up her gloves, tucked them inside her hat, and rose to her feet. "I'd rather eat a bucketful of mud." She grabbed her bag, then stalked across the floor, and disappeared outside.

Cade laced his hands around one upraised knee. Looked to be an interesting journey from this point. *You'll have to help out a bit, Lord. I'm not quite sure yet what my role is supposed to be here.*

But it certainly didn't look like it was destined to be that of confidant.